The Book of Khalid

By

Ameen Fares Rihani

Illustrated By

Khalil Gibran

ISBN: 978-1-78139-143-3

Contents

BOOK THE SECOND IN THE TEMPLE TO NATURE

BOOK THE THIRD IN KULMAKAN
TO GOD

AL-KHATIMAH

AL-FATIHAH

In the Khedivial Library of Cairo, among the Papyri of the Scribe of Amen-Ra and the beautifully illuminated copies of the Korân, the modern Arabic Manuscript which forms the subject of this Book, was found. The present Editor was attracted to it by the dedication and the rough drawings on the cover; which, indeed, are as curious, if not as mystical, as ancient Egyptian symbols. One of these is supposed to represent a New York Skyscraper in the shape of a Pyramid, the other is a dancing group under which is written: "The Stockbrokers and the Dervishes." And around these symbols, in Arabic circlewise, these words:—"*And this is my Book, the Book of Khalid, which I dedicate to my Brother Man, my Mother Nature, and my Maker God.*"

Needless to say we asked at once the Custodian of the Library to give us access to this Book of Khalid, and after examining it, we hired an amanuensis to make a copy for us. Which copy we subsequently used as the warp of our material; the woof we shall speak of in the following chapter. No, there is nothing in this Work which we can call ours, except it be the Loom. But the weaving, we assure the Reader, was a mortal process; for the material is of such a mixture that here and there the raw silk of Syria is often spun with the cotton and wool of America. In other words, the Author dips his antique pen in a modern inkstand, and when the ink runs thick, he mixes it with a slabbering of slang. But we started to write an Introduction, not a Criticism. And lest we end by writing neither, we give here what is more to the point than anything we can say: namely, Al-Fatihah, or the Opening Word of Khalid himself.

With supreme indifference to the classic Arabic proem, he begins by saying that his Book is neither a Memoir nor an Autobiography, neither a Journal nor a Confession.

"Orientals," says he, "seldom adventure into that region of fancy and fabrication so alluring to European and American writers; for, like the eyes of huris, our vanity is soft and demure. This then is a book of travels in an impalpable country, an enchanted country, from which we have all risen, and towards which we are still rising. It is, as it were, the chart and history of one little kingdom of the Soul,—the Soul of a philosopher, poet and criminal. I am all three, I swear, for I have lived both the wild and the social life. And I have thirsted in the desert, and I have thirsted in the city: the springs of the former were dry; the water in the latter was frozen in the pipes. That is why, to save my life, I had to be an incendiary at times, and at others a footpad. And whether on the streets of knowledge, or in the open courts of love, or in the parks of freedom, or in the cellars and garrets of thought and devotion, the only *saki* that would give me a drink without the asking was he who called himself Patience....

"And so, the Book of Khalid was written. It is the only one I wrote in this world, having made, as I said, a brief sojourn in its civilised parts. I leave it now where I wrote it, and I hope to write other books in other worlds. Now understand, Allah keep and guide thee, I do not leave it here merely as a certificate of birth or death. I do not raise it up as an epitaph, a trade-sign, or any other emblem of vainglory or lucre; but truly as a propylon through which my race and those above and below my race, are invited to pass to that higher Temple of mind and spirit. For we are all tourists, in a certain sense, and this world is the most ancient of monuments. We go through life as those pugreed-solar-hatted-Europeans go through Egypt. We are pestered and plagued with guides and dragomans of every rank and shade;—social and political guides, moral and religious dragomans: a Tolstoy here, an Ibsen there, a Spencer above, a Nietzche below. And there thou art left in perpetual confusion and despair. Where wilt thou go? Whom wilt thou follow?

"Or wilt thou tarry to see the work of redemption accomplished? For Society must be redeemed, and many are the redeemers. The Cross, however, is out of fashion, and so is the Dona Dulcinea motive. Howbeit, what an array of Masters and Knights have we, and what a variety! The work can be done, and speedily, if we could but choose. Wagner can do it with music; Bakunin, with dynamite; Karl Marx, with the levelling rod; Haeckel, with an injection of protoplasmic logic; the Pope, with a pinch of salt and chrism; and the Packer-Kings of America, with pork and beef. What wilt thou have? Whom wilt thou employ? Many are the applicants, many are the guides. But if they are all going the way of Juhannam, the Beef-packer I would choose. For verily, a gobbet of beef on the way were better than canned protoplasmic logic or bottled salt and chrism....

"No; travel not on a Cook's ticket; avoid the guides. Take up thy staff and foot it slowly and leisurely; tarry wherever thy heart would tarry. There is no need of hurrying, O my Brother, whether eternal Juhannam or eternal Jannat await us yonder. Come; if thou hast not a staff, I have two. And what I have in my Scrip I will share with thee. But turn thy back to the guides; for verily we see more of them than of the ruins and monuments. Verily, we get more of the Dragomans than of the Show. Why then continue to move and remove at their command?—Take thy guidebook in hand and I will tell thee what is in it.

"No; the time will come, I tell thee, when every one will be his own guide and dragoman. The time will come when it will not be necessary to write books for others, or to legislate for others, or to make religions for others: the time will come when every one will write his own Book in the Life he lives, and that Book will be his code and his creed;—that Life-Book will be the palace and cathedral of his Soul in all the Worlds."

BOOK THE FIRST IN THE EXCHANGE

TO MAN

No matter how good thou art, O my Brother, or how bad thou art, no matter how high or how low in the scale of being thou art, I still would believe in thee, and have faith in thee, and love thee. For do I not know what clings to thee, and what beckons to thee? The claws of the one and the wings of the other, have I not felt and seen? Look up, therefore, and behold this World-Temple, which, to us, shall be a resting-place, and not a goal. On the border-line of the Orient and Occident it is built, on the mountain-heights overlooking both. No false gods are worshipped in it,—no philosophic, theologic, or anthropomorphic gods. Yea, and the god of the priests and prophets is buried beneath the Fountain, which is the altar of the Temple, and from which flows the eternal spirit of our Maker—our Maker who blinketh when the Claws are deep in our flesh, and smileth when the Wings spring from our Wounds. Verily, we are the children of the God of Humour, and the Fountain in His Temple is ever flowing. Tarry, and refresh thyself, O my Brother, tarry, and refresh thyself.

Khalid.

CHAPTER I

PROBING THE TRIVIAL

The most important in the history of nations and individuals was once the most trivial, and vice versa. The plebeian, who is called to-day the man-in-the-street, can never see and understand the significance of the hidden seed of things, which in time must develop or die. A garter dropt in the ballroom of Royalty gives birth to an Order of Knighthood; a movement to reform the spelling of the English language, initiated by one of the presidents of a great Republic, becomes eventually an object of ridicule. Only two instances to illustrate our point, which is applicable also to time-honoured truths and moralities. But no matter how important or trivial these, he who would give utterance to them must do so in cap and bells, if he would be heard nowadays. Indeed, the play is always the thing; the frivolous is the most essential, if only as a disguise.—For look you, are we not too prosperous to consider seriously your ponderous preachment? And when you bring it to us in book form, do you expect us to take it into our homes and take you into our hearts to boot?—Which argument is convincing even to the man in the barn.

But the Author of the Khedivial Library Manuscript can make his Genius dance the dance of the seven veils, if you but knew. It is to be regretted, however, that he has not mastered the most subtle of arts, the art of writing about one's self. He seldom brushes his wings against the dust or lingers among the humble flowers close to the dust: he does not follow the masters in their entertaining trivialities and fatuities. We remember that even Gibbon interrupts the turgid flow of his spirit to tell us in his Autobiography that he really could, and often did, enjoy a game of cards in the evening. And Rousseau, in a suppurative passion, whispers to us in his Confessions that he even kissed the linen of Madame de Warens' bed when he was alone in her room. And Spencer devotes whole pages in his dull and ponderous history of himself to narrate the all-important narration of his constant indisposition,—to assure us that his ill health more than once threatened the mighty task he had in hand. These, to be sure, are most important revelations. But Khalid here misses his cue. Inspiration does not seem to come to him in firefly-fashion.

He would have done well, indeed, had he studied the method of the professional writers of Memoirs, especially those of France. For might he not then have discoursed delectably on The Romance of my Stick Pin, The Tragedy of my Sombrero, The Scandal of my Red Flannel, The Conquest of my Silk Socks, The Adventures of my Tuxedo, and such like? But Khalid is modest only in the things that pertain to the outward self. He wrote of other Romances and other Tragedies. And when his Genius is not dancing the dance of the seven veils, she is either flirting with the monks of the Lebanon hills or setting fire to something in New York. But this is not altogether satisfactory to the present Editor, who, unlike the Author of the Khedivial Library MS., must keep the reader in mind. 'Tis very well to endeavour to unfold a few of the mysteries of one's palingenesis, but why conceal from us his origin? For is it not important, is it not the fashion at least, that one writing his own history should first expatiate on the humble origin of his ancestors and the distant obscure source of his genius? And having done this, should he not then tell us how he behaved in his boyhood; whether or not he made anklets of his mother's dough for his little sister; whether he did not kindle the fire with his father's Korân; whether he did not walk under the rainbow and try to reach the end of it on the hill-top; and whether he did not write verse when he was but five years of age. About these essentialities Khalid is silent. We only know from him that he is a descendant of the brave sea-daring Phœnicians—a title which might be claimed with justice even by the aborigines of Yucatan—and that he was born in the city of Baalbek, in the shadow of the great Heliopolis, a little way from the mountain-road to the Cedars of Lebanon. All else in this direction is obscure.

And the K. L. MS. which we kept under our pillow for thirteen days and nights, was beginning to worry us. After all, might it not be a literary hoax, we thought, and might not this Khalid be a myth. And yet, he does not seem to have sought any material or worldly good from the writing of his Book. Why, then, should he resort to deception? Still, we doubted. And one evening we were detained by the sandomancer, or sand-diviner, who was sitting cross-legged on the sidewalk in front of the mosque. "I know your mind," said he, before we had made up our mind to consult him. And mumbling his "abraca-dabra" over the sand spread on a cloth before him, he took up his bamboo-stick and wrote therein—Khalid! This was amazing. "And I know more," said he. But after scouring the heaven, he shook his head regretfully and wrote in the sand the name of one of the hasheesh-dens of Cairo. "Go thither; and come to see me again to-morrow evening." Saying which, he folded his sand-book of magic, pocketed his fee, and walked away.

In that hasheesh-den,—the reekiest, dingiest of the row in the Red Quarter,—where the etiolated intellectualities of Cairo flock after midnight, the name of Khalid evokes much resounding wit, and sar-casm, and laughter.

"You mean the new Muhdi," said one, offering us his chobok of hasheesh; "smoke to his health and prosperity. Ha, ha, ha."

And the chorus of laughter, which is part and parcel of a hasheesh jag, was tremendous. Every one thereupon had something to say on the subject. The contagion could not be checked. And Khalid was called "the dervish of science" by one; "the rope-dancer of nature" by anoth-er.

"Our Prophet lived in a cave in the wilderness of New York for five years," remarked a third.

"And he sold his camel yesterday and bought a bicycle instead."

"The Young Turks can not catch him now."

"Ah, but wait till England gets after our new Muhdi."

"Wait till his new phthisic-stricken wife dies."

"Whom will our Prophet marry, if among all the virgins of Egypt we can not find a consumptive for him?"

"And when he pulls down the pyramids to build American Sky-scrapers with their stones, where shall we bury then our Muhdi?"

All of which, although mystifying to us, and depressing, was none the less reassuring. For Khalid, it seems, is not a myth. No; we can even see him, we are told, and touch him, and hear him speak.

"Shakib the poet, his most intimate friend and disciple, will bring you into the sacred presence."

"You can not miss him, for he is the drummer of our new Muhdi, ha, ha, ha!"

And this Shakib was then suspended and stoned. But their humour, like the odor and smoke of gunjah, (hasheesh) was become stifling. So, we lay our chobok down; and, thanking them for the entertain-ment, we struggle through the rolling reek and fling to the open air.

In the grill-room of the Mena House we meet the poet Shakib, who was then drawing his inspiration from a glass of whiskey and soda. Nay, he was drowning his sorrows therein, for his Master, alas! has mysteriously disappeared.

"I have not seen him for ten days," said the Poet; "and I know not where he is.—If I did? Ah, my friend, you would not then see me here. Indeed, I should be with him, and though he be in the trap of the Young Turks." And some real tears flowed down the cheeks of the Poet, as he spoke.

The Mena House, a charming little Branch of Civilisation at the gate of the desert, stands, like man himself, in the shadow of two terrible immensities, the Sphinx and the Pyramid, the Origin and the End. And in the grill-room, over a glass of whiskey and soda, we presume to solve in few words the eternal mystery. But that is not what we came for. And to avoid the bewildering depths into which we were led, we suggested a stroll on the sands. Here the Poet waxed more eloquent, and shed more tears.

"This is our favourite haunt," said he; "here is where we ramble, here is where we loaf. And Khalid once said to me, 'In loafing here, I work as hard as did the masons and hod-carriers who laboured on these pyramids.' And I believe him. For is not a book greater than a pyramid? Is not a mosque or a palace better than a tomb? An object is great in proportion to its power of resistance to time and the elements. That is why we think the pyramids are great. But see, the desert is greater than the pyramids, and the sea is greater than the desert, and the heavens are greater than the sea. And yet, there is not in all these that immortal intelligence, that living, palpitating soul, which you find in a great book. A man who conceives and writes a great book, my friend, has done more work than all the helots that laboured on these pyramidal futilities. That is why I find no exaggeration in Khalid's words. For when he loafs, he does so in good earnest. Not like the camel-driver there or the camel, but after the manner of the great thinkers and mystics: like Al-Fared and Jelal'ud-Deen Rumy, like Socrates and St. Francis of Assisi, Khalid loafs. For can you escape being reproached for idleness by merely working? Are you going to waste your time and power in useless unproductive labour, carrying dates to Hajar (or coals to Newcastle, which is the English equivalent), that you might not be called an idler, a loafer?"

"Indeed not," we reply; "for the Poet taking in the sea, or the woods, or the starry-night, the poet who might be just sharing the sunshine with the salamander, is as much a labourer as the stoker or the bricklayer."

And with a few more such remarks, we showed our friend that, not being of india-rubber, we could not but expand under the heat of his grandiosity.

We then make our purpose known, and Shakib is overjoyed. He offers to kiss us for the noble thought.

"Yes, Europe should know Khalid better, and only through you and me can this be done. For you can not properly understand him, unless you read the *Histoire Intime*, which I have just finished. That will give you *les dessous de cartes* of his character."

"*Les dessons*"—and the Poet who intersperses his Arabic with fancy French, explains.—"The lining, the ligaments."—"Ah, that is exactly what we want."

And he offers to let us have the use of his Manuscript, if we link his name with that of his illustrious Master in this Book. To which we cheerfully agree. For after all, what's in a name?

On the following day, lugging an enormous bundle under each arm, the Poet came. We were stunned as he stood in the door; we felt as if he had struck us in the head with them.

"This is the *Histoire Intime*," said he, laying it gently on the table.

And we laid our hand upon it, fetching a deep sigh. Our misgivings, however, were lighted with a happy idea. We will hire a few boys to read it, we thought, and mark out the passages which please them most. That will be just what an editor wants.

"And this," continued the Poet, laying down the other bundle, "is the original manuscript of my forthcoming Book of Poems.—"

Sweet of him, we thought, to present it to us.

"It will be issued next Autumn in Cairo.—"

Fortunate City!

"And if you will get to work on it at once,—"

Mercy!

"You can get out an English Translation in three month, I am sure——"

We sink in our chair in breathless amazement.

"The Book will then appear simultaneously both in London and Cairo."

We sit up, revived with another happy idea, and assure the Poet that his Work will be translated into a universal language, and that very soon. For which assurance he kisses us again and again, and goes away hugging his Muse.

The idea! A Book of Poems to translate into the English language! As if the English language has not enough of its own troubles! Translate it, O Fire, into your language! Which work the Fire did in two minutes. And the dancing, leaping, singing flames, the white and blue and amber flames, were more beautiful, we thought, than anything the Ms. might contain.

As for the *Histoire Intime*, we split it into three parts and got our boys working on it. The result was most satisfying. For now we can show, and though he is a native of Asia, the land of the Prophets, and though he conceals from us his origin after the manner of the Prophets, that he was born and bred and fed, and even thwacked, like all his fellows there, this Khalid.

CHAPTER II

THE CITY OF BAAL

The City of Baal, or Baalbek, is between the desert and the deep sea. It lies at the foot of Anti-Libanus, in the sunny plains of Coele-Syria, a day's march from either Damascus or Beirut. It is a city with a past as romantic as Rome's, as wicked as Babel's; its ruins testify both to its glory and its shame. It is a city with a future as brilliant as any New-World city; the railroad at its gate, the modern agricultural implements in its fields, and the porcelain bath-tubs in its hotels, can testify to this. It is a city that enticed and still entices the mighty of the earth; Roman Emperors in the past came to appease the wrath of its gods, a German Emperor to-day comes to pilfer its temples. For the Acropolis in the poplar grove is a mine of ruins. The porphyry pillars, the statues, the tablets, the exquisite friezes, the palimpsests, the bas-reliefs,—Time and the Turks have spared a few of these. And when the German Emperor came, Abd'ul-Hamid blinked, and the Berlin Museum is now the richer for it.

Of the Temple of Jupiter, however, only six standing columns remain; of the Temple of Bacchus only the god and the Bacchantes are missing. And why was the one destroyed, the other preserved, only the six columns, had they a tongue, could tell. Indeed, how many blustering vandals have *they* conquered, how many savage attacks have they resisted, what wonders and what orgies have they beheld! These six giants of antiquity, looking over Anti-Lebanon in the East, and down upon the meandering Leontes in the South, and across the Syrian steppes in the North, still hold their own against Time and the Elements. They are the dominating feature of the ruins; they tower above them as the Acropolis towers above the surrounding poplars. And around their base, and through the fissures, flows the perennial grace of the seasons. The sun pays tribute to them in gold; the rain, in mosses and ferns; the Spring, in lupine flowers. And the swallows, nesting in the portico of the Temple of Bacchus, above the curious frieze of egg-decoration,—as curious, too, *their* art of egg-making,—pour around the colossal columns their silvery notes. Surely, these swallows and ferns and lupine flowers are more ancient than the Acropolis. And the marvels of extinct nations can not hold a candle to the marvels of Nature.

Here, under the decaying beauty of Roman art, lies buried the monumental boldness of the Phœnicians, or of a race of giants whose extinction even Homer deplores, and whose name even the Phœnicians could not decipher. For might they not, too, have stood here wondering, guessing, even as we moderns guess and wonder? Might not the Phœnicians have asked the same questions that we ask to-day: Who were the builders? and with what tools? In one of the walls of the Acropolis are stones which a hundred bricklayers can not raise an inch from the ground; and among the ruins of the Temple of Zeus are porphyry pillars, monoliths, which fifty horses could barely move, and the quarry of which is beyond the Syrian desert. There, now, solve the problem for yourself.

Hidden in the grove of silver-tufted poplars is the little Temple of Venus, doomed to keep company with a Mosque. But it is a joy to stand on the bridge above the stream that flows between them, and listen to the muazzen in the minaret and the bulbuls in the Temple. Mohammad calling to Venus, Venus calling to Mohammad—what a romance! We leave the subject to the poet that wants it. Another Laus Veneris to another Swinburne might suggest itself.

An Arab Prophet with the goddess, this time—but the River flows between the Temple and the Mosque. In the city, life is one such picturesque languid stream. The shop-keepers sit on their rugs in their stalls, counting their beads, smoking their narghilahs, waiting indifferently for Allah's bounties. And the hawkers shuffle along crying their wares in beautiful poetic illusions,—the flower-seller singing, "Reconcile your mother-in-law! Perfume your spirit! Buy a jasmine for your soul!" the seller of loaves, his tray on his head, his arms swinging to a measured step, intoning in pious thankfulness, "O thou Eternal, O thou Bountiful!" The *sakka* of licorice-juice, clicking his brass cups calls out to the thirsty one, "Come, drink and live! Come, drink and live!" And ere you exclaim, How quaint! How picturesque! a train of laden camels drives you to the wall, rudely shaking your illusion. And the mules and donkeys, tottering under their heavy burdens, upsetting a tray of sweetmeats here, a counter of spices there, must share the narrow street with you and compel you to move along slowly, languidly like themselves. They seem to take Time by the sleeve and say to it, "What's your hurry?" "These donkeys," Shakib writes, quoting Khalid, "can teach the strenuous Europeans and hustling Americans a lesson."

In the City Square, as we issue from the congested windings of the Bazaar, we are greeted by one of those scrub monuments that are found in almost every city of the Ottoman Empire. And in most cases, they are erected to commemorate the benevolence and public zeal of some wali or pasha who must have made a handsome fortune in the promotion of a public enterprise. Be this as it may. It is not our business here to probe the corruption of any particular Government. But we observe that this miserable botch of a monument is to the ruins of the Acropolis, what this modern absolutism, this effete Turkey is to the magnificent tyrannies of yore. Indeed, nothing is duller, more stupid, more prosaic than a modern absolutism as compared with an ancient one. But why concern ourselves with like comparisons? The world is better to-day in spite of its public monuments. These little flights or frights in marble are as snug in their little squares, in front of their little halls, as are the majestic ruins in their poplar groves. In both instances, Nature and Circumstance have harmonised between the subject and the background. Come along. And let the rhymsters chisel on the monument whatever they like about sculptures and the wali. To condemn in this case is to praise.

We issue from the Square into the drive leading to the spring at the foot of the mountain. On the meadows near the stream, is always to be found a group of Baalbekians bibbing *arak* and swaying languidly to the mellow strains of the lute and the monotonous melancholy of Arabic song. Among such, one occasionally meets with a native who, failing as peddler or merchant in America, returns to his native town, and, utilising the chips of English he picked up in the streets of the New-World cities, becomes a dragoman and guide to English and American tourists.

Now, under this sky, between Anti-Libanus rising near the spring, Rasulain, and the Acropolis towering above the poplars, around these majestic ruins, amidst these fascinating scenes of Nature, Khalid spent the halcyon days of his boyhood. Here he trolled his favourite ditties beating the hoof behind his donkey. For he preferred to be a donkey-boy than to be called a donkey at school. The pedagogue with his drivel and discipline, he could not learn to love. The company of muleteers was much more to his liking. The open air was his school; and every-

thing that riots and rejoices in the open air, he loved. Bulbuls and bee-
tles and butterflies, oxen and donkeys and mules,—these were his
playmates and friends. And when he becomes a muleteer, he reaches
in his first venture, we are told, the top round of the ladder. This progressive scale in his trading, we observe. Husbanding his resources,
he was soon after, by selling his donkey, able to buy a sumpter-mule; a
year later he sells his mule and buys a camel; and finally he sells the
camel and buys a fine Arab mare, which he gives to a tourist for a
hundred pieces of English gold. This is what is called success. And
with the tangible symbol of it, the price of his mare, he emigrates to
America. But that is to come.

Let us now turn our "stereopticon on the screen of reminiscence,"
using the pictures furnished by Shakib. But before they can be used to
advantage, they must undergo a process of retroussage. Many of the
lines need be softened, some of the shades modified, and not a few of
the etchings, absolutely worthless, we consign to the flames. Who of
us, for instance, was not feruled and bastinadoed by the town pedagogue? Who did not run away from school, whimpering, snivelling,
and cursing in his heart and in his sleep the black-board and the hornbook? Nor can we see the significance of the fact that Khalid once
smashed the icon of the Holy Virgin for whetting not his wits, for
hearing not his prayers. It may be he was learning then the use of the
sling, and instead of killing his neighbour's laying-hen, he broke the
sacred effigy. No, we are not warranted to draw from these trivialities
the grand results which send Shakib in ecstasies about his Master's
genius. Nor do we for a moment believe that the waywardness of a
genius or a prophet in boyhood is always a significant adumbration.
Shakespeare started as a deer-poacher, and Rousseau as a thief. Yet,
neither the one nor the other, as far as we know, was a plagiarist. This,
however, does not disprove the contrary proposition, that he who begins as a thief or an iconoclast is likely to end as such. But the
actuating motive has nothing to do with what we, in our retrospective
analysis, are pleased to prove. Not so far forth are we willing to piddle
among the knicknacks of Shakib's *Histoire Intime* of his Master.

Furthermore, how can we interest ourselves in his fiction of history
concerning Baalbek? What have we to do with the fact or fable that
Seth the Prophet lived in this City; that Noah is buried in its vicinity;
that Solomon built the Temple of the Sun for the Queen of Sheba; that
this Prince and Poet used to lunch in Baalbek and dine at Istachre in
Afghanistan; that the chariot of Nimrod drawn by four phœnixes from
the Tower of Babel, lighted on Mt. Hermon to give said Nimrod a

chance to rebuild the said Temple of the Sun? How can we bring any of these fascinating fables to bear upon our subject? It is nevertheless significant to remark that the City of Baal, from the Phœnicians and Moabites down to the Arabs and Turks, has ever been noted for its sanctuaries of carnal lust. The higher religion, too, found good soil here; for Baalbek gave the world many a saint and martyr along with its harlots and poets and philosophers. St. Minius, St. Cyril and St. Theodosius, are the foremost among its holy children; Ste. Odicksyia, a Magdalene, is one of its noted daughters. These were as famous in their days as Ashtarout or Jupiter-Ammon. As famous too is Al-Iman ul-Ouzaai the scholar; al-Makrizi the historian; Kallinichus the chemist, who invented the Greek fire; Kosta ibn Luka, a doctor and philosopher, who wrote among much miscellaneous rubbish a treaty entitled, On the Difference Between the Mind and the Soul; and finally the Muazzen of Baalbek to whom "even the beasts would stop to listen." Ay, Shakib relates quoting al-Makrizi, who in his turn relates, quoting one of the octogenarian Drivellers, *Muhaddetheen* (these men are the chief sources of Arabic History) that he was told by an eye and ear witness that when this celebrated Muazzen was once calling the Faithful to prayer, the camels at the creek craned their necks to listen to the sonorous music of his voice. And such was their delight that they forgot they were thirsty. This, by the way of a specimen of the *Muhaddetheen.* Now, about these historical worthies of Baalbek, whom we have but named, Shakib writes whole pages, and concludes——and here is the point—that Khalid might be a descendant of any or all of them! For in him, our Scribe seriously believes, are lusty strains of many varied and opposing humours. And although he had not yet seen the sea, he longed when a boy for a long sea voyage, and he would sail little paper boats down the stream to prove the fact. In truth, that is what Shakib would prove. The devil and such logic had a charm for us once, but no more.

Here is another bubble of retrospective analysis to which we apply the needle. It is asserted as a basis for another astounding deduction that Khalid used to sleep in the ruined Temple of Zeus. As if ruined temples had anything to do with the formation or deformation of the brain-cells or the soul-afflatus! The devil and such logic, we repeat, had once a charm for us. But this, in brief, is how it came about. Khalid hated the pedagogue to whom he had to pay a visit of courtesy every day, and loved his cousin Najma whom he was not permitted to see. And when he runs away from the bastinado, breaking in revenge the icon of the Holy Virgin, his father turns him away from home.

Complaining not, whimpering not, he goes. And hearing the bulbuls calling in the direction of Najma's house that evening, he repairs thither. But the crabbed, cruel uncle turns him away also, and bolts the door. Whereupon Khalid, who was then in the first of his teens, takes a big scabrous rock and sends it flying against that door. The crabbed uncle rushes out, blustering, cursing; the nephew takes up another of those scabrous missiles and sends it whizzing across his shoulder. The second one brushes his ear. The third sends the blood from his temple. And this, while beating a retreat and cursing his father and his uncle and their ancestors back to fifty generations. He is now safe in the poplar grove, and his uncle gives up the charge. With a broken noddle he returns home, and Khalid with a broken heart wends his way to the Acropolis, the only shelter in sight. In relating this story, Shakib mentions "the horrible old moon, who was wickedly smiling over the town that night." A broken icon, a broken door, a broken pate,—a big price this, the crabbed uncle and the cruel father had to pay for thwarting the will of little Khalid. "But he entered the Acropolis a conqueror," says our Scribe; "he won the battle." And he slept in the temple, in the portico thereof, as sound as a muleteer. And the swallows in the niches above heard him sleep.

In the morning he girds his loins with a firm resolution. No longer will he darken his father's door. He becomes a muleteer and accomplishes the success of which we have spoken. His first beau idéal was to own the best horse in Baalbek; and to be able to ride to the camp of the Arabs and be mistaken for one of them, was his first great ambition. Which he realises sooner than he thought he would. For thrift, grit and perseverance, are a few of the rough grains in his character. But no sooner he is possessed of his ideal than he begins to loosen his hold upon it. He sold his mare to the tourist, and was glad he did not attain the same success in his first love. For he loved his mare, and he could not have loved his cousin Najma more. "The realisation is a terrible thing," writes our Scribe, quoting his Master. But when this fine piece of wisdom was uttered, whether when he was sailing paper boats in Baalbek, or unfurling his sails in New York, we can not say.

And now, warming himself on the fire of his first ideal, Khalid will seek the shore and launch into unknown seas towards unknown lands. From the City of Baal to the City of Demiurgic Dollar is not in fact a far cry. It has been remarked that he always dreamt of adventures, of long journeys across the desert or across the sea. He never was satisfied with the seen horizon, we are told, no matter how vast and beautiful. His soul always yearned for what was beyond, above or below, the visible line. And had not the European tourist alienated from him the love of his mare and corrupted his heart with the love of gold, we might have heard of him in Mecca, in India, or in Dahomey. But Shakib prevails upon him to turn his face toward the West. One day, following some tourists to the Cedars, they behold from Dahr'ul-Qadhib the sun setting in the Mediterranean and make up their minds to follow it too. "For the sundown," writes Shakib, "was more appealing to us than the sunrise, ay, more beautiful. The one was so near, the other so far away. Yes, we beheld the Hesperian light that day, and praised Allah. It was the New World's bonfire of hospitality: the sun called to us, and we obeyed."

CHAPTER III

VIA DOLOROSA

In their baggy, lapping trousers and crimson caps, each carrying a bundle and a rug under his arm, Shakib and Khalid are smuggled through the port of Beirut at night, and safely rowed to the steamer. Indeed, we are in a country where one can not travel without a passport, or a password, or a little pass-money. And the boatmen and officials of the Ottoman Empire can better read a gold piece than a passport. So, Shakib and Khalid, not having the latter, slip in a few of the former, and are smuggled through. One more longing, lingering glance behind, and the dusky peaks of the Lebanons, beyond which their native City of Baal is sleeping in peace, recede from view. On the high sea of hope and joy they sail; "under the Favonian wind of enthusiasm, on the friendly billows of boyish dreams," they roll. Ay, and they sing for joy. On and on, to the gold-swept shores of distant lands, to the generous cities and the bounteous fields of the West, to the Paradise of the World—to America.

We need not dwell too much with our Scribe, on the repulsive details of the story of the voyage. We ourselves have known a little of the suffering and misery which emigrants must undergo, before they reach that Western Paradise of the Oriental imagination. How they are huddled like sheep on deck from Beirut to Marseilles; and like cattle transported under hatches across the Atlantic; and bullied and browbeaten by rough disdainful stewards; and made to pay for a leathery gobbet of beef and a slice of black flint-like bread: all this we know. But that New World paradise is well worth these passing privations.

The second day at sea, when the two Baalbekian lads are snug on deck, their rugs spread out not far from the stalls in which Syrian cattle are shipped to Egypt and Arab horses to Europe or America, they rummage in their bags—and behold, a treat! Shakib takes out his favourite poet Al-Mutanabbi, and Khalid, his favourite bottle, the choicest of the Ksarah distillery of the Jesuits. For this whilom donkey-boy will begin by drinking the wine of these good Fathers and then their— blood! His lute is also with him; and he will continue to practise the few lessons which the bulbuls of the poplar groves have taught him. No, he cares not for books. And so, he uncorks the bottle, hands it to Shakib his senior, then takes a nip himself, and, thrumming his lute strings, trolls a few doleful pieces of Arabic song. "In these," he would say to Shakib, pointing to the bottle and the lute, "is real poetry, and not in that book with which you would kill me." And Shakib, in stingless sarcasm, would insist that the music in Al-Mutanabbi's lines is just a little more musical than Khalid's thrumming. They quarrel about this. And in justice to both, we give the following from the *Histoire Intime*.

"When we left our native land," Shakib writes, "my literary bent was not shared in the least by Khalid. I had gone through the higher studies which, in our hedge-schools and clerical institutions, do not reach a very remarkable height. Enough of French to understand the authors tabooed by our Jesuit professors,—the Voltaires, the Rousseaus, the Diderots; enough of Arabic to enable one to parse and analyse the verse of Al-Mutanabbi; enough of Church History to show us, not how the Church wielded the sword of persecution, but how she was persecuted herself by the pagans and barbarians of the earth;—of these and such like consists the edifying curriculum. Now, of this high phase of education, Khalid was thoroughly immune. But his intuitive sagacity was often remarkable, and his humour, sweet and pathetic. Once when I was reading aloud some of the Homeric effusions of Al-Mutanabbi, he said to me, as he was playing his lute, 'In the heart of this,' pointing to the lute, 'and in the heart of me, there be more poetry than in that book with which you would kill me.' And one day, after wandering clandestinely through the steamer, he comes to me with a gesture of surprise and this: 'Do you know, there are passengers who sleep in bunks below, over and across each other? I saw them, billah! And I was told they pay more than we do for such a low passage—the fools! Think on it. I peeped into a little room, a dingy, smelling box, which had in it six berths placed across and above each other like the shelves of the reed manchons we build for our silk-worms at home. I wouldn't sleep in one of them, billah! even though they bribe me. This bovine fragrance, the sight of these fine horses, the rioting of the wind above us, should make us forget the brutality of the stewards. Indeed, I am as content, as comfortable here, as are their Excellencies in what is called the Salon. Surely, we are above them—at least, in the night. What matters it, then, if ours is called the Fourth Class and theirs the Primo. Wherever one is happy, Shakib, there is the Primo.'"

But this happy humour is assailed at Marseilles. His placidity and stolid indifference are rudely shaken by the sharpers, who differ only from the boatmen of Beirut in that they wear pantaloons and intersperse their Arabic with a jargon of French. These brokers, like rapacious bats, hover around the emigrant and before his purse is opened for the fourth time, the trick is done. And with what ceremony, you shall see. From the steamer the emigrant is led to a dealer in frippery, where he is required to doff his baggy trousers and crimson cap, and put on a suit of linsey-woolsey and a hat of hispid felt: end of First Act; open the purse. From the dealer of frippery, spick and span from top to toe, he is taken to the hostelry, where he is detained a fortnight, sometimes a month, on the pretext of having to wait for the best steamer: end of Second Act; open the purse. From the hostelry at last to the steamship agent, where they secure for him a third-class passage on a fourth-class ship across the Atlantic: end of Third Act; open the purse. And now that the purse is almost empty, the poor emigrant is permitted to leave. They send him to New York with much gratitude in his heart and a little trachoma in his eyes. The result being that a month later they have to look into such eyes again. But the purse of the distressed emigrant now being empty,—empty as his hopes and dreams,—the rapacious bats hover not around him, and the door of the verminous hostelry is shut in his face. He is left to starve on the western shore of the Mediterranean.

Ay, even the droll humour and stolidity of Khalid, are shaken, aroused, by the ghoulish greed, the fell inhumanity of these sharpers. And Shakib from his cage of fancy lets loose upon them his hyenas of satire. In a squib describing the bats and the voyage he says: "The voyage to America is the Via Dolorosa of the emigrant; and the Port of Beirut, the verminous hostelries of Marseilles, the Island of Ellis in New York, are the three stations thereof. And if your hopes are not crucified at the third and last station, you pass into the Paradise of your dreams. If they are crucified, alas! The gates of the said Paradise will be shut against you; the doors of the hostelries will be slammed in your face; and with a consolation and a vengeance you will throw yourself at the feet of the sea in whose bosom some charitable Jonah will carry you to your native strands."

And when the emigrant has a surplus of gold, when his capital is such as can not be dissipated on a suit of shoddy, a fortnight's lodging, and a passage across the Atlantic, the ingenious ones proceed with the Fourth Act of *Open Thy Purse.* "Instead of starting in New York as a peddler," they say, unfolding before him one of their alluring schemes, "why not do so as a merchant?" And the emigrant opens his purse for the fourth time in the office of some French manufacturer, where he purchases a few boxes of trinketry,—scapulars, prayer-beads, crosses, jewelry, gewgaws, and such like,—all said to be made in the Holy Land. These he brings over with him as his stock in trade.

Now, Khalid and Shakib, after passing a fortnight in Marseilles, and going through the Fourth Act of the Sorry Show, find their dignity as merchants rudely crushed beneath the hatches of the Atlantic steamer. For here, even the pleasure of sleeping on deck is denied them. The Atlantic Ocean would not permit of it. Indeed, everybody has to slide into their stivy bunks to save themselves from its rising wrath. A fortnight of such unutterable misery is quite supportable, however, if one continues to cherish the Paradise already mentioned. But in this dark, dingy smelling hole of the steerage, even the poets cease to dream. The boatmen of Beirut and the sharpers of Marseilles we could forget; but in this grave among a hundred and more of its kind, set over and across each other, neither the lute nor the little that remained in that Ksarah bottle, could bring us any solace.

We are told that Khalid took up his lute but once throughout the voyage. And this when they were permitted one night to sleep on deck. We are also informed that Khalid had a remarkable dream, which, to our Scribe at least, is not meaningless. And who of us, thou silly Scribe, did not in his boyhood tell his dreams to his mother, who would turn them in her interpretation inside out? But Khalid, we are assured, continued to cherish the belief, even in his riper days, that when you dream you are in Jannat, for instance, you must be prepared to go through Juhannam the following day. A method of interpretation as ancient as Joseph, to be sure. But we quote the dream to show that Khalid should not have followed the setting sun. He should have turned his face toward the desert.

They slept on deck that night. They drank the wine of the Jesuits, repeated, to the mellow strains of the lute, the song of the bulbuls, in-toned the verses of Al-Mutanabbi, and, wrapping themselves in their rugs, fell asleep. But in the morning they were rudely jostled from their dreams by a spurt from the hose of the sailors washing the deck. Complaining not, they straggle down to their bunks to change their clothes. And Khalid, as he is doing this, implores Shakib not to men-tion to him any more that New-World paradise. "For I have dreamt last night," he continues, "that, in the multicoloured robes of an Arab amir, on a caparisoned dromedary, at the head of an immense multitude of people, I was riding through the desert. Whereto and wherefrom, I know not. But those who followed me seemed to know; for they cried, 'Long have we waited for thee, now we shall enter in peace.' And at every oasis we passed, the people came to the gate to meet us, and, prostrating themselves before me, kissed the fringe of my garment. Even the women would touch my boots and kiss their hands, exclaiming, '*Allahu akbar!*' And the palm trees, billah! I could see bending towards us that we might eat of their fruits, and the springs seemed to flow with us into the desert that we might never thirst. Ay, thus in triumph we marched from one camp to another, from one oasis to the next, until we reached the City on the Hills of the Cedar Groves. Outside the gate, we were met by the most beautiful of its tawny women, and four of these surrounded my camel and took the reins from my hand. I was then escorted through the gates, into the City, up to the citadel, where I was awaited by their Princess. And she, taking a necklace of cowries from a bag that hung on her breast, placed it on my head, saying, 'I crown thee King of—' But I could not hear the rest, which was drowned by the cheering of the multitudes. And the cheering, O Shakib, was drowned by the hose of the sailors. Oh, that hose! Is it not made in the paradise you harp upon, the paradise we are coming to? Never, therefore, mention it to me more."

This is the dream, at once simple and symbolic, which begins to worry Khalid. "For in the evening of the day he related it to me," writes Shakib, "I found him sitting on the edge of his bunk brooding over I know not what. It was the first time he had the blues. Nay, it was the first time he looked pensive and profound. And upon asking him the reason for this, he said, 'I am thinking of the paper-boats which I used to sail down the stream in Baalbek, and that makes me sad.'"

How strange! And yet, this first event recorded by our Scribe, in which Khalid is seen struggling with the mysterious and unknown, is most significant. Another instance, showing a latent phase, hitherto dormant, in his character, we note. Among the steerage passengers is a Syrian girl who much resembles his cousin Najma. She was sea-sick throughout the voyage, and when she comes out to breathe of the fresh air, a few hours before they enter the harbour of New York, Khalid sees her, and Shakib swears that he saw a tear in Khalid's eye as he stood there gazing upon her. Poor Khalid! For though we are approaching the last station of the Via Dolorosa, though we are nearing the enchanted domes of the wonder-working, wealth-worshipping City, he is inexplicably sad.

And Shakib, directly after swearing that he saw a tear in his eye, writes the following: "Up to this time I observed in my friend only the dominating traits of a hard-headed, hard-hearted boy, stubborn, impetuous, intractable. But from the time he related to me his dream, a change in his character was become manifest. In fact a new phase was being gradually unfolded. Three things I must emphasise in this connection: namely, the first dream he dreamt in a foreign land, the first time he looked pensive and profound, and the first tear he shed before we entered New York. These are keys to the secret chamber of one's soul."

And now, that the doors, by virtue of our Scribe's open-sesames, are thrown open, we enter, *bismillah.*

CHAPTER IV

ON THE WHARF OF ENCHANTMENT

Not in our make-up, to be sure,—not in the pose which is preceded by the tantaras of a trumpet,—do the essential traits in our character first reveal themselves. But truly in the little things the real self is exteriorised. Shakib observes closely the rapid changes in his co-adventurer's humour, the shadowy traits which at that time he little understood. And now, by applying his palm to his front, he illumines those chambers of which he speaks, and also the niches therein. He helps us to understand the insignificant points which mark the rapid undercurrents of the seemingly sluggish soul of Khalid. Not in vain, therefore, does he crystallise for us that first tear he shed in the harbour of Manhattan. But his gush about the recondite beauty of this pearl of melancholy, shall not be intended upon the gustatory nerves of the Reader. This then we note—his description of New York harbour.

"And is this the gate of Paradise," he asks, "or the port of some subterrestrial city guarded by the Jinn? What a marvel of enchantment is everything around us! What manifestations of industrial strength, what monstrosities of wealth and power, are here! These vessels proudly putting to sea; these tenders scurrying to meet the Atlantic greyhound which is majestically moving up the bay; these barges loading and unloading schooners from every strand, distant and near; these huge lighters carrying even railroads over the water; these fire-boats scudding through the harbour shrilling their sirens; these careworn, grim, strenuous multitudes ferried across from one enchanted shore to another; these giant structures tickling heaven's sides; these cable bridges, spanning rivers, uniting cities; and this superterrestrial goddess, torch in hand—wake up, Khalid, and behold these wonders. Salaam, this enchanted City! There is the Brooklyn Bridge, and here is the Statue of Liberty which people speak of, and which are as famous as the Cedars of Lebanon."

But Khalid is as impassive as the bronze goddess herself. He leans over the rail, his hand supporting his cheek, and gazes into the ooze. The stolidity of his expression is appalling. With his mouth open as usual, his lips relaxed, his tongue sticking out through the set teeth,— he looks as if his head were in a noose. But suddenly he braces up, runs down for his lute, and begins to serenade—Greater New York?

> "On thee be Allah's grace,
> Who hath the well-loved face!"

No; not toward this City does his heart flap its wings of song. He is on another sea, in another harbour. Indeed, what are these wonders as compared with those of the City of Love? The Statue of Eros there is more imposing than the Statue of Liberty here. And the bridges are not of iron and concrete, but of rainbows and—moonshine! Indeed, both these lads are now on the wharf of enchantment; the one on the palpable, the sensuous, the other on the impalpable and unseen. But both, alas, are suddenly, but temporarily, disenchanted as they are jostled out of the steamer into the barge which brings them to the Juhannam of Ellis Island. Here, the unhappy children of the steerage are dumped into the Bureau of Emigration as—such stuff! For even in the land of equal rights and freedom, we have a right to expect from others the courtesy and decency which we ourselves do not have to show, or do not know.

These are sturdy and adventurous foreigners whom the grumpy officers jostle and hustle about. For neither poverty, nor oppression, nor both together can drive a man out of his country, unless the soul within him awaken. Indeed, many a misventurous cowering peasant continues to live on bread and olives in his little village, chained in the fear of dying of hunger in a foreign land. Only the brave and daring spirits hearken to the voice of discontent within them. They give themselves up to the higher aspirations of the soul, no matter how limited such aspirations might be, regardless of the dangers and hardship of a long sea voyage, and the precariousness of their plans and hopes. There may be nothing noble in renouncing one's country, in abandoning one's home, in forsaking one's people; but is there not something remarkable in this great move one makes? Whether for better or for worse, does not the emigrant place himself above his country, his people and his Government, when he turns away from them, when he goes forth propelled by that inner self which demands of him a new life?

And might it not be a better, a cleaner, a higher life? What say our Masters of the Island of Ellis? Are not these straggling, smelling, downcast emigrants almost as clean inwardly, and as pure, as the grumpy officers who harass and humiliate them? Is not that spirit of discontent which they cherish, and for which they carry the cross, so to speak, across the sea, deserving of a little consideration, a little civility, a little kindness?

Even louder than this Shakib cries out, while Khalid open-mouthed sucks his tongue. Here at the last station, where the odours of disinfectants are worse than the stench of the steerage, they await behind the bars their turn; stived with Italian and Hungarian fellow sufferers, uttering such whimpers of expectancy, exchanging such gestures of hope. Soon they shall be brought forward to be examined by the doctor and the interpreting officer; the one shall pry their purses, the other their eyes. For in this United States of America we want clear-sighted citizens at least. And no cold-purses, if the matter can be helped. But neither the eyes, alas, nor the purses of our two emigrants are conformable to the Law; the former are filled with granulations of trachoma, the latter have been emptied by the sharpers of Marseilles. Which means that they shall be detained for the present; and if within a fortnight nothing turns up in their favour, they shall certainly be deported.

Trachoma! a little granulation on the inner surface of the eyelids, what additional misery does it bring upon the poor deported emigrant? We are asked to shed a tear for him, to weep with him over his blasted hopes, his strangled aspirations, his estate in the mother country sold or mortgaged,—in either case lost,—and his seed of a new life crushed in its cotyledon by the physician who might be short-sighted himself, or even blind. But the law must be enforced for the sake of the clear-sighted citizens of the Republic. We will have nothing to do with these poor blear-eyed foreigners.

And thus our grievous Scribe would continue, if we did not exercise the prerogative of our Editorial Divan. Rather let us pursue our narration. Khalid is now in the hospital, awaiting further development in his case. But in Shakib's, whose eyes are far gone in trachoma, the decision of the Board of Emigration is final, irrevocable. And so, after being detained a week in the Emigration pen, the unfortunate Syrian must turn his face again toward the East. Not out into the City, but out upon the sea, he shall be turned adrift. The grumpy officer shall grumpishly enforce the decision of the Board by handing our Scribe to the Captain of the first steamer returning to Europe—if our Scribe can be found! For this flyaway son of a Phœnician did not seem to wait for the decision of the polyglot Judges of the Emigration Board.

And that he did escape, we are assured. For one morning he eludes the grumpy officer, and sidles out among his Italian neighbours who were permitted to land. See him genuflecting now, to kiss the curbstone and thank Allah that he is free. But before he can enjoy his freedom, before he can sit down and chuckle over the success of his escapade, he must bethink him of Khalid. He will not leave him to the mercy of the honourable Agents of the Law, if he can help it. Trachoma, he knows, is a hard case to cure. And in ten days, under the care of the doctors, it might become worse. Straightway, therefore, he puts himself to the dark task. A few visits to the Hospital where Khalid is detained—the patients in those days were not held at Ellis Island—and the intrigue is afoot. On the third or fourth visit, we can not make out which, a note in Arabic is slipt into Khalid's pocket, and with a significant Arabic sign, Shakib takes himself off.

The evening of that very day, the trachoma-afflicted Syrian was absent from the ward. He was carried off by Iblis,—the porter and a few Greenbacks assisting. Yes, even Shakib, who knew only a few English monosyllables, could here make himself understood. For money is one of the two universal languages of the world, the other being love. Indeed, money and love are as eloquent in Turkey and Dahomey as they are in Paris or New York.

And here we reach one of those hedges in the *Histoire Intime* which we must go through in spite of the warning-signs. Between two paragraphs, to be plain, in the one of which we are told how the two Syrians established themselves as merchants in New York, in the other, how and wherefor they shouldered the peddling-box and took to the road, there is a crossed paragraph containing a most significant revelation. It seems that after giving the matter some serious thought, our Scribe came to the conclusion that it is not proper to incriminate his illustrious Master. But here is a confession which a hundred crosses can not efface. And if he did not want to bring the matter to our immediate cognisance, why, we ask, did he not re-write the page? Why did he not cover well that said paragraph with crosses and arabesques? We do suspect him here of chicanery; for by this plausible recantation he would shift the responsibility to the shoulders of the Editor, if the secret is divulged. Be this as it may, no red crosses can conceal from us the astounding confession, which we now give out.

For the two young Syrians, who were smuggled out of their country by the boatmen of Beirut, and who smuggled themselves into the city of New York (we beg the critic's pardon; for, being foreigners ourselves, we ought to be permitted to stretch this term, smuggle, to cover an Arabic metaphor, or to smuggle into it a foreign meaning), these two Syrians, we say, became, in their capacity of merchants, smugglers of the most ingenious and most evasive type.

We now note the following, which pertains to their business. We learn that they settled in the Syrian Quarter directly after clearing their merchandise. And before they entered their cellar, we are assured, they washed their hands of all intrigues and were shrived of their sins by the Maronite priest of the Colony. For they were pious in those days, and right Catholics. 'Tis further set down in the *Histoire Intime*:

"We rented a cellar, as deep and dark and damp as could be found. And our landlord was a Teague, nay, a kind-hearted old Irishman, who helped us put up the shelves, and never called for the rent in the dawn of the first day of the month. In the front part of this cellar we had our shop; in the rear, our home. On the floor we laid our mattresses, on the shelves, our goods. And never did we stop to think who in this case was better off. The safety of our merchandise before our own. But ten days after we had settled down, the water issued forth from the floor and inundated our shop and home. It rose so high that it destroyed half of our capital stock and almost all our furniture. And yet, we continued to live in the cellar, because, perhaps, every one of our compatriot-merchants did so. We were all alike subject to these inundations in the winter season. I remember when the water first rose in our store, Khalid was so hard set and in such a pucker that he ran out capless and in his shirt sleeves to discover in the next street the source of the flood. And one day, when we were pumping out the water he asked me if I thought this was easier than rolling our roofs in Baalbek. For truly, the paving-roller is child's play to this pump. And a leaky roof is better than an inundated cellar."

However, this is not the time for brooding. They have to pump ahead to save what remained of their capital stock. But Khalid, nevertheless, would brood and jabber. And what an inundation of ideas, and what questions!

"Think you," he asks, "that the inhabitants of this New World are better off than those of the Old?—Can you imagine mankind living in a huge cellar of a world and you and I pumping the water out of its bottom?—I can see the palaces on which you waste your rhymes, but mankind live in them only in the flesh. The soul I tell you, still occupies the basement, even the sub-cellar. And an inundated cellar at that. The soul, Shakib, is kept below, although the high places are vacant."

And his partner sputters out his despair; for instead of helping to pump out the water, Khalid stands there gazing into it, as if by some miracle he would draw it out with his eyes or with his breath. And the poor Poet cries out, "Pump! the water is gaining on us, and our shop is going to ruin. Pump!" Whereupon the lazy, absent-minded one resumes pumping, while yearning all the while for the plashing stone-rollers and the purling eaves of his home in Baalbek. And once in a pinch,—they are labouring under a peltering rain,—he stops as is his wont to remind Shakib of the Arabic saying, "From the dripping ceiling to the running gargoyle." He is labouring again under a hurricane of ideas. And again he asks, "Are you sure we are better off here?"

And our poor Scribe, knee-deep in the water below, blusters out curses, which Khalid heeds not. "I am tired of this job," he growls; "the stone-roller never drew so much on my strength, nor did mule-teering. Ah, for my dripping ceiling again, for are we not now under the running gargoyle?" And he reverts into a stupor, leaving the world to the poet and the pump.

For five years and more they lead such a life in the cellar. And they do not move out of it, lest they excite the envy of their compatriots. But instead of sleeping on the floor, they stretch themselves on the counters. The rising tide teaches them this little wisdom, which keeps the doctor and Izräil away. Their merchandise, however,—their crosses, and scapulars and prayer-beads,—are beyond hope of recovery. For what the rising tide spares, the rascally flyaway peddlers carry away. That is why they themselves shoulder the box and take to the road. And the pious old dames of the suburbs, we are told, receive them with such exclamations of joy and wonder, and almost tear their coats to get from them a sacred token. For you must remember, they are from the Holy Land. Unlike their goods, they at least are genuine. And every Saturday night, after beating the hoof in the country and making such fabulous profits on their false Holy-Land gewgaws, they return to their cellar happy and content.

"In three years," writes our Scribe, "Khalid and I acquired what I still consider a handsome fortune. Each of us had a bank account, and a check book which we seldom used.... In spite of which, we continued to shoulder the peddling box and tramp along.... And Khalid would say to me, 'A peddler is superior to a merchant; we travel and earn money; our compatriots the merchants rust in their cellars and lose it.' To be sure, peddling in the good old days was most attractive. For the exercise, the gain, the experience—these are rich acquirements."

And both Shakib and Khalid, we apprehend, have been hitherto most moderate in their habits. The fact that they seldom use their check books, testifies to this. They have now a peddleress, Im-Hanna by name, who occupies their cellar in their absence, and keeps what little they have in order. And when they return every Saturday night from their peddling trip, they find the old woman as ready to serve them as a mother. She cooks *mojadderah* for them, and sews the bed-linen on the quilts as is done in the mother country.

"The linen," says Shakib, "was always as white as a dove's wing, when Im-Hanna was with us."

And in the Khedivial Library Manuscript we find this curious note upon that popular Syrian dish of lentils and olive oil.

"*Mojadderah*," writes Khalid, "has a marvellous effect upon my humour and nerves. There are certain dishes, I confess, which give me the blues. Of these, fried eggplants and cabbage boiled with corn-beef on the American system of boiling, that is to say, cooking, I abominate the most. But *mojadderah* has such a soothing effect on the nerves; it conduces to cheerfulness, especially when the raw onion or the leek is taken with it. After a good round pewter platter of this delicious dish and a dozen leeks, I feel as if I could do the work of all mankind. And I am then in such a beatific state of mind that I would share with all mankind my sack of lentils and my pipkin of olive oil. I wonder not at Esau's extravagance, when he saw a steaming mess of it. For what is a birthright in comparison?"

That Shakib also shared this beatific mood, the following quaint picture of their Saturday nights in the cellar, will show.

"A bank account," he writes, "a good round dish of *mojadderah*, the lute for Khalid, Al-Mutanabbi for me,—neither of us could forego his hobby,—and Im-Hanna, affectionate, devoted as our mothers,—these were the joys of our Saturday nights in our underground diggings. We were absolutely happy. And we never tried to measure our happiness in those days, or gauge it, or flay it to see if it be dead or alive, false or real. Ah, the blessedness of that supreme unconsciousness which wrapped us as a mother would her babe, warming and caressing our hearts. We did not know then that happiness was a thing to be sought. We only knew that peddling is a pleasure, that a bank account is a supreme joy, that a dish of *mojadderah* cooked by Im-Hanna is a royal delight, that our dour dark cellar is a palace of its kind, and that happiness, like a bride, issues from all these, and, touching the strings of Khalid's lute, mantles us with song."

CHAPTER V

THE CELLAR OF THE SOUL

Heretofore, Khalid and Shakib have been inseparable as the Pointers. They always appeared together, went the rounds of their peddling orbit together, and together were subject to the same conditions and restraints. Which restraints are a sort of sacrifice they make on the altar of friendship. One, for instance, would never permit himself an advantage which the other could not enjoy, or a pleasure in which the other could not share. They even slept under the same blanket, we learn, ate from the same plate, puffed at the same narghilah, which Shakib brought with him from Baalbek, and collaborated in writing to one lady-love! A condition of unexampled friendship this, of complete oneness. They had both cut themselves garments from the same cloth, as the Arabic saying goes. And on Sunday afternoon, in garments spick and span, they would take the air in Battery Park, where the one would invoke the Statue of Liberty for a thought, or the gilded domes of Broadway for a metaphor, while the other would be scouring the horizon for the Nothingness, which is called, in the recondite cant of the sophisticated, a vague something.

In the Khedivial Library MS. we find nothing which this Battery Park might have inspired. And yet, we can not believe that Khalid here was only attracted by that vague something which, in his spiritual enceinteship, he seemed to relish. Nothing? Not even the does and kangaroos that adorn the Park distracted or detained him? We doubt it; and Khalid's lute sustains us in our doubt. Ay, and so does our Scribe; for in his *Histoire Intime* we read the following, which we faithfully transcribe.

"Of the many attractions of Battery Park, the girls and the sea were my favourite. For the girls in a crowd have for me a fascination which only the girls at the bath can surpass. I love to lose myself in a crowd, to buffet, so to speak, its waves, to nestle under their feathery crests. For the rolling waves of life, the tumbling waves of the sea, and the fiery waves of Al-Mutanabbi's poetry have always been my delight. In Battery Park I took especial pleasure in reading aloud my verses to Khalid, or in fact to the sea, for Khalid never would listen.

"Once I composed a few stanzas to the Milkmaid who stood in her wagon near the lawn, rattling out milk-punches to the boys. A winsome lass she was, fresh in her sororiation, with fair blue eyes, a celestial flow of auburn hair, and cheeks that suggested the milk and cherry in the glass she rattled out to me. I was reading aloud the stanzas which she inspired, when Khalid, who was not listening, pointed out to me a woman whose figure and the curves thereof were remarkable. 'Is it not strange,' said he, 'how the women here indraw their stomachs and outdraw their hips? And is not this the opposite of the shape which our women cultivate?'

"Yes, with the Lebanon women, the convex curve beneath the waist is frontward, not hindward. But that is a matter of taste, I thought, and man is partly responsible for either convexity. I have often wondered, however, why the women of my country cultivate that shape. And why do they in America cultivate the reverse of it? Needless to say that both are pruriently titillating,—both distentions are damnably suggestive, quite killing. The American woman, from a fine sense of modesty, I am told, never or seldom ventures abroad, when big with child. But in the kangaroo figure, the burden is slightly shifted and naught is amiss. Ah, such haunches as are here exhibited suggest the *aliats* of our Asiatic sheep."

And what he says about the pruriently titillating convexities, whether frontward or hindward, suggests a little prudery. For in his rhymes he betrays both his comrade and himself. Battery Park and the attractions thereof prove fatal. Elsewhere, therefore, they must go, and begin to draw on their bank accounts. Which does not mean, however, that they are far from the snare. No; for when a young man begins to suffer from what the doctors call hebephrenia, the farther he draws away from such snares the nearer he gets to them. And these lusty Syrians could not repel the magnetic attraction of the polypiosis of what Shakib likens to the *aliat* (fattail) of our Asiatic sheep. Surely, there be more devils under such an *aliat* than under the hat of a Jesuit. And Khalid is the first to discover this. Both have been ensnared, however, and both, when in the snare, have been infernally inspired. What Khalid wrote, when he was under the influence of feminine curves, was preserved by Shakib, who remarks that one evening, after returning from the Park, Khalid said to him, 'I am going to write a poem.' A fortnight later, he hands him the following, which he jealously kept among his papers.

> I dreamt I was a donkey-boy again.
> Out on the sun-swept roads of Baalbek, I tramp behind my burro, trolling my *mulayiah*.
> At noon, I pass by a garden redolent of mystic scents and tarry awhile.
> Under an orange tree, on the soft green grass, I stretch my limbs.
> The daisies, the anemones, and the cyclamens are round me pressing:
> The anemone buds hold out to me their precious rubies; the daisies kiss me in the eyes and lips; and the cyclamens shake their powder in my hair.
> On the wall, the roses are nodding, smiling; above me the orange blossoms surrender themselves to the wooing breeze; and on yonder rock the salamander sits, complacent and serene.
> I take a daisy, and, boy as boys go, question its petals:
> Married man or monk, I ask, plucking them off one by one,
> And the last petal says, Monk.
> I perfume my fingers with crumpled cyclamens, cover my face with the dark-eyed anemones, and fall asleep.
> And my burro sleeps beneath the wall, in the shadow of nodding roses.
> And the black-birds too are dozing, and the bulbuls flitting by whisper with their wings, 'salaam.'
> Peace and salaam!
> The bulbul, the black-bird, the salamander, the burro, and the burro-boy, are to each other shades of noon-day sun:
> Happy, loving, generous, and free;—
> As happy as each other, and as free.
> We do what we please in Nature's realm, go where we please;
> No one's offended, no one ever wronged.
> No sentinels hath Nature, no police.
> But lo, a goblin as I sleep comes forth;—

A goblin taller than the tallest poplar, who carries me up-
on his neck to the Park in far New York.
Here women, light-heeled, heavy-haunched, pace up and
down the flags in graceful gait.
My roses these, I cry, and my orange blossoms.
But the goblin placed his hand upon my mouth, and I was
dumb.
The cyclamens, the anemones, the daisies, I saw them, but
I could not speak to them.
The goblin placed his hand upon my mouth, and I was
dumb.
O take me back to my own groves, I cried, or let me
speak.
But he threw me off his shoulders in a huff, among the
daisies and the cyclamens.
Alone among them, but I could not speak.
He had tied my tongue, the goblin, and left me there
alone.
And in front of me, and towards me, and beside me,
Walked Allah's fairest cyclamens and anemones.
I smell them, and the tears flow down my cheeks;
I can not even like the noon-day bulbul
Whisper with my wings, salaam!
I sit me on a bench and weep.
And in my heart I sing
O, let me be a burro-boy again;
O, let me sleep among the cyclamens
Of my own land.

Shades of Whitman! But Whitman, thou Donkey, never weeps.
Whitman, if that goblin tried to silence him, would have wrung his
neck, after he had ridden upon it. The above, nevertheless, deserves
the space we give it here, as it shadows forth one of the essential elements of Khalid's spiritual make-up. But this slight symptom of that
disease we named, this morbidness incident to adolescence, is eventually overcome by a dictionary and a grammar. Ay, Khalid henceforth
shall cease to scour the horizon for that vague something of his
dreams; he has become far-sighted enough by the process to see the
necessity of pursuing in America something more spiritual than peddling crosses and scapulars. Especially in this America, where the
alphabet is spread broadcast, and free of charge. And so, he sets himself to the task of self-education. He feels the embryo stir within him,

and in the squeamishness of enceinteship, he asks but for a few of the fruits of knowledge. Ah, but he becomes voracious of a sudden, and the little pocket dictionary is devoured entirely in three sittings. Hence his folly of treating his thoughts and fancies, as he was treated by the goblin. For do not words often rob a fancy of its tongue, or a thought of its soul? Many of the pieces Khalid wrote when he was devouring dictionaries were finally disposed of in a most picturesque manner, as we shall relate. And a few were given to Shakib, of which that Dream of Cyclamens was preserved.

And Khalid's motto was, "One book at a time." He would not encumber himself with books any more than he would with shoes. But that the mind might not go barefoot, he always bought a new book before destroying the one in hand. Destroying? Yes; for after reading or studying a book, he warms his hands upon its flames, this Khalid, or makes it serve to cook a pot of *mojadderah*. In this extraordinary and outrageous manner, barbarously capricious, he would baptise the ideal in the fire of the real. And thus, glowing with health and confidence and conceit, he enters another Park from which he escapes in the end, sad and wan and bankrupt. Of a truth, many attractions and distractions are here; else he could not forget the peddling-box and the light-heeled, heavy-haunched women of Battery Park. Here are swings for the mind; toboggan-chutes for the soul; merry-go-rounds for the fancy; and many devious and alluring paths where one can lose himself for years. A sanitarium this for the hebephreniac. And like all sanitariums, you go into it with one disease and come out of it with ten. Had Shakib been forewarned of Khalid's mind, had he even seen him at the gate before he entered, he would have given him a few hints about the cross-signs and barbed-cordons therein. But should he not have divined that Khalid soon or late was coming? Did *he* not call enough to him, and aloud? "Get thee behind me on this dromedary," our Scribe, reading his Al-Mutanabbi, would often say to his comrade, "and come from this desert of barren gold, if but for a day,—come out with me to the oasis of poesy."

But Khalid would only ride alone. And so, he begins his course of self-education. But how he shall manage it, in this cart-before-the-horse fashion, the reader shall know. Words before rules, ideas before systems, epigrams before texts,—that is Khalid's fancy. And that seems feasible, though not logical; it will prove effectual, too, if one finally brushed the text and glanced at the rules. For an epigram, when it takes possession of one, goes farther in influencing his thoughts and actions than whole tomes of ethical culture science. You know perhaps how the Arabs conquered the best half of the world with an epi-gram, a word. And Khalid loves a fine-sounding, easy-flowing word; a word of supple joints, so to speak; a word that you can twist and roll out, flexible as a bamboo switch, resilient as a fine steel rapier. But once Shakib, after reading one of Khalid's first attempts, gets up in the night when his friend is asleep, takes from the bottom drawer of the peddling-box the evil-working dictionary, and places therein a gram-mar. This touch of delicacy, this fine piece of criticism, brief and neat, without words withal, Khalid this time is not slow to grasp and appre-ciate. He plunges, therefore, headlong into the grammar, turns a few somersaults in the mazes of Sibawai and Naftawai, and coming out with a broken noddle, writes on the door the following: "What do I care about your theories of nouns and verbs? Whether the one be de-rived from the other, concerns not me. But this I know, after stumbling once or twice in your labyrinths, one comes out parsing the verb, to run. Indeed, verbs are more essential than nouns and adjectives. A noun can be represented pictorially; but how, pictorially, can you rep-resent a noun in motion,—Khalid, for instance, running out of your labyrinths? Even an abstract state can be represented in a picture, but a transitive state never. The richest language, therefore, is not the one which can boast of a thousand names for the lion or two thousand for the camel, but the one whose verbs have a complete and perfect gamut of moods and tenses."

That is why, although writing in Arabic, Khalid prefers English. For the Arabic verb is confined to three tenses, the primary ones only; and to break through any of these in any degree, requires such crow-bars as only auxiliaries and other verbs can furnish. For this and many other reasons Khalid stops short in the mazes of Sibawai, runs out of them exasperated, depressed, and never for a long time after looks in that direction. He is now curious to know if the English language have its Sibawais and Naftawais. And so, he buys him a grammar, and there finds the way somewhat devious, too, but not enough to constitute a maze. The men who wrote these grammars must have had plenty of time to do a little useful work. They do not seem to have walked lei-surely in flowing robes disserting a life-long dissertation on the origin and descent of a preposition. One day Shakib is amazed by finding the grammars page by page tacked on the walls of the cellar and Khalid pacing around leisurely lingering a moment before each page, as if he were in an art gallery. That is how he tackled his subject. And that is why he and Shakib begin to quarrel. The idea! That a fledgling should presume to pick flaws. To Shakib, who is textual to a hair, this is intolerable. And that state of oneness between them shall be subject hereafter to "the corrosive action of various unfriendly agents." For Khalid, who has never yet been snaffled, turns restively from the bit which his friend, for his own sake, would put in his mouth. The rupture follows. The two for a while wend their way in opposite directions. Shakib still cherishing and cultivating his bank account, shoulders his peddling-box and jogs along with his inspiring demon, under whose auspices, he tells us, he continues to write verse and gull with his brummagems the pious dames of the suburbs. And Khalid sits on his peddling-box for hours pondering on the necessity of disposing of it somehow. For now he scarcely makes more than a few peddling-trips each month, and when he returns, he does not go to the bank to add to his balance, but to draw from it. That is why the accounts of the two Syrians do not fare alike; Shakib's is gaining in weight, Khalid's is wasting away.

Yes, the strenuous spirit is a long time dead in Khalid. He is gradually reverting to the Oriental instinct. And when he is not loafing in Battery Park, carving his name on the bench, he is burrowing in the shelves of some second-hand book-shop or dreaming in the dome of some Broadway skyscraper. Does not this seem inevitable, however, considering the palingenetic burden within him? And is not loafing a necessary prelude to the travail? Khalid, of course, felt the necessity of this, not knowing the why and wherefor. And from the vast world of paper-bound souls, for he relished but pamphlets at the start—they do not make much smoke in the fire, he would say—from that vast world he could command the greatest of the great to help him support the loafing while. And as by a miracle, he came out of that chaos of contending spirits without a scratch. He enjoyed the belligerency of pamphleteers as an American would enjoy a prize fight. But he sided with no one; he took from every one his best and consigned him to Im-Hanna's kitchen. Torquemada could not have done better; but Khalid, it is hoped, will yet atone for his crimes.

Monsieur Pascal, with whom he quarrels before he burns, had a particular influence upon him. He could not rest after reading his "Thoughts" until he read the Bible. And of the Prophets of the Old Testament he had an especial liking for Jeremiah and Isaiah. And once he bought a cheap print of Jeremiah which he tacked on the wall of his cellar. From the Khedivial Library MS. we give two excerpts relating to Pascal and this Prophet.

"O Monsieur Pascal,
"I tried hard to hate and detest myself, as you advise,
and I found that I could not by so doing love God. 'Tis in

loving the divine in Man, in me, in you, that we rise to the love of our Maker. And in giving your proofs of the true religion, you speak of the surprising measures of the Christian Faith, enjoining man to acknowledge himself vile, base, abominable, and obliging him at the same time to aspire towards a resemblance of his Maker. Now, I see in this a foreshadowing of the theory of evolution, nay a divine warrant for it. Nor is it the Christian religion alone which unfolds to man the twofold mystery of his nature; others are as dark and as bright on either side of the pole. And Philosophy conspiring with Biology will not consent to the apotheosis of Man, unless he wear on his breast a symbol of his tail.... *Au-revoir*, Monsieur Pascal, Remember me to St. Augustine."

"O Jeremiah,

"Thy picture, sitting among the ruins of the City of Zion, appeals to my soul. Why, I know not. It may be because I myself once sat in that posture among the ruins of my native City of Baal. But the ruins did not grieve me as did the uncle who slammed the door in my face that night. True, I wept in the ruins, but not over them. Something else had punctured the bladderets of my tears. And who knows who punctured thine, O Jeremiah? Perhaps a daughter of Tamar had stuck a bodkin in thine eye, and in lamenting thine own fate—Pardon me, O Jeremiah. Melikes not all these tears of thine. Nor did Zion and her children in Juhannam, I am sure.... Instead of a scroll in thy hand, I would have thee hold a harp. Since King David, Allah has not thought of endowing his prophets with musical talent. Why, think what an honest prophet could accomplish if his message were put into music. And withal, if he himself could sing it. Yes, our modern Jeremiahs should all take music lessons; for no matter how deep and poignant our sorrows, we can always rise from them, harp in hand, to an ecstasy, joyous and divine."

Now, connect with this the following from the *Histoire Intime*, and you have the complete history of this Prophet in Khalid's cellar. For Khalid himself never gives us the facts in the case. Our Scribe, however, comes not short in this.

"The picture of the Prophet Jeremiah," writes he, "Khalid hung on the wall, above his bed. And every night he would look up to it invokingly, muttering I know not what. One evening, while in this posture, he took up his lute and trolled a favourite ditty. For three days and three nights that picture hung on the wall. And on the morning of the fourth day—it was a cold December morning, I remember—he took it down and lighted the fire with it. The Pamphlet he had read a few days since, he also threw into the fire, and thereupon called to me saying, 'Come, Shakib, and warm yourself.'"

And the Pamphlet, we learn, which was thus baptised in the same fire with the Prophet's picture, was Tom Paine's *Age of Reason*.

CHAPTER VI

THE SUMMER AFTERNOON OF A SHAM

For two years and more Khalid's young mind went leaping from one swing to another, from one carousel or toboggan-chute to the next, without having any special object in view, without knowing why and wherefor. He even entered such mazes of philosophy, such labyrinths of mysticism as put those of the Arabian grammaticasters in the shade. To him, education was a sport, pursued in a free spirit after his own fancy, without method or discipline. For two years and more he did little but ramble thus, drawing meanwhile on his account in the bank, and burning pamphlets.

One day he passes by a second-hand book-shop, which is in the financial hive of the city, hard by a church and within a stone's throw from the Stock Exchange. The owner, a shabby venerable, standing there, pipe in mouth, between piles of pamphlets and little pyramids of books, attracts Khalid. He too occupies a cellar. And withal he resembles the Prophet in the picture which was burned with Tom Paine's *Age of Reason*. Nothing in the face at least is amiss. A flowing, serrated, milky beard, with a touch of gold around the mouth; an aquiline nose; deep set blue eyes canopied with shaggy brows; a forehead broad and high; a dome a little frowsy but not guilty of a hair—the Prophet Jeremiah! Only one thing, a clay pipe which he seldom took out of his mouth except to empty and refill, seemed to take from the prophetic solemnity of the face. Otherwise, he is as grim and sullen as the Prophet. In his voice, however, there is a supple sweetness which the hard lines in his face do not express. Khalid nicknames him second-hand Jerry, makes to him professions of friendship, and for many months comes every day to see him. He comes with his bucket, as he would say, to Jerry's well. For the two, the young man and the old man of the cellar, the neophite and the master, would chat about literature and the makers of it for hours. And what a sea of information is therein under that frowsy dome. Withal, second-hand Jerry is a man of ideals and abstractions, exhibiting now and then an heretical twist which is as agreeable as the vermiculations in a mahogany. "We moderns," said he once to Khalid, "are absolutely one-sided. Here, for instance, is my book-shop, there is the Church, and yonder is the Stock Exchange. Now, the men who frequent them, and though their elbows touch, are as foreign to each other as is a jerboa to a polar bear. Those who go to Church do not go to the Stock Exchange; those who spend their days on the Stock Exchange seldom go to Church; and those who frequent my cellar go neither to the one nor the other. That is why our civilisation produces so many bigots, so many philistines, so many pedants and prigs. The Stock Exchange is as necessary to Society as the Church, and the Church is as vital, as essential to its spiritual well-being as my book-shop. And not until man develops his mental, spiritual and physical faculties to what Matthew Arnold calls 'a harmonious perfection,' will he be able to reach the heights from which Idealism is waving to him."

Thus would the master discourse, and the neophite, sitting on the steps of the cellar, smoking his cigarette, listens, admiring, pondering. And every time he comes with his bucket, Jerry would be standing there, between his little pyramids of books, pipe in mouth, hands in pockets, ready for the discourse. He would also conduct through his underworld any one who had the leisure and inclination. But fortunately for Khalid, the people of this district are either too rich to buy second-hand books, or too snobbish to stop before this curiosity shop of literature. Hence the master is never too busy; he is always ready to deliver the discourse.

One day Khalid is conducted into the labyrinthine gloom and mould of the cellar. Through the narrow isles, under a low ceiling, papered, as it were, with pamphlets, between ramparts and mounds of books, old Jerry, his head bowed, his lighted taper in hand, proceeds. And Khalid follows directly behind, listening to his guide who points out the objects and places of interest. And thus, through the alleys and by-ways, through the nooks and labyrinths of these underground temple-ruins, we get to the rear, where the ramparts and mounds crumble to a mighty heap, rising pell-mell to the ceiling. Here, one is likely to get a glimpse into such enchanted worlds as the name of a Dickens or a Balzac might suggest. Here, too, is Shakespeare in lamentable state; there is Carlyle in rags, still crying, as it were, against the filth and beastliness of this underworld. And look at my lord Tennyson shiver-

42

ing in his nakedness and doomed to keep company with the meanest of poetasters. Observe how Emerson is wriggled and ruffled in this crushing crowd. Does he not seem to be still sighing for a little solitude? But here, too, are spots of the rarest literary interest. Close to the vilest of dime novels is an autograph copy of a book which you might not find at Brentano's. Indeed, the rarities here stand side by side with the superfluities—the abominations with the blessings of literature—cluttered together, reduced to a common level. And all in a condition which bespeaks the time when they were held in the affection of some one. Now, they lie a-mouldering in these mounds, and on these shelves, awaiting a curious eye, a kindly hand.

"To me," writes Khalid in the K. L. MS., "there is always something pathetic in a second-hand book offered again for sale. Why did its first owner part with it? Was it out of disgust or surfeit or penury? Did he throw it away, or give it away, or sell it? Alas, and is this how to treat a friend? Were it not better burned, than sold or thrown away? After coming out of the press, how many have handled this tattered volume? How many has it entertained, enlightened, or perverted? Look at its pages, which evidence the hardship of the journey it has made. Here still is a pressed flower, more convincing in its shrouded eloquence than the philosophy of the pages in which it lies buried. On the fly-leaf are the names of three successive owners, and on the margin are lead pencil notes in which the reader criticises the author. Their spirits are now shrouded together and entombed in this pile, where the mould never fails and the moths never die. They too are fallen a prey to the worms of the earth. A second-hand book-shop always reminds me of a Necropolis. It is a kind of Serapeum where lies buried the kings and princes with the helots and underlings of literature. Ay, every book is a mortuary chamber containing the remains of some poor literary wretch, or some mighty genius.... A book is a friend, my brothers, and when it ceases to entertain or instruct or inspire, it is dead. And would you sell a dead friend, would you throw him away? If you can not keep him embalmed on your shelf, is it not the wiser part, and the kinder, to cremate him?"

And Khalid tells old Jerry, that if every one buying and reading books, disposed of them in the end as he himself does, second-hand book-shops would no longer exist. But old Jerry never despairs of business. And the idea of turning his Serapeum into a kiln does not appeal to him. Howbeit, Khalid has other ideas which the old man admires, and which he would carry out if the police would not interfere. "If I were the owner of this shop," thus the neophite to the master, "I would advertise it with a bonfire of pamphlets. I would take a few hundreds from that mound there and give them the match right in front of that Church, or better still before the Stock Exchange. And I would have two sandwich-men stand about the bonfire, as high priests of the Temple, and chant the praises of second-hand Jerry and his second-hand book-shop. This will be the sacrifice which you will have offered to the god of Trade right in front of his sanctuary that he might soften the induration in the breasts of these worthy citizens, your rich neighbours. And if he does not, why, shut up shop or burn it up, and let us go out peddling together."

We do not know, however, whether old Jerry ever adopted Khalid's idea. He himself is an Oriental in this sense; and the business is good enough to keep up, so long as Khalid comes. He is supremely content. Indeed, Shakib asseverates in round Arabic, that the old man of the cellar got a good portion of Khalid's balance, while balancing Khalid's mind. Nay, firing it with free-thought literature. Are we then to consider this cellar as Khalid's source of spiritual illumination? And is this genial old heretic an American avatar of the monk Bohaira? For Khalid is gradually becoming a man of ideas and crotchets. He is beginning to see a purpose in all his literary and spiritual rambles. His mental nebulosity is resolving itself into something concrete, which shall weigh upon him for a while and propel him in the direction of Atheism and Demagogy. For old Jerry once visits Khalid in his cellar, and after partaking of a dish of *mojadderah*, takes him to a political meeting to hear the popular orators of the day.

And in this is ineffable joy for Khalid. Like every young mind he is spellbound by one of those masters of spread-eagle oratory, and for some time he does not miss a single political meeting in his district. We even see him among the crowd before the corner groggery, cheering one of the political spouters of the day.

And once he accompanies Jerry to the Temple of Atheism to behold its high Priest and hear him chant halleluiah to the Nebular Hypothesis. This is wonderful. How easy it is to dereligionise the human race and banish God from the Universe! But after the High Priest

44

had done this, after he had proven to the satisfaction of every atheist that God is a myth, old Jerry turns around and gives Khalid this warning: "Don't believe all he says, for I know that atheist well. He is as eloquent as he is insincere."

And so are all atheists. For at bottom, atheism is either a fad or a trade or a fatuity. And whether the one or the other, it is a sham more pernicious than the worst. To the young mind, it is a shibboleth of cheap culture; to the shrewd and calculating mind, to such orators as Khalid heard, it is a trade most remunerative; and to the scientists, or rather monists, it is the aliment with which they nourish the perversity of their preconceptions. Second-hand Jerry did not say these things to our young philosopher; for had he done so, Khalid, now become edacious, would not have experienced those dyspeptic pangs which almost crushed the soul-fetus in him. For we are told that he is as sedulous in attending these atheistic lectures as he is in flocking with his fellow citizens to hear and cheer the idols of the stump. Once he took Shakib to the Temple of Atheism, but the Poet seems to prefer his *Al-Mutanabby*. In relating of Khalid's waywardness he says:

"Ever since we quarrelled about Sibawai, Khalid and I have seldom been together. And he had become so opinionated that I was glad it was so. Even on Sunday I would leave him alone with Im-Hanna, and returning in the evening, I would find him either reading or burning a pamphlet. Once I consented to accompany him to one of the lectures he was so fond of attending. And I was really surprised that one had to pay money for such masquerades of eloquence as were exhibited that night on the platform. Yes, it occurred to me that if one had not a dollar one could not become an atheist. Billah! I was scandalized. For no matter how irreverent one likes to pose, one ought to reverence at least his Maker. I am a Christian by the grace of Allah, and my ancestors are counted among the martyrs of the Church. And thanks to my parents, I have been duly baptized and confirmed. For which I respect them the more, and love them. Now, is it not absurd that I should come here and pay a hard dollar to hear this heretical speechifier insult my parents and my God? Better the ring of Al-Mutanabbi's scimitars and spears than the clatter of these atheistical bones!"

From which we infer that Shakib was not open to reason on the subject. He would draw his friend away from the verge of the abyss at any cost. "And this," continues he, "did not require much effort. For Khalid like myself is constitutionally incapable of denying God. We are from the land in which God has always spoken to our ancestors."

And the argument between the shrewd verse-maker and the foolish philosopher finally hinges on this: namely, that these atheists are not honest investigators, that in their sweeping generalisations, as in their speciosity and hypocrisy, they are commercially perverse. And Khalid is not long in deciding about the matter. He meets with an accident— and accidents have always been his touchstones of success—which saves his soul and seals the fate of atheism.

One evening, returning from a ramble in the Park, he passes by the Hall where his favourite Mountebank was to lecture on the Gospel of Soap. But not having the price of admittance that evening, and being anxious to hear the orator whom he had idolised, Khalid bravely appeals to his generosity in this quaint and touching note: "My pocket," he wrote, "is empty and my mind is hungry. Might I come to your Table to-night as a beggar?" And the man at the stage door, who carries the note to the orator, returns in a trice, and tells Khalid to lift himself off. Khalid hesitates, misunderstands; and a heavy hand is of a sudden upon him, to say nothing of the heavy boot.

Ay, and that boot decided him. Atheism, bald, bold, niggardly, brutal, pretending withal, Khalid turns from its door never to look again in that direction, Shakib is right. "These people," he growled, "are not free thinkers, but free stinkards. They do need soap to wash their hearts and souls."

An idea did not come to Khalid, as it were, by instalments. In his puerperal pains of mind he was subject to such crises, shaken by such downrushes of light, as only the few among mortals experience. (We are quoting our Scribe, remember.) And in certain moments he had more faith in his instincts than in his reason. "Our instincts," says he, "never lie. They are honest, and though they be sometimes blind." And here, he seems to have struck the truth. He can be practical too. Honesty in thought, in word, in deed—this he would have as the cornerstone of his truth. Moral rectitude he places above all the cardinal virtues, natural and theological. "Better keep away from the truth, O Khalid," he writes, "better remain a stranger to it all thy life, if thou must sully it with the slimy fingers of a mercenary juggler." Now, these brave words, we can not in conscience criticise. But we venture to observe that Khalid must have had in mind that Gospel of Soap and the incident at the stage door.

And in this, we, too, rejoice. We, too, forgetting the dignity of our position, participate of the revelry in the cellar on this occasion. For our editorialship, dear Reader, is neither American nor English. We are not bound, therefore, to maintain in any degree the algidity and indifference of our confrères' sublime attitude. We rejoice in the spiritual safety of Khalid. We rejoice that he and Shakib are now reconciled. For the reclaimed runagate is now even permitted to draw on the poet's balance at the banker. Ay, even Khalid can dissimulate when he needs the cash. For with the assistance of second-hand Jerry and the box-office of the atheistical jugglers, he had exhausted his little saving. He would not even go out peddling any more. And when Shakib asks him one morning to shoulder the box and come out, he replies: "I have a little business with it here." For after having impeached the High Priests of Atheism he seems to have turned upon himself. We translate from the K. L. MS.

"When I was disenchanted with atheism, when I saw somewhat of the meanness and selfishness of its protagonists, I began to doubt in the honesty of men. If these, our supposed teachers, are so vile, so mercenary, so false,—why, welcome Juhannam! But the more I doubted in the honesty of men, the more did I believe that honesty should be the cardinal virtue of the soul. I go so far in this, that an honest thief in my eyes is more worthy of esteem than a canting materialist or a hypocritical free thinker. Still, the voice within me asked if Shakib were honest in his dealings, if I were honest in my peddling? Have I not misrepresented my gewgaws as the atheist misrepresents the truth? 'This is made in the Holy Land,'—'This is from the Holy Sepulchre'—these lies, O Khalid, are upon you. And what is the difference between the jewellery you passed off for gold and the arguments of the atheist-preacher? Are they not both instruments of deception, both designed to catch the dollar? Yes, you have been, O Khalid, as mean, as mercenary, as dishonest as those canting infidels.

"And what are you going to do about it? Will you continue, while in the quagmires yourself, to point contemptuously at those standing in the gutter? Will you, in your dishonesty, dare impeach the honesty of men? Are you not going to make a resolution now, either to keep silent or to go out of the quagmires and rise to the mountain-heights? Be pure yourself first, O Khalid; then try to spread this purity around you at any cost.

"Yes; that is why, when Shakib asked me to go out peddling one day, I hesitated and finally refused. For atheism, in whose false dry light I walked a parasang or two, did not only betray itself to me as a sham, but also turned my mind and soul to the sham I had shouldered for years. From the peddling-box, therefore, I turned even as I did from atheism. Praised be Allah, who, in his providential care, seemed to kick me away from the door of its temple. The sham, although effulgent and alluring, was as brief as a summer afternoon."

As for the peddling-box, our Scribe will tell of its fate in the following Chapter.

CHAPTER VII

IN THE TWILIGHT OF AN IDEA

It is Voltaire, we believe, who says something to the effect that one's mind should be in accordance with one's years. That is why an academic education nowadays often fails of its purpose. For whether one's mind runs ahead of one's years, or one's years ahead of one's mind, the result is much the same; it always goes ill with the mind. True, knowledge is power; but in order to feel at home with it, we must be constitutionally qualified. And if we are not, it is likely to give the soul such a wrenching as to deform it forever. Indeed, how many of us go through life with a fatal spiritual or intellectual twist which could have been avoided in our youth, were we a little less wise. The young *philosophes*, the products of the University Machine of to-day, who go about with a nosegay of -isms, as it were, in their lapels, and perfume their speech with the bottled logic of the College Professor,— are not most of them incapable of honestly and bravely grappling with the real problems of life? And does not a systematic education mean this, that a young man must go through life dragging behind him his heavy chains of set ideas and stock systems, political, social, or religious? (Remember, we are translating from the Khedivial Library MS.) The author continues:

"Whether one devour the knowledge of the world in four years or four nights, the process of assimilation is equally hindered, if the mind is sealed at the start with the seal of authority. Ay, we can not be too careful of dogmatic science in our youth; for dogmas often dam certain channels of the soul through which we might have reached greater treasures and ascended to purer heights. A young man, therefore, ought to be let alone. There is an infinite possibility of soul-power in every one of us, if it can be developed freely, spontaneously, without discipline or restraint. There is, too, an infinite possibility of beauty in every soul, if it can be evoked at an auspicious moment by the proper word, the proper voice, the proper touch. That is why I say, Go thy way, O my Brother. Be simple, natural, spontaneous, courageous, free. Neither anticipate your years, nor lag child-like behind them. For verily, it is as ridiculous to dye the hair white as to dye it black. Ah, be foolish while thou art young; it is never too late to be wise. Indulge thy fancy, follow the bent of thy mind; for in so doing thou canst not possibly do thyself more harm than the disciplinarians can do thee. Live thine own life; think thine own thoughts; keep developing and changing until thou arrive at the truth thyself. An ounce of it found by thee were better than a ton given to thee *gratis* by one who would enslave thee. Go thy way, O my Brother. And if my words lead thee to Juhannam, why, there will be a great surprise for thee. There thou wilt behold our Maker sitting on a flaming glacier waiting for the like of thee. And he will take thee into his arms and poke thee in the ribs, and together you will laugh and laugh, until that glacier become a garden and thou a flower therein. Go thy way, therefore; be not afraid. And no matter how many tears thou sheddest on this side, thou wilt surely be poked in the ribs on the other. Go—thy—but—let Nature be thy guide; acquaint thyself with one or two of her laws ere thou runnest wild."

And to what extent did this fantastic mystic son of a Phœnician acquaint himself with Nature's laws, we do not know. But truly, he was already running wild in the great cosmopolis of New York. From his stivy cellar he issues forth into the plashing, plangent currents of city life. Before he does this, however, he rids himself of all the encumbrances of peddlery which hitherto have been his sole means of support. His little stock of crosses, rosaries, scapulars, false jewellery, mother-of-pearl gewgaws, and such like, which he has on the little shelf in the cellar, he takes down one morning—but we will let our Scribe tell the story.

"My love for Khalid," he writes, "has been severely tried. We could no longer agree about anything. He had become such a dissenter that often would he take the wrong side of a question if only for the sake of bucking. True, he ceased to frequent the cellar of second-hand Jerry, and the lectures of the infidels he no longer attended. We were in accord about atheism, therefore, but in riotous discord about many other things, chief among which was the propriety, the necessity, of doing something to replenish his balance at the banker. For he was now impecunious, and withal importunate. Of a truth, what I had I was always ready to share with him; but for his own good I advised him to take up the peddling-box again. I reminded him of his saying once, 'Peddling is a healthy and profitable business.' 'Come out,' I insisted, 'and though it be for the exercise. Walking is the whetstone of thought.'

"One evening we quarrelled about this, and Im-Hanna sided with me. She rated Khalid, saying, 'You're a good-for-nothing loafer; you don't deserve the *mojadderah* you eat.' And I remember how she took me aside that evening and whispered something about books, and Khalid's head, and Mar-Kizhayiah.[1] Indeed, Im-Hanna seriously believed that Khalid should be taken to Mar-Kizhayiah. She did not know that New York was full of such institutions.[2] Her scolding, however, seemed to have more effect on Khalid than my reasoning. And consenting to go out with me, he got up the following morning, took down his stock from the shelf, every little article of it—he left nothing there—and packed all into his peddling-box. He then squeezed into the bottom drawer, which he had filled with scapulars, the bottle with a little of the Stuff in it. For we were in accord about this, that in New York whiskey is better than arak. And we both took a nip now and then. So I thought the bottle was in order. But why he placed his bank book, which was no longer worth a straw, into that bottom drawer, I could not guess. With these preparations, however, we shouldered our boxes, and in an hour we were in the suburbs. We foot it along then, until we reach a row of cottages not far from the railway station. 'Will you knock at one of these doors,' I asked. And he, 'I do not feel like chaffering and bargaining this morning.' 'Why then did you come out,' I urged. And he, in an air of nonchalance, 'Only for the walk.' And so,

---

[1] A monastery in Mt. Lebanon, a sort of Bedlam, where the exorcising monks beat the devil out of one's head with clouted shoes.—Editor.
[2] And the doctors here practise in the name of science what the exorcising monks practise in the name of religion. The poor devil, or patient, in either case is done to death.—Editor.

we pursued our way in the Bronx, until we reached one of our favourite spots, where a sycamore tree seemed to invite us to its ample shade.

"Here, Khalid, absent-minded, laid down his box and sat upon it, and I stretched my limbs on the grass. But of a sudden, he jumped up, opened the bottom drawer of his case, and drew from it the bottle. It is quite in order now, I mused; but ere I had enjoyed the thought, Khalid had placed his box at a little distance, and, standing there beside it, bottle in hand, delivered himself in a semi-solemn, semi-mocking manner of the following: 'This is the oil,' I remember him saying, 'with which I anoint thee—the extreme unction I apply to thy soul.' And he poured the contents of the bottle into the bottom drawer and over the box, and applied to it a match. The bottle was filled with kerosene, and in a jiffy the box was covered with the flame. Yes; and so quickly, so neatly it was done, that I could not do aught to prevent it. The match was applied to what I thought at first was whiskey, and I was left in speechless amazement. He would not even help me to save a few things from the fire. I conjured him in the name of Allah, but in vain. I clamoured and remonstrated, but to no purpose. And when I asked him why he had done this, he asked me in reply, 'And why have you not done the same? Now, methinks I deserve my *mojadderah.* And not until you do likewise, will you deserve yours, O Shakib. Here are the lies, now turned to ashes, which brought me my bread and are still bringing you yours. Here are our instruments of deception, our poisoned sources of lucre. I am most happy now, O Shakib. And I shall endeavour to keep my blood in circulation by better, purer means.' And he took me thereupon by the shoulders, looked into my face, then pushed me away, laughing the laugh of the hasheesh-smokers.

"Indeed, Im-Hanna was right. Khalid had become too odd, too queer to be sane. Needless to say, I was not prone to follow his example at that time. Nor am I now. *Mashallah!* Lacking the power and madness to set fire to the whole world, it were folly, indeed, to begin with one's self. I believe I had as much right to exaggerate in peddling as I had in writing verse. My license to heighten the facts holds good in either case. And to some extent, every one, a poet be he or a cobbler, enjoys such a license. I told Khalid that the logical and most effective course to pursue, in view of his rigorous morality, would be to pour a gallon of kerosene over his own head and fire himself out of existence. For the instruments of deception and debasement are not in the peddling-box, but rather in his heart. No; I did not think peddling was as bad as other trades. Here at least, the means of deception were reduced to a minimum. And of a truth, if everybody were to judge themselves as strictly as Khalid, who would escape burning? So I turned from him that day fully convinced that my little stock of holy goods was innocent, and my balance at the banker's was as pure as my rich neighbour's. And he turned from me fully convinced, I believe, that I was an unregenerate rogue. Ay, and when I was knocking at the door of one of my customers, he was walking away briskly, his hands clasped behind his back, and his eyes, as usual, scouring the horizon."

And on that horizon are the gilded domes and smoking chimneys of the seething city. Leaving his last friend and his last burden behind, he will give civilised life another trial. Loafer and tramp that he is! For even the comforts of the grand cable-railway he spurns, and foots it from the Bronx down to his cellar near Battery Park, thus cutting the city in half and giving one portion to Izräil and the other to Iblis. But not being quite ready himself for either of these winged Furies, he keeps to his cellar. He would tarry here a while, if but to carry out a resolution he has made. True, Khalid very seldom resolves upon anything; but when he does make a resolution, he is even willing to be carried off by the effort to carry it out. And now, he would solve this problem of earning a living in the great city by honest means. For in the city, at least, success well deserves the compliments which those who fail bestow upon it. What Montaigne said of greatness, therefore, Khalid must have said of success. If we can not attain it, let us denounce it. And in what terms does he this, O merciful Allah! We translate a portion of the apostrophe in the K. L. MS., and not the bitterest, by any means.

"O Success," the infuriated failure exclaims, "how like the Gorgon of the Arabian Nights thou art! For does not every one whom thou favorest undergo a pitiful transformation even from the first bedding with thee? Does not everything suffer from thy look, thy touch, thy breath? The rose loses its perfume, the grape-vine its clusters, the bulbul its wings, the dawn its light and glamour. O Success, our lords of power to-day are thy slaves, thy helots, our kings of wealth. Every one grinds for thee, every one for thee lives and dies.... Thy palaces of silver and gold are reared on the souls of men. Thy throne is mortised with their bones, cemented with their blood. Thou ravenous Gorgon, on what bankruptcies thou art fed, on what failures, on what sorrows! The railroads sweeping across the continents and the steamers ploughing through the seas, are laden with sacrifices to thee. Ay, and millions of innocent children are torn from their homes and from their schools to be offered to thee at the sacrificial-stone of the Factories and Mills.

The cultured, too, and the wise, are counted among thy slaves. Even the righteous surrender themselves to thee and are willing to undergo that hideous transformation. O Success, what an infernal litany thy votaries and high-priests are chanting to thee.... Thou ruthless Gorgon, what crimes thou art committing, and what crimes are being committed in thy name!"

From which it is evident that Khalid does not wish for success. Khalid is satisfied if he can maintain his hold on the few spare feet he has in the cellar, and continue to replenish his little store of lentils and olive oil. For he would as lief be a victim of success, he assures us, as to forego his *mojadderah*. And still having this, which he considers a luxury, he is willing to turn his hand at anything, if he can but preserve inviolate the integrity of his soul and the freedom of his mind. These are a few of the pet terms of Khalid. And in as much as he can continue to repeat them to himself, he is supremely content. He can be a menial, if while cringing before his superiors, he were permitted to chew on his pet illusions. A few days before he burned his peddling-box, he had read Epictetus. And the thought that such a great soul maintained its purity, its integrity, even in bonds, encouraged and consoled him. "How can they hurt me," he asks, "if spiritually I am far from them, far above them? They can do no more than place gilt buttons on my coat and give me a cap to replace this slouch. Therefore, I will serve. I will be a slave, even like Epictetus."

And here we must interpose a little of our skepticism, if but to gratify an habitual craving in us. We do not doubt that Khalid's self-sufficiency is remarkable; that his courage—on paper—is quite above the common; that the grit and stay he shows are wonderful; that his lofty aspirations, so indomitable in their onwardness, are great: but we only ask, having thus fortified his soul, how is he to fortify his stomach? He is going to work, to be a menial, to earn a living by honest means? Ah, Khalid, Khalid! Did you not often bestow a furtive glance on some one else's checkbook? Did you not even exercise therein your skill in calculation? If the bank, where Shakib deposits his little saving, failed, would you be so indomitable, so dogged in your resolution? Would you not soften a trifle, loosen a whit, if only for the sake of your blood-circulation?

Indeed, Shakib has become a patron to Khalid. Shakib the poet, who himself should have a patron, is always ready to share his last dollar with his loving, though cantankerous friend. And this, in spite of all the disagreeable features of a friendship which in the Syrian Colony was become proverbial. But Khalid now takes up the newspapers and scans the Want Columns for hours. The result being a clerkship in a lawyer's office. Nay, an apprenticeship; for the legal profession, it seems, had for a while engaged his serious thoughts.

And this of all the professions is the one on which he would graft his scion of lofty morality? Surely, there be plenty of fuel for a conflagration in a lawyer's office. Such rows of half-calf tomes, such piles of legal documents, all designed to combat dishonesty and fraud, "and all immersed in them, and nourished and maintained by them." In what a sorry condition will your Morality issue out of these bogs! A lawyer's clerk, we are informed, can not maintain his hold on his clerkship, if he does not learn to blink. That is why Khalid is not long in serving papers, copying summonses, and searching title-deeds. In this lawyer's office he develops traits altogether foreign to his nature. He even becomes a quidnunc, prying now and then into the personal affairs of his superiors. Ay, and he dares once to suggest to his employer a new method of dealing with the criminals among his clients. Withal, Khalid is slow, slower than the law itself. If he goes out to serve a summons he does not return for a day. If he is sent to search title-deeds, he does not show up in the office for a week. And often he would lose himself in the Park surrounding the Register's Office, pondering on his theory of immanent morality. He would sit down on one of those benches, which are the anchors of loafers of another type, his batch of papers beside him, and watch the mad crowds coming and going, running, as it were, between two fires. These puckered people are the living, moving chambers of sleeping souls.

Khalid was always glad to come to this Register's Office. For though the searching of title-deeds be a mortal process, the loafing margin of the working hour could be extended imperceptibly, and without hazarding his or his employer's interest. The following piece of speculative fantasy and insight must have been thought out when he should have been searching title-deeds.

"This Register's Office," it is written in the K. L. MS., "is the very bulwark of Society. It is the foundation on which the Trust Companies, the Courts, and the Prisons are reared. Your codes are blind without the miraculous torches which this Office can light. Your judges can not propound the 'laur'—I beg your pardon, the law—without the aid of these musty, smelling, dilapidated tomes. Ay, these are the very constables of the realm, and without them there can be no realm, no legislators, and no judges. Strong, club-bearing constables, these Liebers, standing on the boundary lines, keeping peace between brothers and neighbours.

"Here, in these Liebers is an authority which never fails, never dies—an authority which willy-nilly we obey and in which we place unbounded trust. In any one of these Registers is a potentiality which can always worst the quibbles and quiddities of lawyers and ward off the miserable technicalities of the law. Any of them, when called upon, can go into court and dictate to the litigants and the attorneys, the jury and the judge. They are the deceased witnesses come to life. And without them, the judges are helpless, the marshals and sheriffs too. Ay, and what without them would be the state of our real-estate interests? Abolish your constabulary force, and your police force, and with these muniments of power, these dumb but far-seeing agents of authority and intelligence, you could still maintain peace and order. But burn you this Register's Office, and before the last Lieber turn to ashes, ere the last flame of the conflagration die out, you will have to call forth, not only your fire squads, but your police force and even your soldiery, to extinguish other fires different in nature, but more devouring––and as many of them as there are boundary lines in the land."

And we now come to the gist of the matter.

> "What wealth of moral truth," he continues, "do we find in these greasy, musty pages. When one deeds a piece of property, he deeds with it something more valuable, more enduring. He deeds with it an undying human intelligence which goes down to posterity, saying, Respect my will; believe in me; and convey this respect and this belief to your offspring. Ay, the immortal soul breathes in a deed as in a great book. And the implicit trust we place in a musty parchment, is the mystic outcome of the blind faith, or rather the far-seeing faith which our ancestors had in the morality and intelligence of coming generations. For what avails their deeds if they are not respected?... We are indebted to our forbears, therefore, not for the miserable piece of property they bequeath us, but for the confidence and trust, the faith and hope they had in our innate or immanent morality and intelligence. The will of the dead is law for the living."

Are we then to look upon Khalid as having come out of that Office with soiled fingers only? Or has the young philosopher abated in his clerkship the intensity of his moral views? Has he not assisted his employer in the legal game of quieting titles? Has he not acquired a little of the delusive plausibilities of lawyers? Shakib throws no light on these questions. We only know that the clerkship or rather apprentice-ship was only held for a season. Indeed, Khalid must have recoiled from the practice. Or in his recklessness, not to say obtrusion, he must have been outrageous enough to express in the office of the honoura-ble attorney, or in the neighbourhood thereof, his views about pettifogging and such like, that the said honourable attorney was under the painful necessity of asking him to stay home. Nay, the young Syri-an was discharged. Or to put it in a term adequate to the manner in which this was done, he was "fired." Now, Khalid betakes him back to his cellar, and thrumming his lute-strings, lights up the oppressive gloom with Arabic song and music.

CHAPTER VIII

WITH THE HURIS

From the house of law the dervish Khalid wends his way to that of science, and from the house of science he passes on to that of metaphysics. His staff in hand, his wallet hung on his shoulder, his silver cigarette case in his pocket, patient, confident, content, he makes his way from one place to another. Unlike his brother dervishes, he is clean and proud of it, too. He knocks at this or that door, makes his wish known to the servant or the mistress, takes the crumbs given him, and not infrequently gives his prod to the dogs. In the vestibule of one of the houses of spiritism, he tarries a spell and parleys with the servant. The Mistress, a fair-looking, fair-spoken dame of seven lustrums or more, issues suddenly from her studio, in a curiously designed black velvet dressing-gown; she is drawn to the door by the accent of the foreigner's speech and the peculiar cadence of his voice. They meet: and magnetic currents from his dark eyes and her eyes of blue, flow and fuse. They speak: and the lady asks the stranger if he would not serve instead of begging. And he protests, "I am a Dervish at the door of Allah." "And I am a Spirit in Allah's house," she rejoins. They enter: and the parley in the vestibule is followed by a tête-à-tête in the parlour and another in the dining-room. They agree: and the stranger is made a member of the Spiritual Household, which now consists of her and him, the Medium and the Dervish.

Now, this fair-spoken dame, who dotes on the occult and exotic, delights in the aroma of Khalid's cigarettes and Khalid's fancy. And that he might feel at ease, she begins by assuring him that they have met and communed many times ere now, that they have been friends under a preceding and long vanished embodiment. Which vagary Khalid seems to countenance by referring to the infinite power of Allah, in the compass of which nothing is impossible. And with these mystical circumlocutions of ceremony, they plunge into an intimacy which is bordered by the metaphysical on one side, and the physical on the other. For though the Medium is at the threshold of her climacteric, Khalid afterwards tells Shakib that there be something in her eyes and limbs which always seem to be waxing young. And of a truth, the American woman, of all others, knows best how to preserve her beauty from the ravages of sorrow and the years. That is why, we presume, in calling him, "child," she does not permit him to call her, "mother." Indeed, the Medium and the Dervish often jest, and somewhiles mix the frivolous with the mysterious.

We would still follow our Scribe here, were it not that his pruriency often reaches the edge. He speaks of "the *liaison*" with all the rude simplicity and frankness of the Arabian Nights. And though, as the Mohammedans say, "To the pure everything is pure," and again, "Who quotes a heresy is not guilty of it"; nevertheless, we do not feel warranted in rending the veil of the reader's prudery, no matter how transparent it might be. We believe, however, that the pruriency of Orientals, like the prudery of Occidentals, is in fact only an appearance. On both sides there is a display of what might be called verbal virtue and verbal vice. And on both sides, the exaggerations are configured in a harmless pose. Be this as it may, we at least, shall withhold from Shakib's lasciviousness the English dress it seeks at our hand.

We note, however, that Khalid now visits him in the cellar only when he craves a dish of *mojadderah*; that he and the Medium are absorbed in the contemplation of the Unseen, though not, perhaps, of the Impalpable; that they gallivant in the Parks, attend Bohemian dinners, and frequent the Don't Worry Circles of Metaphysical Societies; that they make long expeditions together to the Platonic North-pole and back to the torrid regions of Swinburne; and that together they perform their *zikr* and drink at the same fountain of ecstasy and devotion. Withal, the Dervish, who now wears his hair long and grows his finger nails like a Brahmin, is beginning to have some manners.

The Medium, nevertheless, withholds from him the secret of her art. If he desires, he can attend the séances like every other stranger. Once Khalid, who would not leave anything unprobed, insisted, importuned; he could not see any reason for her conduct. Why should they not work together in Tiptology, as in Physiology and Metaphysics? And one morning, dervish-like, he wraps himself in his *aba*, and, calling upon Allah to witness, takes a rose from the vase on the table, angrily plucks its petals, and strews them on the carpet. Which portentous sign the Medium understands and hastens to minister her palliatives.

"No, Child, you shall not go," she begs and supplicates; "listen to me, are we not together all the time? Why not leave me alone then with the spirits? One day you shall know all, believe me. Come, sit here," stroking her palm on her lap, "and listen. I shall give up this tiptology business very soon; you and I shall overturn the table. Yes, Child, I am on the point of succumbing under an awful something. So, don't ask me about the spooks any more. Promise not to torment me thus any more. And one day we shall travel together in the Orient; we shall visit the ruins of vanished kingdoms and creeds. Ah, to be in Palmyra with you! Do you know, Child, I am destined to be a Beduin queen. The throne of Zenobia is mine, and yours too, if you will be good. We shall resuscitate the glory of the kingdom of the desert."

To all of which Khalid acquiesces by referring as is his wont to the infinite wisdom of Allah, in whose all-seeing eye nothing is impossible.

And thus, apparently satisfied, he takes the cigarette which she had lighted for him, and lights for her another from his own. But the smoke of two cigarettes dispels not the threatening cloud; it only conceals it from view. For they dine together at a Bohemian Club that evening, where Khalid meets a woman of rare charms. And she invites him to her studio. The Medium, who is at first indifferent, finally warns her callow child. "That woman is a writer," she explains, "and writers are always in search of what they call 'copy.' She in particular is a huntress of male curiosities, *originales*, whom she takes into her favour and ultimately surrenders them to the reading public. So be careful." But Khalid hearkens not. For the writer, whom he afterwards calls a flighter, since she, too, "like the van of the brewer only skims the surface of things," is, in fact, younger than the Medium. Ay, this woman is even beautiful—to behold, at least. So the Dervish, a captive of her charms, knocks at the door of her studio one evening and enters. Ah, this then is a studio! "I am destined to know everything, and to see everything," he says to himself, smiling in his heart.

The charming hostess, in a Japanese kimono receives him somewhat orientally, offering him the divan, which he occupies alone for a spell. He is then laden with a huge scrap-book containing press notices and reviews of her many novels. These, he is asked to go through while she prepares the tea. Which is a mortal task for the Dervish in the presence of the Enchantress. Alas, the tea is long in the making, and when the scrap-book is laid aside, she reinforces him with a lot of magazines adorned with stories of the short and long and middling size, from her fertile pen. "These are beautiful," says he, in glancing over a few pages, "but no matter how you try, you can not with your pen surpass your own beauty. The charm of your literary style can not hold a candle to the charm of your—permit me to read your hand." And laying down the magazine, he takes up her hand and presses it to his lips. In like manner, he tries to read somewhat in the face, but the Enchantress protests and smiles. In which case the smile renders the protest null and void.

Henceforth, the situation shall be trying even to the Dervish who can eat live coals. He oscillates for some while between the Medium and the Enchantress, but finds the effort rather straining. The first climax, however, is reached, and our Scribe thinks it too sad for words. He himself sheds a few rheums with the fair-looking, fair-spoken Dame, and dedicates to her a few rhymes. Her magnanimity, he tells us, is unexampled, and her fatalism pathetic. For when Khalid severs himself from the Spiritual Household, she kisses him thrice, saying, "Go, Child; Allah brought you to me, and Allah will bring you again." Khalid refers, as usual, to the infinite wisdom of the Almighty, and, taking his handkerchief from his pocket, wipes the tears that fell— from her eyes over his. He passes out of the vestibule, silent and sad, musing on the time he first stood there as a beggar.

Now, the horizon of the Enchantress is unobstructed. Khalid is there alone; and her free love can freely pass on from him to another. And such messages they exchange! Such evaporations of the insipidities of free love! Khalid again takes up with Shakib, from whom he does not conceal anything. The epistles are read by both, and sometimes replied to by both! And she, in an effort to seem Oriental, calls the Dervish, "My Syrian Rose," "My Desert Flower," "My Beduin Boy," et cetera, always closing her message with either a strip of Syrian sky or a camel load of the narcissus. Ah, but not thus will the play close. True, Khalid alone adorns her studio for a time, or rather adores in it; he alone accompanies her to Bohemia. But the Dervish, who was always going wrong in Bohemia,—always at the door of the Devil,— ventures one night to escort another woman to her studio. Ah, those studios! The Enchantress on hearing of the crime lights the fire under her cauldron. "Double, double, toil and trouble!" She then goes to the telephone—g-r-r-r you swine—you Phœnician murex—she hangs up the receiver, and stirs the cauldron. "Double, double, toil and trouble!" But the Dervish writes her an extraordinary letter, in which we suspect the pen of our Scribe, and from which we can but transcribe the following:

> "You found in me a vacant heart," he pleads, "and you occupied it. The divan therein is yours, yours alone. Nor shall I ever permit a chance caller, an intruder, to exasperate you.... My breast is a stronghold in which you are well fortified. How then can any one disturb you?... How can I turn from myself against myself? Somewhat of you, the best of you, circulates with my blood; you are my breath of life. How can I then overcome you? How can I turn to another for the sustenance which you alone can give?... If I be thirst personified, you are the living, flowing brook, the everlasting fountain. O for a drink—"

And here follows a hectic uprush about pearly breasts, and honey-sources, and musk-scented arbours, closing with "Your Beduin Boy shall come to-night."

Notwithstanding which, the Enchantress abandons the Syrian Dwelling: she no longer fancies the vacant Divan of which Khalid speaks. Fortress or no fortress, she gives up occupation and withdraws from the foreigner her favour. Not only that; but the fire is crackling under the cauldron, and the typewriter begins to click. Ay, these modern witches can make even a typewriter dance around the fire and join in the chorus. "Double, double, toil and trouble, Fire burn, and cauldron bubble!" and the performance was transformed from the studio to the magazine supplement of one of the Sunday newspapers. There, the Dervish is thrown into the cauldron along with the magic herbs. Bubble—bubble. The fire-eating Dervish, how can he now swallow this double-tongued flame of hate and love? The Enchantress had wrought her spell, had ministered her poison. Now, where can he find an antidote, who can teach him a healing formula? Bruno D'Ast was once bewitched by a sorceress, and by causing her to be burned he was immediately cured. Ah, that Khalid could do this! Like an ordinary pamphlet he would consign the Enchantress to the flames, and her scrap-books and novels to boot. He does well, however, to return to his benevolent friend, the Medium. The spell can be counteracted by another, though less potent. Ay, even witchcraft has its homeopathic remedies.

And the Medium, Shakib tells us, is delighted to welcome back her prodigal child. She opens to him her arms, and her heart; she slays the fatted calf. "I knew that Allah will bring you back to me," she ejaculates; "my prevision is seldom wrong." And kissing her hand, Khalid falters, "Forgiveness is for the sinner, and the good are for forgiveness." Whereupon, they plunge again into the Unseen, and thence to Bohemia. The aftermath, however, does not come up to the expectations of the good Medium. For the rigmarole of the Enchantress about the Dervish in New York had already done its evil work. And—double—double—wherever the Dervish goes. Especially in Bohemia, where many of its daughters set their caps for him.

And here, he is neither shy nor slow nor visionary. Nor shall his theory of immanent morality trouble him for the while. Reality is met with reality on solid, though sometimes slippery, ground. His animalism, long leashed and starved, is eager for prey. His Phœnician passion is awake. And fortunately, Khalid finds himself in Bohemia where the poison and the antidote are frequently offered together. Here the spell of one sorceress can straightway be offset by that of her sister. And we have our Scribe's word for it, that the Dervish went as far and as deep with the huris, as the doctors eventually would permit him. That is why, we believe, in commenting upon his adventures there, he often quotes the couplet,

"In my sublunar paradise
There's plenty of honey—and plenty of flies."

The flies in his cup, however, can not be detected with the naked eye. They are microbes rather—microbes which even the physicians can not manage with satisfaction. For it must be acknowledged that Khalid's immanent morality and intellectualism suffered an interregnum with the huris. Reckless, thoughtless, heartless, he plunges headlong again. It is said in Al-Hadith that he who guards himself against the three cardinal evils, namely, of the tongue (*laklaka*), of the stomach (*kabkaba*), and of the sex (*zabzaba*), will have guarded himself against all evil. But Khalid reads not in the Hadith of the Prophet. And that he became audacious, edacious, and loquacious, is evident from such wit and flippancy as he here likes to display. "Some women," says he, "might be likened to whiskey, others to seltzer water; and many are those who, like myself, care neither for the soda or the whiskey straight. A 'high-ball' I will have."

Nay, he even takes to punch; for in his cup of amour there is a subtle and multifarious mixture. With him, he himself avows, one woman complemented another. What the svelte brunette, for instance, lacked, the steatopygous blonde amply supplied. Delicacy and intensity, effervescence and depth, these he would have in a woman, or a hareem, as in anything else. But these excellences, though found in a hareem, will not fuse, as in a poem or a picture. Even thy bones, thou scented high-lacquered Dervish, are likely to melt away before they melt into one.

It is written in the K. L. MS. that women either bore, or inspire, or excite. "The first and the last are to be met with anywhere; but the second? Ah, well you have heard the story of Diogenes. So take up your lamp and come along. But remember, when you do meet the woman that inspires, you will begin to yearn for the woman that excites."

And here, the hospitality of the Dervish does not belie his Arab blood. In Bohemia, the bonfire of his heart was never extinguished, and the wayfarers stopping before his tent, be they of those who bored, or excited, or inspired, were welcome guests for at least three days and nights. And in this he follows the rule of hospitality among his people.

BOOK THE SECOND IN THE TEMPLE

TO NATURE

O Mother eternal, divine, satanic, all encompassing, all-nourishing, all-absorbing, O star-diademed, pearl-sandaled Goddess, I am thine forever and ever: whether as a child of thy womb, or an embodiment of a spirit-wave of thy light, or a dumb blind personification of thy smiles and tears, or an ignis-fatuus of the intelligence that is in thee or beyond thee, I am thine forever and ever: I come to thee, I prostrate my face before thee, I surrender myself wholly to thee. O touch me with thy wand divine again; stir me once more in thy mysterious alembics; remake me to suit the majestic silence of thy hills, the supernal purity of thy sky, the mystic austerity of thy groves, the modesty of thy slow-swelling, soft-rolling streams, the imperious pride of thy pines, the wild beauty and constancy of thy mountain rivulets. Take me in thine arms, and whisper to me of thy secrets; fill my senses with thy breath divine; show me the bottom of thy terrible spirit; buffet me in thy storms, infusing in me of thy ruggedness and strength, thy power and grandeur; lull me in thine autumn sun-downs to teach me in the arts that enrapture, exalt, supernaturalise. Sing me a lullaby, O Mother eternal! Give me to drink of thy love, divine and diabolic; thy cruelty and thy kindness, I accept both, if thou wilt but whisper to me the secret of both. Anoint me with the chrism of spontaneity that I may be ever worthy of thee.—Withdraw not from me thy hand, lest universal love and sympathy die in my breast.—I implore thee, O Mother eternal, O sea-throned, heaven-canopied Goddess, I prostrate my face before thee, I surrender myself wholly to thee. And whether I be to-morrow the censer in the hand of thy High Priest, or the incense in the censer,—whether I become a star-gem in thy cestus or a sun in thy diadem or even a firefly in thy fane, I am content. For I am certain that it shall be for the best.—**Khalid.**

CHAPTER I

THE DOWRY OF DEMOCRACY

Old Arabic books, printed in Bulaq, generally have a broad margin wherein a separate work, independent of the text, adds gloom to the page. We have before us one of these tomes in which the text treats of the ethics of life and religion, and the margins are darkened with certain adventures which Shahrazad might have added to her famous Nights. The similarity between Khalid's life in its present stage and some such book, is evident. Nay, he has been so assiduous in writing the marginal Work, that ever since he set fire to his peddling-box, we have had little in the Text worth transcribing. Nothing, in fact; for many pages back are as blank as the evil genius of Bohemia could wish them. And how could one with that mara upon him, write of the ethics of life and religion?

Al-Hamazani used to say that in Jorajan the man from Khorasan must open thrice his purse: first, to pay for the rent; second, for the food; and third, for his coffin. And so, in Khalid's case, at least, is Bohemia. For though the purse be not his own, he was paying dear, and even in advance, in what is dearer than gold, for his experience. "O, that the Devil did not take such interest in the marginal work of our life! Why should we write it then, and for whom? And how will it fare with us when, chapfallen in the end and mortified, we stand before the great Task-Master like delinquent school boys with a blank text in our hands?" (Thus Shakib, who has caught the moralising evil from his Master.) And that we must stand, and fall, for thus standing, he is quite certain. At least, Khalid is. For he would not return to the Text to make up for the blank pages therein, if he were not.

"When he returned from his last sojourn in Bohemia," writes our Scribe, "Khalid was pitiful to behold. Even Sindbad, had he seen him, would have been struck with wonder. The tears rushed to my eyes

when we embraced; for instead of Khalid I had in my arms a phantom.
And I could not but repeat the lines of Al-Mutanabbi,

> "So phantom-like I am, and though so near,
> If I spoke not, thou wouldst not know I'm here."

"No more voyages, I trust, O thou Sindbad." And he replied, "Yes,
one more; but to our dear native land this time." In fact, I, too, was
beginning to suffer from nostalgia, and was much desirous of returning
home." But Shakib is in such a business tangle that he could not extricate himself in a day. So, they tarry another year in New York, the one
meanwhile unravelling his affairs, settling with his creditors and collecting what few debts he had, the other brooding over the few blank
pages in his Text.

One day he receives a letter from a fellow traveller, a distinguished
citizen of Tammany Land, whom he had met and befriended in Bohemia, relating to an enterprise of great pith and moment. It was election
time, we learn, and the high post of political canvasser of the Syrian
District was offered to Khalid for a consideration of—but the letter
which Shakib happily preserved, we give in full.

> "Dear Khalid:
> "I have succeeded in getting Mr. O'Donohue to ap-
> point you a canvasser of the Syrian District. You must stir
> yourself, therefore, and try to do some good work, among
> the Syrian voters, for Democracy's Candidate this cam-
> paign. Here is a chance which, with a little hustling on
> your part, will materialise. And I see no reason why you
> should not try to cash your influence among your people.
> This is no mean position, mind you. And if you will come
> up to the Wigwam to-morrow, I'll give you a few sugges-
> tions on the business of manipulating votes.
> "Yours truly,
> "Patrick Hoolihan."

And the said Mr. Hoolihan, the letter shows, is Secretary to Mr.
O'Donohue, who is first henchman to the Boss. Such a letter, if luckily
misunderstood, will fire for a while the youthful imagination. No; not
his Shamrag Majesty's Tammany Agent to Syria, this Canvassership,
you poor phantom-like zany! A high post, indeed, you fond and pitiful
dreamer, on which you must hang the higher aspirations of your soul,
together with your theory of immanent morality. You would not know
this at first. You would still kiss the official notification of Mr. Hooli-

han, and hug it fondly to your breast. Very well. At last—and the gods will not damn thee for musing—you will stand in the band-wagon before the corner groggery and be the object of the admiration of your fellow citizens—perhaps of missiles, too. Very well, Khalid; but you must shear that noddle of thine, and straightway, for the poets are potted in Tammany Land. We say this for your sake.

The orator-dream of youth, ye gods, shall it be realised in this heaven of a dray-cart with its kerosene torch and its drum, smelling and sounding rather of Juhannam? Surely, from the Table of Bohemia to the Stump in Tammany Land, is a far cry. But believe us, O Khalid, you will wish you were again in the gardens of Proserpine, when the silence and darkness extinguish the torch and the drum and the echoes of the shouting crowds. The headaches are certain to follow this inebriation. You did not believe Shakib; you would not be admonished; you would go to the Wigwam for your portfolio. *"High post,"* *"political canvasser,"* *"manipulation of votes,"* you will know the exact meaning of these esoteric terms, when, alas, you meet Mr. Hoolihan. For you must know that not every one you meet in Bohemia is not a Philistine. Indeed, many helots are there, who come from Philistia to spy out the Land.

We read in the *Histoire Intime* of Shakib that Khalid did become a Tammany citizen, that is to say, a Tammany dray-horse; that he was much esteemed by the Honourable Henchmen, and once in the Wigwam he was particularly noticed by his Shamrag Majesty Boss O'Graft; that he was Tammany's Agent to the Editors of the Syrian newspapers of New York, whom he enrolled in the service of the Noble Cause for a consideration which no eloquence or shrewdness could reduce to a minimum; that he also took to the stump and dispensed to his fellow citizens, with rhetorical gestures at least, of the cut-and-dried logic which the Committee of Buncombe on such occasions furnishes its squad of talented spouters; and that—the most important this—he was subject in the end to the ignominy of waiting in the lobby with tuft-hunters and political stock-jobbers, until it pleased the Committee of Buncombe and the Honourable Treasurer thereof to give him—a card of dismissal!

But what virtue is there in waiting, our cynical friend would ask. Why not go home and sleep? Because, O cynical friend, the Wigwam now is Khalid's home. For was he not, in creaking boots and a slouch hat, ceremoniously married to Democracy? Ay, and after spending their honeymoon on the Stump and living another month or two with his troll among her People, he returns to his cellar to brood, not over the blank pages in his Text, nor over the disastrous results of the Campaign, but on the weightier matter of divorce. For although Politics and Romance, in the History of Human Intrigue, have often known and enjoyed the same yoke, with Khalid they refused to pull at the plough. They were not sensible even to the goad. Either the yoke in his case was too loose, or the new yoke-fellow too thick-skinned and stubborn.

Moreover, the promise of a handsome dowry, made by the Shamrag Father-in-Law or his Brokers materialised only in the rotten eggs and tomatoes with which the Orator was cordially received on his honeymoon trip. Such a marriage, O Mohammad, and such a honeymoon, and such a dowry!—is not this enough to shake the very sides of the Kaaba with laughter? And yet, in the Wigwam this not uncommon affair was indifferently considered; for the good and honourable Tammanyites marry off their Daughters every day to foreigners and natives alike, and with like extraordinary picturesque results.

Were it not wiser, therefore, O Khalid, had you consulted your friend the Dictionary before you saw exact meaning of canvass and manipulation, before you put on your squeaking boots and slouch hat and gave your hand and heart to Tammany's Daughter and her Father-in-Law O'Graft? But the Dictionary, too, often falls short of human experience; and even Mr. O'Donohue could at best but hint at the meaning of the esoteric terms of Tammany's political creed. These you must define for yourself as you go along; and change and revise your definitions as you rise or descend in the Sacred Order. For canvass here might mean eloquence; there it might mean shrewdness; lower down, intimidation and coercion; and further depthward, human sloth and misery. It is but a common deal in horses. Ay, in Tammany Land it is essentially a trade honestly conducted on the known principle of supply and demand. These truths you had to discover for yourself, you say; for neither the Dictionary, nor your friend and fellow traveller in Bohemia, Mr. Hoolihan, could stretch their knowledge or their conscience to such a compass. And you are not sorry to have made such a discovery? Can you think of the Dowry and say that? We are, indeed, sorry for you. And we would fain insert in letter D of the Dictionary a new definition: namely, Dowry, n. (Tammany Land Slang). The odoriferous missiles, such as eggs and tomatoes, which are showered on an Orator-Groom by the people.

But see what big profits Khalid draws from these small shares in the Reality Stock Company. You remember, good Reader, how he was kicked away from the door of the Temple of Atheism. The stogies of that inspired Doorkeeper were divine, according to his way of viewing things, for they were at that particular moment God's own boots. Ay, it was God, he often repeats, who kicked him away from the Temple of his enemies. And now, he finds the Dowry of Democracy, with all its wonderful revelations, as profitable in its results, as divine in its purpose. And in proof of this, we give here a copy of his letter to Boss O'Graft, written in that downright manner of his contemporaries, the English original of which we find in the *Histoire Intime*.

"From Khalid to Boss O'Graft.

"Right *Dis*honourable Boss:

"I have just received a check from your Treasurer, which by no right whatever is due me, having been paid for my services by Him who knows better than you and your Treasurer what I deserve. The voice of the people, and their eggs and tomatoes, too, are, indeed, God's. And you should know this, you who dare to remunerate me in what is not half as clean as those missiles. I return not your insult of a check, however; but I have tried to do your state some service in purchasing the few boxes of soap which I am now dispatching to the Wigwam. You need more, I know, you and your Honourable Henchmen or Hashmen. And instead of canvassing and orating for Democracy's illustrious Candidate and the Noble Cause, *mashallah!* one ought to do a little canvassing for Honesty and Truth among Democracy's leaders, tuft-hunters, political stock-jobbers, and such like. O, for a higher stump, my Boss, to preach to those who are supporting and degrading the stumps and the stump-orators of the Republic!"

And is it come to this, you poor phantom-like dreamer? Think you a Tammany Boss is like your atheists and attorneys and women of the studio, at whom you could vent your ire without let or hindrance? These harmless humans have no constables at their command. But his Shamrag Majesty—O wretched Khalid, must we bring one of his myrmidons to your cellar to prove to you that, even in this Tammany Land, you can not with immunity give free and honest expression to your thoughts? Now, were you not summoned to the Shamrag's presence to answer for the crime of *lèse-majesté*? And were you not, for your audacity, left to brood ten days and nights in gaol? And what tedium we have in Shakib's History about the charge on which he was arrested. It is unconscionable that Khalid should misappropriate Party funds. Indeed, he never even touched or saw any of it, excepting, of course, that check which he returned. But the Boss was still in power. And what could Shakib do to exonerate his friend? He did much, and he tells as much about it. With check-boot in his pocket, he makes his way through aldermen, placemen, henchmen, and other questionable political species of humanity, up to the Seat of Justice—but such detail, though of the veracity of the writer nothing doubting, we gladly set aside, since we believe with Khalid that his ten days in gaol were akin to the Boots and the Dowry in their motive and effect.

But our Scribe, though never remiss when Khalid is in a pickle, finds much amiss in Khalid's thoughts and sentiments. And as a further illustration of the limpid shallows of the one and the often opaque depths of the other, we give space to the following:

"When Khalid was ordered to appear before the Boss," writes Shakib, "such curiosity and anxiety as I felt at that time made me accompany him. For I was anxious about Khalid, and curious to see this great Leader of men. We set out, therefore, together, I musing on an incident in Baalbek when we went out to meet the Pasha of the Lebanons and a droll old peasant, having seen him for the first time, cried out, 'I thought the Pasha to be a Pasha, but he's but a man.' And I am sorry, after having seen the Boss, I can not say as much for him."

Here follows a little philosophising, unbecoming of our Scribe, on men and names and how they act and react upon each other. Also, a page about his misgivings and the effort he made to persuade Khalid not to appear before the Boss. But skipping over these, "we reach the Tammany Wigwam and are conducted by a thick-set, heavy-jowled, heavy-booted citizen through the long corridor into a little square room occupied by a little square-faced clerk. Here we wait a half hour and more, during which the young gentleman, with his bell before him and his orders to minor clerks who come and go, poses as somebody of some importance. We are then asked to follow him from one room into another, until we reach the one adjoining the private office of the Boss. A knock or two are executed on the door of Greatness with a nauseous sense of awe, and 'Come in,' Greatness within huskily replies. The square-faced clerk enters, shuts the door after him, returns in a trice, and conducts us into the awful Presence. Ye gods of Baalbek, the like of this I never saw before. Here is a room sumptuously furnished with sofas and fauteuils, and rugs from Ispahan. On the walls are pictures of Washington, Jefferson, and the great Boss Tweed; and right under the last named, behind that preciously carved mahogany desk, in that soft rolling mahogany chair, is the squat figure of the big Boss. On the desk before him, besides a plethora of documents, lay many things pell-mell, among which I noticed a box of cigars, the Criminal Code, and, most prominent of all, the Boss' feet, raised there either to bid us welcome, or to remind us of his power. And the rich Ispahan rug, the cuspidor being small and overfull, receives the richly coloured matter which he spurts forth every time he takes the cigar out of his mouth. O, the vulgarity, the bestiality of it! Think of those poor patient Persian weavers who weave the tissues of their hearts into such beautiful work, and of this proud and paltry Boss, whose office should have been furnished with straw. Yes, with straw; and the souls of those poor artist-weavers will sleep in peace. O, the ignominy of having such precious pieces of workmanship under the feet and spittle of such vulgar specimens of humanity. But if the Boss had purchased these rugs himself, with money earned by his own brow-sweat, I am sure he would appreciate them better. He would then know, if not their intrinsic worth, at least their market value. Yes, and they were presented to him by some one *needing, I suppose, police connivance and protection.* The first half of this statement I had from the Boss himself; the second, I base on Khalid's knowingness and suspicion. Be this, however, as it may.

"When we entered this sumptuously furnished office, the squat figure in the chair under the picture of Boss Tweed, remained as immobile as a fixture and did not as much as reply to our *salaam.* But he pointed disdainfully to seats in the corner of the room, saying, 'Sit down there,' in a manner quite in keeping with his stogies raised on the desk directly in our face. Such freedom, nay, such bestiality, I could never tolerate. Indeed, I prefer the suavity and palaver of Turkish officials, no matter how crafty and corrupt, to the puffing, spitting manners of these come-up-from-the-shamble men. But Khalid could sit there as immobile as the Boss himself, and he did so, billah! For he was thinking all the while, as he told me when we came out, not of such matters as grate on the susceptibilities of a poet, but on the one sole idea of how such a bad titman could lead by the nose so many good people."

Shakib then proceeds to give us a verbatim report of the interview. It begins with the Boss' question, "What do you mean by writing such a letter?" and ends with this other, "What do you mean by immanent morality?" The reader, given the head and tail of the matter, can supply the missing parts. Or, given its two bases, he can construct this triangle of Politics, Ethics, and the Constable, with Khalid's letter, offended Majesty, and a prison cell, as its three turning points. We extract from the report, however, the concluding advice of the Boss. For when he asked Khalid again what he meant by immanent morality, he continued in a crescendo of indignation: "You mean the morality of hayseeds, and priests, and philosophical fools? That sort of morality will not as much as secure a vote during the campaign, nor even help to keep the lowest clerk in office. That sort of morality is good for your mountain peasants or other barbarous tribes. But the free and progressive people of the United States must have something better, nobler, more practical. You'd do well, therefore, to get you a pair of rings, hang them in your ears, and go preach, your immanent morality to the South African Pappoos. But before you go, you shall taste of the rigour of our law, you insolent, brazen-faced, unmannerly scoundrel!"

And we are assured that the Boss did not remain immobile as be spurted forth this mixture of wrath and wisdom, nor did the stogies; for moved by his own words, he rose promptly to his feet. "And what of it," exclaims our Scribe. "Surely, I had rather see those boots perform any office, high or low, as to behold their soles raised like mirrors to my face." But how high an office they performed when the Boss came forward, we are not told. All that our Scribe gives out about the matter amounts to this: namely, that he walked out of the room, and as he looked back to see if Khalid was following, he saw him brushing with his hands—his hips! And on that very day Khalid was summoned to appear before the Court and give answer to the charge of misappropriation of public funds. The orator-dream of youth—what a realisation! He comes to Court, and after the legal formalities are performed, he is delivered unto an officer who escorts him across the Bridge of Sighs to gaol. There, for ten days and nights,—and it might have been ten months were it not for his devoted and steadfast friend,—we leave Khalid to brood on Democracy and the Dowry of Democracy. A few extracts from the Chapter in the K. L. MS. entitled "In Prison," are, therefore, appropriate.

> "So long as one has faith," he writes, "in the general moral summation of the experience of mankind, as the philosophy of reason assures us, one should not despair. But the material fact of the Present, the dark moment of no-morality, consider that, my suffering Brothers. And reflect further that in this great City of New York the majority of citizens consider it a blessing to have a *rojail* (titman) for their boss and leader.... How often have I mused that if Ponce de Leon sought the Fountain of

Youth in the New World, I, Khalid, sought the Fountain of Truth, and both of us have been equally successful!

"But the Americans are neither Pagans—which is consoling—nor fetish-worshipping heathens: they are all true and honest votaries of Mammon, their great God, their one and only God. And is it not natural that the Demiurgic Dollar should be the national Deity of America? Have not deities been always conceived after man's needs and aspirations? Thus in Egypt, in a locality where the manufacture of pottery was the chief industry, God was represented as a potter; in agricultural districts, as a god of harvest; among warring tribes as an avenger, a Jehovah. And the more needs, the more deities; the higher the aspirations, the better the gods. Hence the ugly fetish of a savage tribe, and the beautiful mythology of a Greek Civilisation. Change the needs and aspirations of the Americans, therefore, and you will have changed their worship, their national Deity, and even their Government. And believe me, this change is coming; people get tired of their gods as of everything else. Ay, the time will come, when man in this America shall not suffer for not being a seeker and lover and defender of the Dollar....

"Obedience, like faith, is a divine gift; but only when it comes from the heart: only when prompted by love and sincerity is it divine. If you can not, however, reverence what you obey, then, I say, withhold your obedience. And if you prefer to barter your identity or ego for a counterfeit coin of ideology, that right is yours. For under a liberal Constitution and in a free Government, you are also at liberty to sell your soul, to open a bank account for your conscience. But don't blame God, or Destiny, or Society, when you find yourself, after doing this, a brother to the ox. Herein, we Orientals differ from Europeans and Americans; we are never bribed into obedience. We obey either from reverence and love, or from fear. We are either power-worshippers or cowards but never, never traders. It might be said that the masses in the East are blind slaves, while in Europe and America they are become blind rebels. And which is the better part of valour, when one is blind—submission or revolt?...

"No; popular suffrage helps not the suffering individual; nor does it conduce to a better and higher morality. Why, my Masters, it can not as much as purge its own channels. For what is the ballot box, I ask again, but a modern vehicle of corruption and debasement? The ballot box, believe me, can not add a cubit to your frame, nor can it shed a modicum of light on the deeper problems of life. Of course, it is the exponent of the will of the majority, that is to say, the will of the Party that has more money at its disposal. The majority, and Iblis, and Juhannam—ah, come out with me to the new gods!..."

But we must make allowance for these girds and gibes at Democracy, of which we have given a specimen. Khalid's irony bites so deep at times as to get at the very bone of truth. And here is the marrow of it. We translate the following prophecy with which he closes his Chapter "In Prison," and with it, too, we close ours.

"But my faith in man," he swears, "is as strong as my faith in God. And as strong, too, perhaps, is my faith in the future world-ruling destiny of America. To these United States shall the Nations of the World turn one day for the best model of good Government; in these United States the well-springs of the higher aspirations of the soul shall quench the thirst of every race-traveller on the highway of emancipation; and from these United States the sun and moon of a great Faith and a great Art shall rise upon mankind. I believe this, billah! and I am willing to go on the witness stand to swear to it. Ay, in this New World, the higher Superman shall rise. And he shall not be of the tribe of Overmen of the present age, of the beautiful blond beast of Zarathustra, who would riddle mankind as they would riddle wheat or flour; nor of those political moralists who would reform the world as they would a parish.

"From his transcendental height, the Superman of America shall ray forth in every direction the divine light, which shall mellow and purify the spirit of Nations and strengthen and sweeten the spirit of men, in this New World, I tell you, he shall be born, but he shall not be an American in the Democratic sense. He shall be nor of the Old World nor of the New; he shall be, my Brothers, of both. In him shall be reincarnated the Asiatic spirit of origination, of Poesy and Prophecy, and the European spirit of Art, and the American spirit of Invention. Ay, the Nation that leads the world to-day in material progress shall lead it, too, in the future, in the higher things of the mind and soul. And when you reach that height, O beloved America, you will be far from the majority-rule, and Iblis, and Juhannam. And you will then conquer those 'enormous mud Megatheriums' of which Carlyle makes loud mention."

CHAPTER II

SUBTRANSCENDENTAL

Deficiencies in individuals, as in States, have their value and import. Indeed, that sublime impulse of perfectibility, always vivacious, always working under various forms and with one underlying purpose, would be futile without them, and fatuous. And what were life without this incessant striving of the spirit? What were life without its angles of difficulty and defeat, and its apices of triumph and power? A banality this, you will say. But need we not be reminded of these wholesome truths, when the striving after originality nowadays is productive of so much quackery? The impulse of perfectibility, we repeat, whether at work in a Studio, or in a Factory, or in a Prison Cell, is the most noble of all human impulses, the most divine.

Of that Chapter, In Prison, we have given what might be called the exogenous bark of the Soul, or that which environment creates. And now we shall endeavour to show the reader somewhat of the ludigenous process, by which the Soul, thrumming its own strings or eating its own guts, develops and increases its numbers. For Khalid in these gaol-days is much like Hamlet's player, or even like Hamlet himself—always soliloquising, tearing a passion to rags. And what mean these outbursts and objurgations of his, you will ask; these suggestions, fugitive, rhapsodical, mystical; this furibund allegro about Money, Mediums, and Bohemia; these sobs and tears and asseverations, in which our Lady of the Studio and Shakib are both expunged with great billahs;—the force and significance of these subliminal uprushes, dear Reader, we confess we are, like yourself, unable to understand, without the aid of our Interpreter. We shall, therefore, let him speak.

"When in prison," writes Shakib, "Khalid was subject to spasms and strange hallucinations. One day, when I was sweating in the effort to get him out of gaol, he sends me word to come and see him. I go;

and after waiting a while at the Iron gate, I behold Khalid rushing down the isle like an angry lion. 'What do you want,' he growled, 'why are you here?' And I, amazed, 'Did you not send for me?' And he snapped up, 'I did; but you should not have come. You should withhold from me your favours.' Life of Allah, I was stunned. I feared lest his mind, too, had gone in the direction of his health, which was already sorrily undermined. I looked at him with dim, tearful eyes, and assured him that soon he shall be free. 'And what is the use of freedom,' he exclaimed, 'when it drags us to lower and darker depths? Don't think I am miserable in prison. No; I am not—I am happy. I have had strange visions, marvellous. O my Brother, if you could behold the sloughs, deeper and darker than any prison-cell, into which *you* have thrown me. Yes, *you*—and another. O, I hate you both. I hate my best lovers. I hate You—no—no, no, no.' And he falls on me, embraces me, and bathes my cheeks with his tears. After which he falters out beseechingly, 'Promise, promise that you will not give me any more money, and though starving and in rags you find me crouching at your door, promise.' And of a truth, I acquiesced in all he said, seeing how shaken in body and mind he was. But not until I had made a promise under oath would he be tranquillised. And so, after our farewell embrace, he asked me to come again the following day and bring him some books to read. This I did, fetching with me Rousseau's *Emile* and Carlyle's *Hero-Worship*, the only two books he had in the cellar. And when he saw them, he exclaimed with joy, 'The very books I want! I read them twice already, and I shall read them again. O, let me kiss you for the thought.' And in an ecstasy he overwhelms me again with suffusing sobs and embraces.

"What a difference, I thought, between Khalid of yesterday and Khalid of to-day. What a transformation! Even I who know the turn and temper of his nature had much this time to fear. Surely, an alienist would have made a case of him. But I began to get an inkling into his cue of passion, when he told me that he was going to start a little business again, if I lend him the necessary capital. But I reminded him that we shall soon be returning home. 'No, not I,' he swore; 'not until I can pay my own passage, at least. I told you yesterday I'll accept no more money from you, except, of course, the sum I need to start the little business I am contemplating.' 'And suppose you lose this money,' I asked.—'Why, then *you* lose *me*. But no, you shall not. For I know, I believe, I am sure, I swear that my scheme this time will not be a failure in any sense of the word. I have heavenly testimony on that.'— 'And what was the matter with you yesterday? Why were you so queer?' 'O, I had nightmares and visions the night before, and you came too early in the morning. See this.' And he holds down his head to show me the back of his neck. 'Is there no swelling here? I feel it. Oh, it pains me yet. But I shall tell you about it and about the vision when I am out.'—And at this, the gaoler comes to inform us that Khalid's minutes are spent and he must return to his cell."

All of which from our Interpreter is as clear as God Save the King. And from which we hope our Reader will infer that those outbursts and tears and rhapsodies of Khalid did mean somewhat. They did mean, even when we first approached his cell, that something was going on in him—a revolution, a *coup d'état*, so to speak, of the spirit. For a Prince in Rags, but not in Debts and Dishonour, will throttle the Harpy which has hitherto ruled and degraded his soul.

But the dwelling, too, of that soul is sorely undermined. And so, his leal and loving friend Shakib takes him later to the best physician in the City, who after the tapping and auscultation, shakes his head, writes his prescriptions, and advises Khalid to keep in the open air as much as possible, or better still, to return to his native country. The last portion of the advice, however, Khalid can not follow at present. For he will either return home on his own account or die in New York. "If I can not in time save enough money for the Steamship Company," he said to Shakib, "I can at least leave enough to settle the undertaker's bill. And in either case, I shall have paid my own passage out of this New World. And I shall stand before my Maker in a shroud, at least, which I can call my own."

To which Shakib replies by going to the druggist with the prescriptions. And when he returns to the cellar with a package of four or five medicine bottles for rubbing and smelling and drinking, he finds Khalid sitting near the stove—we are now in the last month of Winter—warming his hands on the flames of the two last books he read. *Emile* and *Hero-Worship* go the way of all the rest. And there he sits, meditating over Carlyle's crepitating fire and Rousseau's writhing, sibilating flame. And it may be he thought of neither. Perhaps he was brooding over the resolution he had made, and the ominous shaking of the doctor's head. Ah, but his tutelar deities are better physicians, he thought. And having made his choice, he will pitch the medicine bottles into the street, and only follow the doctor's advice by keeping in the open air.

Behold him, therefore, with a note in hand, applying to Shakib, in a formal and business-like manner, for a loan; and see that noble benefactor and friend, after gladly giving the money, throw the note into the fire. And now, Khalid is neither dervish nor philosopher, but a man of business with a capital of twenty-five dollars in his pocket. And with one-fifth of this capital he buys a second-hand push-cart from his Greek neighbour, wends his way with it to the market-place, makes a purchase there of a few boxes of oranges, sorts them in his cart into three classes,—"there is no equality in nature," he says, while doing this,—sticks a price card at the head of each class, and starts, in the name of Allah, his business. That is how he will keep in the open air twelve hours a day.

But in the district where he is known he does not long remain. The sympathy of his compatriots is to him worse than the doctor's medicines, and those who had often heard him speechifying exchanged significant looks when he passed. Moreover, the police would not let him set up his stand anywhere. "There comes the push-cart orator," they would say to each other; and before our poor Syrian stops to breathe, one of them grumpishly cries out, "Move on there! Move on!" Once Khalid ventures to ask, "But why are others allowed to set up their stands here?" And the "copper" (we beg the Critic's pardon again) coming forward twirling his club, lays his hand on Khalid's shoulder and calmly this: "Don't you think I know you? Move on, I say." O Khalid, have you forgotten that these "coppers" are the minions of Tammany? Why tarry, therefore, and ask questions? Yes, make a big move at once—out of the district entirely.

Now, to the East Side, into the Jewish Quarter, Khalid directs his cart. And there, he falls in with Jewish fellow push-cart peddlers and puts up with them in a cellar similar to his in the Syrian Quarter. But only for a month could he suffer what the Jew has suffered for centuries. Why? There is this difference between the cellar of the Semite Syrian and that of the Semite Jew: in the first we eat *mojadderah*, in the second, *kosher* but stinking flesh; in the first we read poetry and play the lute, in the second we fight about the rent and the division of the profits of the day; in the first we sleep in linen "as white as the wings of the dove," in the second on pieces of smelly blankets; the first is redolent of ottar of roses, Shakib's favourite perfume, the second is especially made insufferable by that stench which is peculiar to every Hebrew hive. For these and other reasons, Khalid separates himself from his Semite fellow peddlers, and makes this time a bigger move than the first.

Ay, even to the Bronx, where often in former days, shouldering the peddling-box, he tramped, will he now push his orange-cart and his hopes. There, between City and Country, nearer to Nature, and not far from the traffic of life, he fares better both in health and purse. It is much to his liking, this upper end of the City. Here the atmosphere is more peaceful and soothing, and the police are more agreeable. No, they do not nickname and bully him in the Bronx. And never was he ordered to move on, even though he set up his stand for months at the same corner. "Ah, how much kinder and more humane people become," he says, "even when they are not altogether out of the City, but only on the outskirts of the country expanse."

Khalid passes the Spring and Summer in the Bronx and keeps in the open air, not only in the day, but also in the night. How he does this, is told in a letter which he writes to Shakib. But does he sleep at all, you ask, and how, and where? Reader, we thank you for your anxiety about Khalid's health. And we would fain show you the Magic Carpet which he carries in the lock-box of his push-cart. But see for yourself, here be neither Magic Carpet, nor Magic Ring. Only his papers, a few towels, a blanket, some underwear, and his coffee utensils, are here. For Khalid could forego his *mojadderah*, but never his coffee, the Arab that he is. But an Arab on the wayfare, if he finds himself at night far from the camp, will dig him a ditch in the sands and lie there to sleep under the living stars. Khalid could not do thus, neither in the City nor out of it. And yet, he did not lodge within doors. He hired a place only for his push-cart; and this, a small padlock-booth where he deposits his stock in trade. But how he lived in the Bronx is described in the following letter:

"My loving Brother Shakib,

"I have been two months here, in a neighbourhood familiar to you. Not far from the place where I sleep is the sycamore tree under which I burned my peddling-box. And perhaps I shall yet burn there my push-cart too. But for the present, all's well. My business is good and my health is improving. The money-order I am enclosing with this, will cancel the note, but not the many debts, I owe you. And I hope to be able to join you again soon, to make the voyage to our native land together. Meanwhile I am working, and laying up a little something. I make from two to three dollars a day, of which I never spend more than one. And this on one meal only; for my lodging and my lunch and breakfast cost next to nothing. Yes, I can be a push-cart peddler in the day; I can sleep out of doors at night; I can do with coffee and oranges for lunch and breakfast; but in the evening I will assert my dignity

and do justice to my taste: I will dine at the Hermitage
and permit you to call me a fool. And why not, since my
purse, like my stomach, is now my own? Why not go to
the Hermitage since my push-cart income permits of it?
But the first night I went there my shabbiness attracted
the discomforting attention of the fashionable diners, and
made even the waiters offensive. Indeed, one of them
came to ask if I were looking for somebody. 'No,' I replied with suppressed indignation; 'I'm looking for a
place where I can sit down and eat, without being eaten
by the eyes of the vulgar curious.' And I pass into an ar-
bor, which from that night becomes virtually my own,
followed by a waiter who from that night, too, became my
friend. For every evening I go there, I find my table unoc-
cupied and my waiter ready to receive and serve me. But
don't think he does this for the sake of my black eyes or
my philosophy. That disdainful glance of his on the first
evening I could never forget, billah. And I found that it
could be baited and mellowed only by a liberal tip. And
this I make in advance every week for both my comfort
and his. Yes, I am a fool, I grant you, but I'm not out of
my element there.

"After dinner I take a stroll in the Flower Gardens, and
crossing the rickety wooden bridge over the river, I enter
the hemlock grove. Here, in a sequestered spot near the
river bank, I lay me on the grass and sleep for the night. I
always bring my towels with me; for in the morning I take
a dip, and at night I use them for a pillow. When the
weather requires it, I bring my blankets too. And hanging
one of them over me, tied to the trees by the cords sown
to its corners, I wrap myself in the other, and praise Allah.

"These and the towels, after taking my bath, I leave at
the Hermitage; my waiter minds them for me. And so, I
suspect I am happy—if, curse it! I could but breathe better. O, come up to see me. I'll give you a royal dinner at
the Hermitage, and a royal bed in the hemlock grove on
the river-bank. Do come up, the peace of Allah upon thee.
Read my salaam to Im-Hanna."

And during his five months in the Bronx he did not sleep five
nights within doors, we are told, nor did he once dine out of the Hermitage. Even his hair, a fantastic fatuity behind a push-cart, he did not

take the trouble to cut or trim. It must have helped his business. But this constancy, never before sustained to such a degree, must soon cease, having laid up, thanks to his push-cart and the people of the Bronx, enough to carry him, not only to Baalbek, but to *Aymakanenkan*.

CHAPTER III

THE FALSE DAWN

What the Arabs always said of Andalusia, Khalid and Shakib said once of America: a most beautiful country with one single vice—it makes foreigners forget their native land. But now they are both suffering from nostalgia, and America, therefore, is without a single vice. It is perfect, heavenly, ideal. In it one sees only the vices of other races, and the ugliness of other nations. America herself is as lovely as a dimpled babe, and as innocent. A dimpled babe she. But wait until she grows, and she will have more than one vice to demand forgetfulness.

Shakib, however, is not going to wait. He begins to hear the call of his own country, now that his bank account is big enough to procure for him the Pashalic of Syria. And Khalid, though his push-cart had developed to a stationary fruit stand,—and perhaps for this very reason,—is now desirous of leaving America anon. He is afraid of success overtaking him. Moreover, the Bronx Park has awakened in him his long dormant love of Nature. For while warming himself on the flames of knowledge in the cellar, or rioting with the Bassarides of Bohemia, or canvassing and speechifying for Tammany, he little thought of what he had deserted in his native country. The ancient historical rivers flowing through a land made sacred by the divine madness of the human spirit; the snow-capped mountains at the feet of which the lily and the oleander bloom; the pine forests diffusing their fragrance even among the downy clouds; the peaceful, sun-swept multi-coloured meadows; the trellised vines, the fig groves, the quince orchards, the orangeries: the absence of these did not disturb his serenity in the cellar, his voluptuousness in Bohemia, his enthusiasm in Tammany Land.

And we must not forget to mention that, besides the divine voice of Nature and native soil, he long since has heard and still hears the still sweet voice of one who might be dearer to him than all. For Khalid, after his return from Bohemia, continued to curse the huris in his dreams. And he little did taste of the blessings of "sore labour's bath, balm of hurt minds." Ay, when he was not racked and harrowed by nightmares, he was either disturbed by the angels of his visions or the succubi of his dreams. And so, he determines to go to Syria for a night's sleep, at least, of the innocent and just. His cousin Najma is there, and that is enough. Once he sees her, the huris are no more.

Now Shakib, who is more faithful in his narration than we first thought—who speaks of Khalid as he is, extenuating nothing—gives us access to a letter which he received from the Bronx a month before their departure from New York. In these Letters of Khalid, which our Scribe happily preserved, we feel somewhat relieved of the dogmatism, fantastic, mystical, severe, which we often meet with in the K. L. MS. In his Letters, our Syrian peddler and seer is a plain blunt man unbosoming himself to his friend. Read this, for instance.

"My loving Brother:

"It is raining so hard to-night that I must sleep, or in fact keep, within doors. Would you believe it, I am no more accustomed to the luxuries of a soft spring-bed, and I can not even sleep on the floor, where I have moved my mattress. I am sore, broken in mind and spirit. Even the hemlock grove and the melancholy stillness of the river, are beginning to annoy me. Oh, I am tired of everything here, tired even of the cocktails, tired of the push-cart, tired of earning as much as five dollars a day. Next Sunday is inauguration day for my stationary fruit stand; but I don't think it's going to stand there long enough to deserve to be baptized with champagne. If you come up, therefore, we'll have a couple of steins at the Hermitage and call it square.—O, I would square myself with the doctors by thrusting a poker down my windpipe: I might be able to breathe better then. I pause to curse my fate.—Curse it, Juhannam-born, curse it!—

"I can not sleep, nor on the spring-bed, nor on the floor. It is two hours past midnight now, and I shall try to while away the time by scrawling this to you. My brother, I can not long support this sort of life, being no more fit for rough, ignominious labor. 'But why,' you will ask, 'did you undertake it?' Yes, why? Strictly speaking, I made a mistake. But it's a noble mistake, believe me—a mistake which everybody in my condition ought to make, if but once in their life-time. Is it not something to be able to make an honest resolution and carry it out? I have heard strange voices in prison; I have hearkened to them; but I find that one must have sound lungs, at least, to be able to do the will of the immortal gods. And even if he had, I doubt if he could do much to suit them in America. O, my greatest enemy and benefactor in the whole world is this dumb-hearted mother, this America, in whose iron loins I have been spiritually conceived. Paradoxical, this? But is it not true? Was not the Khalid, now writing to you, born in the cellar? Down there, in the very loins of New York? But alas, our spiritual Mother devours, like a cat, her own children. How then can we live with her in the same house?

"I need not tell you now that the ignominious task I set my hands to, was never to my liking. But the ox under the yoke is not asked whether he likes it or not. I have been yoked to my push-cart by the immortal gods; and soon my turn and trial will end. It must end. For our country is just beginning to speak, and I am her chosen voice. I feel that if I do not respond, if I do not come to her, she will be dumb forever. No; I can not remain here any more. For I can not be strenuous enough to be miserably happy; nor stupid enough to be contentedly miserable. I confess I have been spoiled by those who call themselves spiritual sisters of mine. The huris be dam'd. And if I don't leave this country soon, I'll find myself sharing the damnation again—in Bohemia.—

"The power of the soul is doubled by the object of its love, or by such labor of love as it undertakes. But, here I am, with no work and nobody I can love; nay, chained to a task which I now abominate. If a labor of love doubles the power of the soul, a labor of hate, to use an antonym term, warps it, poisons it, destroys it. Is it not a shame that in this great Country,—this Circe with her golden horns of plenty,—one can not as much as keep his blood in circulation without damning the currents of one's soul? O America, equally hated and beloved of Khalid, O Mother of prosperity and spiritual misery, the time will come when you shall see that your gold is but pinchbeck, your gilt-edge bonds but death decrees, and your god of wealth a carcase enthroned upon a dung-hill. But you can not see this now; for you are yet in the false dawn, floundering tumultuously, worshipping your mammoth carcase on a dung-hill—and devouring your spiritual children. Yes, America is now in the false dawn, and as sure as America lives, the true dawn must follow.

"Pardon, Shakib. I did not mean to end my letter in a rhapsody. But I am so wrought, so broken in body, so inflamed in spirit. I hope to see you soon. No, I hope to see myself with you on board of a Transatlantic steamer."

And is not Khalid, like his spiritual Mother, floundering, too, in the false dawn of life? His love of Nature, which was spontaneous and free, is it not likely to become formal and scientific? His love of Country, which begins tremulously, fervently in the woods and streams, is it not likely to end in Nephelococcygia? His determination to work, which was rudely shaken at a push-cart, is it not become again a determination to loaf? And now, that he has a little money laid up, has he not the right to seek in this world the cheapest and most suitable place for loafing? And where, if not in the Lebanon hills, "in which it seemed always afternoon," can he rejoin the Lotus-Eaters of the East? This man of visions, this fantastic, rhapsodical—but we must not be hard upon him. Remember, good Reader, the poker which he would thrust down his windpipe to broaden it a little. With asthmatic fits and tuberous infiltrations, one is permitted to commune with any of Allah's ministers of grace or spirits of Juhannam. And that divine spark of primal, paradisical love, which is rapidly devouring all others—let us not forget that. Ay, we mean his cousin Najma. Of course, he speaks, too, of his nation, his people, awaking, lisping, beginning to speak, waiting for him, the chosen Voice! Which reminds us of how he was described to us by the hasheesh-smokers of Cairo.

In any event, the Reader will rejoice with us, we hope, that Khalid will not turn again toward Bohemia. He will agree with us that, whether on account of his health, or his love, or his mission, it is well, in his present fare of mind and body, that he is returning to the land "in which it seemed always afternoon."

CHAPTER IV

THE LAST STAR

Is it not an ethnic phenomenon that a descendant of the ancient Phœnicians can not understand the meaning and purport of the Cash Register in America? Is it not strange that this son of Superstition and Trade can not find solace in the fact that in this Pix of Business is the Host of the Demiurgic Dollar? Indeed, the omnipresence and omnipotence of it are not without divine significance. For can you not see that this Cash Register, this Pix of Trade, is prominently set up on the altar of every institution, political, moral, social, and religious? Do you not meet with it everywhere, and foremost in the sanctuaries of the mind and the soul? In the Societies for the Diffusion of Knowledge; in the Social Reform Propagandas; in the Don't Worry Circles of Metaphysical Gymnasiums; in Alliances, Philanthropic, Educational; in the Board of Foreign Missions; in the Sacrarium of Vaticinatress Eddy; in the Church of God itself;—is not the Cash Register a divine symbol of the *credo*, the faith, or the idea?

"To trade, or not to trade," Hamlet-Khalid exclaims, "that is the question: whether 'tis nobler in the mind to suffer, etc., or to take arms against the Cash Registers of America, and by opposing end—" What? Sacrilegious wretch, would you set your face against the divinity in the Holy Pix of Trade? And what will you end, and how will You end by it? An eternal problem, this, of opposing and ending. But before you set your face in earnest, we would ask you to consider if the vacancy or chaos which is sure to follow, be not more pernicious than what you would end. If you are sure it is not, go ahead, and we give you Godspeed. If you have the least doubt about it—but Khalid is incapable now of doubting anything. And whether he opposes his theory of immanent morality to the Cash Register, or to Democracy, or to the ruling powers of Flunkeydom, we hope He will end well. Such is the

penalty of revolt against the dominating spirit of one's people and ancestors, that only once in a generation is it attempted, and scarcely
with much success. In fact, the first who revolts must perish, the second, too, and the third, and the fourth, until, in the course of time and
by dint of repetition and resistance, the new species of the race can
overcome the forces of environment and the crushing influence of con-
formity. This, we know, is the biological law, and Khalid must suffer
under it. For, as far as our knowledge extends, he is the first Syrian,
the ancient Lebanon monks excepted, who revolted against the ruling
spirit of his people and the dominant tendencies of the times, both in
his native and his adopted Countries.

Yes, the *êthos* of the Syrians (for once we use Khalid's philosophic
term), like that of the Americans, is essentially money-seeking. And
whether in Beirut or in New York, even the moralists and reformers,
like the hammals and grocers, will ask themselves, before they undertake to do anything for you or for their country, "What will this profit
us? How much will it bring us?" And that is what Khalid once thought
to oppose and end. Alas, oppose he might—and End He Must. How
can an individual, without the aid of Time and the Unseen Powers,
hope to oppose and end, or even change, this monstrous mass of
things? Yet we must not fail to observe that when we revolt against a
tendency inimical to our law of being, it is for our own sake, and not
the race's, that we do so. And we are glad we are able to infer, if not
from the K. L, MS., at least from his Letters, that Khalid is beginning
to realise this truth. Let us not, therefore, expatiate further upon it.

If the reader will accompany us now to the cellar to bid our Syrian
friends farewell, we promise a few things of interest. When we first
came here some few years ago in Winter, or to another such underground dwelling, the water rose ankle-deep over the floor, and the
mould and stench were enough to knock an ox dead. Now, a scent of
ottar of roses welcomes us at the door and leads us to a platform in the
centre, furnished with a Turkish rug, which Shakib will present to the
landlord as a farewell memento.

And here are our three Syrians making ready for the voyage.
Shakib is intoning some verses of his while packing; Im-Hanna is
cooking the last dish of *mojadderah*; and Khalid, with some vague
dream in his eyes, and a vaguer, far-looming hope in his heart, is sitting on his trunk wondering at the variety of things Shakib is
cramming into his. For our Scribe, we must not fail to remind the
Reader, is contemplating great things of State, is nourishing a great
political ambition. He will, therefore, bethink him of those in power at

home. Hence these costly presents. Ay, besides the plated jewellery—the rings, bracelets, brooches, necklaces, ear-rings, watches, and chains—of which he is bringing enough to supply the peasants of three villages, see that beautiful gold-knobbed ebony stick, which he will present to the vali, and this precious gold cross with a ruby at the heart for the Patriarch, and these gold fountain pens for his literary friends, and that fine Winchester rifle for the chief of the tribe Anezah. These he packs in the bottom of his trunk, and with them his precious dilapidated copy of Al-Mutanabbi, and—what MS. be this? What, a Book of Verse spawned in the cellar? Indeed, the very embryo of that printed copy we read in Cairo, and which Shakib and his friends would have us translate for the benefit of the English reading public.

For our Scribe is the choragus of the Modern School of Arabic poetry. And this particular Diwan of his is a sort of rhymed inventory of all the inventions and discoveries of modern Science and all the wonders of America. He has published other Diwans, in which French morbidity is crowned with laurels from the Arabian Nights. For this Modern School has two opposing wings, moved by two opposing forces, Science being the motive power of the one, and Byron and De Musset the inspiring geniuses of the other. We would not be faithful to our Editorial task and to our Friend, if we did not give here a few luminant examples of the Diwan in question. We are, indeed, very sorry, for the sake of our readers, that space will not allow us to give them a few whole qasïdahs from it. To those who are so fortunate as to be able to read and understand the Original, we point out the Ode to the Phonograph, beginning thus:

> "O Phonograph, thou wonder of our time,
> Thy tongue of wax can sing like me in rhyme."

And another to the Brooklyn Bridge, of which these are the opening lines:

> "O Brooklyn Bridge, how oft upon thy back
> I tramped, and once I crossed thee in a hack."

And finally, the great Poem entitled, On the Virtue and Benefit of Modern Science, of which we remember these couplets:

> "Balloons and airships, falling from the skies,
> Will be as plenty yet as summer flies.
>
> *   *   *   *   *
>
> "Electricity and Steam and Compressed Air

95

Will carry us to heaven yet, I swear."

Here be rhymed truth, at least, which can boast of not being poetry. Ay, in this MS. which Shakib is packing along with Al-Mutanabbi in the bottom of his trunk to evade the Basilisk touch of the Port officials of Beirut, is packed all the hopes of the Modern School. Pack on, Shakib; for whether at the Mena House, or in the hasheesh-dens of Cairo, the Future is drinking to thee, and dreaming of thee and thy School its opium dreams. And Khalid, the while, sits impassive on his trunk, and Im-Hanna is cooking the last dinner of *mojadderah*.

Emigration has introduced into Syria somewhat of the three prominent features of Civilisation: namely, a little wealth, a few modern ideas, and many strange diseases. And of these three blessings our two Syrians together are plentifully endowed. For Shakib is a type of the emigrant, who returns home prosperous in every sense of the word. A Book of Verse to lure Fame, a Letter of Credit to bribe her if necessary, and a double chin to praise the gods. This is a complete set of the prosperity, which Khalid knows not. But he has in his lungs what Shakib the poet can not boast of; while in his trunk he carries but a little wearing apparel, his papers, and his blankets. And in his pocket, he has his ribbed silver cigarette case—the only object he can not part with—a heart-shaped locket with a little diamond star on its face—the only present he is bringing with him home,—and a third-class passage across the Atlantic. For Khalid will not sleep in a bunk, even though it be furnished with eiderdown cushions and tiger skins.

And since he is determined to pass his nights on deck, it matters little whether he travels first class, or second or tenth. Shakib, do what he may, cannot prevail upon him to accept the first-class passage he had bought in his name. "Let us not quarrel about this," says he; "we shall be together on board the same ship, and that settles the question. Indeed, the worse way returning home must be ultimately the best. No, Shakib, it matters not how I travel, if I but get away quickly from this pandemonium of Civilisation. Even now, as I sit on this trunk waiting for the hour of departure, I have a foretaste of the joy of being away from the insidious cries of hawkers, the tormenting bells of the ragman, the incessant howling of children, the rumbling of carts and wagons, the malicious whir of cable cars, the grum shrieks of ferry boats, and the thundering, reverberating, smoking, choking, blinding abomination of an elevated railway. A musician might extract some harmony from this chaos of noises, this jumble of sounds. But I—extract me quickly from them!"

Ay, quickly please, especially for our sake and the Reader's. Now, the dinner is finished, the rug is folded and presented to our landlord with our salaams, the trunks are locked and roped, and our Arabs will silently steal away. And peacefully, too, were it not that an hour before sailing a capped messenger is come to deliver a message to Shakib. There is a pleasant dilative sensation in receiving a message on board a steamer, especially when the messenger has to seek you among the Salon passengers. Now, Shakib dilates with pride as he takes the envelope in his hand; but when he opens it, and reads on the enclosed card, "Mr. Isaac Goldheimer wishes you a *bon voyage*," he turns quickly on his heels and goes on deck to walk his wrath away. For this Mr. Goldheimer is the very landlord who received the Turkish rug. Reflect on this, Reader. Father Abraham would have walked with us to the frontier to betoken his thanks and gratitude. "But this modern Jew and his miserable card," exclaims Shakib in his teeth, as he tears and throws it in the water,—"who asked him to send it, and who would have sued him if he didn't?"

But Shakib, who has lived so long in America and traded with its people, is yet ignorant of some of the fine forms and conventions of Civilisation. He does not know that fashionable folk, or those aping the dear fashionable folk, have a right to assert their superiority at his expense.—I do not care to see you, but I will send a messenger and card to do so for me. You are not my equal, and I will let you know this, even at the hour of your departure, and though I have to hire a messenger to do so.—Is there no taste, no feeling, no gratitude in this? Don't you wish, O Shakib,—but compose yourself. And think not so ill of your Jewish landlord, whom you wish you could wrap in that rug and throw overboard. He certainly meant well. That formula of card and messenger is so convenient and so cheap. Withal, is he not too busy, think you, to come up to the dock for the puerile, prosaic purpose of shaking hands and saying ta-ta? If you can not consider the matter in this light, try to forget it. One must not be too visceral at the hour of departure. Behold, your skyscrapers and your Statue of Liberty are now receding from view; and your landlord and his card and messenger will be further from us every while we think of them, until, thanks to Time and Space and Steam! they will be too far away to be remembered.

Here, then, with our young Seer and our Scribe, we bid New York farewell, and earnestly hope that we do not have to return to it again, or permit any of them to do so. In fact, we shall not hereafter consider, with any ulterior material or spiritual motive, any more of such disparaging, denigrating matter, in the two MSS. before us, as has to pass through our reluctant hands "touchin' on and appertainin' to" the great City of Manhattan and its distinguished denizens. For our part, we have had enough of this painful task. And truly, we have never before undergone such trials in sailing between—but that Charybdis and Scylla allusion has been done to death. Indeed, we love America, and in the course of our present task, which we also love, we had to suffer Khalid's shafts to pass through our ken and sometimes really through our heart. But no more of this. Ay, we would fain set aside our pen from sheer weariness of spirit and bid the Reader, too, farewell. Truly, we would end here this Book of Khalid were it not that the greater part of the most important material in the K. L. MS. is yet intact, and the more interesting portion of Shakib's History is yet to come. Our readers, though we do not think they are sorry for having come out with us so far, are at liberty either to continue with us, or say good-bye. But for the Editor there is no choice. What we have begun we must end, unmindful of the influence, good or ill, of the Zodiacal Signs under which we work.

"Our Phœnician ancestors," says Khalid, "never left anything they undertook unfinished. Consider what they accomplished in their days, and the degree of culture they attained. The most beautiful fabrications in metals and precious stones were prepared in Syria. Here, too, the most important discoveries were made: namely, those of glass and purple. As for me, I can not understand what the Murex trunculus is; and I am not certain if scholars and archæologists, or even mariners and fishermen, will ever find a fossil of that particular species. But murex or no murex, Purple was discovered by my ancestors. Hence the purple passion, that is to say the energy and intensity which coloured everything they did, everything they felt and believed. For whether in bemoaning Tammuz, or in making tear-bottles, or in trading with the Gauls and Britons, the Phœnicians were the same superstitious, honest, passionate, energetic people. And do not forget, you who are now enjoying the privilege of setting down your thoughts in words, that on these shores of Syria written language received its first development.

"It is also said that they discovered and first navigated the Atlantic Ocean, my Phœnicians; that they worked gold mines in the distant isle of Thasos and opened silver mines in the South and Southwest of Spain. In Africa, we know, they founded the colonies of Utica and Carthage. But we are told they went farther than this. And according to some historians, they rounded the Cape, they circumnavigated Africa. And according to recent discoveries made by an American archæologist, they must have discovered America too! For in the ruins of the Aztecs of Mexico there are traces of a Phœnician language and religion. This, about the discovery of America, however, I can not verify with anything from Sanchuniathon. But might they not have made this discovery after the said Sanchuniathon had given up the ghost? And if they did, what can We, their worthless descendants do for them now? Ah, if we but knew the name of their Columbus! No, it is not practical to build a monument to a whole race of people. And yet, they deserve more than this from us, their descendants.

"These dealers in tin and amber, these manufacturers of glass and purple, these developers of a written language, first gave the impetus to man's activity and courage and intelligence. And this activity of the industry and will is not dead in man. It may be dead in us Syrians, but not in the Americans. In their strenuous spirit it rises uppermost. After all, I must love the Americans, for they are my Phœnician ancestors incarnate. Ay, there is in the nature of things a mysterious recurrence which makes for a continuous, everlasting modernity. And I believe that the spirit which moved those brave sea-daring navigators of yore, is still working lustily, bravely, but alas, not joyously—bitterly, rather, selfishly, greedily—behind the steam engine, the electric motor, the plough, and in the clinic and the studio as in the Stock Exchange. That spirit in its real essence, however, is as young, as puissant to-day as it was when the native of Byblus first struck out to explore the seas, to circumnavigate Africa, to discover even America!"

And what in the end might Khalid discover for us or for himself, at least, in his explorations of the Spirit-World? What Colony of the chosen sons of the young and puissant Spirit, on some distant isle beyond the seven seas, might he found? To what far, silent, undulating shore, where "a written language is the instrument only of the lofty expressions and aspirations of the soul" might he not bring us? What Cape of Truth in the great Sea of Mystery might we not be able to circumnavigate, if only this were possible of the language of man?

"Not with glass," he exclaims, "not with tear-bottles, not with purple, not with a written language, am I now concerned, but rather with what those in Purple and those who make this written language their capital, can bring within our reach of the treasures of the good, the true, and the beautiful. I would fain find a land where the soul of man, and the heart of man, and the mind of man, are as the glass of my ancestors' tear-bottles in their enduring quality and beauty. My ancestors' tear-bottles, and though buried in the earth ten thousand years, lose not a grain of their original purity and transparency, of their soft and iridescent colouring. But where is the natural colour and beauty of these human souls, buried in bunks under hatches? Or of those moving in high-lacquered salons above?...

"O my Brothers of the clean and unclean species, of the scented and smelling kind, of the have and have-not classes, there is but one star in this vague dusky sky above us, for you as for myself. And that star is either the last in the eternal darkness, or the first in the rising dawn. It is either the first or the last star of night. And who shall say which it is? Not the Church, surely, nor the State; not Science, nor Sociology, nor Philosophy, nor Religion. But the human will shall influence that star and make it yield its secret and its fire. Each of you, O my Brothers, can make it light his own hut, warm his own heart, guide his own soul. Never before in the history of man did it seem as necessary as it does now that each individual should think for himself, will for himself, and aspire incessantly for the realisation of his ideals and dreams. Yes, we are to-day at a terrible and glorious turning point, and it depends upon us whether that one star in the vague and dusky sky of modern life, shall be the harbinger of Jannat or Juhannam."

CHAPTER V

PRIESTO-PARENTAL

If we remember that the name of Khalid's cousin is Najma (Star), the significance to himself of the sign spoken of in the last Chapter, is quite evident. But what it means to others remains to be seen. His one star, however, judging from his month's experience in Baalbek, is not promising of Jannat. For many things, including parental tyranny and priestcraft and Jesuitism, will here conspire against the single blessedness of him, which is now seeking to double itself.

"Where one has so many Fathers," he writes, "and all are pretending to be the guardians of his spiritual and material well-being, one ought to renounce them all at once. It was not with a purpose to rejoin my folk that I first determined to return to my native country. For, while I believe in the Family, I hate Familism, which is the curse of the human race. And I hate this spiritual Fatherhood when it puts on the garb of a priest, the three-cornered hat of a Jesuit, the hood of a monk, the gaberdine of a rabbi, or the jubbah of a sheikh. The sacredness of the Individual, not of the Family or the Church, do I proclaim. For Familism, or the propensity to keep under the same roof, as a social principle, out of fear, ignorance, cowardice, or dependence, is, I repeat, the curse of the world. Your father is he who is friendly and reverential to the higher being in you; your brothers are those who can appreciate the height and depth of your spirit, who hearken to you, and believe in you, if you have any truth to announce to them. Surely, one's value is not in his skin that you should touch him. Are there any two individuals more closely related than mother and son? And yet, when I Khalid embrace my mother, mingling my tears with hers, I feel that my soul is as distant from her own as is Baalbek from the Dog-star. And so I say, this attempt to bind together under the principle of Familism conflicting spirits, and be it in the name of love or religion or anything else more or less sacred, is in itself a very curse, and should straightway end. It will end, as far as I am concerned. And thou my Brother, whether thou be a son of the Morning or of the Noontide or of the Dusk,—whether thou be a Japanese or a Syrian or a British man—if thou art likewise circumstanced, thou shouldst do the same, not only for thine own sake, but for the sake of thy family as well."

No; Khalid did not find that wholesome plant of domestic peace in his mother's Nursery. He found noxious weeds, rather, and brambles galore. And they were planted there, not by his father or mother, but by those who have a lien upon the souls of these poor people. For the priest here is no peeled, polished affair, but shaggy, scrubby, terrible, forbidding. And with a word he can open yet, for such as Khalid's folk, the gate which Peter keeps or the other on the opposite side of the Universe. Khalid must beware, therefore, how he conducts himself at home and abroad, and how, in his native town, he delivers his mind on sacred things, and profane. In New York, for instance, or in Turabu for that matter, he could say in plain forthright speech what he thought of Family, Church or State, and no one would mind him. But where these Institutions are the rottenest existing he will be minded too well, and reminded, too, of the fate of those who preceded him.

The case of Habib Ish-Shidiak at Kannubin is not yet forgotten. And Habib, be it known, was only a poor Protestant neophite who took pleasure in carrying a small copy of the Bible in his hip pocket, and was just learning to roll his eyes in the pulpit and invoke the "laud." But Khalid, everybody out-protesting, is such an intractable protestant, with, neither Bible in his pocket nor pulpit at his service. And yet, with a flint on his tongue and a spark in his eyes, he will make the neophite Habib smile beside him. For the priesthood in Syria is not, as we have said, a peeled, polished, pulpy affair. And Khalid's father has been long enough in their employ to learn somewhat of their methods. Bigotry, cruelty, and tyranny at home, priestcraft and Jesuitism abroad,— these, O Khalid, you will know better by force of contact before you end. And you will begin to pine again for your iron-loined spiritual Mother. Ay, and the scelerate Jesuit will even make capital of your mass of flowing hair. For in this country, only the native priests are privileged to be shaggy and scrubby and still be without suspicion. But we will let Shakib give us a few not uninteresting details of the matter.

"Not long after we had rejoined our people," he writes, "Khalid comes to me with a sorry tale. In truth, a fortnight after our arrival in Baalbek—our civility towards new comers seldom enjoys a longer lease—the town was alive with rumours and whim-whams about my friend. And whereso I went, I was not a little annoyed with the tehees and grunts which his name seemed to invoke. The women often came to his mother to inquire in particular why he grows his hair and shaves his mustaches; the men would speak to his father about the change in his accent and manners; the children teheed and tittered whenever he passed through the town-square; and all were of one mind that Khalid was a worthless fellow, who had brought nothing with him from the Paradise of the New World but his cough and his fleece. Such tattle and curiosity, however, no matter what degree of savage vulgarity they reach, are quite harmless. But I felt somewhat uneasy about him, when I heard the people asking each other, "Why does he not come to Church like honest folks?" And soon I discovered that my apprehensions were well grounded; for the questioning was noised at Khalid's door, and the fire crackled under the roof within. The father commands; the mother begs; the father objurgates, threatens, curses his son's faith; and the mother, prostrating herself before the Virgin, weeps, and prays, and beats her breast. Alas, and my Khalid? he goes out on the terrace to search in the Nursery for his favourite Plant. No, he does not find it; brambles are there and noxious weeds galore. The thorny, bitter reality he must now face, and, by reason of his lack of savoir-faire, be ultimately out-faced by it. For the upshot of the many quarrels he had with his father, the prayers and tears of the mother not availing, was nothing more or less than banishment. You will either go to Church like myself, or get out of this house: this the ultimatum of Abu-Khalid. And needless to say which alternative the son chose.

"I still remember how agitated he was when he came to tell me of the fatal breach. His words, which drew tears from my eyes, I remember too. 'Homeless I am again,' said he, 'but not friendless. For besides Allah, I have you.—Oh, this straitness of the chest is going to kill me. I feel that my windpipe is getting narrower every day. At least, my father is doing his mighty best to make things so hard and strait.— Yes, I would have come now to bid you farewell, were it not that I still have in this town some important business. In the which I ask your help. You know what it is. I have often spoken to you about my cousin Najma, the one star in my sky. And now, I would know what is its significance to me. No, I can not leave Baalbek, I can not do anything, until that star unfolds the night or the dawn of my destiny. And you Shakib—'

"Of course, I promised to do what I could for him. I offered him such cheer and comfort as my home could boast of, which he would not accept. He would have only my terrace roof on which to build a booth of pine boughs, and spread in it a few straw mats and cushions. But I was disappointed in my calculations; for in having him thus near me again, I had hoped to prevail upon him for his own good to temper his behaviour, to conform a little, to concede somewhat, while he is among his people. But virtually he did not put up with me. He ate outside; he spent his days I know not where; and when he did come to his booth, it was late in the night. I was informed later that one of the goatherds saw him sleeping in the ruined Temple near Ras'ul-Ain. And the muazzen who sleeps in the Mosque adjacent to the Temple of Venus gave out that one night he saw him with a woman in that very place."

A woman with Khalid, and in the Temple of Venus at night? Be not too quick, O Reader, to suspect and contemn; for the Venus-worship is not reinstated in Baalbek. No tryst this, believe us, but a scene pathetic, more sacred. Not Najma this questionable companion, but one as dear to Khalid. Ay, it is his mother come to seek him here. And she begs him, in the name of the Virgin, to return home, and try to do the will of his father. She beats her breast, weeps, prostrates herself before him, beseeches, implores, cries out, 'dakhilak (I am at your mercy), come home with me.' And Khalid, taking her up by the arm, embraces her and weeps, but says not a word. As two statues in the Temple, silent as an autumn midnight, they remain thus locked in each other's arms, sobbing, mingling their sighs and tears. The mother then, 'Come, come home with me, O my child.' And Khalid, sitting on one of the steps of the Temple, replies, 'Let him move out of the house, and I will come. I will live with you, if he will keep at the Jesuits.'

For Khalid begins to suspect that the Jesuits are the cause of his banishment from home, that his father's religious ferocity is fuelled and fanned by these good people. One day, before Khalid was banished, Shakib tells us, one of them, Father Farouche by name, comes to pay a visit of courtesy, and finds Khalid sitting cross-legged on a mat writing a letter.

The Padre is received by Khalid's mother who takes his hand, kisses it, and offers him the seat of honour on the divan. Khalid continues writing. And after he had finished, he turns round in his cross-legged posture and greets his visitor. Which greeting is surely to be followed by a conversation of the sword-and-shield kind.

"How is your health?" this from Father Farouche in miserable Arabic.

"As you see: I breathe with an effort, and can hardly speak."

"But the health of the body is nothing compared with the health of the soul."

"I know that too well, O Reverend" (Ya Muhtaram).

"And one must have recourse to the physician in both instances."

"I do not believe in physicians, O Reverend."

"Not even the physician of the soul?"

"You said it, O Reverend."

The mother of Khalid serves the coffee, and whispers to her son a word. Whereupon Khalid rises and sits on the divan near the Padre.

"But one must follow the religion of one's father," the Jesuit resumes.

"When one's father has a religion, yes; but when he curses the religion of his son for not being ferociously religious like himself—"

"But a father must counsel and guide his children."

"Let the mother do that. Hers is the purest and most disinterested spirit of the two."

"Then, why not obey your mother, and—"

Khalid suppresses his anger.

"My mother and I can get along without the interference of our neighbours."

"Yes, truly. But you will find great solace in going to Church and ceasing your doubts."

Khalid rises indignant.

"I only doubt the Pharisees, O Reverend, and their Church I would destroy to-day if I could."

"My child—"

"Here is your hat, O Reverend, and pardon me—you see, I can hardly speak, I can hardly breathe. Good day."

And he walks out of the house, leaving Father Farouche to digest his ire at his ease, and to wonder, with his three-cornered hat in hand, at the savage demeanour of the son of their pious porter. "Your son," addressing the mother as he stands under the door-lintel, "is not only an infidel, but he is also crazy. And for such wretches there is an asylum here and a Juhannam hereafter."

And the poor mother, her face suffused with tears, prostrates herself before the Virgin, praying, beating her breast, invoking with her tongue and hand and heart; while Farouche returns to his coop to hatch under his three-cornered hat, the famous Jesuit-egg of intrigue. That hat, which can outwit the monk's hood and the hundred fabled devils under it, that hat, with its many gargoyles, a visible symbol of the leaky conscience of the Jesuit, that hat, O Khalid, which you would have kicked out of your house, has eventually succeeded in ousting YOU, and will do its mighty best yet to send you to the Bosphorus. Indeed, to serve their purpose, these honest servitors of Jesus will even act as spies to the criminal Government of Abd'ul-Hamid. Read Shakib's account.

"About a fortnight after Khalid's banishment from home," he writes, "a booklet was published in Beirut, setting forth the history of Ignatius Loyola and the purports and intents of Jesuitism. On the cover it was expressly declared that the booklet is translated from the English, and the Jesuits, who are noted for their scholarly attainments, could have discovered this for themselves without the explicit declaration. But they did not deem it necessary to make such a discovery then. It seemed rather imperative to maintain the contrary and try to prove it. Now, Khalid having received a copy of this booklet from a friend in Beirut, reads it and writes back, saying that it is not a translation but a mutilation, rather, of one of Thomas Carlyle's Latter-Day Pamphlets entitled *Jesuitism*. This letter must have reached them together with Father Farouche's report on Khalid's infidelity, just about the time the booklet was circulating in Baalbek. For in the following Number of their *Weekly Journal* an article, stuffed and padded with execrations and anathema, is published against the book and its anonymous author. From this I quote the following, which is by no means the most erring and most poisonous of their shafts.

"'Such a Pamphlet,' exclaims the scholarly Jesuit Editor, 'was never written by Thomas Carlyle, as some here, from ignorance or malice, assert. For that philosopher, of all the thinkers of his day, believed in God and in the divinity of Jesus His Son, and could never descend to these foul and filthy depths. He never soiled his pen in the putrescence of falsehood and incendiarism. The author of this blasphemous and pernicious Pamphlet, therefore, in trying to father his infidelity, his sedition, and his lies, on Carlyle, is doubly guilty of a most heinous crime. And we suspect, we know, and for the welfare of the community we hope to be able soon to point out openly, who and where this vile one is. Yes, only an atheist and anarchist is capable of such villainous mendacity, such unutterable wickedness and treachery. Now, we would especially call upon our readers in Baalbek to be watchful and vigilant, for among them is one, recently come back from America, who harbours under his bushy hair the atheism and anarchy of decadent Europe, etc, etc.'

"And this is followed by secret orders from their Head Office to the Superior of their Branch in Zahleh, to go on with the work hinted in the article aforesaid. Let it not be supposed that I make this statement in jaundice or malice. For the man who was instigated to do this foul work subsequently sold the secret. And the Kaimkam, my friend, when speaking to me of the matter, referred to the article in question, and told me that Khalid was denounced to the Government by the Jesuits as an anarchist. 'And lest I be compelled,' he continued, 'to execute such orders in his case as I might receive any day, I advise you to spirit him away at once.'"

But though the Jesuits have succeeded in kicking Khalid out of his home, they did not succeed, thanks to Shakib, in sending him to the Bosphorus. Meanwhile, they sit quiet, hatching another egg.

CHAPTER VI

FLOUNCES AND RUFFLES

Now, that there is a lull in the machinations of Jesuitry, we shall turn a page or two in Shakib's account of the courting of Khalid. And apparently everything is propitious. The fates, at least, in the beginning, are not unkind. For the feud between Khalid's father and uncle shall now help to forward Khalid's love-affair. Indeed, the father of Najma, to spite his brother, opens to the banished nephew his door and blinks at the spooning which follows. And such an interminable yarn our Scribe spins out about it, that Khalid and Najma do seem the silliest lackadaisical spoonies under the sun. But what we have evolved from the narration might have for our readers some curious alien phase of interest.

Here then are a few beads from Shakib's romantic string. When Najma cooks *mojadderah* for her father, he tells us, she never fails to come to the booth of pine boughs with a platter of it. And this to Khalid was very manna. For never, while supping on this single dish, would he dream of the mensal and kitchen luxuries of the Hermitage in Bronx Park. In fact, he never envied the pork-eating Americans, the beef-eating English, or the polyphagic French. "Here is a dish of lentils fit for the gods," he would say....

When Najma goes to the spring for water, Khalid chancing to meet her, takes the jar from her shoulder, saying, "Return thou home; I will bring thee water." And straightway to the spring hies he, where the women there gathered fill his ears with tittering, questioning tattle as he is filling his jar. "I wish I were Najma," says one, as he passes by, the jar of water on his shoulder. "Would you cement his brain, if you were?" puts in another. And thus would they gibe and joke every time Khalid came to the spring with Najma's jar....

One day he comes to his uncle's house and finds his betrothed rib-boning and beading some new lingerie for her rich neighbour's daughter. He sits down and helps her in the work, writing meanwhile, between the acts, an alphabetic ideology on Art and Life. But as they are beading the vests and skirts and other articles of richly laced linen underwear, Najma holds up one of these and naïvely asks, "Am I not to have some such, *ya habibi* (O my Love)?" And Khalid, affecting like bucolic innocence, replies, "What do we need them for, my heart?" With which counter-question Najma is silenced, convinced.

Finally, to show to what degree of ecstasy they had soared without searing their wings or losing a single feather thereof, the following deserves mention. In the dusk one day, Khalid visits Najma and finds her oiling and lighting the lamp. As she beholds him under the door-lintel, the lamp falls from her hands, the kerosene blazes on the floor, and the straw mat takes fire. They do not heed this—they do not see it—they are on the wings of an ecstatic embrace. And the father, chancing to arrive in the nick of time, with a curse and a cuff, saves them and his house from the conflagration.

Aside from these curious and not insignificant instances, these radiations of a giddy hidden flame of heart-fire, this melting gum of spooning on the bark of the tree of love, we turn to a scene in the Temple of Venus which unfolds our future plans—our hopes and dreams. But we feel that the Reader is beginning to hanker for a few pieces of description of Najma's charms. Gentle Reader, this Work is neither a Novel, nor a Passport. And we are exceeding sorry we can not tell you anything about the colour and size of Najma's eyes; the shape and curves of her brows and lips; the tints and shades in her cheeks; and the exact length of her figure and hair. Shakib leaves us in the dark about these essentials, and we must needs likewise leave you. Our Scribe thinks he has said everything when he speaks of her as a huri. But this paradisal title among our Arabic writers and verse-makers is become worse than the Sultan's Medjidi decorations. It is bestowed alike on every drab and trollop as on the very few who really deserve it. Let us rank it, therefore, with the Medjidi decorations and pass on.

But Khalid, who has seen enough of the fair, would not be attracted to Najma, enchanted by her, if she were not endowed with such of the celestial treasures as rank above the visible lines of beauty. Our Scribe speaks of the "purity and naïvete of her soul as purest sources of felicity and inspiration." Indeed, if she were not constant in love, she would not have spurned the many opportunities in the absence of Khalid; and had she not a fine discerning sense of real worth, she would not have surrendered herself to her poor ostracised cousin; and if she were not intuitively, preternaturally wise, she would not marry an enemy of the Jesuits, a bearer withal of infiltrated lungs and a shrunken windpipe. "There is a great advantage in having a sickly husband," she once said to Shakib, "it lessons a woman in the heavenly virtues of our Virgin Mother, in patient endurance and pity, in charity, magnanimity, and pure love." What, with these sublimities of character, need we know of her visible charms, or lack of them? She might deserve the title Shakib bestows upon her; she might be a real huri, for all we know? In that event, the outward charms correspond, and Khalid is a lucky dog—if some one can keep the Jesuits away.

This, then, is our picture of Najma, to whom he is now relating, in the Temple of Venus, of the dangers he had passed and the felicities of the beduin life he has in view. It is evening. The moon struggles through the poplars to light the Temple for them, and the ambrosial breeze caresses their cheeks.

"No," says Khalid; "we can not live here, O my Heart, after we are formally married. The curse in my breast I must not let you share, and only when I am rid of it am I actually your husband. By the life of this blessed night, by the light of these stars, I am inalterably resolved on this, and I shall abide by my resolution. We must leave Baalbek as soon as the religious formalities are done. And I wish your father would have them performed under his roof. That is as good as going to Church to be the central figures of the mummery of priests. But be this as You will. Whether in Church or at home, whether by your father or by gibbering Levites the ceremony is performed, we must hie us to the desert after it is done. I shall hire the camels and prepare the necessary set-out for the wayfare a day or two ahead. No, I must not be a burden to you, my Heart. I must be able to work for you as for myself. And Allah alone, through the ministration of his great Handmaid Nature, can cure me and enable me to share with you the joys of life. No, not before I am cured, can I give you my whole self, can I call myself your husband. Into the desert, therefore, to some oasis in its very heart, we shall ride, and there crouch our camels and establish ourselves as husbandmen. I shall even build you a little home like your own. And you will be to me an aura of health, which I shall breathe with the desert air, and the evening breeze. Yes, our love shall dwell in a palace of health, not in a hovel of disease. Meanwhile, we shall buy with what money I have a little patch of ground which we shall cultivate together. And we shall own cattle and drink camel milk. And we shall doze in the afternoon in the cool shade of the palms, and in the evening, wrapt in our cloaks, we'll sleep on the sands under the living stars. Yes, and Najma shall be the harbinger of dawn to Khalid.—Out on that little farm in the oasis of our desert, far from the world and the sanctified abominations of the world, we shall live near to Allah a life of purest joy, of true happiness. We shall never worry about the hopes of to-morrow and the gone blessings of yesterday. We shall not, while labouring, dream of rest, nor shall we give a thought to our tasks while drinking of the cup of repose: each hour shall be to us an epitome of eternity. The trials and troubles of each day shall go with the setting sun, never to rise with him again. But I am unkind to speak of this. For your glances banish care, and we shall ever be together. Ay, my Heart, and when I take up the lute in the evening, you'll sing *mulayiah* to me, and the stars above us shall dance, and the desert breeze shall house us in its whispers of love...."

And thus interminably, while Najma, understanding little of all this, sits beside him on a fallen column in the Temple and punctuates his words with assenting exclamations, with long eighs of joy and wonder. "But we are not going to live in the desert all the time, are we?" she asks.

"No, my Heart. When I am cured of my illness we shall return to Baalbek, if you like."

"Eigh, good. Now, I want to say—no. I shame to speak about such matters."

"Speak, *ya Gazalty* (O my Doe or Dawn or both); your words are like the scented breeze, like the ethereal moon rays, which enter into this Temple without permission. Speak, and light up this ruined Temple of thine."

"How sweet are Your words, but really I can not understand them. They are like the sweetmeats my father brought with him once from Damascus. One eats and exclaims, 'How delicious!' But one never knows how they are made, and what they are made of. I wish I could speak like you, *ya habibi*. I would not shame to say then what I want."

"Say what you wish. My heart is open, and your words are silvery moonbeams."

"Do not blame me then. I am so simple, you know, so foolish. And I would like to know if you are going to Church on our wedding day in the clothes you have on now."

"Not if you object to them, my Heart."

"Eigh, good! And must I come in my ordinary Sunday dress? It is so plain; it has not a single ruffle to it."

111

"And what are ruffles for?"

"I never saw a bride in a plain gown; they all have ruffles and flounces to them. And when I look at your lovely hair—O let people say what they like! A gown without ruffles is ugly.—So, you will buy me a sky-blue silk dress, *ya habibi* and a pink one, too, with plenty of ruffles on them? Will you not?"

"Yes, my Heart, you shall have what you desire. But in the desert you can not wear these dresses. The Arabs will laugh at you. For the women there wear only plain muslin dipped in indigo."

"Then, I will have but one dress of sky-blue silk for the wedding."

"Certainly, my Heart. And the ruffles shall be as many and as long as you desire them."

And while the many-ruffled sky-blue dress is being made, Khalid, inspired by Najma's remarks on his hair, rhapsodises on flounces and ruffles. Of this striking piece of fantasy, in which are scintillations of the great Truth, we note the following:

"What can you do without your flounces? How can you live without your ruffles? Ay, how can you, without them, think, speak, or work? How can you eat, drink, walk, sleep, pray, worship, moralise, sentimentalise, or love, without them? Are you not ruffled and flounced when you first see the light, ruffled and flounced when you last see the darkness? The cradle and the tomb, are they not the first and last ruffles of Man? And between them what a panoramic display of flounces! What clean and attractive visible Edges of unclean invisible common Skirts! Look at your huge elaborate monuments, your fancy sepulchers, what are they but the ruffles of your triumphs and defeats? The marble flounces, these, of your cemeteries, your Pantheons and Westminster Abbeys. And what are your belfries and spires and chimes, your altars and reredoses and such like, but the sanctified flounces of your churches. No, these are not wholly adventitious sanctities; not empty, superfluous growths. They are incorporated into Life by Time, and they grow in importance as our Æsthetics become more inutile, as our Religions begin to exude gum and pitch for commerce, instead of bearing fruits of Faith and Love and Magnanimity.

"The first church was the forest; the first dome, the welkin; the first altar, the sun. But that was, when man went forth in native buff, brother to the lion, not the ox, without ruffles and without faith. His spirit, in the course of time, was born; it grew and developed zenithward and nadirward, as the cycles rolled on. And in spiritual pride, and pride of power and wealth as well, it took to ruffling and flouncing to such an extent that at certain epochs it disappeared, dwindled into nothingness, and only the appendages remained. These were significant appendages, to be sure; not altogether adscititious. Ruffles these, indeed, endowed, as it were, with life, and growing on the dead Spirit, as the grass on the grave.

"And is it not noteworthy that our life terrene at certain epochs seems to be made up wholly of these? That as the great Pine falls, the noxious weeds, the brambles and thorny bushes around it, grow quicker, lustier, luxuriating on the vital stores in the earth that were its own––is not this striking and perplexing, my rational friends? Surely, Man is neither the featherless biped of the Greek Philosopher, nor the tool-using animal of the Sage of Chelsea. For animals, too, have their tools, and man, in his visible flounces, has feathers enough to make even a peacock gape. Both my Philosophers have hit wide of the mark this time. And Man, to my way of thinking, is a flounce-wearing Spirit. Indeed, flounces alone, the invisible ones in particular, distinguish us from the beasts. For like ourselves they have their fashions in clothes; their peculiar speech; their own hidden means of intellection, and, to some extent, of imagination: but flounces they have not, they know not. These are luxuries, which Man alone enjoys.

"Ah, Man,—thou son and slave of Allah, according to my Oriental Prophets of Heaven; thou exalted, apotheosised ape, according to my Occidental Prophets of Science;—how much thou canst suffer, how much thou canst endure, under what pressure and in what Juhannam depths thou canst live; but thy flounces thou canst not dispense with for a day, nor for a single one-twelfth part of a day. Even in thy suffering and pain, the agonised spirit is wrapped, bandaged, swathed in ruffles. It is assuaged with the flounces of thy lady's caresses, and the scalloped intonations of her soft and soothing voice. It is humbugged into health by the malodorous flounces of the apothecary and the medicinal ruffles of the doctor.

"Ay, we live in a phantasmagoric, cycloramic economy of flounces and ruffles. The human Spirit shirks nudity as it shirks pain. Even your modern preacher of the Simple Life is at best suggesting the moderate use of ruffles.... Indeed, we can suffer anything, everything, but the naked and ugly reality. Alas, have I not listened for years to what I mistook to be the strong, pure voice of the naked Truth? And have I not discovered, to my astonishment, that the supposed scientific Nudity is but an indurated thick Crust under which the Lie lies hidden. Why strip Man of his fancy appendages, his adventitious sanctities, if you are going to give him instead only a few yards of shoddy? No, I tell you; this can not be done. Your brambles and thorn hedges will continue to grow and luxuriate, will even shut from your view the Temple in the Grove, until the great Pine rises again to stunt, and ultimately extirpate, them.

"Behold, meanwhile, how the world parades in ruffles before us. What a bewildering phantasmagoria this: a very Dress Ball of the human race. See them pass: the Pope of Christendom, in his three hats and heavy trailing gowns, blessing the air of heaven; the priest, in his alb and chasuble, dispensing of the blessings of the Pope; the judge, in his wig and bombazine, endeavouring to reconcile divine justice with the law's mundane majesty; the college doctor, in cap and gown, anointing the young princes of knowledge; the buffoon, in his cap and bells, dancing to the god of laughter; mylady of the pink-tea circle, in her huffing, puffing gasoline-car, fleeing the monster of ennui; the bride and bridegroom at the altar or before the mayor putting on their already heavy-ruffled garments the sacred ruffle of law or religion; the babe brought to church by his mother and kindred to have the priest-tailor sew on his new garment the ruffle of baptism; the soldier in his gaudy uniform; the king in his ermine with a crown and sceptre appended; the Nabob of Ind in his gorgeous and multi-colored robes; and the Papuan with horns in his nostrils and rings in his ears: see them all pass.

"And wilt thou still add to the bewildering variety of the pageant? Or wilt have another of the higher things of the mind? Lo, the artist this, wearing his ruffles of hair over his shoulders; and here, too, is the man of the sombrero and red flannel, which are the latest flounces of a certain set of New World poets. Directly behind them is Dame Religion with her heavy ruffled robes, her beribboned and belaced bodices, her ornaments and sacred gewgaws. And billah, she has stuffings and paddings, too. And false teeth and foul breath! Never mind. Pass on, and let her pass. But tarry thou a moment here. Behold this pyrotechnic display, these buntings and flags; hear thou this music and these shouts and cheers; on yonder stump is an orator dispensing to his fellow citizens spread-eagle rhetoric as empty as yonder drum: these are the elaborate and attractive ruffles of politics. And among the crowd are genial and honest citizens who have their own way of ruffling your temper with their coarse flounces of linsey-woolsey freedom. Wilt thou have more?"

Decidedly not, we reply. For how can we even keep company with Khalid, who has become such a maniac on flounces? And was this fantastic, phantasmagoric rhapsody all inspired by Najma's simple remark on his hair? Fruitful is thy word, O woman!

But being so far away now from the Hermitage in the Bronx, what has the "cherry in the cocktail" and "the olive in the oyster patty" to do with all this? Howbeit, the following deserves a place as the tail-flounce of his Fantasy.

"Your superman and superwoman," says he, with philosophic calm, "may go Adam-and-Eve like if they choose. But can they, even in that chaste and splendid nudity, dispense with ruffles and flounces? Pray, tell me, did not our first parents spoon and sentimentalise in the Paradise, before the Serpent appeared? And would they not often whisper unto each other, 'Ah, Adam, ah, Eve!' sighing likewise for sweeter things? And what about those fatal Apples, those two sour fruits of their Love?—I tell thee every new-born babe is the magnificent flesh-flounce of a shivering, trembling, nudity. And I Khalid, what am I but the visible ruffle of an invisible skirt? Verily, I am; and thou, too, my Brother. Yea, and this aquaterrestrial globe and these sidereal heavens are the divine flounces of the Vesture of Allah."

CHAPTER VII

THE HOWDAJ OF FALSEHOOD

"Humanity is so feeble in mind," says Renan, "that the purest thing has need of the co-operation of some impure agent." And this, we think, is the gist of Khalid's rhapsody on flounces and ruffles. But how is he to reconcile the fact with the truth in his case? For a single sanctified ruffle—a line of type in the canon law—is likely to upset all his plans. Yes, a priest in alb and chasuble not only can dispense with the blessings of his Pope, but—and here is the rub—he can also withhold such blessings from Khalid. And now, do what he may, say what he might, he must either revise his creed, or behave, at least, like a Christian.

Everything is ready, you say? The sky-blue, many-ruffled wedding gown; the set-out for the wayfare; the camel and donkeys; the little stock of books; the coffee utensils; the lentils and sweet oil;—all ready? Very well; but you can not set forth to-morrow, nor three weeks from to-morrow. Indeed, before the priest can give you his blessings—and what at this juncture can you do without them?—the dispensations of the ban must be performed. In other words, your case must now be laid before the community. Every Sunday, for three such to come, the intended marriage of Khalid to Najma will be published in the Church, and whoso hath any objection to make can come forth and make it. Moreover, there is that little knot of consanguinity to be considered. And your priest is good enough to come and explain this to you. Understand him well. "An alm of a few gold pieces," says he, "will remove the obstacle; the unlawfulness of your marriage resulting from consanguinity will cease on payment of five hundred piasters."

All of which startles Khalid, stupefies him. He had not, heretofore, thought of such a matter. Indeed, he was totally ignorant of these forms, these prohibitions and exemptions of the Church. And the father of Najma, though assenting, remarks nevertheless that the alms demanded are much. "Why," exclaims Khalid, "I can build a house for five hundred piasters."

The priest sits down cross-legged on the divan, lights the cigarette which Najma had offered with the coffee, and tries to explain.

"And where have you this, O Reverend, about consanguinity, prohibition, and alms!" Khalid asks.

"Why, my child, in the Canons of our Church, Catholic and Apostolic. Every one knows that a marriage between cousins can not be effected, without the sanction of the Bishop."

"But can we not obtain this sanction without paying for it?"

"You are not paying for it, my child; you are only contributing some alms to the Church."

"You come to us, therefore, as a beggar, not as a spiritual father and guide."

"That is not good speaking. You misunderstand my purpose."

"And pray, tell me, what is the purpose of prohibiting a marriage between cousins; what chief good is there in such a ban?"

"Much good for the community."

"But I have nothing to do with the community. I'm going to live with my wife in the desert."

"The good of your souls is chiefly concerned."

"Ah, the good of our souls!"

"And there are other reasons which can not be freely spoken of here."

"You mean the restriction and prohibition of sexual knowledge between relatives. That is very well. But let us return to what concerns us properly: the good of my soul, and the spiritual well-being of the community,—what becomes of these, when I pay the prescribed alms and obtain the sanction of the Bishop?"

"No harm then can come to them—they'll be secure."

"Secure, you say? Are they not hazarded, sold by your Church for five hundred piasters? If my marriage to my cousin be wrong, unlawful, your Bishop in sanctioning same is guilty of perpetuating this wrong, this unlawfulness, is he not?"

"But what the Church binds only the Church can loosen."

"And what is the use of binding, O Reverend Father, when a little sum of money can loosen anything you bind? It seems to me that these prohibitions of the Church are only made for the purpose of collecting alms. In other words, you bind for the sake of loosening, when a good bait is on the hook, do you not? Pardon, O my Reverend Father, pardon. I can not, to save my soul and yours, reconcile these contradictions. For if Mother Church be certain that my marriage to my cousin is contrary to the Law of God, is destructive of my spiritual well-being, then let her by all means prohibit it. Let her restrain me, compel me to obey. Ay, and the police ought to interfere in case of disobedience. In her behalf, in my behalf, in the behalf of my cousin's soul and mine, the police ought to do the will of God, if the Church knows what it is, and is certain and honest about it. Compel me to stop, I conjure you, if you know I am going in the way of damnation. O my Father, what sort of a mother is she who would sell two of her children to the devil for a few hundred piasters? No, billah! no. What is unlawful by virtue of the Divine Law the wealth of all the Trust-Kings of America can not make lawful. And what is so by virtue of your Canon Law concerns not me. You may angle, you and your Church, as long as you please in the murky, muddy waters of Bind-and-Loosen, I have nothing to do with you."...

But the priests, O Khalid, have yet a little to do with you. Such arguments about the Divine Law and the Canon Law, about alms and spiritual beggars, might cut the Gordian knot with your uncle, but—and whether it be good or bad English, we say it—they cut no ice with the Church. Yes, Mother Church, under whose wings you and your cousin were born and bred, and under whose wings you and your cousin would be married, can not take off for the sweet sake of your black eyes the ruffles and flounces of twenty centuries. Think well on it, you who have so extravagantly and not unwisely delivered yourself on flounces and ruffles. But to think, when in love, were, indeed, disastrous. O Love, Love, what Camels of wisdom thou canst force to pass through the needle's eye! What miracles divine are thine! Khalid himself says that to be truly, deeply, piously in love, one must needs hate himself. How true, how inexorably true! For would he be always inviting trouble and courting affliction, would he be always bucking against the dead wall of a Democracy or a Church, if he did not sincerely hate himself—if he were not religiously, fanatically in love—in love with Najma, if not with Truth?

Now, on the following Sunday, instead of publishing the intended marriage of Khalid and Najma, the parish priest places a ban upon it. And in this, ye people of Baalbek, is food enough for tattle, and cause enough for persecution. Potent are the ruffles of the Church! But why, we can almost hear the anxious Reader asking, if the camels are ready, why the deuce don't they get on and get them gone? But did we not say once that Khalid is slow, even slower than the law itself? Nevertheless, if this were a Novel, an elopement would be in order, but we must repeat, it is not. We are faithful transcribers of the truth as we find it set down in Shakib's *Histoire Intime*.

True, Khalid did ask Najma to throw with him the handful of dust, to steal out of Baalbek and get married on the way, say in Damascus. But poor Najma goes over to his mother instead, and mingling their tears and prayers, they beseech the Virgin to enlighten the soul and mind of Khalid. "Yes, we must be married here, before we go to the desert," says she, "for think, O my mother, how far away we shall be from the world and the Church if anything happens to us."

And they would have succeeded, the mother and cousin of Khalid, in persuading the parish priest to accept from them the prescribed alms and perform the wedding ceremony, had not the Jesuits, in the interest of the Faith and the Church, been dogging Khalid still. For if they have failed in sending him to the Bosphorus, they will succeed in sending him elsewhither. And observe how this is done.

After communicating with the Papal Legate in Mt. Lebanon about that fatal Latter Day Pamphlet of Thomas Carlyle, the Adjutant-General, or Adjutant-Bird, stalks up there one night in person and lays before the Rt. Rev. Mgr. his devil's brief in Khalid's case. It has already been explained that this Pamphlet was fathered on Khalid by the Jesuits. For if they can not punish the Voice which is still pursuing them—and in their heart of hearts they must have recognised its thunder, even in a Translation—they will make the man smart for it who first mentioned Carlyle in this connection.

"And besides this pernicious booklet," says the Adjutant-Bird, "the young man's heretical opinions are notorious. He was banished from home on that account. And now, after corrupting and deluding his cousin, he is going to marry her despite the ban of the Church. Something, Monseigneur, ought to be done, and quickly, to protect the community against the poison of this wretch." And Monseigneur, nodding his accord, orders his Secretary to write a note to the Patriarch, enclosing the aforesaid devil's brief, and showing the propriety, nay, the necessity of excommunicating Khalid the Baalbekian. The Adjutant-Bird, with the Legate's letter in his pocket, skips over to the Patriarch on the other hill-top below, and after a brief interview—our dear good Ancient of the Maronites must willy-nilly obey Rome—the fate of Khalid the Baalbekian is sealed.

Indeed, the upshot of these Jesuitic machinations is this: on the very day when Khalid's mother and cousin are pleading before the parish priest for justice, for mercy,—offering the prescribed alms, beseeching that the ban be revoked, the marriage solemnised,—a messenger from the Bishop of the Diocese enters, kisses his Reverence's hand, and delivers an imposing envelope. The priest unseals it, unfolds the heavy foolscap sheet therein, reads it with a knitting of the brow, a shaking of the beard, and, clapping one hand upon the other, tells the poor pleaders to go home.

"It is all finished. There is no more hope for you and your cousin." And he shows the Patriarchal Bull, and explains.

Whereupon, Najma and Khalid's mother go out weeping, wailing, beating their breasts and cheeks, calling upon Allah to witness their sorrow and the outrageous tyranny of the priests.

"What has my son done to be excommunicated? Hear it, ye people, hear it. And be just to me and my son. What has he done to deserve the anathema of the Church? What has he done?" And thus frantic, mad, she runs through the main street of the town, making wild gestures and clamours,—publishing, as it were, the Patriarchal Bull, before it was read by the priest on the following day, and tacked on the door of the Church.

Of this Bull, tricked with the stock phrases of the Church of the Middle Ages, such as "anathema be he," or "banned be he," who speaks with, deals with, and so forth, we have a copy before us. But our readers will not pardon us, we fear, if further space and consideration be here given to its contents. Suffice it to say, however, that Khalid comes to church on that fatal day, takes the foolscap sheet down from the door, and, going with it to the town-square, burns it there before the multitudes.

And it came to pass, when the Bull is burned in the town-square of Baalbek, in the last year of the reign of Abd'ul-Hamid, some among the multitudes shout loud shouts of joy, and some cast stones.

Then, foul, vehement speaking falleth between the friends and the enemies of him who wrought evil in the sight of the Lord;

And every one thereupon brandisheth a stick or taketh up a stone and the battle ensueth.

Now, the mighty troops of the Sultan of the Ottomans come forth like the Yaman wind and stand in the town-square like rocks;

And the battle rageth still, and the troops who are come forth to part the fighting multitudes, having gorged themselves at the last meal, can not as much as speak their part:

And it came to pass, when the clubs and spades are veiled and the battle subsideth of itself, the good people return to their respective callings and trades;

But the perverse recalcitrants which remain—and Khalid the Baal-bekian is among them—are taken by the aforesaid overfed troops to the City Hall and thence to the *velayet* prison in Damascus.

And here endeth our stichometrics of the Battle of the Bull.

Now, Shakib may wear out his shoes this time, his tongue, too, and his purse, but to no purpose. Behold, your friend the *kaimkam* is gloomy and impassive as a camel; what can you do? Whisper in his ear? The Padres have done that before you. Slip a purse into his pocket? They have done that, too, and overdone it long since. Yes, the City Hall of every city in the Empire is an epitome of Yildiz Kiosk. And your *kaimkams*, and *valis*, and *viziers*, have all been taught in the same Text-Book, at the same Political School, and by the same Professor. Let Khalid rest, therefore and ponder these matters in silence. For in the City Hall and during the month he passes in the prison of Damascus, we are told, he does not utter a word. His partisans in prison ask to be taught his creed, and among these are some Mohammadans: "We'll burn the priests and their church yet and follow you. By our Prophet Mohammad we will ..." Khalid makes no reply. Even Shakib, when he comes to visit him, finds him dumb as a stone, slain by adversity and disease. Nothing can be done now. The giant excommunicated, incommunicative soul, struggling in a prison of sore flesh, we must leave, alas, with his friends and partisans to pass his thirty days and nights in the second prison of stone.

Now, let us return to the Jesuits, who, having worsted Khalid, or the Devil in Khalid, as they charitably put it, will also endeavour to do somewhat in the interest of his intended bride. For the Padres, in addition to their many crafts and trades, are matrimonial brokers of honourable repute. And in their meddling and making, their baiting and mating, they are as serviceable as the Column Personal of an American newspaper. Whoso is matrimonially disposed shall whisper his mind at the Confessional or drop his advertisement in the pocket of the visiting Columns of their Bride-Dealer, and he shall prosper. She as well as he shall prosper.

Now, Father Farouche is commissioned to come all the way from Zahleh to visit the brother of Abu-Khalid their porter, and bespeak him in the interest of his daughter. All their faculties of persuasion shall be exerted in behalf of Najma. She must be saved at any cost. Hence they volunteer their services. And while Khalid is lingering in prison at Damascus, they avail themselves of the opportunity to further the suit of their pickle-herring candidate for Najma's love.

The Reverend Farouche, therefore, holds a secret conference with her father.

"No," says he, "God would never have forgiven you for giving your daughter to one utterly destitute of morality, religion, money, and health. But praise Allah! the Church has come to her rescue. She shall be saved, wrested from the hands of Iblis. Yes, Holy Church, through us, will guide her to find a god-fearing life-companion; one worthy of her charms, her virtues, her fine qualities of heart and mind. The young man we recommend is rich, respected in the community; is an official of the Government with a third-class Medjidi decoration and the title of Bey; and is free from all diseases. Moreover, he is a good Catholic. Consider these advantages. A relation this, which no father would reject, if he loves his daughter and is solicitous of her future well-being. Speak to her, therefore, and let us know soon your mind."

And our Scribe, in relating of this, loses his temper.—"An Official of the Government, a Bey with a third-class Medjidi decoration from the Sultan! As if Officialdom could not boast of a single scoundrel—as if any rogue in the Empire, with a few gold coins in his purse, were not eligible to the Hamidian decorations! And a third-class decoration! Why, I have it on good authority that these Medjidi Orders were given to a certain Patriarch in a bushel to distribute among his minions...."

But to our subject. Abu-Najma does not look upon it in this light. A decorated and titled son-in-law were a great honour devoutly to be wished. And some days after the first conference, the Padre Farouche comes again, bringing along his Excellency the third-class Medjidi Bey; but Najma, as they enter and salaam, goes out on the terrace roof to weep. The third time the third-class Medjidi Dodo comes alone. And Najma, as soon as she catches a glimpse of him, takes up her earthen jar and hies her to the spring.

"O the hinny! I'll rope noose her (hang her) to-night," murmurs the father. But here is his Excellency with his Sultan's green button in his lapel. Abu-Najma bows low, rubs his hands well, offers a large cushion, brings a *masnad* (leaning pillow), and blubbers out many unnecessary apologies.

"This honour is great, your Excellency—overlook our shortcomings—our *beit* (one room house) can not contain our shame—it is not becoming your Excellency's high rank—overlook—you have condescended to honour us, condescend too to be indulgent.—My daughter? yes, presently. She is gone to church, to mass, but she'll return soon."

But Najma is long gone; returns not; and the third-class Dodo will call again to-morrow. Now, Abu-Najma brings out his rope, soaps it well, nooses and suspends it from the rafter in the ceiling. And when his daughter returns from the spring, he takes her by the arm, shows her the rope, and tells her laconically to choose between his Excellency and this. Poor Najma has not the courage to die, and so soon. Her cousin Khalid is in prison, is excommunicated—what can she do? Run away? The Church will follow her—punish her. There's something satanic in Khalid—the Church said so—the Church knows. Najma rolls these things in her mind, looks at her father beseechingly. Her father points to the noose. Najma falls to weeping. The noose serves well its purpose.

For hereafter, when the Dodo comes decorated, SHE has to offer him the cushion, bring him the *masnad*, make for him the coffee. And eventually, as the visits accumulate, she goes with him to the dress-maker in Beirut. The bridal gown shall be of the conventional silk this time; for his Excellency is travelled, and knows and reverences the fashion. But why prolong these painful details?

"Allah, in the mysterious working of his Providence," says Shakib, "preordained it thus: Khalid, having served his turn in prison, Najma begins her own; for a few days after he was set free, she was placed in bonds forged for her by the Jesuits. Now, when Khalid returned from Damascus, he came straightway to me and asked that we go to see Najma and try to prevail upon her, to persuade her to go with him, to run away. They would leave on the night-train to Hama this time, and thence set forth towards Palmyra. I myself did not know what had happened, and so I approved of his plan. But alas! as we were coming down the main Street to Najma's house, we heard the sound of tomtoms in the distance and the shrill ulluluing of women. We continued apace until we reached the by-way through which we had to pass, and lo, we find it choked by the *zeffah* (wedding procession) of none but she and the third-class Medjidi...."

But we'll no more of this! Too tragic, too much like fiction it sounds, that here abruptly we must end this Chapter.

CHAPTER VIII

THE KAABA OF SOLITUDE

Disappointed, distraught, diseased,—worsted by the Jesuits, ex-communicated, crossed in love,—but with an eternal glint of sunshine in his breast to open and light up new paths before him, Khalid, after the fatal episode, makes away from Baalbek. He suddenly disappears. But where he lays his staff, where he spends his months of solitude, neither Shakib nor our old friend the sandomancer can say. Some-whither he still is, indeed; for though he fell in a swoon as he saw Najma on her caparisoned palfrey and the decorated Excellency coming up along side of her, he was revived soon after and persuaded to return home. But on the following morning, our Scribe tells us, coming up to the booth, he finds neither Khalid there, nor any of his few worldly belongings. We, however, have formed a theory of our own, based on certain of his writings in the K. L. MS., about his mysterious levitation; and we believe he is now somewhither whittling arrows for a coming combat. In the Lebanon mountains perhaps. But we must not dog him like the Jesuits. Rather let us reverence the privacy of man, the sacredness of his religious retreat. For no matter where he is in the flesh, we are metaphysically certain of his existence. And instead of filling up this Chapter with the bitter bickerings of life and the wick-edness and machination of those in power, let us consecrate it to the divine peace and beauty of Nature. Of a number of Chapters in the Book of Khalid on this subject, we choose the one entitled, My Native Terraces, or Spring in Syria, symbolising the natural succession to Khalid's Winter of destiny. In it are signal manifestations of the tri-umph of the soul over the diseases and adversities and sorrows of mortal life. Indeed, here is an example of faith and power and love which we reckon sublime.

Ameen Fares Rihani

"The inhabitants of my terraces and terrace walls," we translate, "dressed in their Sunday best, are in the doorways lounging or peeping idly through their windows. And why not? It is Spring, and to these delicate, sweet little creatures, Spring is the one Sunday of the year. Have they not hugged the damp, dark earth long enough? Hidden from the wrath of Winter, have they not squatted patiently round the primitive, smokeless fire of the mystic depths? And now, the rain having partly extinguished the inner, hidden flame, they come out to bask in the sun, and drink deeply of the ambrosial air. They come, almost slain with thirst, to the Mother Fountain. They come out to worship at the shrine of the sweet-souled, God-absorbed Rabia of Attar. In their bright, glowing faces what a delectable message from the under world of romance and enchantment! Their lips are red with the kisses of love, in whose alembics, intangible, unseen, the dark and damp of the earth are translated into warmth and colour and shade. Ay, these dear little children, unfolding their soft green scrolls and reading aloud such odes on Modesty and Beauty, are as inspiring as the star-crowned night. And every chink in my terrace walls seems to breathe a message of sweetness and light and love.

"Know you not the anecdote about the enchanting Goddess Rabia, as related by Attar in his *Biographies of Sufi Mystics and Saints*? Here it is. Rabia was asked if she hated the devil, and she replied, 'No.' Asked again why, she said, 'Being absorbed in love, I have no time to hate.' Now, all the inhabitants of my terraces and fields seem to echo this sublime sentiment of their Goddess. The air and sunshine, nay, the very rocks are imbued with it. See, how the fissures in the boulders yonder seem to sympathise with the gaps in the terrace walls: the cyclamen leaves in the one are salaaming the cyclamen flowers in the other. O, these terraces would have delighted the heart of the American naturalist Thoreau. He could not have desired stone walls with more gaps in them. But mind you, these are not dark, ugly, hollow, hopeless chinks. Behind every one of them lurks a mystery. Far back in the niches I can see the busts of the poets who wrote the poems which these beautiful wild flowers are reading to me. Yes, the authors are dead, and what I behold now are the flowers of their amours. These are the offspring of their embraces, the crystallised dew of their love. Yes, this one single, simple act of love brings forth an infinite variety of flowers to celebrate the death of the finite outward shape and the eternal essence of life perennial. In complete surrender lies the divineness of things eternal. This is the key-note of the Oriental mystic poets. And I incline to the belief that they of all bards have sung best the song of love. In rambling through the fields with these beautiful children of the terraces, I know not what draws me to Al-Fared, the one erotic-mystic poet of Arabia, whose interminable rhymes have a perennial charm. Perhaps such lines as these,—

> 'All that is fair is fairer when she rises,
> All that is sweet is sweeter when she is here;
> And every form of beauty she surprises
> With one brief word she whispers in its ear:

> 'Thy wondrous charms, O let them not deceive thee;
> They are but borrowed from her for a while;
> Thine outward guise and loveliness would grieve thee,
> If in thine inmost soul she did not smile.

> 'All colours, forms, into each other merging,
> Are woven on her Loom of Unity;
> For she alone is One in All diverging,
> And she alone is absolute and free.'

"Now, I will bring you to a scene most curiously suggestive. Behold that little knot of daisies pressing around the alone anemone beneath the spreading leaves of the colocasia. Here is a rout at the Countess Casiacole's, and these are the débutantes crowding around the Celebrity of the day. But would they do so if they were sensible of their own worth, if they knew that their idol, flaunting the crimson crown of popularity, had no more, and perhaps less, of the pure essence of life than any of them? But let Celebrity stand there and enjoy her hour; to-morrow the Ploughman will come.

"The sage, with its spikes of greyish blue flowers, its fibrous, velvety leaves, its strong, pungent perfume, which is not squandered or repressed, is the stoic of my native terraces. It responds generously to the personal touch, and serves the Lebanonese, rich and poor alike, with a little luxury. Ay, who of us, wandering on foreign strands, does not remember the warm foot-bath, perfumed with sage leaves, his mother used to give him before going to bed? Our dear mothers!"— And here, Khalid goes in raptures and tears about his sorry experience in Baalbek and the anguish and sorrow of his poor mother. "But while I stand," he continues, "let me be like the sage, a live-oak among shrubs, indifferent as the oak or pine to the winds and storms. And as the sun is setting, find you no solace in the thought, O Khalid, that some angel herb-gatherer will preserve the perfume in your leaves, to refresh therewith in other worlds your dear poor mother?

"My native terraces are rich with faith and love, luxuriant with the life divine and the wondrous symbols thereof. And the grass here is not cut and trimmed as in the artificial gardens and the cold dull lawns of city folk, whose love for Nature is either an experiment, a sport, a business, or a fad. 'A dilettantism in Nature is barren and unworthy,' says Emerson. But of all the lovers of Nature, the children are the least dilettanteish. And every day here I see a proof of this. Behold them wading to their knees in that lusty grass, hunting the classic lotus with which to deck their olive branches for the high mass and ceremony of Palm Sunday. But alas, my lusty grass and my beautiful wild flowers do not enjoy the morning of Spring. Here, the ploughman comes, carrying his long plough and goad on his shoulder, and with him his wife lugging the yoke and his boy leading the oxen. Alas, the sun shall not set on these bright, glowing, green terraces, whose walls are very ramparts of flowers. There, the boy with his scythe is paving the way for his father's plough; the grass is mowed and given to the oxen as a bribe to do the ugly business. And all for the sake of the ugly mulberries, which are cultivated for the ugly silk-worms. Come, let us to the heath, where the hiss of the scythe and the 'ho-back' and 'oho' of the ploughman are not heard.

"But let us swing from the road. Come, the hedges of Nature are not as impassable as the hedges of man. Through these scrub oaks and wild pears, between this tangle of thickets, over the clematis and blackberry bush,—and here we are under the pines, the lofty and majestic pines. How different are these natural hedges, growing in wild disorder, from the ugly cactus fences with which my neighbours choose to shut in their homes, and even their souls. But my business now is not with them. There are my friends the children again gathering the pine-needles of last summer for lighting the fire of the silkworm nursery. And down that narrow foot-path, meandering around the boulders and disappearing among the thickets, see what big loads of brushwood are moving towards us. Beneath them my swarthy and hardy peasants are plodding up the hill asweat and athirst. When I first descended to the wadi, one such load of brushwood emerging suddenly from behind a cliff surprised and frightened me. But soon I was reminded of the moving forest in Macbeth. The man bowed beneath the load was hidden from view, and the boy directly behind was sweating under a load as big as that of his father. '*Awafy!*' (Allah give you strength), I said, greeting them. 'And increase of health to you,' they replied. I then asked the boy how far down do they have to go for their brushwood, and laying down his load on a stone to rest, he points below, saying, 'Here, near the river.' But this 'Here, near the river' is more than four hours' walk from the village.—Allah preserve you in your strength, my Brothers. And they pass along, plodding slowly under their overshadowing burdens. A hard-hearted Naturalist, who goes so deep into Nature as to be far from the vital core even as the dilettante, might not have any sympathy to throw away on such occasions. But of what good is the love of Nature that consists only in classification and dissection? I carry no note-book with me when I go down the wadi or out into the fields. I am content if I bring back a few impressions of some reassuring instance of faith, a few pictures, and an armful of wild flowers and odoriferous shrubs. Let the learned manual maker concern himself with the facts; he is content with jotting down in his note-book the names and lineage of every insect and every herb.

"But Man? What is he to these scientific Naturalists? If they meet a stranger on the road, they pass him by, their eyes intent on the breviary of Nature, somewhat after the fashion of my priests, who are fond of praying in the open-air at sundown. No, I do not have to prove to my Brothers that my love of Nature is but second to my love of life. I am interested in my fellow men as in my fellow trees and flowers. 'The beauty of Nature,' Emerson again, 'must always seem unreal and mocking until the landscape has human figures, that are as good as itself.' And 'tis well, if they are but half as good. To me, the discovery of a woodman in the wadi were as pleasing as the discovery of a woodchuck or a woodswallow or a woodbine. For in the soul of the woodman is a song, I muse, as sweet as the rhythmic strains of the goldfinch, if it could be evoked. But the soul plodding up the hill under its heavy overshadowing burden, what breath has it left for song? The man bowed beneath the load, the soul bowed beneath the man! Alas, I seem to behold but moving burdens in my country. And yet, my swarthy and shrunken, but firm-fibred people plod along, content, patient, meek; and when they reach the summit of the hill with their crushing burdens, they still have breath enough to troll a favourite ditty or serenade the night.

> 'I come to thee, O Night,
> I'm at thy feet;
> I can not see, O Night,
> But thy breath is sweet.'

"And so is the breath of the pines. Here, the air is surcharged with perfume. In it floats the aromatic soul of many a flower. But the perfume-soul of the pines seems to tower over all others, just as its material shape lifts its artistic head over the oak, the cercis, and the terabinth. And though tall and stately, my native pines are not forbidding. They are so pruned that the snags serve as a most convenient ladder. Such was my pleasure mounting for the green cones, the salted pinons of which are delicious. But I confess they seem to stick in the stomach as the pitch of the cones sticks on the hands. This, however, though it remains for days, works no evil; but the pinons in the stomach, and the stomach on the nerves,—that is a different question.

"The only pines I have seen in the United States are those in front of Emerson's house in Concord; but compared with my native trees, they are scrubby and mean. These pine parasols under which I lay me, forgiving and forgetting, are fit for the gods. And although closely planted, they grow and flourish without much ado. I have seen spots not exceeding a few hundred square feet holding over thirty trees, and withal stout and lusty and towering. Indeed, the floor of the Tent seems too narrow at times for its crowded guests; but beneath the surface there is room for every root, and over it, the sky is broad enough for all.

"Ah, the bewildering vistas through the variegated pillars, taking in a strip of sea here, a mountain peak there, have an air of enchantment from which no human formula can release a pilgrim-soul. They remind me—no; they can not remind me of anything more imposing. But when I was visiting the great Mosques of Cairo I was reminded of them. Yes, the pine forests are the great mosques of Nature. And for art-lovers, what perennial beauty of an antique art is here. These majestic pillars arched with foliage, propping a light-green ceiling, from which cones hang in pairs and in clusters, and through which curiously shaped clouds can be seen moving in a cerulean sky; and at night, instead of the clouds, the stars—the distant, twinkling, white and blue stars—what to these are the decorations in the ancient mosques? There, the baroques, the arabesques, the colourings gorgeous, are dead, at least inanimate; here, they palpitate with life. The moving, swelling, flaming, flowing life is mystically interwoven in the evergreen ceiling and the stately colonnades. Ay, even the horizon yonder, with its planets and constellations rising and setting ever, is a part of the ceiling decoration.

"Here in this grand Mosque of Nature, I read my own Korân. I, Khalid, a Beduin in the desert of life, a vagabond on the highway of thought, I come to this glorious Mosque, the only place of worship open to me, to heal my broken soul in the perfumed atmosphere of its celestial vistas. The mihrabs here are not in this direction nor in that. But whereso one turns there are niches in which the living spirit of Allah is ever present. Here, then, I prostrate me and read a few Chapters of MY Holy Book. After which I resign myself to my eternal Mother and the soft western breezes lull me asleep. Yea, and even like my poor brother Moslem sleeping on his hair-mat in a dark corner of his airy Mosque, I dream my dream of contentment and resignation and love.

"See the ploughman strutting home, his goad in his hand, his plough on his shoulder, as if he had done his duty. Allah be praised, the flowers in the terrace-walls are secure. That is why, I believe, my American brother Thoreau liked walls with many gaps in them. The sweet wild daughters of Spring can live therein their natural life without being molested by the scythe or the plough. Allah be praised a hundred times and one."

CHAPTER IX

SIGNS OF THE HERMIT

Although we claim some knowledge of the Lebanon mountains, having landed there in our journey earthward, and having since then, our limbs waxing firm and strong, made many a journey through them, we could not, after developing, through many readings, Khalid's spiritual films, identify them with the vicinage which he made his Kaaba. On what hill, in what wadi, under what pines did he ruminate and extravagate, we could not from these idealised pictures ascertain. For a spiritual film is other than a photographic one. A poet's lens is endowed with a seeing eye, an insight, and a faculty to choose and compose. Hence the difficulty in tracing the footsteps of Fancy—in locating its cave, its nest, or its Kaaba. His pine-mosque we could find anywhere, at any altitude; his vineyards, too, and his glades; for our mountain scenery, its beauty alternating between the placid and the rugged—the tame terrace soil and the wild, forbidding majesty—is allwhere almost the same. But where in these rocky and cavernous recesses of the world can we to-day find the ancient Lebanon troglodyte, whom Khalid has seen, and visited in his hut, and even talked with? It is this that forces us to seek his diggings, to trace, if possible, his footsteps.

In the K. L. MS., as we have once remarked and more than once hinted, we find much that is unduly inflated, truly Oriental; much that is platitudinous, ludicrous, which we have suppressed. But never could we question the Author's veracity and sincerity of purpose. Whether he crawled like a zoöphyte, soared like an eagle, or fought, like Ali, the giants of the lower world, he is genuine, and oft-times amusingly truthful. But the many questionable pages on this curious subject of the eremite, what are we to do with them? If they are imaginary, there is too much in this Book against quackery to daunt us. And yet, if

Khalid has found the troglodyte, whom we thought to be an extinct species, he should have left us a few legends about it.

We have visited the ancient caverns of the Lebanon troglodytes in the cliffs overhanging the river of Wadi Kadeesha, and found nothing there but blind bats, and mosses, and dreary vacuity. No, not a vestage of the fossil is there, not a skull, not a shinbone. We have also inquired in the monasteries near the Cedars, and we were frankly told that no monk to-day fancies such a life. And if he did, he would not give his brother monks the trouble of carrying his daily bread to a cave in those forbidden cliffs. And yet, Simeon Stylites, he of the Pillar, who remained for thirty years perched on the top of it, was a Syrian shepherd. But who of his descendants to-day would as much as pass one night on the top of that pillar? Curious eleemosynary phases of our monkish system, these modern times reveal.

On our way from a journey to the Cedars, while engaged in the present Work, we passed through a pine forest, in which were some tangled bushes of the clematis. The muleteer stops near one of these and stoops to reach something he had seen therein. No treasure-trove, alas, as he supposed; but merely a book for which he lacerated his hands and which he cursed and handed to us, saying, "This must be the breviary of some monk."

No, it was an English book, and of American origin, and of a kind quite rare in America. Indeed, here were a find and surprise as agreeable as Khalid's sweetbrier bush. Henry Thoreau's *Week*! What a miracle of chance. Whose this mutilated copy of the *Week*, we thought? Who in these mountains, having been in America, took more interest in the Dreamer of Walden Woods than in peddling and trading? We walk our mule, looking about in vague, restless surprise, as if seeking in the woods a lost companion, and lo, we reach a monarch pine on which is carved the name of—Khalid! This book, then, must be his; the name on the pine tree is surely his own; we know his hand as well as his turn of mind. But who can say if this be his Kaaba, this his pine-mosque? Might he not only have passed through these glades to other parts? Signs, indeed, are here of his feet and hands, if not of his tent-pegs. And what signifies his stay? No matter how long he might have put up here, it is but a passage, deeply considered: like Thoreau's passage through Walden woods, like Mohammad's through the desert.

This leisure hour is the nipple of the soul. And fortunate they who are not artificially suckled, who know this hour no matter how brief, who get their nipple at the right time. If they do not, no pabulum ever after, will their indurated tissues assimilate. Do you wonder why the world is full of crusty souls? and why to them this infant hour, this suckling while, is so repugnant? But we must not intrude more of such remarks about mankind. Whether rightly suckled or not, we manage to live; but whether we do so marmot-like or Maronite-like, is not the question here to be considered. To pray for your bread or to burrow in the earth for it, is it not the same with most people? Given a missionary with a Bible in his hip-pocket or a peasant with a load of brushwood on his back and the same gastric coefficient, and you will have in either case a resulting expansion for six feet of coffin ground and a fraction of Allah's mercy. Our poor missionary, is it worth while to cross the seas for this? Marmot-like or Maronite-like—but soft you know! Here is our peasant with his overshadowing load of brushwood. And there is another, and another. They are carrying fuel to the lime-pit ahead of us yonder. What brow-sweat, what time, what fire, what suffering and patient toil, the lime-washing, or mere liming, of our houses and sepulchres, requires. That cone structure there, that artificial volcano, with its crackling, flaming bowels and its fuliginous, coruscating crater, must our hardy peasants feed continually for twenty days and nights.

But the book and the name on the pine, we would know more of these signs, if possible. And so, we visit the labourers of the kiln. They are yödling, the while they work, and jesting and laughing. The stokers, with flaming, swollen eyes, their tawny complexion waxing a brilliant bronze, their sweat making golden furrows therein, with their pikes and pitchforks busy, are terribly magnificent to behold. Here be men who would destroy Bastilles for you, if it were nominated in the bond. And there is the monk-foreman—the kiln is of the monastery's estate—reading his breviary while the lime is in making. Indeed, these sodalities of the Lebanons are not what their vows and ascetic theologies would make them. No lean-jowled, hungry-looking devotees, living in exiguity and droning in exinanition their prayers,—not by any means. Their flesh-pots are not a few, and their table is a marvel of ascetism! And why not, if their fat estates—three-quarter of the lands here is held in mortmain by the clergy—can yield anything, from silk cocoons to lime-pits? They will clothe you in silk at least; they will lime-wash your homes and sepulchres, if they cannot lime-wash anything else. Thanks to them so long as they keep some reminiscence of business in their heads to keep the Devil out of it.

The monk-foreman is reading with one eye and watching with the other. "Work," cries he, "every minute wasted is stolen from the abbey. And whoso steals, look in the pit: its fire is nothing compared with Juhannam." And the argument serves its purpose. The labourers hurry hither and thither, bringing brushwood near; the first stoker pitches to the second, the second to the third, and he feeds the flaming, smoking, coruscating volcano. "*Yallah!*" (Keep it up) exclaims the monk-foreman. "Burn the devil's creed," cries one. "Burn hell," cries another. And thus jesting in earnest, mightily working and enduring, they burn the mountains into lime, they make the very rocks yield somewhat.—Strength and blessings, brothers.

After the usual inquiry of whence and whither, his monkship offers the snuff-box. "No? roll you, then, a cigarette," taking out a plush pouch containing a mixture of the choicest native roots. These, we were told, are grown on the monastery's estate. We speak of the co-coon products of the season.

"Beshrew the mulberries!" exclaims the monk. "We are turning all our estates into fruit orchards and orangeries. The cultivation of the silk-worm is in itself an abomination. And while its income to-day is not as much as it was ten years ago, the expenditure has risen twofold. America is ruining our agriculture; and soon, I suppose, we have to send to China for labourers. Why, those who do not emigrate demand twice as much to-day for half the work they used to do five years ago; and those who return from America strut about like country gentlemen deploring the barrenness of their native soil."

And one subject leading to another, for our monk is a glib talker, we come to the cheese-makers, the goatherds. "Even these honest rustics," says he, "are becoming sophisticated (*mafsudin*). Their cheese is no longer what it was, nor is their faith. For Civilisation, passing by their huts in some shape or other, whispers in their ears something about cleverness and adulteration. And mistaking the one for the other, they abstract the butter from the milk and leave the verdigris in the utensils. This lust of gain is one of the diseases which come from Europe and America,—it is a plague which even the goatherd cannot escape. Why, do you know, wherever the cheese-monger goes these days ptomaine poison is certain to follow."

"And why does not the Government interfere?" we ask.

"Because the Government," replies our monk in a dry, droll air and gesture, "does not eat cheese."

And the monks, we learned, do not have to buy it. For this, as well as their butter, olive oil, and wine, is made on their own estates, under their own supervision.

"Yes," he resumes, placing his breviary in his pocket and taking out the snuff-box; "not long ago one who lived in these parts—a young man from Baalbek he was, and he had his booth in the pine forest yonder—bought some cheese from one of these muleteer cheese-mongers, and after he had eaten of it fell sick. It chanced that I was passing by on my way to the abbey, when he was groaning and retching beneath that pine tree. It was the first time I saw that young man, and were I not passing by I know not what would have become of him. I helped him to the abbey, where he was ministered to by our physician, and he remained with us three days. He ate of our cheese and drank of our wine, and seemed to like both very much. And ever since, while he was here, he would come to the abbey with a basket or a tray of his own make—he occupied himself in making wicker-baskets and trays—and ask in exchange some of our cheese and olive oil. He was very intelligent, this fellow; his eyes sometimes were like the mouth of this pit, full of fire and smoke. But he was queer. The clock in him was not wound right—he was always ahead or behind time, always complaining that we monks did not reckon time as he did. Nevertheless, I liked him much, and often would I bring him some of our cookery. But he never accepted anything without giving something in exchange."

Unmistakable signs.

"And his black turban," continues the monk, "over his long flowing hair made him look like our hermit." (Strange coincidence!) "On your way here have you not stopped to visit the hermit? Not far from the abbey, on your right hand coming here, is the Hermitage."

We remember passing a pretty cottage surrounded by a vineyard in that rocky wilderness; but who would mistake that for a troglodyte's cave? "And this young man from Baalbek," we ask, "how did he live in this forest?"

"Yonder," points the monk, "he cleared and cleaned for himself a little space which he made his workshop. And up in the pines he constructed a platform, which he walled and covered with boughs. And when he was not working or walking, he would be there among the branches, either singing or asleep. I used to envy him that nest in the pines."

"And did he ever go to church?"

"He attended mass twice in our chapel, on Good Friday and on Easter Sunday, I think."

"And did he visit the abbey often?"

"Only when he wanted cheese or olive oil." (Shame, O Khalid!) "But he often repaired to the Hermitage. I went with him once to listen

135

to his conversation with the Hermit. They often disagreed, but never quarrelled. I like that young man in spite of his oddities of thought, which savoured at times of infidelity. But he is honest, believe me; never tells a lie; and in a certain sense he is as pious as our Hermit, I think. Roll another cigarette."

"Thank you. And the Hermit, what is your opinion of him?"

"Well, h'm—h'm—go visit him. A good man he is, but very simple. And between us, he likes money too much. H'm, h'm, go visit him. If I were not engaged at present, I would accompany you thither."

We thank our good monk and retrace our steps to the Hermitage, rolling meanwhile in our mind that awful remark about the Hermit's love of money. Blindness and Plague! even the troglodyte loves and worships thee, thou silver Demiurge! We can not believe it. The grudges of monks against each other often reach darker and more fatal depths. Alas, if the faith of the cheese-monger is become adulterated, what shall we say of the faith of our monkhood? If the salt of the earth—but not to the nunnery nor to the monkery, we go. Rather let us to the Hermitage, Reader, and with an honest heart; in earnest, not in sport.

CHAPTER X

THE VINEYARD IN THE KAABA

This, then, is the cave of our troglodyte! Allah be praised, even the hermits of the Lebanon mountains, like the prophets of America and other electric-age species, are subject to the laws of evolution. A cottage and chapel set in a vineyard, the most beautiful we have yet seen, looms up in this rocky wilderness like an oasis in a desert. For many miles around, the vicinage presents a volcanic aspect, wild, barren, howlingly dreary. At the foot of Mt. Sanneen in the east, beyond many ravines, are villages and verdure; and from the last terrace in the vineyard one overlooks the deep chasm which can boast of a rivulet in winter. But in the summer its nakedness is appalling. The sun turns its pocket inside out, so to speak, exposing its boulders, its little windrows of sands, and its dry ditches full of dead fish spawn. And the cold, rocky horizon, rising so high and near, shuts out the sea and hides from the Hermit the glory of the sundown. But we can behold its effects on Mt. Sanneen, on the clouds above us, on the glass casements in the villages far away. The mountains in the east are mantled with etherial lilac alternating with mauve; the clouds are touched with purple and gold; the casements in the distance are scintillating with mystical carbuncles: the sun is setting in the Mediterranean,—he is waving his farewell to the hills.

We reach the first gate of the Hermitage; and the odour peculiar to monks and monkeries, a mixed smell of mould and incense and burning oil, greets us as we enter into a small open space in the centre of which is a Persian lilac tree. To the right is a barbed-wire fence shutting in the vineyard; directly opposite is the door of the chapel; and near it is a wicket before which stands a withered old woman. Against the wall is a stone bench where another woman is seated. As we enter, we hear her, standing at the wicket, talking to some one behind the scene. "Yes, that is the name of my husband," says she. "Allah have mercy on his soul," sighs an exiguous voice within; "pray for him, pray for him." And the woman, taking to weeping, blubbers out, "Will thirty masses do, think your Reverence?" "Yes, that will cheer his soul," replies the oracle.

The old woman thereupon enters the chapel, pays the priest or serving-monk therein, one hundred piasters for thirty masses, and goes away in tears. The next woman rises to the gate. "I am the mother of—," she says. "Ah, the mother of—," repeats the exiguous voice. "How are you? (She must be an old customer.) How is your husband? How are your children? And those in America, are they well, are they prosperous? Yes, yes, your deceased son. Well, h'm—h'm—you must come again. I can not tell you anything yet. Come again next week." And she, too, visits the chapel, counts out some money to the serving-monk, and leaves the Hermitage, drying her tears.

The Reader, who must have recognised the squeaking, snuffling, exiguous voice, knows not perhaps that the Hermit, in certain moments of *inkhitaf* (abstraction, levitation) has glimpses into the spirit-world and can tell while in this otherworldliness how the Christian souls are faring, and how many masses those in Purgatory need before they can rejoin the bosom of Father Abraham. And those who seek consolation and guidance through his occult ministrations are mostly women. But the money collected for masses, let it here be said, as well as the income of the vineyard, the Hermit touches not. The monks are the owners of the occult establishment, and they know better than he what to do with the revenue. But how far this ancient religious Medium can go in the spirit-world, and how honest he might be in his otherworldliness, let those say who have experience in spookery and table-rapping.

Now, the women having done and gone, the wicket is open, and the serving-monk ushers us through the dark and stivy corridor to the rear, where a few boxes marked "Made in America"—petroleum boxes, these—are offered us as seats. Before the door of the last cell are a few potsherds in which sweet basil plants are withering from thirst. Presently, the door squeaks, and one, not drooping like the plants, comes out to greet us. This is Father Abd'ul-Messiah (Servitor of the Christ), as the Hermit is called. Here, indeed, is an up-to-date hermit, not an antique troglodyte. Lean and lathy, he is, but not hungry-looking; quick of eye and gesture; quick of step, too. He seems always on the alert, as if surrounded continually with spirits. He is young, withal, or keeps so, at least, through the grace and ministration of Allah and the

Virgin. His long unkempt hair and beard are innocent of a single white line. And his health? "Through my five and twenty years of seclusion," said he, "I have not known any disease, except, now and then, in the spring season, when the sap begins to flow, I am visited by Allah with chills and fever.—No; I eat but one meal a day.—Yes; I am happy, Allah be praised, quite happy, very happy."

And he lifts his eyes heavenward, and sighs and rubs his hands in joyful satisfaction. To us, this Servitor of the Christ seemed not to have passed the climacteric. But truly, as he avowed, he was entering the fifth lustrum beyond it. Such are the advantages of the ascetic life, and of such ascetics the Kingdom of Heaven. A man of sixty can carry twenty years in his pocket, and seem all honesty, and youth, and health, and happiness.

We then venture a question about the sack-cloth, a trace of which was seen under his tunic sleeve. And fetching a deep sigh, he gazes on the drooping sweet basils in silence. No, he likes not to speak of these mortifications of the flesh. After some meditation he tells us, however, that the sack-cloth on the first month is annoying, torturing. "But the flesh," he continues naïvely, "is inured to it, as the pile, in the course of time, is broken and softened down." And with an honest look in his eyes, he smiled and sighs his assurance. For his Reverence always punctuates his speech with these sweet sighs of joy. The serving-monk now comes to whisper a word in his ear, and we are asked to "scent the air" a while in the vineyard.

This lovely patch of terrace-ground the Hermit tills and cultivates alone. And so thoroughly the work is done that hardly a stone can be seen in the soil. And so even and regular are the terrace walls that one would think they were built with line and plummet. The vines are handsomely trimmed and trellised, and here and there, to break the monotony of the rows, a fig, an apricot, an almond, or an olive, spreads its umbrageous boughs. Indeed, it is most cheering in the wilderness, most refreshing to the senses, this lovely vineyard, the loveliest we have seen.

Father Abd'ul-Messiah might be a descendant of Simeon of the Pillar for all we know; but instead of perching on the top of it, he breaks it down and builds with its stones a wall of his vineyard. Here he comes with his serving-monk, and we resume the conversation under the almond tree.

"You should come in the grape season to taste of my fruits," says he.

"And do you like the grape?" we ask.

"Yes, but I prefer to cultivate it."

"Throughout the season," the serving-monk puts in, "and though the grapes be so plentiful, he tastes them not."

"No?"

The Hermit is silent; for, as we have said, he is reluctant in making such confessions. Virtue, once bragged about, once you pride yourself upon it, ceases to be such.

In his vineyard the Hermit is most thorough, even scientific. One would think that he believed only in work. No; he does not sprinkle the vines with holy water to keep the grubs away. Herein he has sense enough to know that only in *kabrit* (sulphur) is the phylactery which destroys the phylloxera.

"And what do you do when you are not working in your vineyard or praying?"

"I have always somewhat to do, always. For to be idle is to open the door for Iblis. I might walk up and down this corridor, counting the slabs therein, and consider my time well spent." Saying which he rises and points to the sky. The purple fringes of the clouds are gone to sable; the lilac tints on the mountains are waxing grey; and the sombre twilight with his torch—the evening star had risen—is following in the wake of day; 'tis the hour of prayer.

But before we leave him to his devotion, we ask to be permitted to see his cell. Ah, that is against the monastic rules. We insist. And with a h'm, h'm, and a shake of the head, he rubs his hands caressingly and opens the door. Yes, the Reader shall peep into this eight by six cell, which is littered all around with rubbish, sacred and profane. In the corner is a broken stove with a broken pipe attached,—broken to let some of the smoke into the room, we are told. "For smoke," quoth the Hermit, quoting the Doctor, "destroys the microbes—and keeps the room warm after the fire goes out."

In the corner opposite the stove is a little altar with the conventional icons and gewgaws and a number of prayer books lying pell-mell around. Nearby is an old pair of shoes, in which are stuck a few candles and St. Anthony's Book of Contemplations. In the corner behind the door is a large cage, a pantry, suspended middleway between the floor and ceiling, containing a few earthen pots, an oil lamp, and a jar, covered with a cloth. Between the pantry and the altar, on a hair-mat spread on the floor, sleeps his Reverence. And his bed is not so hard as you might suppose, Reader; for, to serve your curiosity, we have been rude enough to lift up a corner of the cloth, and we found underneath a substantial mattress! On the bed is his book of accounts, which, being opened, when we entered, he hastened to close.

"You keep accounts, too, Reverence?"

"Indeed, so. That is a duty devolved on every one with mortal memory."

Let it not be supposed, however, that he has charge of the crops. In his journal he keeps the accounts of his masses? And here be evil sufficient for the day.

This, then, is the inventory of Abd'ul-Messiah's cell. And we do not think we have omitted much of importance. Yes; in the fourth corner, which we have not mentioned, are three or four petroleum cans containing provisions. From one of these he brings out a handful of dried figs, from another a pinch of incense, which he gives us as a token of his love and blessing. One thing we fain would emphasise, before we conclude our account. The money part of this eremitic business need not be harshly judged; for we must bear in mind that this honest Servitor of Christ is strong enough not to have his will in the matter. And remember, too, that the abbey's bills of expenses run high. If one of the monks, therefore, is blessed with a talent for solitude and seclusion, his brother monks shall profit by it. Indeed, we were told, that the income of the Hermitage, that is, the sum total in gold of the occult and the agricultural endeavours of Abd'ul-Messiah, is enough to defray the yearly expenditures of the monkery. Further, we have nothing to say on the subject. But Khalid has. And of his lengthy lucubration on *The Uses of Solitude*, we cull the following:

"Every one's life at certain times," writes he, "is either a Temple, a Hermitage, or a Vineyard: every one, in order to flee the momentary afflictions of Destiny, takes refuge either in God, or in Solitude, or in Work. And of a truth, work is the balm of the sore mind of the world. God and Solitude are luxuries which only a few among us nowadays can afford. But he who lives in the three, though his life be that of a silk larva in its cocoon, is he not individually considered a good man? Is he not a mystic, though uncreative, centre of goodness? Surely, his influence, his Me alone considered, is living and benign, and though it is not life-giving. He is a flickering taper under a bushel; and this, *billah*, were better than the pissasphaltum-souls which bushels of quackery and pretence can not hide. But alas, that a good man by nature should be so weak as to surrender himself entirely to a lot of bad men. For the monks, my brother Hermit, being a silk worm in its cocoon, will asphyxiate the larva after its work is done, and utilise the silk. Ay, after the Larva dies, they pickle and preserve it in their chapel

141

for the benefit of those who sought its oracles in life. Let the beef-packers of America take notice; the monks of my country are in the market with 'canned hermits!'

"And this Larva, be it remembered, is not subject to decay; a saint does not decompose in the flesh like mortal sinners. One of these, I have been told, dead fifty years ago and now canonised, can be seen yet in one of the monasteries of North Lebanon, keeping well his flesh and bones together—divinely embalmed. It has been truly said that the work of a good man never dies; and these leathery hermits continue in death as in life to counsel and console the Faithful.

"In the past, these Larvæ, not being cultivated for the market, con-tinued their natural course of development and issued out of their silk prisons full fledged moths. But those who cultivate them to-day are in sore need. They have masses and indulgences to sell; they have big bills to pay. But whether left to grow their wings or not, their solitude is that of a cocoon larva, narrow, stale, unprofitable to the world. While that of a philosopher, a Thoreau, for instance, might be called Nature's filter; and one, issuing therefrom benefited in every sense, morally, physically, spiritually, can be said to have been filtered through Solitude."

"The study of life at a distance is inutile; the study of it at close range is defective. The only method left, therefore, and perhaps the true one, is that of the artist at his canvas. He works at his picture an hour or two, and retires a little to study and criticise it from a distance. It is impossible to withdraw entirely from life and pretend to take an interest in it. Either like my brother Hermit in these parts, a spiritual larva in its cocoon, or like a Thoreau, who during his period of seclu-sion, peeped every fortnight into the village to keep up at least his practice of human speech. Else what is the use of solitude? A life of fantasy, I muse, is nearer to the heart of Nature and Truth than a life in sack-cloth and ashes....

"And yet, deeply considered, this eremitic business presents anoth-er aspect. For does not the eremite through his art of prayer and devotion, seek an ideal? Is he not a transcendentalist, at least in the German sense of the word? Is not his philosophy above all the senses, as the term implies, and common sense included? For through Mother Church, and with closed eyes, he will attain the ideal, of which my German philosopher, through the logic-mill, and with eyes open, hard-ly gets a glimpse.

"The devout and poetic souls, and though they walk among the crowd, live most of their lives in solitude. Through Mother Sorrow, or

Mother Fancy, or Mother Church, they are ever seeking the ideal, which to them is otherwise unattainable. And whether a howler of Turabu or a member of the French Academy, man, in this penumbra of faith and doubt, of superstition and imagination, is much the same. 'The higher powers in us,' says Novalis, 'which one day, as Genii, shall fulfil our will, are for the present, Muses, which refresh us on our toilsome course with sweet remembrances.' And the jinn, the fairies, the angels, the muses, are as young and vivacious to-day as they were in the Arabian and Gaelic Ages of Romance.

"But whether Mother Church or Poetry or Philosophy or Music be the magic-medium, the result is much the same if the motive be not religiously sincere, sincerely religious, piously pure, lofty, and humane. Ay, my Larva-Hermit, with all his bigotry and straitness of soul, stands higher than most of your artists and poets and musicians of the present day. For a life sincerely spent between the Temple and the Vineyard, between devotion and honest labour, producing to one man of all mankind some positive good, is not to be compared with the life which oscillates continuously between egoism and vanity, quackery and cowardice, selfishness and pretence, and which never rises, do what it may, above the larva state....

"Let every one cultivate with pious sincerity some such vineyard as my Hermit's and the world will not further need reform. For through all the vapour and mist of his ascetic theology, through the tortuous chasm of his eremitic logic, through the bigotry and crass superstition of his soul, I can always see the Vineyard on the one side of his cell, and the Church on the other, and say to myself: Here be a man who is never idle; here be one who loves the leisure praised by Socrates, and hates the sluggishness which Iblis decks and titivates. And if he crawls between his Church and his Vineyard, and burrows in both for a solution of life, nay, spins in both the cocoon of his ideal, he ought not to be judged from on high. Come thou near him; descend; descend a little and see: has he not a task, and though it be of the taper-under-the-bushel kind? Has he not a faith and a sincerity which in a Worm of the Earth ought to be reckoned sublime? 'If there were sorrow in heaven,' he once said to me, 'how many there would continuously lament the time they wasted in this world?'

"O my Brothers, build your Temples and have your Vineyards, even though it be in the rocky wilderness."

BOOK THE THIRD IN KULMAKAN

TO GOD[1]

In the religious systems of mankind, I sought thee, O God, in vain; in their machine-made dogmas and theologies, I sought thee in vain; in their churches and temples and mosques, I sought thee long, and long in vain; but in the Sacred Books of the World, what have I found? A letter of thy name, O God, I have deciphered in the Vedas, another in the Zend-Avesta, another in the Bible, another in the Korân. Ay, even in the Book of the Royal Society and in the Records of the Society for Psychical Research, have I found the diacritical signs which the infant races of this Planet Earth have not yet learned to apply to the consonants of thy name. The lisping infant races of this Earth, when will they learn to pronounce thy name entire? Who shall supply the Vowels which shall unite the Gutturals of the Sacred Books? Who shall point out the dashes which compound the opposite loadstars in the various regions of thy Heaven? On the veil of the eternal mystery are palimpsests of which every race has deciphered a consonant. And through the diacritical marks which the seers and paleologists of the future shall furnish, the various dissonances in thy name shall be reduced, for the sake of the infant races of the Earth, to perfect harmony.—**Khalid**.

---

[1] Arabic Symbol.

CHAPTER I

THE DISENTANGLEMENT OF THE ME

"Why this exaggerated sense of thine importance," Khalid asks himself in the K. L. MS., "when a little ptomaine in thy cheese can poison the source of thy lofty contemplations? Why this inflated conception of thy Me, when an infusion of poppy seeds might lull it to sleep, even to stupefaction? What avails thy logic when a little of the Mandragora can melt the material universe into golden, unfolding infinities of dreams? Why take thyself so seriously when a leaf of henbane, taken by mistake in thy salad, can destroy thee? But the soul is not dependent on health or disease. The soul is the source of both health and disease. And life, therefore, is either a healthy or a diseased state of the soul.

"One day, when I was rolling these questions in my mind, and working on a reed basket to present to my friend the Hermit as a farewell memento, his serving-monk brings me some dried figs in a blue kerchief and says, 'My Master greets thee and prays thee come to him.' I do so the following morning, bringing with me the finished basket, and as I enter the Hermitage court, I find him repairing a stone wall in the vineyard. As he sees me, he hastens to put on his cloak that I might not remark the sack-cloth he wore, and with a pious smile of assurance and thankfulness, welcomes and embraces me, as is his wont. We sit down in the corridor before the chapel door. The odorous vapor of what was still burning in the censer within hung above us. The holy atmosphere mantled the dread silence of the place. And the slow, insinuating smell of incense, like the fumes of gunga, weighed heavy on my eyelids and seemed to brush from my memory the cobwebs of time. A drowsiness possessed me; I felt like one awaking from a dream. I asked for the water jug, which the Hermit hastened to bring. And looking through the door of the chapel, I saw on the altar a burning cresset flickering like the planet Mercury on a December morning. How often did I light such a cresset when a boy, I mused. Yes, I was an acolyte once. I swang the censer and drank deep of the incense fumes as I chanted in Syriac the service. And I remember when I made a mistake one day in reading the Epistle of Paul, the priest, who was of an irascible humour, took me by the ear and made me spell the words I could not pronounce. And the boys in the congregation tittered gleefully. In my mortification was honey for them. Such was my pride, nevertheless, such the joy I felt, when, of all the boys that gathered round the lectern at vespers, I was called upon to read in the *sinksar* (hagiography) the Life of the Saint of the day.

"I knew then that to steal, for instance, is a sin; and yet, I emptied the box of wafers every morning after mass and shared them with the very boys who laughed at my mistakes. One day, in the purest intention, I offered one of these wafers to my donkey and he would not eat it. I felt insulted, and never after did I pilfer a wafer. Now, as I muse on these sallies of boyish waywardness I am impressed with the idea that the certainty and daring of Ignorance, or might I say Innocence, are great. Indeed, to the pure everything is pure. But strange to relate that as I sat in the corridor of the Hermitage and saw the light flickering on the altar, I hankered for a wafer, and was tempted to go into the chapel and filch one. What prevented me? Alas, knowledge makes sceptics and cowards of us all. And the pursuit of knowledge, according to my Hermit, nay, the noblest pursuit, even the serving of God, ceases to be a virtue the moment we begin to enjoy it.

"'It is necessary to conquer, not only our instincts,' he continued, 'but our intellectual and our spiritual passions as well. To force our will in the obedience of a higher will, to leave behind all our mundane desires in the pursuit of the one great desire, herein lies the essence of true virtue. St. Anthony would snatch his hours of devotion from the Devil. Even prayer to him was a struggle, an effort not to feel the joy of it. Yes, we must always disobey our impulses, and resist the tyranny of our desires. When I have a strong desire to pray, I go out into the vineyard and work. When I begin to enjoy my work in the vineyard, I cease to do it well. Therefore, I take up my breviary. Do that which you must not do, when you are suffering, and you will not want to do it again, when you are happy. The other day, one who visited the Hermitage, spoke to me of you, O Khalid. He said you were what is called an anarchist. And after explaining to me what is meant by this—I never heard of such a religion before—I discovered to my surprise that I, too, am an anarchist. But there is this difference between us: I obey only God and the authority of God, and you obey your instincts and what is called the authority of reason. Yours, O Khalid, is a narrow conception of anarchy. In truth, you should try to be an anarchist like me: subordinate your personality, your will and mind and soul, to a higher will and intelligence, and resist with all your power everything else. Why do you not come to the Hermitage for a few days and make me your confessor?'

"'I do not confess in private, and I can not sleep within doors.'

"'You do not have to do so; the booth under the almond tree is at your disposal. Come for a spiritual exercise of one week only.'

"'I have been going through such an exercise for a year, and soon I shall leave my cloister in the pines.'

"'What say you? You are leaving our neighbourhood? No, no; remain here, O Khalid. Come, live with me in the Hermitage. Come back to Mother Church; return not to the wicked world. O Khalid, we must inherit the Kingdom of Allah, and we can not do so by being anarchist like the prowlers of the forest. Meditate on the insignificance and evanescence of human life.'

"'But it lies within us, O my Brother, to make it significant and eternal.'

"'Yes, truly, in the bosom of Mother Church. Come back to your Mother—come to the Hermitage—let us pass this life together.'

"'And what will you do, if in the end you discover that I am in the right?'

"Here he paused a moment, and, casting on me a benignant glance, makes this reply: 'Then, I will rejoice, rejoice,' he gasped; 'for we shall both be in the right. You will become an anarchist like me and not against the wretched authorities of the world, but against your real enemies, Instinct and Reason.'

"And thus, now and then, he would salt his argument with a pinch of casuistic wit. Once he was hard set, and, to escape the alternatives of the situation, he condescended to tell me the story of his first and only love.

"'In my youth,' said the Hermit, 'I was a shoemaker, and not a little fastidious as a craftsman. In fact, I am, and always have been, an extremist, a purist. I can not tolerate the cobblings of life. Either do your work skilfully, devotedly, earnestly, or do it not. So, as a shoemaker, I succeeded very well. Truth to tell, my work was as good, as neat, as elegant as that of the best craftsman in Beirut. And you know, Beirut is noted for its shoemakers. Yes, I was successful as any of them, and I counted among my customers the bishop of the diocese himself. One day, forgive me, Allah! a young girl, the daughter of a peasant neighbour, comes into the shop to order a pair of shoes. In taking the measure of her foot—but I must not linger on these details. A shoemaker can not fail to notice the shape of his customer's foot. Well, I measured, too, her ankle—ah, forgive me, Allah!

"'In brief, when the shoes were finished—I spent a whole day in the finishing touches—I made her a present of them. And she, in recognition of my favor, made a plush tobacco bag, on which my name was worked in gold threads, and sent it to me, wrapped in a silk handkerchief, with her brother. Now, that is the opening chapter. I will abruptly come to the last, skipping the intermediate parts, for they are too silly, all of them. I will only say that I was as earnest, as sincere, as devoted in this affair of love as I was in my craft. Of a truth, I was mad about both.

"'Now the closing chapter. One day I went to see her—we were engaged—and found she had gone to the spring for water. I follow her there and find her talking to a young man, a shoemaker like myself. No, he was but a cobbler. On the following day, going again to see her, I find this cobbler there. I remonstrate with her, but in vain. And what is worse, she had sent to him the shoes I made, to be repaired. He was patching my own work! I swallowed my ire and went back to my shop. A week later, to be brief, I went there again, and what I beheld made my body shiver. She, the wench. Forgive me, Allah! had her hands around his neck and her lips—yes, her lying lips, on his cheek! No, no; even then I did not utter a word. I could but cry in the depth of my heart. How can woman be so faithless, so treacherous—in my heart I cried.

"'It was a terrible shock; and from it I lay in bed for days with chills and fever. Now, when I recovered, I was determined on pursuing a new course of life. No longer would I measure women's feet. I sold my stock, closed my shop, and entered the monastery. I heard afterwards that she married that young cobbler; emigrated with him to America; deserted him there; returned to her native village; married again, and fled with her second husband to South Africa. Allah be praised! even He appreciates the difference between a shoemaker and a cobbler; and the bad woman He gives to the bad craftsman. That is why I say, Never be a cobbler, whatever you do.

"'But in the monastery—draw near, I will speak freely—in the monastery, too, there are cobblers and shoemakers. There, too, is much ungodliness, much treachery, much cobbling. Ah me, I must not speak thus. Forgive me, Allah! But I promised to tell you the whole story.

Therefore, I will speak freely. After passing some years in the monastery, years of probation and grief they were, I fell sick with a virulent fever. The abbot, seeing that there was little chance of my recovery, would not send for the physician. And so, I languished for weeks, suffering from thirst and burning pains and hunger. I raved and chattered in my delirium. I betrayed myself, too, they told me. The monks my brothers, even during my suffering, made a scandal of the love affair I related. They said that I exposed my wounds and my broken heart before the Virgin, that I sinned in thought and word on my death-bed. Allah forgive them. It may be, however; for I know not what I said and what I did. But when I recovered, I was determined not to remain in the monastery, and not to return to the world. The wicked world, I disentangled myself absolutely from its poisoned meshes. I came to the Hermitage, to this place. And never, since I made my second remove until now, have I known disease, or sorrow, nor treachery, which is worse than both. Allah be praised! One's people, one's brothers, one's lovers and friends, are a hindrance and botheration. We are nothing, nothing: God is everything. God is the only reality. And in God alone is my refuge. That is my story in brief. If I did not like you, I would not have told it, and so freely. Meditate upon it, and on the insignificance and evanescence of human life. The world is a snare, and a bad snare, at that. For it can not hold us long enough in it to learn to like it. It is a cobbler's snare. The world is full of cobblers, O Khalid. Come away from it; be an ideal craftsman—be an extremist—be a purist—come live with me. Let us join our souls in devotion, and our hearts in love. Come, let us till and cultivate this vineyard together.'

"And taking me by the hand, he shows me a cell furnished with a hair-mat, a *masnad* (leaning pillow), and a chair. 'This cell,' says he, 'was occupied by the Bishop when he came here for a spiritual exercise of three weeks. It shall be yours if you come; it's the best cell in the Hermitage. Now, let us visit the chapel.' I go in with him, and as we are coming out, I ask him child-like for a wafer. He brings the box straightway, begs me to take as much as I desire, and placing his hand on my shoulder, encircles me with one of his benignant glances, saying, 'Allah illumine thy heart, O Khalid.' 'Allah hear thy prayer,' I reply. And we part in tears."

Here Khalid bursts in ecstasy about the higher spiritual kingdom, and chops a little logic about the I and the not-I, the Reality and the non-Reality.—"God," says the Hermit. "Thought," says the Idealist, "that is the only Reality." And what is Thought, and what is God, and what is Matter, and what is Spirit? They are the mysterious vessels of

Life, which are always being filled by Love and emptied by Logic. "The external world," says the Materialist—"Does not exist," says the Idealist. "'Tis immaterial if it does or not," says the Hermit. And what if the three are wrong? The Universe, knowable and unknowable, will it be affected a whit by it? If the German Professor's Chair of Logic and Philosophy were set up in the Hermitage, would anything be gained or lost? Let the *I* deny the stars, and they will nevertheless roll in silence above it. Let the not-I crush this I, this "thinking reed," and the higher universal I, rising above the stars and flooding the sidereal heavens with light, will warm, remold, and regenerate the world.

"I can conceive of a power," writes Khalid in that vexing Manuscript, "which can create a beautiful parti-colored sun-flower of the shattered fragments of Idealism, Materialism, and my Hermit's theology. Why not, if in the New World—" And here, of a sudden, to surprise and bewilder us, he drags in Mrs. Eddy and the Prophet Dowie yoked under the yoke of Whitman. He marks the *Key to Scripture* with blades from *Leaves of Grass*, and such fuel as he gathers from both, he lights with an ember borrowed from the chariot to Elijah. And thus, for ten whole pages, beating continually, now in the dark of Metaphysics, now in the dusk of Science; losing himself in the tangled bushes of English Materialism, and German Mysticism, and Arabic Sufism; calling now to Berkeley, now to Hackel; meeting with Spencer here, with Al-Gazzaly there; and endeavoring to extricate himself in the end with some such efforts as "the Natural being Negativity, the Spiritual must be the opposite of that, and both united in God form the Absolute," etc., etc. But we shall not give ourselves further pain in laying before the English reader the like heavy and unwieldy lumber. Whoever relishes such stuff, and can digest it, need not apply to Khalid; for, in this case, he is but a poor third-hand caterer. Better go to the Manufacturers direct; they are within reach of every one in this Age of Machinery and Popular Editions. But there are passages here, of which Khalid can say, 'The Mortar at least is mine.' And in this Mortar he mixes and titrates with his Neighbour's Pestle some of his fantasy and insight. Of these we offer a sample:

"I say with psychologists, as the organism, so is the personality. The revelation of the Me is perfect in proportion to the sound state of the Medium. But according to the Arabic proverb, the jar oozes of its contents. If these be of a putridinous mixture, therefore, no matter how sound the jar, the ooze is not going to smell of ambergris and musk. So, it all depends on the contents with which the Potter fills his jugs and pipkins, I assure you. And if the contents are good and the jar is sound, we get such excellence of soul as is rare among mortals. If the contents are excellent and the jar is cracked, the objective influence will then predominate, and putrescence, soon or late, will set in. Now, the Me in the majority of mankind comes to this world in a cracked pipkin, and it oozes out entirely as soon as it liquifies in youth. The pipkin, therefore, goes through life empty and cracked, ever sounding flat and false. While in others the Me is enclosed in a sealed straw-covered flask and can only be awakened by either evaporation or de-capitation, in other words, by a spiritual revolution. And in the very few among mortals, it emerges out of the iron calyx of a flower of red-hot steel, or flows from the transparent, odoriferous bosom of a rose of light. In the first we have a Cæsar, an Alexander, a Napoleon; in the second, a Buddha, a Socrates, a Christ.

"But consider that Science, in the course of psychological analysis, speaks of Christ, Napoleon, and Shakespeare, as patients. Such exalted states of the soul, such activity of the mind, such exuberance of spir-itual strength, are but the results of the transformation of the Me in the subject, we are told, and this transformation has its roots in the organ-ism. But why, I ask, should there be such a gulf between individuals, such a difference in their Mes, when a difference in the organism is a trifle in comparison? How account for the ebb and flow in the souls, or let us say, in the expression of the individualities, of Mohammad the Prophet, for instance, and Mohammad the camel-herd? And why is it in psychological states that are similar, the consciousness of the one is like a mountain peak, so to speak, and that of the other like a cave?

"A soldier is severely wounded in battle and a change takes place in his nervous organism, by reason of which he loses his organic con-sciousness; or, to speak in the phraseology of the psychologist, he loses the sense of his own body, of his physical personality. The cause of this change is probably the wound received; but the nature of the change can be explained only by hypotheses, which are become mat-ters of choice and taste—and sometimes of personal interest among scientists. Now, when the question is resolved by hypothesis, is not even a layman free to offer one? If I say the Glass is shattered and the Me within is sadly reflected, or in a more tragic instance the light of the Me runs out, would I not be offering thee a solution as dear and tenable as that of the professor of psychology?"

CHAPTER II

THE VOICE OF THE DAWN

Breathless but scathless, we emerge from the mazes of metaphysics and psychology where man and the soul are ever playing hide-and-seek; and where Khalid was pleased to display a little of his killing skill in fencing. To those mazes, we promise the Reader, we shall not return again. In our present sojourn, however, it is necessary to go through the swamps and Jordans as well as the mountains and plains. Otherwise, we would not have lingered a breathing while in the lowlands of mystery. But now we know how far Khalid went in seeking health, and how deep in seeking the Me, which he would disentangle from the meshes of philosophy and anchoretism, and bring back to life, triumphant, loving, joyous, free. And how far he succeeded in this, we shall soon know.

On the morning of his last day in the pines, meanwhile, we behold him in the chariot of Apollo serenading the stars. He no longer would thrust a poker down his windpipe; for he breathes as freely as the mountain bears and chirps as joyously as the swallows. And his lungs? The lungs of the pines are not as sound. And his eyes? Well, he can gaze at the rising sun without adverting the head or squinting or shedding a tear. Now, as a sign of this healthy state of body and mind, and his healthier resolve to return to the world, to live opposite his friend the Hermit on the other antipode of life, and furthermore, as a relief from the exhausting tortuosities of thought in the last Chapter, we give here a piece of description notably symbolical.

"I slept very early last night; the lights in the chapel of the abbey were still flickering, and the monks were chanting the complines. The mellow music of a drizzle seemed to respond sombrely to the melancholy echo of the choir. About midnight the rain beat heavily on the pine roof of the forest, and the thunder must have struck very near, between me and the monks. But rising very early this morning to commune for the last time with the pensive silence of dawn in the pines, I am greeted, as I peep out of my booth, by a knot of ogling stars. But where is the opaque breath of the storm, where are the clouds? None seem to hang on the horizon, and the sky is as limpid and clear as the dawn of a new life. Glorious, this interval between night and dawn. Delicious, the flavour of the forest after a storm. Intoxicating, the odours of the earth, refreshed and satisfied. Divine, the whispers of the morning air, divine!

"But where is the rain, and where are the thunderbolts of last night? The forest and the atmosphere retain but the sweet and scented memories of their storming passion. Such a December morning in these mountain heights is a marvel of enduring freshness and ardour. All round one gets a vivid illusion of Spring. The soft breezes caressing the pines shake from their boughs the only evidence of last night's storm. And these are more like the dew of Summer than the lees of the copious tears of parting Autumn. A glorious morning, too glorious to be enjoyed by a solitary soul. But near the rivulet yonder stands a fox sniffing the morning air. Welcome, my friend. Welcome to my coffee, too.

"I gather my mulberry sticks, kindle them with a handful of dried pine needles, roast my coffee beans, and grind them while the water boils in the pot. In half an hour I am qualified to go about my business. The cups and coffee utensils I wash and restore to the chest—and what else have I to do to-day? Pack up? Allah be praised, I have little packing to do. I would pack up, if I could, a ton of the pine air and the forest perfume, a strip of this limpid sky, and a cluster of those stars. Never at such an hour and in this season of the year did I enjoy such transporting limpidity in the atmosphere and such reassuring expansiveness on the horizon. Why, even the stars, the constellations, and the planets, are all here to enjoy this with me. Not one of them, I think, is absent.

"The mountains are lost in the heavens. They are seeking, as it were, the sisters of the little flowers sleeping at their feet. The moon, resembling a crushed orange, is sinking in the Mediterranean. The outlines of earth and sky all round are vague, indistinct. Were not the sky so clear and the atmosphere so rare, thus affording the planets and the constellations to shed their modicum of light, the dusk of this hour would have deprived the scene of much of its pensive beauty of colour and shade. But there is Pegasus, Andromeda, Aldebaran, not to mention Venus and Jupiter and Saturn,—these alone can conquer the right

wing of darkness. And there is Mercury, like a lighted cresset shaken
by the winds, flapping his violet wings above the Northeastern horizon; and Mars, like a piece of gold held out by the trembling hand of a
miser, is sinking in the blue of the sea with Neptune; the Pleiades are
stepping on the trail of the blushing moon; the Balance lingers behind
to weigh the destinies of the heroes who are to contend with the dawn;
while Venus, peeping from her tower over Mt. Sanneen, is sending
love vibrations to all. I would tell thee more if I knew. But I swear to
thee I never read through the hornbook of the heavens. But if I can not
name and locate more of the stars, I can tell thee this about them all:
they are the embers of certainty eternally glowing in the ashes of
doubt.

"The Eastern horizon is yet lost in the dusk; the false dawn is
spreading the figments of its illusion; the trees in the distance seem
like rain-clouds; and the amorphous shadows of the monasteries on the
mountain heights and hilltops all around, have not yet developed into
silhouettes. Everything, except the river in the wadi below, is yet
asleep. Not even the swallows are astir. Ah, but my neighbour yonder
is; the light in the loophole of his hut sends a struggling ray through
the mulberries, and the tintinnabulations of his daughter's loom are
like so many stones thrown into this sleeping pond of silence. The
loom-girl in these parts is never too early at her harness and shuttle. I
know a family here whose loom and spinning wheel are never idle: the
wife works at the loom in the day and her boy at the wheel; while in
the night, her husband and his old mother keep up the game. And this
hardly secures for them their flour and lentils the year round. But I
concern not myself now with questions of economy.

"There, another of my neighbours is awake; and the hinges of his
door, shrieking terribly, fiendishly, startle the swallows from their
sleep. And here are the muleteers, yodling, as they pass by, their

> 'Dhome, Dhome, Dhome,
> O mother, he is come;
> Hide me, hide me quickly,
> And say I am not home.'

"Lo, the horizon is disentangling itself from the meshes of darkness. The dust of haze and dusk on the scalloped edges of the
mountains, is blown away by the first breath of dawn. The lighter grey
of the horizon is mirrored in the clearer blue of the sea. But the darkness seems to gather on the breast of the sloping hills. Conquered on

the heights, it retreats into the wadi. Ay, the darkest hour is nearest the dawn.

"Now the light grey is become a lavender; the outlines of earth and sky are become more distinct; the mountain peaks, the dusky veil being rent, are separating themselves from the heaven's embrace; the trees in the distance no longer seem like rain-clouds; and the silhouettes of the monasteries are casting off the cloak of night. The lavender is melting now into heliotrope, and the heliotrope is bursting here and there in pink; the stars are waning, the constellations are dying out, and the planets are following in their wake. The darkness, too, which has not yet retreated from the wadi, must soon follow; for the front guard of the dawn is near. Behold the shimmer of their steel! And see, in the dust of the retreating darkness, the ochre veins of the lime cliffs are now perceptible. And that huge pillar, which looked like the standard-bearer of Night, is transformed into a belfry; and a monk can be seen peeping through the ogive beneath it. Mt. Sanneen, its black and ochre scales thrown in relief on a coat of grey, is like a huge panther sleeping over the many-throated ravine of Kisrawan. Ah, the pink flower of dawn is bursting in golden glory, thrilling in orange and saffron, flaming with the ardency of love and hope. The dawn! The glow and glamour of the Eastern dawn!...

"The dawn of a new life, of a better, purer, healthier, higher spiritual kingdom. I would have its temples and those of the vast empire of wealth and material well-being, stand side by side. Ay, I would even rear an altar to the Soul in the temple of Materialism, and an altar to Materialism in the temple of the Soul. Each shall have its due, each shall glory in the sacred purity and strength of life; each shall develop and expand, but never at the expense of the other. I will have neither the renunciation which ends in a kind of idiocy dignified with a philosophic or a theologic name, nor the worldliness which ends in bestiality. I am a citizen of two worlds—a citizen of the Universe; I owe allegiance to two kingdoms. In my heart are those stars and that sun, and the LIGHT of those stars and that sun.

"Yes, I am equally devoted both to the material and the spiritual. And when the two in me are opposed to each other, conflicting, inimical, obdurate, my attitude towards them is neither that of my friend the Hermit nor that of my European superman. I sit down, shut my eyes, compose myself, and concentrate my mind on the mobility of things. If the clouds are moving, why, I have but to sit down and let them move away. I let my No-will, in this case, dominate my will, and that serves my purpose well. To be sure, every question tormenting us would resolve itself favourably, or at least indifferently, if we did not always rush in, wildly, madly, and arrogate to ourselves such claims of authority and knowledge as would make Olympus shake with laughter. The resignation and passiveness of the spirit should always alternate equitably with the terrible strivings of the will. For the dervish who whirls himself into a foaming ecstasy of devotion and the strenuous American who works himself up to a sweating ecstasy of gain, are the two poles of the same absurdity, the two ends of one evil. Indeed, to my way of thinking, the man on the Stock Exchange and the demagogue on the stump, for instance, are brothers to the blatant corybant."

CHAPTER III

THE SELF ECSTATIC

To graft the strenuosity of Europe and America upon the ease of the Orient, the materialism of the West upon the spirituality of the East,—this to us seems to be the principal aim of Khalid. But often in his wanderings and divagations of thought does he give us fresh proof of the truism that no two opposing elements meet and fuse without both losing their original identity. You may place the bit of contentment in the mouth of ambition, so to speak, and jog along in your sterile course between the vast wheat fields groaning under the thousand-toothed plough and the gardens of delight swooning with devotion and sensuality. But cross ambition with contentment and you get the hinny of indifference or the monster of fatalism. We do not say that indifference at certain passes of life, and certain stages, is not healthy, and fatalism not powerful; but both we believe are factors as potent in commerce and trade as pertinacity and calculation. "But is there not room in the garden of delight for a wheat field?" asks Khalid. "Can we not apply the bow to the telegraph wires of the world and make them the vehicle of music as of stock quotations? Can we not simplify life as we are simplifying the machinery of industry? Can we not consecrate its Temple to the Trinity of Devotion, Art, and Work, or Religion, Romance, and Trade?"

This seems to be the gist of Khalid's gospel. This, through the labyrinths of doubt and contradiction, is the pinnacle of faith he would reach. And often in this labyrinthic gloom, where a gleam of light from some recess of thought or fancy reveals here a Hermit in his cloister, there an Artist in his studio, below a Nawab in his orgies, above a Broker on the Stock Exchange, we have paused to ask a question about these glaring contrarieties in his life and thought. And always would he make this reply: "I have frequently moved and removed between extremes; I have often worked and slept in opposing camps. So, do not expect from me anything like the consistency with which the majority of mankind solder and shape their life. Deep thought seems often, if not always, inconsistent at the first blush. The intensity and passiveness of the spirit are as natural in their attraction and repulsion as the elements, whose harmony is only patent on the surface. Consistency is superficial, narrow, one-sided. I am both ambitious, therefore, and contented. My ambition is that of the earth, the ever producing and resuscitating earth, doing the will of God, combatting the rasure of time; and my contentment is that of the majestic pines, faring alike in shade and sunshine, in calm and storm, in winter as in spring. Ambition and Contentment are the night and day of my life-journey. The day makes room for the fruits of solacement which the night brings; and the night gives a cup of the cordial of contentment to make good the promise of day to day.

"Ay, while sweating in the tortuous path, I never cease to cherish the feeling in which I was nourished; the West for me means ambition, the East, contentment: my heart is ever in the one, my soul, in the other. And I care not for the freedom which does not free both; I seek not the welfare of the one without the other. But unlike my Phœnician ancestors, the spiritual with me shall not be limited by the natural; it shall go far above it, beyond or below it, saturating, sustaining, purifying what in external nature is but a symbol of the invisible. Nor is my idea of the spiritual developed in opposition to nature, and in a manner inimical to its laws and claims, as in Judaism and Christianity.

"The spiritual and natural are so united, so inextricably entwined around each other, that I can not conceive of them separately, independently. And both in the abstract sense are purportless and ineffectual without Consciousness. They are blind, dumb forces, beautiful, barbaric pageants, careering without aim or design through the immensities of No-where and No-time, if they are not impregnated and nourished with Thought, that is to say, with Consciousness, vitalised and purified. You may impregnate them with philosophy, nourish them with art; they both emanate from them, and remain as skidding clouds, as shining mirages, as wandering dust, until they find their exponent in Man.

"I tell thee then that Man, that is to say Consciousness, vitalised and purified, in other words Thought—that alone is real and eternal. And Man is supreme, only when he is the proper exponent of Nature, and spirit, and God: the three divine sources from which he issues, in which he is sustained, and to which he must return. Nature and the spiritual, without this embodied intelligence, this somatic being, called man or angel or ape, are as ermine on a wax figure. The human factor, the exponent intelligence, the intellective and sensuous faculties, these, my Brothers, are whole, sublime, holy, only when, in a state of continuous expansion, the harmony among themselves and the affirmative ties between them and Nature, are perfect and pure. No, the spiritual ought not and can not be free from the sensuous, even the sensual. The true life, the full life, the life, pure, robust, sublime, is that in which all the nobler and higher aspirations of the soul AND THE BODY are given free and unlimited scope, with the view of developing the divine strain in Man, and realising to some extent the romantic as well as the material hopes of the race. God, Nature, Spirit, Passion—Passion, Spirit, Nature, God—in some such panorama would I paint the life of a highly developed being. Any of these elements lacking, and the life is wanting, defective, impure.

"I have no faith in men who were conceived in a perfunctory manner, on a pragmatical system, so to speak; the wife receiving her husband in bed as she would a tedious guest at an afternoon tea. Only two flames uniting produce a third; but a flame and a name, or a flame and a spunge, produce a hiff and nothing. Oh, that the children of the race are all born phœnix-like in the fire of noble and sacred passion, in the purgatory, as it were, of Love. What a race, what a race we should have. What men, what women! Yes, that is how the children of the earth should be conceived, not on a pragmatical system, in an I-don't-care-about-the-issue manner. I believe in evoking the spirit, in dreaming a little about the gods of Olympus, and a little, too, about the gods of the abysmal depths, before the bodily communion. And in earnest, O my Brother, let us do this, despite what old Socrates says about the propriety and wisdom of approaching your wife with prudence and gravity...."

And thus, if we did not often halloo, Khalid, like a huntsman pursuing his game, would lose himself in the pathless, lugubrious damp of the forest. If we did not prevent him at times, holding firmly to his coat-tail, he would desperately pursue the ghost of his thoughts even on such precipitous paths to those very depths in which Socrates and Montaigne always felt at home. But he, a feverish, clamorous, obstreperous stripling of a Beduin, what chance has he in extricating his barbaric instincts from such thorny hedges of philosophy? And had he not quoted Socrates in that last paragraph, it would have been expunged. No, we are not utterly lost to the fine sense of propriety of this chaste and demure age. But no matter how etiolated and sickly the thought, it regains its colour and health when it breathes the literary air. Prudery can not but relish the tang of lubricity when flavoured with the classical. Moreover, if Socrates and Montaigne speak freely of these midnight matters, why not Khalid, if he has anything new to say, any good advice to offer. But how good and how new are his views let the Reader judge.

'Tis very well to speak "of evoking the spirit before the bodily communion," but those who can boast of a deeper experience in such matters will find in Socrates' dictum, quoted by Montaigne, the very gist of reason and wisdom. Those wise ones were as far-sighted as they were far gone. And moderation, as it was justly said once, is the respiration of the philosopher. But Khalid, though always invoking the distant luminary of transcendentalism for light, can not arrogate to himself this high title. The expansion of all the faculties, and the reduction of the demands of society and the individual to the lowest term;—this, as we understand it, is the aim of transcendentalism. And Khalid's distance from the orbit of this grand luminary seems to vary with his moods; and these vary with the librations and revolutions of the moon. Hallucinated, moonstruck Khalid, your harmonising and affinitative efforts do not always succeed. That is our opinion of the matter. And the Reader, who is no respecter of editors, might quarrel with it, for all we know.

Only by standing firmly in the centre can one preserve the equilibrium of one's thoughts. But Khalid seldom speaks of equilibrium: he cares not how he fares in falling on either side of the fence, so he knows what lies behind. Howbeit, we can not conceive of how the affinity of the mind and soul with the senses, and the harmony between these and nature, are possible, if not exteriorised in that very superman whom Khalid so much dreads, and on whom he often casts a lingering glance of admiration. So there you are. We must either rise to a higher consciousness on the ruins of a lower one, of no-consciousness, rather, or go on seeming and simulating, aspiring, perspiring, and suffering, until our turn comes. Death denies no one. Meanwhile, Khalid's rhapsodies on his way back to the city, we shall heed and try to echo.

"On the high road of the universal spirit," he sings, "the world, the whole world before me, thrilling and radiating, chanting of freedom, faith, hope, health and power, and joy. Back to the City, O Khalid,— the City where Truth, and Faith, and Honesty, and Wisdom, are ever suffering, ever struggling, ever triumphing. No, it matters not with me if the spirit of intelligence and power, of freedom and culture, which

166

must go the rounds of the earth, is always dominated by the instinct of self-interest. That must be; that is inevitable. But the instinct of self-interest, O my Brother, goes with the flesh; the body-politic dies; nations rise and fall; and the eternal Spirit, the progenitor of all ideals, passes to better or worse hands, still chastening and strengthening itself in the process.

"The Orient and Occident, the male and female of the Spirit, the two great streams in which the body and soul of man are refreshed, invigorated, purified—of both I sing, in both I glory, to both I consecrate my life, for both I shall work and suffer and die. My Brothers, the most highly developed being is neither European nor Oriental; but rather he who partakes of the finer qualities of both the European genius and the Asiatic prophet.

"Give me, ye mighty nations of the West, the material comforts of life; and thou, my East, let me partake of thy spiritual heritage. Give me, America, thy hand; and thou, too, Asia. Thou land of origination, where Light and Spirit first arose, disdain not the gifts which the nations of the West bring thee; and thou land of organisation and power, where Science and Freedom reign supreme, disdain not the bounties of the sunrise.

"If the discoveries and attainments of Science will make the body of man cleaner, healthier, stronger, happier, the inexhaustible Oriental source of romantic and spiritual beauty will never cease to give the soul of man the restfulness and solacement it is ever craving. And remember, Europa, remember, Asia, that foreign culture is as necessary to the spirit of a nation as is foreign commerce to its industries. Elsewise, thy materialism, Europa, or thy spiritualism, Asia, no matter how trenchant and impregnable, no matter how deep the foundation, how broad the superstructure thereof, is vulgar, narrow, mean—is nothing, in a word, but parochialism.

"I swear that neither religious nor industrial slavery shall forever hold the world in political servitude. No; the world shall be free of the authority, absolute, blind, tyrannical, of both the Captains of Industry and the High Priests of the Temple. And who shall help to free it? Science alone can not do it; Science and Faith must do it.

"I say with thee, O Goethe, 'Light, more light!' I say with thee, O Tolstoi, 'Love, more love!' I say with thee, O Ibsen, 'Will, more will!' Light, Love, and Will—the one is as necessary as the other; the one is dangerous without the others. Light, Love, and Will, are the three eternal, vital sources of the higher, truer, purer cosmic life.

"Light, Love, and Will—with corals and pearls from their seas would I crown thee, O my City. In these streams would I baptise thy children, O my City. The mind, and the heart, and the soul of man I would baptise in this mountain lake, this high Jordan of Truth, on the flourishing and odoriferous banks of Science and Religion, under the sacred *sidr* of Reason and Faith.

"Ay, in the Lakes of Light, Love, and Will, I would baptise all mankind. For in this alone is power and glory, O my European Brothers; in this alone is faith and joy, O my Brothers of Asia.

"The Hudson, the Mississippi, the Amazon, the Thames, the Seine, the Rhine, the Danube, the Euphrates, the Ganges—every one of these great streams shall be such a Jordan in the future. In every one of them shall flow the confluent Rivers of Light, Love, and Will. In every one of them shall sail the barks of the higher aspirations and hopes of mankind.

"I come now to be baptised, O my City. I come to slake my thirst in thy Jordan. I come to launch my little skiff, to do my little work, to pay my little debt.

"In thy public-squares, O my City, I would raise monuments to Nature; in thy theatres to Poesy and Thought; in thy bazaars to Art; in thy homes, to Health; in thy temples of worship, to universal Goodwill; in thy courts, to Power and Mercy; in thy schools, to Simplicity; in thy hospitals, to Faith; and in thy public-halls to Freedom and Culture. And all these, without Light, Love, and Will, are but hollow affairs, high-sounding inanities. Without Light, Love, and Will, even thy Nabobs in the end shall curse thee; and with these, thy hammals under their burdens shall thank the heavens under which thy domes and turrets and minarets arise."

CHAPTER IV

ON THE OPEN HIGHWAY

And Khalid, packing his few worldly belongings in one of his reed baskets, gives the rest to his neighbours, leaves his booth in the pines to the swallows, and bids the monks and his friend the Hermit farewell. The joy of the wayfaring! Now, where is the jubbah, the black jubbah of coarse wool, which we bought from one of the monks? He wraps himself in it, tightens well his shoe-strings, draws his fur cap over his ears, carries his basket on his back, takes up his staff, lights his cigarette, and resolutely sets forth. The joy of the wayfaring! We accompany him on the open highway, through the rocky wilderness, down to the fertile plains, back to the city. For the account he gives us of his journey enables us to fill up the lacuna in Shakib's *Histoire Intime*, before we can have recourse to it again.

"From the cliffs 'neath which the lily blooms," he muses as he issues out of the forest and reaches the top of the mountain, "to the cliffs round which the eagles flit,—what a glorious promontory! What a contrast at this height, in this immensity, between the arid rocky haunts of the mountain bear and eagle and the spreading, vivifying verdure surrounding the haunts of man. On one side are the sylvan valleys, the thick grown ravines, the meandering rivulets, the fertile plains, the silent villages, and on the distant horizon, the sea, rising like a blue wall, standing like a stage scene; on the other, a howling immensity of boulders and prickly shrubs and plants, an arid wilderness—the haunt of the eagle, the mountain bear, and the goatherd. One step in this direction, and the entire panorama of verdant hills and valleys is lost to view. Its spreading, riant beauty is hidden behind that little cliff. I penetrate through this forest of rocks, where the brigands, I am told, lie in ambush for the caravans traveling between the valley of the Leontes and the villages of the lowland. But the brigands can not harm a dervish; my penury is my amulet—my salvation.

"The horizon, as I proceed, shrinks to a distance of ten minutes' walk across. And thus, from one circle of rocks to another, I pass through ten of them before I hear again the friendly voice of the rill, and behold again the comforting countenance of the sylvan slopes. I reach a little grove of slender poplars, under the brow of a little hill, from which issues a little limpid stream and runs gurgling through the little ferns and bushes down the heath. I swing from the road and follow this gentle rill; I can not find a better companion now. But the wanton lures me to a village far from the road on the other side of the gorge. Now, I must either retrace my steps to get to it by a long detour, or cross the gorge, descending to the deep bottom and ascending in a tangled and tortuous path to reach the main road on the breast of the opposite escarpment. Here is a short-cut which is long and weary. It lures me as the stream; it cheats me with a name. And when I am again on the open road, I look back with a sigh of relief on the dangers I had passed. I can forgive the luring rill, which still smiles to me innocently from afar, but not the deluding, ensnaring ravine. The muleteer who saw me struggling through the tangled bushes up the pathless, hopeless steep, assures me that my mother is a pious woman, else I would have slipped and gone into an hundred pieces among the rocks below. 'Her prayers have saved thee,' quoth he; 'thank thy God.'

"And walking together a pace, he points to the dizzy precipice around which I climbed and adds: 'Thou seest that rock? I hallooed to thee when thou wert creeping around it, but thou didst not hear me. From that same rock a woodman fell last week, and, falling, looked like a potted bird. He must have died before he reached the ground. His bones are scattered among those rocks. Thank thy God and thy mother. Her prayers have saved thee.'

"My dear mother, how long since I saw thee, how long since I thought of thee. My loving mother, even the rough, rude spirit of a muleteer can see in the unseen the beauty and benevolence of such devotion as thine. The words of this dusky son of the road, coming as through the trumpet of revelation to rebuke me, sink deep in my heart and draw tears from mine eyes. For art thou not ever praying for thy grievous son, and for his salvation? How many beads each night dost thou tell, how many hours dost thou prostrate thyself before the Virgin, sobbing, obsecrating, beating thy breast? And all for one, who until now, ever since he left Baalbek, did not think on thee.—Let me kiss thee, O my Brother, for thy mild rebuke. Let me kiss thee for reminding me of my mother.—No, I can not further with thee; I am waygone; I must sit me a spell beneath this pine—and weep. O Khalid, wretched that thou art, can the primitive soul of this muleteer be better than thine? Can there be a sounder intuitiveness, a healthier sense of love, a grander sympathy, beneath that striped aba, than there is within thy cloak? Wilt thou not beat thy cheeks in ignominy and shame, when a stranger thinks of thy mother, and reverently, ere thou dost? No matter how low in the spiritual circles she might be, no matter how high thou risest, her prayer and her love are always with thee. If she can not rise to thee on the ladder of reason, she can soar on the wings of affection. Yea, I prostrate myself beneath this pine, bury my forehead in its dust, thanking Allah for my mother. Oh, I am waygone, but joyous. The muleteer hath illumined thee, O Khalid.—

"There, the snow birds are passing by, flitting to the lowland. The sky is overcast; there is a lull in the wind. Hark, I hear the piping of the shepherd and the tinkling bell of the wether. Yonder is his flock; and there sits he on a rock blowing his doleful reed. I am almost slain with thirst. I go to him, and cheerfully does he milk for me. I do not think Rebekah was kinder and sweeter in Abraham's servant's eyes than was this wight in mine. 'Where dost thou sleep?' I ask, 'Under this rock,' he replies. And he shows me into the cave beneath it, which is furnished with a goat-skin, a masnad, and a little altar for the picture of the Virgin. Before this picture is an oil lamp, ever burning, I am told. 'And this altar,' quoth the shepherd, 'was my mother's. When she died she bequeathed it to me. I carry it with me in the wilderness, and keep the oil burning in her memory.' Saying which he took to weeping. Even the shepherd, O Khalid, is sent to rebuke thee. I thank him, and resume my march.

"At eventide, descending from one hilltop to another, I reach a village of no mean size. It occupies a broad deep steep, in which the walnut and poplar relieve the monotony of the mulberries. I hate the mulberry, which is so suggestive of worms; and I hate worms, and though they be of the silk-making kind. I hate them the more, because the Lebanon peasant seems to live for the silk-worms, which he tends and cultivates better than he does his children.

"When I stood on the top of the steep, the village glittering with a thousand lights lay beneath like a strip of the sidereal sky. It made me feel I was above the clouds, even above the stars. The gabled houses overtopping each other, spreading in clusters and half-circles, form here an aigrette, as it were, on the sylvan head of the mountain, there a necklace on its breast, below a cestus brilliant with an hundred lights. I descend into the village and stop before the first house I reach. The door is wide open; and the little girl who sees me enter runs in fright to tell her mother. Straightway, the woman and her son, a comely and lusty youth, come out in a where-is-the-brigand manner, and, as they see me, stand abashed, amazed. The young man who wore a robe-de-chambre and Turkish slippers worked in gold, returns my salaam courteously and invites me up to the divan. There is a spark of intelligence in his eyes, and an alien affectation in his speech. I foresaw that he had been in America. He does not ask me the conventional questions about my religious persuasion; but after his inquiries of whence and whither, he offers me an Egyptian cigarette, and goes in to order the coffee. It did not occur to him that I was his guest for the night.—

"Ah me, I no longer know how to recline on a cushion, and a rug under my feet seems like a sheet of ice. But with my dust and mud I seem like Diogenes trampling upon Plato's pride. I survey the hall, which breathes of rural culture and well-being, and in which is more evidence of what I foresaw. On the wall hung various photographs and oil prints, among which I noticed those of the King and Queen of England, that of Theodore Roosevelt, a framed cartoon by an American artist, an autographed copy of an English Duke's, and a large photograph of a banquet of one of the political Clubs of New York. On the table were a few Arabic magazines, a post-card album, and a gramophone! Yes, mine host was more than once in the United States. And knowing that I, too, had been there, he is anxious to display somewhat of his broken English. His father, he tells me, speaks English even as good as he does, having been a dragoman for forty years.

"After supper, he orders me a narghilah, and winds for my entertainment that horrible instrument of torture." Khalid did not seem to mind it; but he was anxious about the sacred peace of the hills, sleeping in the bosom of night. My Name is Billy Muggins, I Wish I Had a Pal Like You, Tickle Me, Timothy, and such like ragtime horrors come all the way from America to violate the antique grandeur and beauty of the Lebanon hills. That is what worried Khalid. And he excuses himself, saying, "I am waygone from the day's wayfaring." The instrument of torture is stopped, therefore, and he is shown into a room where a mattress is spread for him on the floor.

"In the morning," he continues, "mine host accompanies me through the populous village, which is noted for its industries. Of all the Lebanon towns, this is, indeed, the busiest; its looms, its potteries, and its bell foundries, are never idle. And the people cultivate little of the silk worm; they are mostly artisans. American cotton they spin, and dye, and weave into substantial cloth; Belgian iron they melt and cast into bells; and from their native soil they dig the clay which they mould into earthenware. The tintinnabulations of the loom can be heard in other parts of the Lebanons; but no where else can the vintner buy a dolium for his vine, or the housewife, a pipkin for her oil, or the priest, a bell for his church. The sound of these foundries' anvils, translated into a wild, thrilling, far-reaching music, can be heard in every belfry and bell-cote of Syria.

"We descend to the potteries below, not on the carriage road which serpentines through the village, and which is its only street, but sheer down a steep path, between the noise of the loom and spinning wheel and the stench of the dyeing establishments. And here is the real potter and his clay, not the symbol thereof. And here is the pottery which is illustrated in the Bible. For in the world to-day, if we except the un-glazed tinajas of the Pueblo Indians, nothing, above ground at least, can be more ancient and primitive. Such a pitcher, I muse, did Rebek-ah carry to the well; with such a Jar on her shoulder did Hagar wander in the wilderness; and in such vessels did the widow, by Elijah's mira-cle, multiply her jug of oil.

"The one silk-reeling factory of the village, I did not care to visit; for truly I can not tolerate the smell of asphyxiated larvas and boiling cocoons. 'But the proprietor,' quoth mine host, 'is very honourable, and of a fine wit.' As honourable as a sweater can be, I thought. No, no; these manufacturers are all of a piece. I know personally one of them, who is a Scrooge, and of the vilest. I watched him one day buy-ing cocoons from the peasants. He does not trust any of his employees at the scales; they do not know how to press their hand over the weights in the pan. Ay, that little pressure of his chubby hand on the weights makes a difference in his favour of more than ten per cent. of what he buys. That little pressure of his hand is five or six piasters out of the peasant's pocket, who, with five or six piasters, remember, can satisfy his hunger on bread and olives and pulverised thyme, for five or six days. So, we visit not the cocoon-man, about whom the priest of his private chapel—he prays at home like the Lebanon Amirs of old, this khawaja—tells me many edifying things. Of these, I give out the most curious and least injurious. As the sheikh (squire) of the town, he is generous; as the operator of a silk-reeling factory, he is grasping, niggardly, mean. For, to misgovern well, one must open his purse as often as he forces the purses of others. He was passing by in his car-riage this great khawaja, when we were coming out of the pottery. And of a truth, his paunch and double chin and ruddy cheeks seemed to illustrate what the priest told me about his usurious propensities.

"What a contrast between him and the swarthy, leathery, hungry-looking potters. I can not think that Nature has aught to do with these naked inequalities. I can not believe that, to produce one roseate complexion, she must etiolate a thousand. I can not see how, in drinking from the same gushing spring, and breathing the same mountain air, and basking in the same ardent sun, the khawaja gets a double chin and the peasant a double curse. But his collops and his ruddiness are due to the fact that he misgoverns as well as his Pasha and his Sultan. He battens, even like a Tammany chief, on political jobbery, on extortion, on usury. His tree is better manured, so to speak; manured by the widows and tended by the orphans of his little kingdom. In a word, this great khawaja is what I call a political coprophagist. Hence, his suspicious growth, his lustre and lustiness.

"But he is not the only example in the village of this superabundance of health; the priests are many more. For I must not fail to mention that, in addition to its potteries and founderies, the town is blessed with a dozen churches. Every family, a sort of tribe, has its church and priests; and consequently, its feuds with all the others. It is a marvel how the people, in the lethal soot and smoke of strife and dissension, can work and produce anything. Farewell, ye swarthy people! Farewell, O village of bells and potteries! Were it not for the khawaja who misgoverns thee, and the priests who sow their iniquity in thee, thou shouldst have been an ideal town. I look back, as I descend into the wadi, and behold, thou art as beautiful in the day as thou art in the night. Thy pink gables under a December sky seem not as garish as they do in summer. And the sylvan slopes, clustered with thy white-stone homes, peeping here through the mulberries, standing there under the walnuts and poplars, rising yonder in a group like a mottled pyramid, this most picturesque slope, whereon thou art ever beating the anvil, turning the wheel, throwing the shuttle, moulding the clay, and weltering withal in the mud of strife and dissension, this beautiful slope seems, nevertheless, from this distance, like an altar raised to Nature. I look not upon thee more; farewell.

"I descend in the wadi to the River Lykos of the ancients; and crossing the stone-bridge, an hour's ascent brings me to one of the villages of Kisrawan. On the grey horizon yonder, is the limed bronze Statue of Mary the Virgin, rising on its sable pedestal, and looking, from this distance, like a candle in a bronze candle-stick. That Statue, fifty years hence, the people of the Lebanons will rebaptise as the

Statue of Liberty. Masonry, even to-day, raises around it her mace. But whether these sacred mountains will be happier and more prosperous under its régime, I can not say. The Masons and the Patriarch of the Maronites are certainly more certain. Only this I know, that between the devil and the deep sea, Mary the Virgin shall hold her own. For though the name be changed, and the alm-box thrown into the sea, she shall ever be worshipped by the people. The Statue of the Holy Virgin of Liberty it will be called, and the Jesuits and priests can go a-begging. Meanwhile, the Patriarch will issue his allocutions, and the Jesuits, their pamphlets, against rationalism, atheism, masonry, and other supposed enemies of their Blessed Virgin, and point them out as enemies of Abd'ul-Hamid. 'Tis curious how the Sultan of the Ottomans can serve the cause of the Virgin!

"I visit the Statue for the love of my mother, and mounting to the top of the pedestal, I look up and behold my mother before me. The spectre of her, standing before the monument, looks down upon me, reproachfully, piteously, affectionately. I sit down at the feet of the Virgin Mary and bury my face in my hands and weep. I love what thou lovest, O my mother, but I can see no more what thou seest. For thy love, O my mother, these kisses and tears. For thy love, I stand here like a child, and look up to this inanimate figure as I did when I was an acolyte. My intellect, O my mother, I would drown in my tears, and thy faith I would stifle with my kisses. Only thus is reconciliation possible.

"Leaving this throne of modern mythology, I cross many wadis, descend and ascend many hills, pass through many villages, until I reach, at Ghina and Masshnaka, the tomb of the mythology of the ancients. At Ghina are ruins and monuments, of which Time has spared enough to engage the interest of archæologists. Let the Pères Jesuit, Bourquenoud and Roz, make boast of their discoveries and scholarship; I can only boast of the fact that the ceremonialisms of worship are the same to-day as they were in the days of my Phœnician ancestors. Which, indeed, speaks well for THEM. This tablet, representing an armed figure and a bear, commemorates, it is said, the death of Tammuz. And the figure of the weeping woman near it is probably that of Ashtaroth. Other figures there are; but nothing short of the scholarship of Bourquenoud and Roz can unveil their marble mystery.

"At Masshnaka, overlooking the River Adonis, are ruins of an ancient temple in which can still be seen a few Corinthian columns. This, too, we are told, was consecrated to Tammuz; and in this valley the women of Byblus bemoaned every year the fate of their god. Isis and

Osiris, Tammuz and Ashtaroth, Venus and Adonis,—these, I believe, are one and the same. Their myth borrowed from the Phœnicians, the Egyptians, and the Romans, from either of the two. But the Venus of Rome is cheerful, joyous, that of the Phœnicians is sad and sorrowful. Even mythology triumphs in its evolution.

"Here, where my forebears deliquesced in sensuality, devotion, and grief, where the ardency of the women of Byblus flamed on the altar of Tammuz, on this knoll, whose trees and herbiage are fed perchance with their dust, I build my *athafa* (little kitchen), Arab-like, and cook my noonday meal. On the three stones, forming two right angles, I place my skillet, kindle under it a fire, pour into it a little sweet oil, and fry the few eggs I purchased in the village. I abominate the idea of frying eggs in water as the Americans do.[1] I had as lief fry them in vinegar or syrup, where neither olive oil nor goat-butter is obtainable. But to fry eggs in water? O the barbarity of it! Why not, my friend, take them boiled and drink a little hot water after them? This savours of originality, at least, and is just as insipid, if not more. Withal, they who boil cabbage, and heap it in a plate over a slice of corn-beef, and call it a dish, can break a few boiled eggs in a cup of hot water and call them fried. Be this as it may. The Americans will be solesistically simple even in their kitchen.

"Now, my skillet of eggs being ready, I draw out of my basket a cake of cheese, a few olives, an onion, and three paper-like loaves, rather leaves, of bread, and fall to. With what relish, I need not say. But let it be recorded here, that under the karob tree, on the bank of the River Adonis, in the shadow of the great wall surrounding the ruins of the temple of Tammuz, I Khalid, in the thirty-fourth year of the reign of Abd'ul-Hamid, gave a banquet to the gods—who, however, were content in being present and applauding the devouring skill of the peptic host and toast-master. Even serene Majesty at Yieldiz would give away, I think, an hundred of its sealed dishes for such a skillet of eggs in such an enchanted scene. But for it, alas! such wild and simple joy is a sealed book. Poor Serene Majesty! Now, having gone through the fruit course—and is not the olive a fruit?—I fill my jug at the River to

---

[1] Khalid would speak here of poached eggs, we believe. And the Americans, to be fair, are not so totally ignorant of the art of frying. They have lard— much worse than water—in which they cook, or poach, or fry—but the change in the name does not change the taste. So, we let Khalid's stricture on fried eggs and boiled cabbage stand.—Editor.

make my coffee. And here I ask, In what Hotel Cecil or Waldorf or Savoy, or in what Arab tent in the desert, can one get a better cup of coffee than this, which Khalid makes for himself? The gods be praised, before and after. Ay, even in washing my pots and dishes I praise the good gods.

"And having done this, I light my cigarette, lug my basket on my back, and again set forth. In three hours, on my way to Byblus, I reach a hamlet situated in a deep narrow wadi, closed on all sides by huge mountain walls. The most sequestered, the most dreary place, I have yet seen. Here, though unwilling, the dusk of the December day having set in, I lay down the staff of wayfare. And as I enter the little village, I am greeted by the bleat of sheep and the low of the kine. The first villager I meet is an aged woman, who stands in her door before which is a pomegranate tree, telling her beads. She returns my salaam graciously, and invites me, saying, 'Be kind to tarry overnight.' But can one be kinder than such an hostess? Seeing that I laid down my burden, she calls to her daughter to light the seraj (naphtha lamp) and bring some water for the stranger. 'Methinks thou wouldst wash thy feet,' quoth she. Indeed, that is as essential and refreshing, after a day's walk, as washing one's face. I sit me down, therefore, under the pomegranate, take off my shoes and stockings, and the little girl, a winsome, dark-eyed, quick-witted lass, pours to me from the pitcher. I try to take it from her; but she would not, she said, be deprived of the pleasure of serving the stranger. Having done, I put on my stockings, and, leaving my shoes and basket near the door, enter a beit (one-room house) meagrely but neatly furnished. The usual straw mats are spread on the winter side, behind the door; in the corner is a little linen-covered divan with trimming of beautiful hand-made lace, the work of the little girl; and nearby are a few square cushions on the floor and a crude chair. The seraj, giving out more smoke and smell than light, is placed on a little shelf attached to the central pillar of the beit. Near the door is a bench for the water jars, and in the other corner are the mattresses and quilts, and the earthen tub containing the round leaves of bread. Of these consist the furniture and provision of mine hostess.

"Her son, a youth of not more than two score years, returns from his day's labour a while after I had arrived. And as he stands in the door, his pick-axe and spade on his shoulder, his sister runs to meet him, and whispers somewhat about the stranger. Sitting on the threshold, he takes off his spats of cloth and his clouted shoes, while she gets the pitcher of water. After having washed, he enters, salaams graciously, and squats on the floor. The mother then brings a wicker tray on which is set the supper, consisting of only bread and olives. 'Thou wilt overlook our penury,' she falters out; 'here be all we have.' In truth, my hostess is of the poorest of the Lebanon peasants; even her sweet-oil pipkin and her jars of lentils and beans, are empty. She lays the tray before her son and invites me to partake of the repast. I go to my basket, bring forth the few onions and the two cakes of cheese I had left, lay them with an apology on the tray—the mother, abashed, protests—and we sit down cross-legged in a circle to supper. When we rise, the little girl lights a little fire, and they enjoy the cup of coffee I make for them. And the mother, in taking hers, tells me naïvely, and with a sigh, that it is five years now since she had had a cup of coffee. Indeed, she had seen better days. And 'tis sorrow, forestalling Time, which furrows her cheeks and robs her black eyes of their lustre and spark.

"She had once cattle, and a beit of her own, and rugs, too, and jars full of provision. But now she is a tenant. And her husband, ever since he emigrated to America, did not send a single piaster or even write a letter. From necessity she becomes a prey of usurers; for those Lebanon Moths, of which we saw a specimen in the village of bells and potteries, fall mostly in the wardrobe of women. They are locusts rather, who visit only the wheat fields of the poor. Her home was mortgaged to one such, and failing to meet her obligation, the mortgage is closed and he takes possession. Soon after she is evicted, her son, the first-born, a youth of much promise, dies.

"'He could read and write, my son,' quoth she, sobbing; 'of a sharp wit he was, and very assiduous in his studies. Once he accompanied the priest of the village on a visit to the Patriarch, and read there a eulogium of his own composition, for which he received a silver medal. The Patriarch then sent him to a Seminary; he was to become a priest, my son. He wrote a beautiful hand—both Arabic and French; he was of a fine wit, sharp, quick, brilliant. Ah, me, but those who are of such minds never live!'

"She then tells me how they lost their last head of cattle. An excellent sheep it was; which one night they forgot outside; and the wolf, visiting the village, sees it tied to the mulberry, howls for joy, and carries it off. And thus Death robs the poor woman of her son; America, of her husband; the Shylock of the village, of her home; and the wolf, of her last head of cattle. And this were enough to age even a Spartan woman. Late in the evening, after she had related at length of her sorrows, three mattresses—all she had—are laid on the straw mat near each other, and the little girl had to sleep with her mother.

"Early in the morning I bid them farewell, and pass on my way to Amsheet, where Henriette Renan, the sister of Ernest, is buried. An hour's walk, and the incarcerated wadi and its folk lie concealed behind. I breathe again the open air of the mountain expanse; I behold again the emerald stretch of water on the horizon, where the baggalas and saics, from this distance, seem like doves basking in the morning sun. I cross the last rill, mount the last hilltop on my journey, and lo, at the foot of the gently sloping heath are the orchards and palms of Amsheet. Further below is Jbail, or ancient Byblus, looking like a clutter of cliffs on the shore. Farewell to the mountain heights, and the arid wilderness! Welcome the fertile plains, and hopeful strands. In half an hour I reach the immense building—the first or the last of the village, according to your direction—which, from the top of the hill, I thought to be a fortress. A huge structure this, still a-building, and of an architecture altogether different from the conventional Lebanon type. No plain square affair, with three pointed arches in the façade, and a gable of pink tiles; but here are quoins, oriels, embrasures, segmental arches, and other luxuries of architecture. Out of place in these wilds, altogether out of place. Hard by are two primitive flat-roofed beits, standing grimly there as a rebuke to the extravagant tendencies of the age. I go there in the hope of buying some cheese and eggs, and behold a lady of severe beauty smoking a narghilah and giving orders to a servant. She returns my salaam seated in her chair, and tells me in an injured air, after I had made known to her my desire, that eggs and cheese are sold in the stores.

"'You may come in for breakfast,' she adds; and clapping for the servant, orders him to lay the table for me. I enter the beit, which is partitioned into a kitchen, a dining-room, and a parlour. On the table is spread the usual breakfast of a Lebanonese of affluence: namely, cheese, honey, fig-jam, and green olives. The servant, who is curious to know my name, my religion, my destination, and so forth, tells me afterwards that Madame is the wife of the kaiemkam, and the castle, which is building, is their new home.

"Coming out, I thank Madame, and ask her about the grave of Renan's sister. She pauses amazed, blows her narghilah smoke in my face, surveys me from top to toe, and puts to me those same questions with which I was tormented by her servant. Indeed, I had answered ten of hers, before I got this answer to mine: 'The sister of whom, thou sayst? That Frenchman who came here in the sixties for antiquities? Yes; his sister died and was buried here, but no Christian remembers her for good. She must have been a bad one like her brother, who was an infidel, they say, and did not know or fear God.—What wouldst thou see there? Art like the idiot Franje (Europeans) who come here and carry away from around the grave some stones and dust? Go thou with him—(this to the servant) and show him the vault of the Toubei-yahs, where she was buried.' This, in a supercilious air, while she drew from the narghilah the smoke, which I could not relish.

"We come to the cemetery near the church in the centre of the town. The vault where Henriette was laid, a plain, plastered square cell, is not far from an oak which in the morning envelopes it with its shadow; and directly across are palms, whose shades at sundown, make a vain effort to kiss its dust. No grass, no flowers around; but much of the dust of neglect. And of this I take up a handful, like 'the idiot Franje'; but instead of carrying it away, I press therein my lips and leave my planted kisses near the vault.—When the mothers and the sisters of these sacred hills, O Henriette, can see the flowers of these kisses in thy dust, when they can appreciate the sacred purity of thy spirit and devotion, what mothers then we shall have, and what sisters!

"I pass through the village descending on the carriage road to Jbail, or Byblus. In these diggings the shrewd antiquary digs for those precious tear-bottles of my ancestors. And everywhere one turns are tombs in which the archæologist finds somewhat to noise abroad. His, indeed, is a scholarship which is essentially necrophagous. For consider, what would become of it, if a necropolis, for instance, did not yield somewhat of nourishment,—a limb, a torso, a palimpsest, or even an earthen lamp, a potsherd, or a coin? I rail not at these scholarly grave-diggers because I can not interest myself in their work; that were unwise and unfair. But truly, I abominate this business of 'cashing,' as it were, the ruins and remains, the ashes and dust, of our ancestors. Archæology for archæology's sake is pardonable; archæology for the sake of writing a book is intolerable; and archæology for lucre is abominable.

"At Jbail I visited the citadel, said to be of Phœnician origin, which is occupied by the mudir of the District. Entering the gate, near which is a chapel consecrated to Our Lady of that name, where litigants, when they can not prove their claims, are made to swear to them, we pass through a court between rows of Persian lilac trees, into a dark, stivy arcade on both sides of which are dark, stivy cells used as stables. Reaching the citadel proper, we mount a high stairway to the loft occupied by the mudir. This, too, is partitioned, but with cotton sheeting, into various apartments.

"The zabtie, in zouave uniform, at the door, would have me wait standing in the corridor outside; for his Excellency is at dinner. And Excellency, as affable as his zabtie, hearing the parley without, growls behind the scene and orders me gruffly to go to the court. 'This is not the place to make a complaint,' he adds. But the stranger at thy door, O gracious Excellency, complains not against any one in this world; and if he did, assure thee, he would not complain to the authorities of this world. This, or some such plainness of distemper, the zouave communicates to his superior behind the cotton sheeting, who presently comes out, his anger somewhat abated, and, taking me for a monk— my jubbah is responsible for the deception—invites me to the sitting-room in the enormous loophole of the citadel. He himself was beginning to complain of the litigants who pester him at his home, and apologise for his ill humour, when suddenly, disabused on seeing my trousers beneath my jubbah, he subjects me to the usual cross-examination. I could not refrain from thinking that, not being of the cowled gentry, he regretted having honoured me with an apology.

"But after knowing somewhat of the pilgrim stranger, especially that he had been in America, Excellency tempers the severity of his expression and evinces an agreeable curiosity. He would know many things of that distant country; especially about a Gold-Mining Syndicate, or Gold-Mining Fake, in which he invested a few hundred pounds of his fortune. And I make reply, 'I know nothing about Gold Mines and Syndicates, Excellency: but methinks if there be gold in such schemes, the grubbing, grabbing Americans would not let it come to Syria.' 'Indeed, so,' he murmurs, musing; 'indeed, so.' And clapping for the serving-zabtie—the mudirs and kaiemkams of the Lebanon make these zabties, whose duty is to serve papers, serve, too, in their homes—he orders for me a cup of coffee. And further complaining to me, he curses America for robbing the country of its men and labourers.—'We can no more find tenants for our estates, despite the fact that they get more of the income than we do. The shreek (partner), or tenant, is rightly called so. For the owner of an estate that yields fifty pounds, for instance, barely gets half of it; while the shreek, he who tills and cultivates the land, gets away with the other half, sniffing and grumbling withal. Of a truth, land-tenants are not so well-off anywhere. And if the land but yields a considerable portion, any one with a few grains of the energy of those Americans, would prefer to be a shreek than a real-estate owner.' Thus, his Excellency, complaining of the times, regretting his losses, cursing America and its

The Book of Khalid

Gold Mines; and having done, drops the narghilah tube from his hand and dozes on the divan.

"I muse meanwhile on Time, who sees in a citadel of the ancient Phœnicians, after many thousand years, that same propensity for gold, that same instinct for trade. The Phœnicians worked gold mines in Thrace, and the Syrians, their descendants, are working gold mines in America. But are we as daring, as independent, as honest? I am not certain, however, if those Phœnicians had anything to do with bubbles. My friend Sanchuniathon writes nothing on the subject. History records not a single instance of a gold-mine bubble in Thrace, or a silver ditto in Africa. Apart from this, have we, the descendants of those honest Phœnicians, any of their inventive skill and bold initiative? They taught other nations the art of ship-building; we can not as much as learn from other nations the art of building a gig. They transmitted to the people of the West a knowledge of mathematics, weights, and measures; we can not as much as weigh or measure the little good Europe is transmitting to us. They always fought bravely against their conquerors, always gave evidence of their love of independence; and we dare not raise a finger or whisper a word against the red Tyrant by whom we are degraded and enslaved. We are content in paying tribute to a criminal Government for pressing upon our necks the yoke and fettering hopelessly our minds and souls—and my brave Phœnicians, ah, how bravely they thought and fought. What daring deeds they accomplished! what mysteries of art and science they unveiled!

"On these shores they hammered at the door of invention, and, entering, showed the world how glass is made; how colours are extracted from pigments; how to measure, and count, and communicate human thought. The swarthy sons of the eternal billows, how shy they were of the mountains, how enamoured of the sea! For the mountains, it was truly said, divide nations, and the seas connect them. And my Phœnicians, mind you, were for connection always. Everywhere, they lived on the shores, and ever were they ready to set sail.

"In this mammoth loophole, measuring about ten yards in length,— this the thickness of the wall—I muse of another people skilled in the art of building. But between the helots who built the pyramids and the freemen who built this massive citadel, what a contrast! The Egyptian mind could only invent fables; the Phœnician was the vehicle of commerce and the useful arts. The Egyptians would protect their dead from the tyranny of Time; the Phœnicians would protect themselves, the living, from the invading enemy: those based their lives on the vagaries of the future; these built it on the solid rock of the present...."

But we have had enough of Khalid's gush about the Phœnicians, and we confess we can not further walk with him on this journey. So, we leave his Excellency the mudir snoring on the divan, groaning under the incubus of the Gold Mine Fake, bemoaning his losses in America; pass the zabtie in zouave uniform, who is likewise snoring on the door-step; and, hurrying down the stairway and out through the stivy arcade, we say farewell to Our Lady of the Gate, and get into one of the carriages which ply the shore between Junie and Jbail. We reach Junie about sundown, and Allah be praised! Even this toy of a train brings us, in thirty minutes, to Beirut.

CHAPTER V

UNION AND PROGRESS

Had not Khalid in his retirement touched his philosophic raptures with a little local colouring, had he not given an account of his tramping tour in the Lebanons, the hiatus in Shakib's *Histoire Intime* could not have been bridged. It would have remained, much to our vexation and sorrow, somewhat like the ravine in which Khalid almost lost his life. But now we return, after a year's absence, to our Scribe, who at this time in Baalbek is soldering and hammering out rhymes in praise of Niazi and Enver, Abd'ul-Hamid and the Dastur (Constitution).

"When Khalid, after his cousin's marriage, suddenly disappeared from Baalbek," writes he, "I felt that something had struck me violently on the brow, and everything around me was dark. I could not withhold my tears: I wept like a child, even like Khalid's mother. I remember he would often speak of suicide in those days. And on the evening of that fatal day we spent many hours discussing the question. 'Why is not one free to kill himself,' he finally asked, 'if one is free to become a Jesuit?' But I did not believe he was in earnest. Alas, he was. For on the morning of the following day, I went up to his tent on the roof and found nothing of Khalid's belongings but a pamphlet on the subject, 'Is Suicide a Sin?' and right under the title the monosyllable LA (no) and his signature. The frightfulness of his intention stood like a spectre before me. I clapped one hand upon the other and wept. I made inquiries in the city and in the neighbouring places, but to no purpose. Oh, that dreadful, dismal day, when everywhither I went something seemed to whisper in my heart, 'Khalid is no more.' It was the first time in my life that I felt the pangs of separation, the sting of death and sorrow. The days and months passed, heartlessly confirming my conjecture, my belief.

"One evening, when the last glimmer of hope passed away, I sat down and composed a threnody in his memory. And I sent it to one of the newspapers of Beirut, in the hope that Khalid, if he still lived, might chance to see it. It was published and quoted by other journals here and in Egypt, who, in their eulogies, spoke of Khalid as the young Baalbekian philosopher and poet. One of these newspapers, whose editor is a dear friend of mine, and of comely ancient virtue, did not mention, from a subtle sense of tender regard for my feelings, the fact that Khalid committed suicide. 'He died,' the Notice said, 'of a sudden and violent defluxion of rheums,[1] which baffled the physician and resisted his skill and physic.' Another journal, whose editor's religion is of the Jesuitical pattern, spoke of him as a miserable God-abandoned wretch who was not entitled to the right of Christian burial; and fulminated at its contemporaries for eulogising the youthful infidel and moaning his death, thus spreading and justifying his evil example.

"And so, the days passed, and the months, and Khalid was still dead. In the summer of this year, when the Constitution was proclaimed, and the country was rioting in the saturnalia of Freedom and Equality, my sorrow was keener, deeper than ever. Not I alone, but the cities and the deserts of Syria and Arabia, missed my loving friend. How gloriously he would have filled the tribune of the day, I sadly mused.... O Khalid, I can never forgive this crime of thine against the sacred rites of Friendship. Such heartlessness, such inexorable cruelty, I have never before observed in thee. No matter how much thou hast profited by thy retirement to the mountains, no matter how much thy solitude hath given thee of health and power and wisdom, thy cruel remissness can not altogether be drowned in my rejoicing. To forget those who love thee above everything else in the world,—thy mother, thy cousin, thine affectionate brother—"

And our Scribe goes on, blubbering like a good Syrian his complaint and joy, gushing now in verse, now in what is worse, in rhymed prose, until he reaches the point which is to us of import. Khalid, in the winter of the first year of the Dastur (Constitution) writes to him many

---

[1] In some parts of Syria, as in Arabia, almost every ill and affection is attributed to the rheums, or called so. Rheumatism, for instance, is explained by the Arab quack as a defluxion of rheums, failing to discharge through the upper orifices, progress downward, and settling in the muscles and joints, produce the affection. And might there not be more truth in that than the diagnosis of him who is a Membre de la Faculté de Medicine de France?— Editor.

letters from Beirut, of which he gives us not less than fifty! And of these, the following, if not the most piquant and interesting, are the most indispensable to our History.

Letter I (As numbered in the Original)

My loving Brother Shakib:

To whom, if not to you, before all, should I send the first word of peace, the first sign of the resurrection? To my mother? To my cousin Najma? Well, yes. But if I write to them, my letters will be brought to you to be read and answered. So I write now direct, hoping that you will convey to them these tidings of joy. 'Tis more than a year now since I slinked out of Baalbek, leaving you in the dark about me. Surely, I deserve the chastisement of your bitterest thoughts. But what could I do? Such is the rigour of the sort of life I lived that any communication with the outside world, especially with friends and lovers, would have marred it. So, I had to be silent as the pines in which I put up, until I became as healthy as the swallows, my companions there. When we meet, I shall recount to you the many curious incidents of my solitude and my journey in the sacred hills of Lebanon. To these auspicious mountains, my Brother, I am indebted for the health and joy and wisdom that are now mine; and yours, too, if you consider.

Strange, is it not, that throughout my journey, and I have passed in many villages, nothing heard I of this great political upheaval in the Empire. Probably the people of the Lebanons cherish not the Revolution. There is so much in common, I find, between them and the Celtic races, who always in such instances have been more royalists than the king. And I think Mt. Lebanon is going to be the Vendée of the Turks.

I have been in Beirut but a few days. And truly, I could not believe my eyes, when in the Place de la Concorde (I hope the Turks are not going to follow in the steps of the French Revolutionists in all things), I could not believe my eyes, when, in this muddy Square, on the holy Stump of Liberty, I beheld my old friend the Spouter dispensing to the turbaned and tarboushed crowd, among which were cameleers and muleteers with their camels and mules, of the blessing of that triple political abraca-dabra of the France of more than a century passed. Liberty, Fraternity, Equality!—it's a shame that the show has been running for six months now and I did not know it. I begin by applauding the Spouters of Concord Square, the donkey that I am. But how, with my cursed impulsiveness, can I always keep on the sidewalk of reason? I, who have suckled of the milk of freedom and broke the bottle, too, on my Nurse's head, I am not to blame, if from sheer joy, I cheer those who are crowning her on a dung-hill with wreaths of stable straw. It's better, billah, than breaking the bottle on her head, is it not? And so, let the Spouters spout. And let the sheikh and the priest and the rabbi embrace on that very Stump and make up. Live the Era of Concord and peace and love! Live the Dastur! Hurrah for the Union and Progress Heroes! Come down to Beirut and do some shouting with your fellow citizens.

Letter V

No; I do not approve of your idea of associating with that young Mohammedan editor. You know what is said about the tiger and its spots. Besides, I had another offer from a Christian oldtimer; but you might as well ask me to become a Jesuit as to became a Journalist. I wrote last week a political article, in which I criticised Majesty's Address to the Parliament, and mauled those oleaginous, palavering, mealy-mouthed Representatives, who would not dare point out the lies in it. They hear the Chief Clerk read of "the efforts made by the Government during the past thirty years in the interest of education," and applaud; while at the Royal Banquet they jostle and hustle each other to kiss the edge of Majesty's frock-coat. The abject slaves!

The article was much quoted and commented upon; I was flouted by many, defended by a few, these asked: "Was the Government of Abd'ul-Hamid, committing all its crimes in the interest of education, were we being trained by the Censorship and the Bosphorus Terror for the Dastur?" "But the person of Majesty, the sacredness of the Khalifate," cried the others. And a certain one, in the course of his attack, denies the existence of Khalid, who died, said he, a year ago. And what matters it if a dead man can stir a whole city and blow into the nostrils of its walking spectres a breath of life?

I spoke last night in one of the music halls and gave the Mohammedans a piece of my mind. The poor Christians!—they feared the Government in the old régime; they cower before the boatmen in this. For the boatmen of Beirut have not lost their prestige and power. They are a sort of commune and are yet supreme. Yes, they are always riding the whirlwind and directing the storm. And who dares say a word against them? Every one of them, in his swagger and bluster, is an Abd'ul-Hamid. Alas, everything is yet in a chaotic state. The boatman's shriek can silence the Press and make the Spouters tremble.

I am to lecture in the Public Hall of one of the Colleges here on the "Moral Revolution." Believe me, I would not utter a word or write a line if I were not impelled to it. And just as soon as some one comes to the front to champion in this land spiritual and moral freedom, I'll go "way back and sit down." For why should I then give myself the trouble? And the applause of the multitude, mind you, brings me not a single olive.

Letter XXII

I had made up my mind to go to Cairo, and I was coming up to say farewell to you and mother. For I like not Beirut, where one in winter must go about in top-boots, and in a dust-coat in summer. I wonder what Rousseau, who called Paris the city of mud, would have said of this? Besides, a city ruled by boatmen is not a city for gentlemen to live in. So, I made up my mind to get out of it, and quickly. But yesterday morning, before I had taken my coffee, some one knocked at my door. I open, and lo, a policeman in shabby uniform, makes inquiry about Khalid. What have I done, I thought, to deserve this visit? And before I had time to imagine the worst, he delivers a card from the Deputy to Syria of the Union and Progress Society of Salonique. I am desired in this to come at my earliest convenience to the Club to meet this gentleman. There, I am received by an Army Officer and a certain Ahmed Bey. And after the coffee and the formalities of civility are over, I am asked to accompany them on a tour to the principal cities of upper Syria—to Damascus, Homs, Hama, and Aleppo. The young Army Officer is to speechify in Turkish, I, in Arabic, and Ahmed Bey, who is as oleaginous as a Turk could be, will take up, I think, the collection. Seeing in this a chance to spread the Idea among our people, I accept, and in a fortnight we shall be in Damascus. You must come there, for I am burning to meet and embrace you.

Letter XXV

Whom do you think I met yesterday? Why, nothing gave me greater pleasure ever since I have been here than this: I was crossing the Square on my way to the Club, when some one plucking at my jubbah angrily greets me. I look back, and behold our dear old Im-Hanna, who has just returned from New York. She stood there waving her hand wildly and rating me for not returning her salaam. "You know no one any more, O Khalid," she said plaintively; "I call to you three times and you look not, hear not. No matter, O Khalid." Thereupon, she embraces me as fondly as my mother. "And why," she inquired, "do you wear this black jubbah? Are you now a monk? Were it not for that long hair and that cap of yours, I would not have known you. Let me see, isn't that the cap I bought you in New York?" And she takes it off my head to examine it. "Yes, that's it. How good of you to keep it. Well, how are you now? Do you cough any more? Are you still crazy about books? I don't think so, for you have rosy cheeks now." And sobbing for joy, she embraces me again and again.

She is neatly dressed, wears a silk fiché, and is as alert as ever. In the afternoon, I visit her at the Hotel, and she asks me to accompany her to the Bank, where she cashes three bills of exchange for three hundred pounds each! I ask her what she is going to do with all this money, and she tells me that she is going to build a little home for her grandson and send him to the College of the Americans here.

"And is there like America in all the world?" she exclaims. "Ah, my heart for America!" And on asking her why she did not remain there: "Fear not; just as soon as I

build my house and place my son in the College I am going back to New York. What, O Khalid, will you return
with me?" She then takes some gold pieces in her hand,
and lowering her voice: "May be you need some money;
take, take these." Dear old Im-Hanna, I would not refuse
her favour, and I would not accept one such. What was I
to do? Coming through the Jewellers' bazaar I hit upon an
idea, and with the money she slipped into my pocket, I
bought a gold watch in one of the stores and charged her
to present it to her grandson. "Say it is from his brother,
your other grandson Khalid." She protests, scolds, and finally takes the watch, saying, "Well, nothing is changed
in you: still the same crazy Khalid."

To-morrow she is coming to see my room, and to cook
for me a dish of *mojadderah*! Ah, the old days in the cellar!

In the thirtieth Letter, one of considerable length, dated March, is
an exceedingly titillating divagation on the *gulma* (oustraation of animals), called forth, we are told, "by the rut of the d——d cats in the
yard." Poor Khalid can not sleep. One night he jumps out of bed and
chases them away with his skillet, saying, "Why don't I make such a
row, ye wantons?" They come again the following night, and Khalid
on the following morning moves to a Hotel which, by good or ill
chance, is adjacent to the lupanars of the city. His window opens on
another yard in which other cats, alas!—of the human species this
time—are caterwauling, harrowing the soul of him and the night. He
makes a second remove, but finds himself disturbed this time by the
rut of a certain roebuck within. Nature, O Khalid, will not be cheated,
no more than she will be abused, without retaliating soon or late. True,
you got out of many ruts heretofore; but this you can not get out of
except you go deeper into it. Your anecdotes from Ad-Damiry and
your quotations from Montaigne shall not help you. And your allu-
sions to March-cats and March-Khalids are too pitiful to be humorous.
Indeed, were not the tang of lubricity in this Letter too strong, we
would have given in full the confession it contains.

We now come to the last of this Series, in which Khalid speaks of a
certain American lady, a Mrs. Goodfree, or Gotfry, who is a votary of
Ebbas Effendi, the Pope of Babism at Heifa. Mrs. Gotfry may not be a
Babist in the strict sense of the word; but she is a votary and worship-
per of the Bab. To her the personal element in a creed is of more
importance than the ism. Hence, her pilgrimage every year to Heifa.

She comes with presents and gold; and Ebbas Effendi, who is not impervious to the influence of other gods than his own, permits her into the sanctuary, where she shares with him the light of divine revelation and returns to the States, as the Priestess of the Cult, to bless and console the Faithful. Khalid was dining with Ahmed Bey at the Grand Hotel—but here is a portion of the Letter.

By a devilish mischance she occupied the seat opposite to mine. And in this trap of Iblis was decoy enough for a poor mouse like me. It is an age since I beheld such an Oriental gem in an American setting; or such a strange Southern beauty in an exotic frame. For one would think her from the South, or further down from Mexico. Nay, of Andalusian, and consequently of Arabian, origin she must be. Her hair and her eyes are of the richest jet; her glance, voluptuous, mysterious; her complexion, neither white nor olive, but partakes of both,—a gauze-like shade of heliotrope, as it were, over a pink and straw surface, if you can imagine that; and her expression, a play between devotion and diabolism—now a question mark to love, now an exclamation to sorrow, and at times a dash between both. By what mysterious medium of romance and adventure did America produce such a beauty, I can not tell. Perhaps she, too, can not. If you saw her, O Shakib, you'd do nothing for months but dedicate odes to her eyes,—to the deep, dark infinity of their luring, devouring beauty,—which seem to drop honey and poison from every arched hair of their fulsome lashes. Withal,— another devilish mischance,—she was dressed in black and wore a white silk ruffle, like myself. And her age? Well, she can not have passed her sixth lustrum. And really, as the Novelist would say in his Novel, she looks ten years younger.... To say we were attracted to each other were presumptuous: but *I was* taken.... Near her sat a Syrian gentleman of my acquaintance, with whom she was conversing when we entered. That is the lady whose beauty, when she was sitting, I described to you: but when she got up to leave the table,—alas, and *ay me*, and all the other expressions of regret and sorrow. That such a beautiful face should be denied a corresponding beauty of figure. And what is more pitiable about her, she is lame in the right leg. Poor dear Misfortune, I wish it were in my power to add an inch of my limb to hers.

And Khalid goes on limping, drooling, alassing, to the end. After dinner he is introduced to his "poor dear Misfortune" by his Syrian friend. But being with Ahmed Bey he can not remain this evening. On the following day, however, he is invited to lunch; and on the terrace facing the sea, they pass the afternoon discussing various subjects.

Mrs. Gotfry is surprised how a Syrian of Khalid's mind can not see the beauties of Babism, or Buhaism, as it is now called, and the lofty spirituality of the Bab. But she forgives him his lack of faith, gives him her card, and invites him to her home, if he ever returns to the United States.

Now, maugre the fact that, in a postscript to this Letter, Khalid closes with these words, "And what have I to do with priests and priestesses?" we can not but harbour a suspicion that his "Union and Progress" tour is bound to have more than a political significance. By ill or good hap those words are beginning to assume a double meaning; and maugre all efforts to the contrary, the days must soon unfold the twofold tendency and result of the "Union and Progress" ideas of Khalid.

CHAPTER VI

REVOLUTIONS WITHIN AND WITHOUT

"Even Carlyle can be longwinded and short-sighted on occasions. 'Once in destroying the False,' says he, 'there was a certain inspiration.' And always there is, to be sure, my Master. For the world is not Europe, and the final decision on Who Is and What Is To Rule, was not delivered by the French Revolution. The Orient, the land of origination and prophecy, must yet solve for itself this eternal problem of the Old and New, the False and True. And whether by Revolutions, Speculations, or Constitutions, ancient Revelation will be purged and restored to its original pristine purity: the superannuated lumber that accumulated around it during centuries of apathy, fatalism, and sloth, must go: the dust and mould and cobwebs of the Temple will be swept away. Indeed, 'a war must be eternally waged on evils eternally renewed.' The genius of destruction has done its work, you say, O my esteemed Master? and there is nothing more to destroy? The gods might say this of other worlds than ours. In Europe, as in Asia, there is to be considered and remembered: if this mass of things we call humanity and civilisation were as healthy as the eternal powers would have them, the healthiest of the race would not be constantly studying and dissecting our social and political ills.

"In a certain sense, we are healthier to-day than the Europeans; but our health is that of the slave and not the master: it is of more benefit to others than it is to ourselves. We are doomed to be the drudges of neurasthenic, psychopathic, egoistic masters, if we do not open our minds to the light of science and truth. 'Every age has its Book,' says the Prophet. But every book, if it aspires to be a guide to life, must contain of the eternal truth what was in the one that preceded it. We can not afford to let aught of this die. Leave the principal original altar in the Temple, and destroy all the others. Light on that altar the torch of science, which the better mind and cleaner hand of Europe are transmitting to us, and place your foot upon its false and unspeakable divinities. The gods of wealth, of egoism, of alcohol, of fornication, we must not acknowledge; nay, we must resist unto death their malign influence and power. But alas, what are we doing to-day? Instead of looking up to the pure and lofty souls of Europe for guidance, we welter in the mud with the lowest and most degenerate. We are beginning to know and appreciate English whiskey, but not English freedom; we know the French grisettes, but not the French sages; we guzzle German beer, but of German wisdom we taste not a drop.

"O my Brothers, let us cease rejoicing in the Dastur; for at heart we know no freedom, nor truth, nor order. We elect our representatives to Parliament, but not unlike the Europeans; we borrow from France what the deeper and higher mind of France no longer believes; we imitate England in what England has long since discarded; but our Books of Revelation, which made France and Germany and England what they are, and in which is the divine essence of truth and right and freedom, we do not rightly understand. A thousand falsehoods are cluttered around the truth to conceal it from us. I call you back, O my Brothers, to the good old virtues of our ancestors. Without these the Revolution will miscarry and our Dastur will not be worth a datestone. Our ancestors,—they never bowed their proud neck to tyranny, whether represented in an autocrat or in a body of autocrats; they never betrayed their friends; they never soiled their fingers with the coin of usury; they never sacrificed their manhood to fashion; they never endangered in the cafés and lupanars their health and reason. The Mosque and the Church, notwithstanding the ignorance and bigotry they foster, are still better than lunatic asylums. And Europe can not have enough of these to-day.

"Continence, purity of heart, fidelity, simplicity, a sense of true manhood, magnanimity of spirit, a healthiness of body and mind,—these are the beautiful ancient virtues. These are the supreme truths of the Books of Revelation: in these consists the lofty spirituality of the Orient. But through what thick, obscene growths we must pass to-day, through what cactus hedges and thistle-fields we must penetrate, before we rise again to those heights.

"'There can be no Revolution without a Reformation,' says a German philosopher. And truly so. For the fetters which bind us can not be shaken off, before the conscience is emancipated. A political revolution must always be preceded by a spiritual one, that it might have some enduring effect. Otherwise, things will revert to their previous state of rottenness as sure as Allah lives. But mind you, I do not say, Cut down the hedges; mow the thistle-fields; uproot the obscene plants; no: I only ask you to go through them, and out of them, to return no more. Sell your little estate there, if you have one; sell it at any price: give it away and let the dead bury their dead. Cease to work in those thorny fields, and God and nature will do the rest.

"I am for a reformation by emigration. And quietly, peacefully, this can be done. Nor fire, nor sword bring I: only this I say: Will and do; resolve and act upon your resolution. The emigration of the mind before the revolution of the state, my Brothers. The soul must be free, and the mind, before one has a right to be a member of a free Government, before one can justly enjoy his rights and perform his duties as a subject. But a voting slave, O my Brothers, is the pitifulest spectacle under the sun. And remember that neither the Dastur, nor the Unionists, nor the Press, can give you this spiritual freedom, if you do not awake and emigrate. Come up to the highlands: here is a patrimony for each of you; here are vineyards to cultivate. Leave the thistle-fields and marshes behind; regret nothing. Come out of the superstitions of the sheikhs and ulema; of the barren mazes of the sufis; of the deadly swamps of theolougues and priests: emigrate! Every one of us should be a Niazi in this moral struggle, an Enver in this spiritual revolution. A little will-power, a little heroism, added to those virtues I have named, the solid virtues of our ancestors, and the Orient will no longer be an object of scorn and gain to commercial Europe. We shall then stand on an equal footing with the Europeans. Ay, with the legacy of science which we shall learn to invest, and with our spirituality divested of its cobwebs, and purified, we shall stand even higher than the Americans and Europeans."—

On the following day Damascus was simmering with excitement— Damascus, the stronghold of the ulema—the learned fanatics—whom Khalid has lightly pinched. But they scarcely felt it; they could not believe it. Now, the gentry of Islam, the sheikhs and ulema, would hear this lack-beard dervish, as he was called. But they disdain to stand with the rabble in the Midan or congregate with the *Mutafarnejin* (Europeanised) in the public Halls. Nowhere but at the Mosque, therefore, can they hear what this Khalid has to say. This was accordingly decided upon, and, being approved by all parties concerned,—the Mufti, the Vali, the Deputies of the Holy Society and the speaker,—a day was set for the great address at the great Mosque of Omaiyah.

Meanwhile, the blatant Officer, the wheedling Politician, and the lack-beard Dervish, are feasted by the personages and functionaries of

Damascus. The Vali, the Mufti, Abdallah Pasha,—he who owns more than two score villages and has more than five thousand braves at his beck and call,—these, and others of less standing, vie with each other in honouring the distinguished visitors. And after the banqueting, while Ahmed Bey retires to a private room with his host to discuss the political situation, Khalid, to escape the torturing curiosity of the bores and quidnuncs of the evening, goes out to the open court, and under an orange tree, around the gurgling fountain, breathes again of quietude and peace. Nay, breathes deeply of the heavy perfume of the white jasmines of his country, while musing of the scarlet salvias of a distant land.

And what if the salvia, as by a miracle, blossoms on the jasmine? What if the former stifles the latter? Indeed, one can escape boredom, but not love. One can flee the quidnuncs of the salon, but not the questioning perplexity of one's heart. A truce now to ambiguities.

'Tis high time that we give a brief account of what took place after Khalid took leave of Mrs. Gotfry. Many "devilish mischances" have since then conspired against Khalid's peace of mind. For when they were leaving Beirut, only a few minutes before the train started, Mrs. Gotfry, who was also going to Damascus, steps into the same carriage, which he and his companions occupied: mischance first. Arriving in Damascus they both stay at the same Hotel: mischance second. At table this time he occupies the seat next to hers, and once, rising simultaneously, their limbs touch: mischance third. And the last and worst, when he retires to his room, he finds that her own is in the same side-hall opposite to his. Now, who could have ordered it thus, of all the earthly powers? And who can say what so many mischances might not produce? True, a thousand thistles do not make a rose; but with destiny this logic does not hold. For every new mischance makes us forget the one preceding; and the last and worst is bound to be the harbinger of good fortune. Yes, every people, we imagine, has its aphorisms on the subject: Distress is the key of relief, says the Arabic proverb; The strait leads to the plain, says the Chinese; The darkest hour is nearest the dawn, says the English.

But we must not make any stipulations with time, or trust in aphorisms. We do not know what Mrs. Gotfry's ideas are on the subject. Nor can we say how she felt in the face of these strange coincidences. In her religious heart, might there not be some shadow of an ancient superstition, some mystical, instinctive strain, in which the preternatural is resolved? That is a question which neither our Scribe nor his Master will help us to answer. And we, having been faithful so far in the discharge of our editorial duty, can not at this juncture afford to fabricate.

We know, however, that the Priestess of Buhaism and the beardless, long-haired Dervish have many a conversation together: in the train, in the Hotel, in the parks and groves of Damascus, they tap their hearts and minds, and drink of each other's wine of thought and fancy.

"I first mistook you for a Mohammedan," she said to him once; and he assured her that she was not mistaken.

"Then, you are not a Christian?"

"I am a Christian, too."

And he relates of the Buha when he was on trial in Rhodes. "Of what religion are you," asks the Judge. "I am neither a Camel-driver nor a Carpenter," replies the Buha, alluding thereby to Mohammad and Christ. "If you ask me the same question," Khalid continues—"but I see you are uncomfortable." And he takes up the cushion which had fallen behind the divan, and places it under her arm. He then lights a cigarette and holds it up to her inquiringly. Yes? He, therefore, lights another for himself, and continues. "If you ask me the same question that was asked the Buha, I would not hesitate in saying that I am both a Camel-driver and Carpenter. I might also be a Buhaist in a certain sense. I renounce falsehood, whatsoever be the guise it assumes; and I embrace truth, wheresoever I find it. Indeed, every religion is good and true, if it serves the high purpose of its founder. And they are false, all of them, when they serve the low purpose of their high priests. Take the lowest of the Arab tribes, for instance, and you will find in their truculent spirit a strain of faith sublime, though it is only evinced at times. The Beduins, rovers and raveners, manslayers and thieves, are in their house of moe-hair the kindest hosts, the noblest and most generous of men. They receive the wayfarer, though he be an enemy, and he eats and drinks and sleeps with them under the same root, in the assurance of Allah. If a religion makes a savage so good, so kind, it has well served its purpose. As for me, I admire the grand passion in both the Camel-driver and the Carpenter: the barbaric grandeur, the magnanimity and fidelity of the Arab as well as the sublime spirituality, the divine beauty, of the Nazarene, I deeply reverence. And in one sense, the one is the complement of the other: the two combined are *my* ideal of a Divinity."

And now we descend from the chariot of the empyrean where we are riding with gods and apostles, and enter into one drawn by mortal coursers. We go out for a drive, and alight from the carriage in the poplar grove, to meander in its shades, along its streams. But digressing from one path into another, we enter unaware the eternal vista of love. There, on a boulder washed by the murmuring current, in the shade of the silver-tufted poplars, Khalid and Mrs. Gotfry sit down for a rest.

"Everything in life must always resolve itself into love," said Khalid, as he stood on the rock holding out his hand to his friend. "Love is the divine solvent. Love is the splendour of God."

Mrs. Gotfry paused at the last words. She was startled by this image. Love, the splendour of God? Why, the Bab, the Buha, is the splendour of God. Buha mean splendour. The Buha, therefore, is love. Love is the new religion. It is the old religion, the eternal religion, the only religion. How came he by this, this young Syrian? Would he rival the Buha? Rise above him? They are of kindred races—their ancestors, too, may be mine. Love the splendour of God—God the splendour of Love. Have I been all along fooling myself? Did I not know my own heart?

These, and more such, passed through Mrs. Gotfry's mind, as shuttles through a loom, while Khalid was helping her up to her seat on the boulder, which is washed by the murmuring current.

"If life were such a rock under our feet," said he, pressing his lips upon her hand, "the divine currents around it will melt it, soon or late, into love."

They light cigarettes. A fresh breeze is blowing from the city. It is following them with the perfume of its gardens. The falling leaves are whispering in the grove to the swaying boughs. The narcissus is nodding to the myrtle across the way. And the bulbuls are pouring their golden splendour of song. Khalid speaks.

"Beauty either detains, repels, or enchants. The first is purely external, linear; the second is an imitation of the first, its artistic artificial ideal, so to speak; and the third"—He is silent. His eyes, gazing into hers, take up the cue.

Mrs. Gotfry turns from him exhausted. She looks into the water.

"See the rose-beds in the stream; see the lovely pebbles dancing around them."

"I can see everything in your eyes, which are like limpid lakes shaded with weeping-willows. I can even hear bulbuls singing in your brows.—Turn not from me your eyes. They reflect the pearls of your soul and the flowers of your body, even as those crystal waters reflect the pebbles and rose-beds beneath."

"Did you not say that love is the splendour of God?"

"Yes."

"Then, why look for it in my eyes?"

"And why look for it in the heart of the heavens, in the depths of the sea—in the infinities of everything that is beautiful and terrible—in the breath of that little flower, in the song of the bulbul, in the whispers of your silken lashes, in—"

"Shut your eyes, Khalid; be more spiritual."

"With my eyes open I see but one face; with my eyes closed I see a million faces: they are all yours. And they are loving, and sweet, and kind. But I am content with one, with the carnate symbol of them, with you, and though you be cold and cruel. The divine splendour is here, and here and here—"

"Why, your ardour is exhausting."

But on their way back to the Hotel, Khalid gives her this from Swedenborg: "'Do you love me' means 'do you see the same truth that I see?'"

There is no use. Khalid is impossible.

CHAPTER VII

A DREAM OF EMPIRE

"I'm not starving for pleasure," Khalid once said to Shakib; "nor for the light free love of an exquisite caprice. Those little flowers that bloom and wither in the blush of dawn are for the little butterflies. The love that endures, give me that. And it must be of the deepest divine strain,—as deep and divine as maternal love. Man is of Eternity, not of Time; and love, the highest attribute of man, must be likewise. With me it must endure throughout all worlds and immensities; else I would not raise a finger for it. Pleasure, Shakib, is for the child within us; sexual joy, for the animal; love, for the god. That is why I say when you set your seal to the contract, be sure it is of the kind which all the gods of all the future worlds will raise to their lips in reverence."

But Khalid's child-spirit, not to say childishness, is not, as he would have us believe, a thing of the past. Nor are the animal and the god within him always agreed as to what is and what is not a love divine and eternal. In New York, to be sure, he often brushed his wings against those flowerets that "bloom and wither in the blush of dawn." And he was not a little pleased to find that the dust which gathers on the wings adds a charm to the colouring of life. But how false and trivial it was, after all. The gold dust and the dust of the road, could they withstand a drop of rain? A love dust-deep, as it were, close to the earth; too mean and pitiful to be carried by the storm over terrible abysses to glorious heights. A love, in a word, without pain, that is to say impure. In Baalbek, on the other hand, he drank deep of the pain, but not of the joy, of love. He and his cousin Najma had just lit in the shrine of Venus the candles of the altar of the Virgin, when a villainous hand that of Jesuitry, issuing from the darkness, clapped over them the snuffer and carried his Happiness off. Here was a love divine, the promised bliss of which was snatched away from him.

And now in Damascus, he feels, for the first time, the exquisite pain and joy of a love which he can not yet fathom; a love, which like the storm, is carrying him over terrible abysses to unknown heights. The bitter sting of a Nay he never felt so keenly before. The sleep-stifling torture and joy of suspense he did not fully experience until now. But if he can not sleep, he will work. He has but a few days to prepare his address. He can not be too careful of what he says, and how he says it. To speak at the great Mosque of Omaiyah is a great privilege. A word uttered there will reach the furthermost parts of the Mohammedan world. Moreover, all the ulema and all the heavy-turbaned fanatics will be there.

But he can not even work. On the table before him is a pile of newspapers from all parts of Syria and Egypt—even from India—and all simmering, as it were, with Khalid's name, and Khalidism, and Khalid scandals. He is hailed by some, assailed by others; glorified and vilified in tawdry rhyme and ponderous prose by Christians and Mohammedans alike. "Our new Muhdi," wrote an Egyptian wit (one of those pallid prosers we once met in the hasheesh dens, no doubt), "our new Muhdi has added to his hareem an American beauty with an Oriental leg."

What he meant by this only the hasheesh smokers know. "An instrument in the hands of some American speculators, who would build sky-scrapers on the ruins of our mosques," wrote another. "A lever with which England is undermining Al-Islam," cried a voice in India. "A base one in the service of some European coalition, who, under the pretext of preaching the spiritualities, is undoing the work of the Revolution. The gibbet is for ordinary traitors; for him the stake," etc., etc.

On the other hand, he is hailed as the expected one,—the true leader, the real emancipator,—"who has in him the soul of the East and the mind of the West, the builder of a great Asiatic Empire." Of course, the foolish Damascene editor who wrote this had to flee the country the following day. But Khalid's eyes lingered on that line. He read it and reread it over and over again—forward and backward, too. He juggled, so to speak, with its words.

How often people put us, though unwittingly, on the path we are seeking, he thought. How often does a chance word uttered by a stranger reveal to us our deepest aims and purposes.

Before him was ink and paper. He took up the pen. But after scrawling and scribbling for ten minutes, the sheet was filled with circles and arabesques, and the one single word Dowla (Empire).

He could not think: he could only dream. The soul of the East—
The mind of the West—the builder of a great Empire. The triumph of
the Idea, the realisation of a great dream: the rise of a great race who
has fallen on evil days; the renaissance of Arabia; the reclaiming of
her land; the resuscitation of her glory;—and why not? especially if
backed with American millions and the love of a great woman. He is
enraptured. He can neither sleep nor think: he can but dream. He puts
on his jubbah, refills his cigarette box, and walks out of his room. He
paces up and down the hall, crowning his dream with wreaths of
smoke. But the dim lights seemed to be ogling each other and smiling,
as he passed. The clocks seemed to be casting pebbles at him. The silence horrified him. He pauses before a door. He knocks—knocks
again.

The occupant of that room was not yet asleep. In fact, she, too,
could not sleep. The clock in the hall outside had just struck one, and
she was yet reading. After inquiring who it was that knocked, she puts
on a kimono and opens the door. She is surprised.

"Anything the matter with you?"

"No; but I can not sleep."

"That is amusing. And do you take me for a soporific? If you think
you can sleep here, stretch yourself on the couch and try." Saying
which, she laughed and hurried back to her bed.

"I did not come to sleep."

"What then? How lovely of you to wake me up so early.—No, no;
don't apologise. For truly, I too, could not sleep. You see, I was still
reading. Sit on the couch there and talk to me.—Of course, you may
smoke.—No, I prefer to sit in bed."

Khalid lights another cigarette and sits down. On the table before
him are some antique colour prints which Mrs. Gotfry had bought in
the Bazaar. These one can only get in Damascus. And—strange coincidence!—they represented some of the heroes of Arabia—Antar, Ali,
Saladin, Harûn ar-Rashid—done in gorgeous colouring, and in that
deliciously ludicrous angular style which is neither Arabic nor Egyptian, but a combination perhaps of both. Khalid reads the poetry under
each of them and translates it into English. Mrs. Gotfry is charmed.
Khalid is lost in thought. He lays the picture of Saladin on the table,
lights another cigarette, looks intently upon his friend, his face beam-
ing with his dream.

"Jamilah." It was the first time he called her by her first name—an
Arabic name which, as a Bahaist she had adopted. And she was neither
surprised nor displeased.

"We need another Saladin to-day,—a Saladin of the Idea, who will wage a crusade, not against Christianity or Mohammedanism, but against those Tataric usurpers who are now toadying to both."

"Whom do you mean?"

"I mean the Turks. They were given a last chance to rise; they tried and failed. They can not rise. They are demoralised; they have no stamina, no character; no inborn love for truth and art; no instinctive or acquired sense of right and justice. Whiskey and debauch and high-sounding inanities about fraternity and equality can not regenerate an Empire. The Turk must go: he will go. But out in those deserts is a race which is always young, a race that never withers; a strong, healthy, keen-eyed, quick-witted race; a fighting, fanatical race; a race that gave Europe a civilisation, that gave the world a religion; a race with a past as glorious as Rome's; and with a future, too, if we had an Ali or a Saladin. But He who made those heroes will make others like them, better, too. He may have made one already, and that one may be wandering now in the desert. Now think what can be done in Arabia, think what the Arabs can accomplish, if American arms and an up-to-date Korân are spread broadcast among them. With my words and your love and influence, with our powers united, we can build an Arab Empire, we can resuscitate the Arab Empire of the past. Abd'ul-Wahhab, you know, is the Luther of Arabia; and Wahhabism is not dead. It is only slumbering in Nejd. We will wake it; arm it; infuse into it the living spirit of the Idea. We will begin by building a plant for the manufacture of arms on the shore of the Euphrates, and a University in Yaman. The Turk must go—at least out of Arabia. And the Turk in Europe, Europe will look after. No; the Arab will never be virtually conquered. Nominally, maybe. And I doubt if any of the European Powers can do it. Why? Chiefly because Arabia has a Prophet. She produced one and she will produce more. Cannons can destroy Empires; but only the living voice, the inspired voice can build them."

Mrs. Gotfry is silent. In Khalid's vagaries is a big idea, which she can not wholly grasp. And she is moreover devoted to another cause— the light of the world—the splendour of God—Buhaism. But why not spread it in Arabia as in America? She will talk to Ebbas Effendi about Khalid. He is young, eloquent, rising to power. And with her love, and influence superadded, what might he not do? what might he not accomplish? These ideas flashed through her mind, while Khalid was pacing up and down the room, which was already filled with smoke. She is absorbed in thought. Khalid comes near her bed, bends over her, and buries his face in her wealth of black hair.

Mrs. Gotfry is startled as from a dream.

"I can not see all that you see."

"Then you do not love me."

"Why do you say that? Here, now go sit down. Oh, I am suffocating. The smoke is so thick in the room I can scarcely see you. And it is so late.—No, no. Give me time to think on the subject. Now, come."

And Mrs. Gotfry opens the door and the window to let out Khalid and his smoke.

"Go, Khalid, and try to sleep. And if you can not sleep, try to write. And if you can not write, read. And if you can neither read nor write nor sleep, why, then, put on your shoes and go out for a walk. Good night. There. Good night. But don't forget, we must visit Sheikh Taleb to-morrow."

The astute Mrs. Gotfry might have added, And if you do not feel like walking, take a dip in the River Barada. But in her words, to be sure, were a douche cold enough for Khalid. Now, to be just and comprehensive in our History we must record here that she, too, did not, and could not sleep that night. The thought that Khalid would make a good apostle of Buhaism and incidentally a good companion, insinuated itself between the lines on every page of the book she was trying to read.

On the following day they visit Sheikh Taleb, who is introduced to us by Shakib in these words:

"A Muslem, like Socrates, who educates not by lesson, but by going about his business. He seldom deigns to write; and yet, his words are quoted by every writer of the day, and on every subject sacred and profane. His good is truly magnetic. He is a man who lives after his own mind and in his own robes; an Arab who prays after no Imam, but directly to Allah and his Apostle; a scholar who has more dryasdust knowledge on his finger ends than all the ulema of Cairo and Damascus; a philosopher who would not give an orange peel for the opinion of the world; an ascetic who flees celebrity as he would the plague; a sage who does not disdain to be a pedagogue; an eccentric withal to amuse even a Diogenes:—this is the noted Sheikh Taleb of Damascus, whom Mrs. Gotfry once met at Ebbas Effendy's in Akka, and whom she was desirous of meeting again. When we first went to visit him, this charming lady and Khalid and I, we had to knock at the door until his neighbour peered from one of the windows above and told us that the Sheikh is asleep, and that if we would see him, we must come in the evening. I learned afterwards that he, reversing the habitual practice of mankind, works at night and sleeps during the day.

Ameen Fares Rihani

"We return in the evening. And the Sheikh, with a lamp in his hand, peers through a small square opening in the door to see who is knocking. He knew neither Khalid nor myself; but Mrs. Gotfry— 'Eigh!' he mused. And as he beheld her face in the lamplight he exclaimed 'Marhaba (welcome)! Marhaba!' and hastened to unbolt the door. We are shown through a dark, narrow hall, into a small court, up to his study. Which is a three-walled room—a sort of stage—opening on the court, and innocent of a divan or a settle or a chair. While he and Mrs. Gotfry were exchanging greetings in Persian, I was wondering why in Damascus, the city of seven rivers and of poetry and song, should there be a court guilty like this one of a dry and dilapidated fountain. I learned afterwards, however, that the Sheikh can not tolerate the noise of the water; and so, suffering from thirst and neglect, the fountain goes to ruin.

"On the stage, which is the study, is a clutter of old books and pamphlets; in the corner is the usual straw mat, a cushion, and a sort of stool on which are ink and paper. This he clears, places the cushion upon it, and offers to Mrs. Gotfry; he himself sits down on the mat; and we are invited to arrange for ourselves some books. Indeed, the Sheikh is right; most of these tomes are good for nothing else.

"Mrs. Gotfry introduces us.

"'Ah, but thou art young and short of stature,' said he to Khalid; 'that is ominous. Verily, there is danger in thy path.'

"'But he will embrace Buhaism,' put in Mrs. Gotfry.

"'That might save him. Buhaism is the old torch, relighted after many centuries, by Allah.'

"Meanwhile Khalid was thinking of second-hand Jerry of the second-hand book-shop of New York. The Sheikh reminded him of his old friend.

"And I was holding in my hand a book on which I chanced while arranging my seat. It was Debrett's Baronetage, Knightage, and Companionage. How did such a book find its way into the Sheikh's rubbish, I wondered. But birds of a feather, thought I.

"'That book was sent to me,' said he, 'by a merchant friend, who found it in the Bazaar. They send me all kinds of books, these simple of heart. They think I can read in all languages and discourse on all subjects. Allah forgive them.'

"And when I tell him, in reply to his inquiry, that the book treats of Titles, Orders, and Degrees of Precedence, he utters a sharp whew, and with a quick gesture of weariness and disgust, tells me to take it. 'I have my head full of our own ansab (pedigrees),' he adds, 'and I have

205

no more respect for a green turban (the colour of the Muslim nobility) than I have for this one,' pointing to his, which is white.

"Mrs. Gotfry then asks the Sheikh what he thinks of Wahhabism.

"'It is Islam in its pristine purity; it is the Islam of the first great Khalifs. "Mohammed is dead; but Allah lives," said Abu Bekr to the people on the death of the Prophet. And Wahhabism is a direct telegraph wire between mortal man and his God.

"'But why should these Wahhabis of Nejd be the most fanatical, when their doctrines are the most pure?' asked Khalid.

"'In thy question is the answer to it. They are fanatical *because* of their purity of doctrine, and withal because they live in Nejd. If there were a Wahhabi sect in Barr'ush-Sham (Syria), it would not be thus, assure thee.'

"And expressing his liking for Khalid, he advises him to be careful of his utterances in Damascus, if he believes in self-preservation. 'I am old,' he continues; 'and the ulema do not think my flesh is good for sacrifice. But thou art young, and plump—a tender yearling—ah, be careful sheikh Khalid. Then, I do not talk to the people direct. I talk to them through holy men and dervishes. The people do not believe in a philosopher; but the holy man, and though he attack the most sacred precepts of the Faith, they will believe. And Damascus is the very hive of turbans, green and otherwise. So guard thee, my child.'

"Mrs. Gotfry then asks for a minute's privacy with the Sheikh. And before he withdraws with her to the court, he searches through a heap of mouldy tomes, draws from beneath them a few yellow pamphlets on the Comparative Study of the Semetic Alphabets and on The Rights of the Khalifate—such is the scope of his learning—and dusting these on his knee, presents them to us, saying, 'Judge us not severely.'

"This does not mean that he cares much if we do or not. But in our country, in the Orient, even a Diogenes does not disdain to handle the coin of affability. We are always meekly asked, even by the most supercilious, to overlook shortcomings, and condone.

"I could not in passing out, however, overlook the string of orange peels which hung on a pole in the court. Nor am I sensible of an indecorum if I give out that the Sheikh lives on oranges, and preserves the peels for kindling the fire. And this, his only article of food, he buys at wholesale, like his robes and undergarments. For he never changes or washes anything. A robe is worn continually, worn out in the run, and discarded. He no more believes in the efficacy of soap than in the efficacy of a good reputation. 'The good opinion of men,' he says, 'does not wash our hearts and minds. And if these be clean, all's clean.'

"That is why, I think, he struck once with his staff a journalist for inserting in his paper a laudatory notice on the Sheikh's system of living and thinking and speaking of him as 'a deep ocean of learning and wisdom.' Even in travelling he carries nothing with him but his staff, that he might the quicker flee, or put to flight, the vulgar curious. He puts on a few extra robes, when he is going on a journey, and in time, becoming threadbare, sheds them off as the serpent its skin...."

And we pity our Scribe if he ever goes back to Damascus after this, and the good Sheikh chances upon him.

CHAPTER VIII

ADUMBRATIONS

"In the morning of the eventful day," it is set forth in the *Histoire Intime*, "I was in Khalid's room writing a letter, when Ahmed Bey comes in to confer with him. They remain together for some while during which I could hear Khalid growl and Ahmed Bey gently whispering, 'But the Dastur, the Unionists, Mother Society,'—this being the burden of his song. When he leaves, Khalid, with a scowl on his brow, paces up and down the room, saying, 'They would treat me like a school boy; they would have me speak by rule, and according to their own dictation. They even espy my words and actions as if I were an enemy of the Constitution. No; let them find another. The servile spouters in the land are as plenty as summer flies. After I deliver my address to-day, Shakib, we will take the first train for Baalbek. I want to see my mother. No, billah! I can not go any further with these Turks. Why, read this.' And he hands me the memorandum, or outline of the speech given to him by Ahmed Bey."

And this, we learn, is a litany of praises, beginning with Abd'ul-Hamid and ending with the ulema of Damascus; which litany the Society Deputies would place in the mouth of Khalid for the good of all concerned. Ay, for his good, too, if he but knew. If he but looked behind him, he would have yielded a whit, this Khalid. The deep chasm between him and the Deputy, however, justifies the conduct of each on his side: the lack of gumption in the one and the lack of depth in the other render impossible any sort of understanding between them. While we recommend, therefore, the prudence of the oleaginous Ahmed, we can not with justice condemn the perversity of our fretful Khalid. For he who makes loud boast of spiritual freedom, is, nevertheless, a slave of the Idea. And slavery in some shape or shade will clutch at the heart of the most powerful and most developed of mortals. Poor Khalid! if Truth commands thee to destroy the memorandum of Ahmed Bey, Wisdom suggests that thou destroy, too, thine address. And Wisdom in the person of Sheikh Taleb now knocks at thy door.

The Sheikh is come to admonish Khalid, not to return his visit. For at this hour of the day he should have been a-bed; but his esteem for Mrs. Gotfry, billah, his love, too, for her friend Khalid, and his desire to avert a possible danger, banish sleep from his eyes.

"My spirit is perturbed about thee," thus further, "and I can not feel at ease until I have given my friendly counsel. Thou art free to follow it or not to follow it. But for the sake of this beard Sheikh Khalid, do not speak at the Mosque to-day. I know the people of this City: they are ignorant, obtuse, fanatical, blind. 'God hath sealed up their hearts and their hearing.' They will not hear thee; they can not understand thee. I know them better than thou: I have lived amongst them for forty years. And what talk have we wasted. They will not hear; they can not see. It's a dog's tail, Sheikh Khalid. And what Allah hath twisted, man can not straighten. So, let it be. Let them wallow in their ignorance. Or, if thou wilt help them, talk not to them direct. Use the medium of the holy man, like myself. This is my advice to thee. For thine own sake and for the sake of that good woman, thy friend and mine, I give it. Now, I can go and sleep. Salaam."

And the grey beard of Sheikh Taleb and his sharp blue eyes were animated, as he spoke, agitated like his spirit. What he has heard abroad and what he suspects, are shadowed forth in his friendly counsel. Let Khalid reflect upon it. Our Scribe, at least, is persuaded that Sheikh Taleb spoke as a friend. And he, too, suspects that something is brewing abroad. He would have Khalid hearken, therefore, to the Sheikh.

But Khalid in silence ponders the matter. And at table, even Mrs. Gotfry can not induce him to speak. She has just returned from the bazaar; she could hardly make her way through the choked arcade leading to the Mosque; the crowd is immense and tumultuous; and a company of the Dragoons is gone forth to open the way and maintain order. "But I don't think they are going to succeed," she added. Silently, impassively, Khalid hears this. And after going through the second course, eating as if he were dreaming, he gets up and leaves the table. Mrs. Gotfry, somewhat concerned, orders her last course, takes her thimble-full of coffee at a gulp, and, leaving likewise, hurries upstairs and calls Khalid, who was pacing up and down the hall, into her room.

"What is the matter with you?"

"Nothing, nothing," murmured Khalid absent-mindedly.

"That's not true. Everything belies your words. Why, your actions, your expression, your silence oppresses me. I know what is disturbing you. And I would prevail upon you, if I could, to give up this afternoon's business. Don't go; don't speak. I have a premonition that things are not going to end well. Why, even my dragoman says that the Mohammedan mob is intent upon some evil business. Be advised. And since you are going to break with your associates, why not do so now. The quicker the better. Come, make up your mind. And we'll not wait for the morning train. We'll leave for Baalbek in a special carriage this afternoon. What say you?"

Just then the brass band in front of the Hotel struck up the Dastur march in honour of the Sheikhs who come to escort the Unionist Deputies and the speaker to the Mosque.

"I have made up my mind. I have given my word."

And being called, Mrs. Gotfry, though loath to let him go, presses his hand and wishes him good speed.

And here we are in the carriage on the right of the green-turbaned Sheikh. We look disdainfully on the troops, the brass band, and the crowd of nondescripts that are leading the procession. We cross the bridge, pass the Town-Hall, and, winding a narrow street groaning with an electric tramway, we come to the grand arcade in which the multitudes on both sides are pressed against the walls and into the stalls by the bullying Dragoons. We drive through until we reach the arch, where some Khalif of the Omayiahs used to take the air. And descending from the carriage, we walk a few paces between two rows of book-shops, and here we are in the court of the grand Mosque Omayiah.

We elbow our way through the pressing, distressing multitudes, following Ahmed Bey into the Mosque, while the Army Officer mounts a platform in the court and dispenses to the crowd there of his Turkish blatherskite. We stand in the Mosque near the heavy tapestried square which is said to be the sarcophagus of St. John. Already a Sheikh is in the pulpit preaching on the excellences of liberty, chopping out definitions of equality, and quoting from Al-Hadith to prove that all men are Allah's children and that the most favoured in Allah's sight is he who is most loving to his brother man. He then winds up with an encomium on the heroes of the day, curses vehemently the reactionaries and those who curse them not (the Mosque resounds with "Curse the reactionists, curse them all!"), tramples beneath his heel every spy and informer of the New Era, invokes the great Allah and his Apostle to watch over the patriots and friends of the Ottoman nation, to visit with grievous punishment its enemies, and—descends.

The silence of expectation ensues. The Mosque is crowded; and the press of turbans is such that if a pea were dropt from above it would not reach the floor. From the pulpit the great Mohammedan audience, with its red fezes, its green and white turbans, seemed to Khalid like a verdant field overgrown with daisies and poppies. "It is the beginning of Arabia's Spring, the resuscitation of the glory of Islam," and so forth; thus opening with a flourish of flattery like the spouting tricksters whom he so harshly judges. And what shall we say of him? It were not fair quickly to condemn, to cry him down at the start. Perhaps he was thus inspired by the august assembly; perhaps he quailed and thought it wise to follow thus far the advice of his friends. "It was neither this nor that," say our Scribe. "For as he stood in the tribune, the picture of the field of daisies and poppies suggested the picture of Spring. A speaker is not always responsible for the frolics of his fancy. Indeed, an audience of some five thousand souls, all intent upon this opaque, mysterious Entity in the tribune, is bound to reach the very heart of it; for think what five thousand rays focussed on a sensitive plate can do." Thus our Scribe, apologetically.

But after the first contact and the vibrations of enthusiasm and flattery that followed, Khalid regains his equilibrium and reason, and strikes into his favourite theme. He begins by arraigning the utilitarian spirit of Europe, the rank materialism which is invading our very temples of worship. God, Truth, Virtue, with them, is no longer esteemed for its own worth, but for what it can yield of the necessities and luxuries of life. And with these cynical materialistic abominations they would be supreme even in the East; they would extinguish with their dominating spirit of trade every noble virtue of the soul. And yet, they make presumption of introducing civilisation by benevolent assimilation, rather dissimulation. For even an Englishman in our country, for instance, is unlike himself in his own. The American, too, who is loud-lunged about democracy and shirt-sleeve diplomacy, wheedles and truckles as good as the wiliest of our pashas. And further he exclaims:

"Not to Christian Europe as represented by the State, therefore, or by the industrial powers of wealth, or by the alluring charms of decadence in art and literature, or by missionary and educational institutions, would I have you turn for light and guidance. No: from these plagues of civilisation protect us, Allah! No: let us have nothing to do with that practical Christianity which is become a sort of divine key to Colonisation; a mint, as it were, which continually replenishes the treasuries of Christendom. Let us have nothing to do with their propagandas for the propagation of supreme Fakes. No, no. Not this Europe, O my Brothers, should we take for our model or emulate: not the Europe which is being dereligionised by Material Science; disorganised by Communion and Anarchy; befuddled by Alcoholism; enervated by Debauch. To another Europe indeed, would I direct you––a Europe, high, noble, healthy, pure, and withal progressive. To the deep and inexhaustible sources of genius there, of reason and wisdom and truth, would I have you advert the mind. The divine idealism of German philosophy, the lofty purity of true French art, the strength and sterling worth of English freedom,—these we should try to emulate; these we should introduce into the gorgeous besottedness of Oriental life, and literature, and religion...."

And thus, until he reaches the heart of his subject; while the field of daisies and poppies before him gently sways as under a soft morning breeze; nods, as it were, its approbation.

"Truly," he continues, "religion is purely a work of the heart,—the human heart, and the heart of the world as well. For have not the three monotheistic religions been born in this very heart of the world, in Arabia, Syria, and Palestine? And are not our Books of Revelation the truest guides of life hitherto known to man? How then are we to keep this Heart pure, to free it, in other words, from the plagues I have named? And how, on the other hand, are we to strengthen it, to quicken its sluggish blood? In a word, how are we to attain to the pinnacle of health, and religion, and freedom,—of power, and love, and light? By political revolutions, and insurrections, and Dasturs? By blindly adopting the triple political tradition of France, which after many years of terror and bloodshed, only gave Europe a new Yoke, a new Tyranny, a new grinding Machine? No, my Brothers; not by political nomenclature, not by political revolutions alone, shall the nations be emancipated."

Whereupon Ahmed Bey begins to knit his brows; Shakib shakes his head, biting his nether lip; and here and there in the audience is heard a murmur about retrogression and reaction. Khalid proceeds with his allegory of the Muleteer and the Pack-Mule.

"See, the panel of the Mule is changed; the load, too; and a few short-cuts are made in the rocky winding road of statecraft and tyranny. Ah, the stolid, patient, drudging Mule always exults in a new Panel, which, indeed, seems necessary every decade, or so. For the old one, when, from a sense of economy, or from negligence or stupidity, is kept on for a length of time, makes the back sore, and the Mule becomes kickish and resty. Hence, the plasters of conservative homeopa-thists, the operations suggested by political leeches, the radical cures of social quacks, and such like. But the Mule continues to kick against the pricks; and the wise Muleteer, these days, when he has not the price of a new Panel, or knows not how to make one, sells him to the first bidder. And the new owner thereupon washes the sores and wounds, applies to them a salve of the patent kind, buys his Mule a new Panel, and makes him do the work. That is what I understand by a political revolution.... And are the Ottoman people free to-day? Who in all Syria and Arabia dare openly criticise the new Owner of the Mule?

"Ours in a sense is a theocratic Government. And only by reform-ing the religion on which it is based, is political reform in any way possible and enduring." And here he argues that the so-called Refor-mation of Islam, of which Jelal ud-Dïn el-Afghani and Mohammed Abdu are the protagonists, is false. It is based on theological juggling and traditional sophisms. Their Al-Gazzali, whom they so much prize and quote, is like the St. Augustine of the Christians: each of these theologians finds in his own Book of Revelation a divine criterion for measuring and judging all human knowledge. No; a scientific truth can not be measured by a Korânic epigram: the Korân, a divine guide to life; a work of the heart should not attempt to judge a work of the mind or should be judged by it.

"But I would brush the cobwebs of interpretation and sophism from this Work of the heart," he cries; "every spider's web in the Mosque, I would sweep away. The garments of your religion, I would have you clean, O my Brothers. Ay, even the threadbare adventitious wrappag-es, I would throw away. From the religiosity and cant of to-day I call you back to the religion pure of the heart...."

But the Field of poppies and daisies begins to sway as under a gale. It is swelling violently, tumultuously.

"I would free al-Islam," he continues, "from its degrading customs, its stupefying traditions, its enslaving superstitions, its imbruting cants."

Here several voices in the audience order the speaker to stop. "In-novation! Infidelity!" they cry.

"The yearly pestiferous consequences of the Haji"—But Khalid no longer can be heard. On all sides zealotry raises and shakes a protest-ing hand; on all sides it shrieks, objurgating, threatening. Here it asks, "We would like to know if the speaker be a Wahhabi." From another part of the Mosque comes the reply: "Ay, he is a Wahhabi." And the voice of the speaker thundering above the storm: "Only in Wahhabism pure and simple is the reformation of al-Islam possible."... Finis.

Zealotry is set by the ear; the hornet's nest is stirred. Your field of poppies and daisies, O Khalid, is miraculously transformed into a pit of furious grey spectres and howling red spirits. And still you wait in the tribune until the storm subside? Fool, fool! Art now in a civilised assembly? Hast thou no eyes to see, no ears to hear?

"Reactionist! Infidel! Innovator! Wahhabi! Slay him! Kill him!"— Are these likely to subside the while thou wait? By the tomb of St. John there, get thee down, and quickly. Bravo, Shakib!—He rushes to the tribune, drags him down by the jubbah, and, with the help of another friend, hustles him out of the Mosque. But the thirst for blood pursues them. And Khalid receives in the court outside a stiletto-thrust in the back and a slash in the forehead above the brow down to the ear. Which, indeed, we consider a part of his good fortune. Like the muleteer of his Lebanon tour, we attribute his escape with two wounds to the prayers of his good mother. For he is now in the carriage with Shakib, the blood streaming down his back and over his face. With difficulty the driver makes his way through the crowds, issues out of the arcade, and—crack the whip! Quickly to the Hotel.

The multitudes behind us, both inside and outside the Mosque, are violently divided; for the real reactionists of Damascus, those who are hostile to the Constitution and the statochratic Government, are always watching for an opportunity to give the match to the dry sedges of sedition. And so, the liberals, who are also the friends of Khalid, and the fanatical mobs of the ulema, will have it out among themselves. They call each other reactionists, plotters, conspirators; and thereupon the bludgeons and poniards are brandished; the pistols here and there are fired; the Dragoons hasten to the scene of battle—but we are not writing now the History of the Ottoman Revolution. We leave them to have it out among themselves as best they can, and accompany our Khalid to the Hotel.

Here the good Mrs. Gotfry washes the blood from his face, and Shakib, after helping him to bed, hastens to call the surgeon, who, having come straightway, sews and dresses the wounds and assures us that they are not dangerous. In the evening a number of Sheikhs of an enlightened and generous strain, come to inquire about him. They tell us that one of the assailants of Khalid, a noted brigand, and ten of the reactionists, are now in prison. The Society Deputies, however, do not seem much concerned about their wounded friend. Yes, they are concerned, but in another direction and on weightier matters. For the

telegraph wires on the following day were kept busy. And in the afternoon of the second day after the event, the man who helped Shakib to
save Khalid from the mob, comes to save Khalid's life. The Superin-
tendent of the Telegraph himself is here to inform us that Khalid was
accused to the Military Tribunal as a reactionist, and a cablegram, in
which he is summoned there, is just received.

"Had I delivered this to the Vali," he continues, "you would have
been now in the hands of the police, and to-morrow on your way to
Constantinople. But I shall not deliver it until you are safe out of the
City. And you must fly or abscond to-day, because I can not delay the
message until to-morrow."

Now Khalid and Shakib and Mrs. Gotfry take counsel together. The
one train for Baalbek leaves in the morning; the carriage road is ruined
from disuse; and only on horseback can we fly. So, Mrs. Gotfry orders
her dragoman to hire horses for three,—nay, for four, since we must
have an extra guide with us,—and a muleteer for the baggage.

And here Shakib interposes a suggestion: "They must not come to
the Hotel. Be with them on the road, near the first bridge, about the
first hour of night."

At the office of the Hotel the dragoman leaves word that they are
leaving for a friend's house on account of their patient.

And after dinner Mrs. Gotfry and Khalid set forth afoot, accompanied by Shakib. In five minutes they reach the first bridge; the
dragoman and the guide, with their horses and lanterns, are there waiting. Shakib helps Khalid to his horse and bids them farewell. He will
leave for Baalbek by the first train, and be there ahead of them.

And now, Reader, were we really romancing, we should here dilate
of the lovely ride in the lovely moonlight on the lovely road to Baalbek. But truth to tell, the road is damnable, the welkin starless, the
night pitch-black, and our poor Dreamer is suffering from his wounds.

CHAPTER IX

THE STONING AND FLIGHT

"And whence the subtle thrill of joy in suffering for the Truth," asks Khalid. "Whence the light that flows from the wounds of martyrs? Whence the rapture that triumphs over their pain? In the thick of night, through the alcoves of the mountains, over their barren peaks, down through the wadi of oblivion, silently they pass. And they dream. They dream of appearance in disappearance; of triumph in surrender; of sunrises in the sunset.

"A mighty tidal wave leaves high upon the beach a mark which later on becomes the general level of the ocean. And so do the great thinkers of the world,—the poets and seers, the wise and strong and self-denying, the proclaimers of the Religion of Man. And I am but a scrub-oak in this forest of giants, my Brothers. A scrub-oak which you might cut down, but not uproot. Lop off my branches; apply the axe to my trunk; make of my timber charcoal for the censers of your temples of worship; but the roots of me are deep, deep in the soil, beyond the reach of mortal hands. They are even spreading under your tottering palaces and temples....

"I dream of the awakening of the East; of puissant Orient nations rising to glorify the Idea, to build temples to the Universal Spirit—to Art, and Love, and Truth, and Faith. What if I am lost in the alcoves of the hills, if I vanish forever in the night? The sun that sets must rise. It is rising and lighting up the dark and distant continents even when setting. Think of that, ye who gloat over the sinking of my mortal self.

"No; an idea is never too early annunciated. The good seed will grow among the rocks, and though the heavens withhold from it the sunshine and rain. It is because I will it, nay, because a higher Will than mine wills it, that the spirit of Khalid shall yet flow among your pilgrim caravans, through the fertile deserts of Arabia, down to the fountain-head of Faith, to Mecca and Medina," et cetera.

This, perhaps the last of the rhapsodies of Khalid's, the Reader considering the circumstances under which it was written, will no doubt condone. Further, however, in the K. L. MS. we can not now proceed. Certainly the Author is not wanting in the sort of courage which is loud-lunged behind the writing table; his sufficiency of spirit is remarkable, unutterable. But we would he knew that the strong do not exult in their strength, nor the wise in their wisdom. For to fly and philosophize were one thing, and to philosophize in prison were another. Khalid this time does not follow closely in the way of the Masters. But he would have done so, if we can believe Shakib in this, had not Mrs. Gotfry persuaded him to the contrary. He would have stood in the Turkish Areopagus at Constantinople, defended himself somewhat Socratic before his judges, and hung out his tung on a rickety gibbet in the neighborhood of St. Sophia. But Mrs. Gotfry spoiled his great chance. She cheated him of the glory of dying for a noble cause.

"The Turks are not worth the sacrifice," Shakib heard her say, when Khalid ejaculated somewhat about martyrdom. And when she offered to accompany him, the flight did not seem shameful in his eyes. Nay, it became necessary; and under the circumstances it was, indeed, cowardice not to fly. For is it not as noble to surrender one's self to Love as to the Turks or any other earthly despotism? Gladly, heroically, he adventures forth, therefore, and philosophizes on the way about the light that flows from the wounds of persecution. But we regret that this celestial stream is not unmixed; it is accompanied by blood and pus; by distention and fever, and other inward and outward sores.

In this grievous state, somewhat like Don Quixote after the Battle of the Mill, our Khalid enters Baalbek. If the reader likes the comparison between the two Knights at this juncture, he must work it out for himself. We can not be so uncharitable as that; especially that our Knight is a compatriot, and is now, after our weary journeyings together, become our friend.—Our poor grievous friend who must submit again to the surgeon's knife.

Mrs. Gotfry would not let him go to his mother, for she herself would nurse him. So, the doctor is called to the Hotel. And after opening, disinfecting, and dressing the wounds, he orders his patient to keep in bed for some days. They will then visit the ruins and resume their journeying to Egypt. Khalid no longer would live in Syria,—in a country forever doomed to be under the Turkish yoke, faring, nay, misfaring alike in the New Era as in the Old.

Now, his mother, tottering with age and sorrow, comes to the Hotel, and begs him in a flood of tears to come home; for his father is now with the Jesuits of Beirut and seldom comes to Baalbek. And his cousin Najma, with a babe on her arm and a tale of woe in her eyes, comes also to invite her cousin Khalid to her house.

She is alone; her father died some months ago; her husband, after the dethronement of Abd'ul-Hamid, being implicated in the reaction-movement, fled the country; and his relatives, to add to her affliction, would deprive her of her child. She is alone; and sick in the lungs. She coughs, too, the same sharp, dry, malignant cough that once plagued Khalid. Ay, the same disease which he buried in the pine forest of Mt. Lebanon, he beholds the ghost of it now, more terrible and heart-rending than anything he has yet seen or experienced. The disease which he conquered is come back in the person of his cousin Najma to conquer him. And who can assure Khalid that it did not steal into her breast along with his kisses? And yet, he is not the only one in Baalbek who returned from America with phthisis. O, but that thought is horri-fying. Impossible—he can not believe it.

But whether it be from you or from another, O Khalid, there is the ghost of it beckoning to you. Look at it. Are those the cheeks, those the eyes, this the body which a year ago was a model of rural charm and beauty and health? Is this the compensation of love? Is there any-thing like it dreamt of in your philosophy? There she is, who once in the ruined Temple of Venus mixed the pomegranate flower of her cheeks with the saffron of thy sickly lips. Wasted and dejected broken in body and spirit, she sits by your bedside nursing her baby and coughing all the while. And that fixed expression of sadness, so habit-ual among the Arab women who carry their punks and their children on their backs and go a-begging, it seems as if it were an hundred au-tumns old, this sadness. But right there, only a year ago, the crimson poppies dallied with the laughing breeze; the melting rubies dilated of health and joy.

And now, deploring, imploring, she asks: "Will you not come to me, O Khalid? Will you not let me nurse you? Come; and your moth-er, too, will live with us. I am so lonesome, so miserable. And at night the boys cast stones at my door. My husband's relatives put them to it because I would not give them the child. And they circulate all kinds of calumnies about me too."

Khalid promises to come, and assures her that she will not long remain alone. "And Allah willing," he adds, "you will recover and be happy again."

She rises to go, when Mrs. Gotfry enters the room. Khalid introduces his cousin as his dead bride. "What do you mean?" she inquires. He promises to explain. Meanwhile, she goes to her room, brings some sweetmeats in a round box inlaid with mother-of-pearl for Khalid's guests. And taking the babe in her arms, she fondles and kisses it, and gives its mother some advice about suckling. "Not whenever the child cries, but only at stated times," she repeats.

So much about Khalid's mother and cousin. A few days after, when he is able to leave his room, he goes to see them. His cousin Najma he would take with him to Cairo. He would not leave her behind, a prey to the cruelty of loneliness and disease. He tells her this. She is overjoyed. She is ready to go whenever he says. To-morrow? Please Allah, yes. But—

Please Allah, ill-luck is following. For on his way back to the Hotel, a knot of boys, lying in wait in one of the side streets, cast stones at him. He looks back, and a missile whizzes above his head, another hits him in the forehead almost undoing the doctor's work. Alas, that wound! Will it ever heal? Khalid takes shelter in one of the shops; a cameleer rates the boys and chases them away. The stoning was repeated the following day, and the cause of it, Shakib tells us, is patent. For when it became known in Baalbek that Khalid, the excommunicated one, is living in the Hotel, and with an American woman! the old prejudices against him were aroused, the old enemies were astirring. The priests held up their hands in horror; the women wagged their long tongues in the puddle of scandal; and the most fanatical shrieked out, execrating, vituperating, threatening even the respectable Shakib, who persists in befriending this muleteer's son. Excommunicated, he now comes with this Americaniyah (American woman) to corrupt the community. Horrible! We will even go farther than this boy's play of stoning. We present petitions to the kaiemkam demanding the expulsion of this Khalid from the Hotel, from the City.

From other quarters, however, come heavier charges against Khalid. The Government of Damascus has not been idle ever since the seditious lack-beard Sheikh disappeared. The telegraph wires, in all the principal cities of Syria, are vibrating with inquiries about him, with orders for his arrest. One such the kaiemkam of Baalbek had just received when the petition of the "Guardians of the Morals of the Community" was presented to him. To this, the kaiemkam, in a perfunctory manner, applies his seal, and assures his petitioners that it will promptly be turned over to the proper official. But Turk as Turks go, he "places it under the cushion," when they leave. Which expression, translated into English means, he quashes it.

Now, by good chance, this is the same kaiemkam who sent Khalid a year ago to prison, maugre the efforts and importunities and other inducements of Shakib. And this time, he will do him and his friend a good turn. He was thinking of the many misfortunes of this Khalid, and nursing a little pity for him, when Shakib entered to offer a written complaint against a few of the more noted instigators of the assailants of his friend. His Excellency puts this in his pocket and withdraws with Shakib into another room. A few minutes after, Shakib was hurrying to the Hotel to confer with his brother Khalid and Mrs. Gotfry.

"I saw the Order with these very eyes," said Shakib, almost poking his two forefingers into them. "The kaiemkam showed it to me."

Hence, the secret preparations inside the Hotel and out of it for a second remove, for a final flight. Shakib packs up; Najma is all ready. And Khalid cuts his hair, doffs his jubbah, and appears again in the ordinary attire of civilised mortals. For how else can he get out of Beirut and the telegraph wires throughout Syria are flowing with orders for his arrest? In a hat and frock-coat, therefore (furnished by Shakib), he enters into the carriage with Mrs. Gotfry about two hours after midnight; and, with their whole retinue, make for Riak, and thence by train for Beirut. Here Shakib obtains passports for himself and Najma, and together with Mrs. Gotfry and her dragoman, they board in the afternoon the Austrian Liner for Port-Said; while, in the evening, walking at the side of one of the boatmen, Khalid, passportless, stealthily passes through the port, and rejoins his friends.

CHAPTER X

THE DESERT

We remember seeing once a lithographic print representing a Christmas legend of the Middle Ages, in which a detachment of the Heavenly Host—big, ugly, wild-looking angels—are pursuing, with sword and pike, a group of terror-stricken little devils. The idea in the picture produced such an impression that one wished to see the helpless, pitiful imps in heaven and the armed winged furies, their pursuers, in the other place. Now, as we go through the many pages of Shakib's, in which he dilates of the mischances, the persecutions, and the flights of Khalid, and of which we have given an abstract, very brief but comprehensive, in the preceding Chapters, we are struck with the similarity in one sense between his Dastur-legend, so to speak, and that of the Middle Ages to which we have alluded. The devils in both pictures are distressing, pitiful; while the winged persecutors are horribly muscular, and withal atrociously armed.

Indeed, this legend of the Turkish angels of Fraternity and Equality, pursuing the Turkish little devils of reaction, so called, is most killing. But we can not see how the descendants of Yakut and Seljuk Khan, whether pursuers or pursued, whether Dastur winged furies they be, or Hamidian devils, are going to hold their own in face of the fell Dragon which soon or late must overtake them. That heavy, slow-going, slow-thinking Monster—and it makes little difference whether he comes from the North or from the West—will wait until the contending parties exhaust their strength and then—but this is not our subject. We would that this pursuing business cease on all sides, and that everybody of all parties concerned pursue rather, and destroy, the big strong devil within them. Thus sayeth the preacher. And thus, for once, we, too. For does not every one of these furious angels of Equality, whether in Constantinople, in Berlin, in Paris, in London, or in New York, sit on his wings and reveal his horns when he rises to power? We are tired of wings that are really nothing but horns, misshaped and misplaced.

Look at our French-swearing, whiskey-drinking Tataric angels of the Dastur! Indeed, we rejoice that our poor little Devil is now beyond the reach of their dripping steel and rickety second-hand gibbets. And yet, not very far; for if the British Government consent or blink, Khalid and many real reactionists whom Cairo harbours, would have to seek an asylum elsewhere. And the third flight might not be as successful as the others. But none such is necessary. On the sands of the Libyan desert, not far from Cairo and within wind of Helwan, they pitch their tents. And Mrs. Gotfry is staying at Al-Hayat, which is a stone's throw from their evening fire. She would have Khalid live there too, but he refuses. He will live with his cousin and Shakib for a while. He is captivated, we are told, by that little cherub of a babe. But this does not prevent him from visiting his friend the Buhaist Priestess every day and dining often with her at the Hotel.

She, too, not infrequently comes to the camp. Indeed, finding the solitude agreeable she has a tent pitched near theirs. And as a relief from the noise and bustle of tourists and the fatiguing formalities of Hotel life, she repairs thither for a few days every week.

Now, in this austere delicacy of the desert, where allwhere is the softness of pure sand, Khalid is perfectly happy. Never did he seem so careless, our Scribe asserts, and so jovial and child-like in his joys. Far from the noise and strife of politics, far from the bewildering tangle of thought, far from the vain hopes and dreams and ambitions of life, he lives each day as if it were the last of the world. Here are joys manifold for a weary and persecuted spirit: the joy of having your dearest friend and comrade with you; the joy of nursing and helping to restore to health and happiness the woman dearest to your heart; the joy of a Love budding in beauty and profusion; and—this, the rarest and sublimest for Khalid—the joy of worshipping at the cradle—of fondling, caressing, and bringing up one of the brightest, sweetest, loveliest of babes.

Najib is his name—it were cruel to neutralise such a prodigy—and he is just learning to walk and lisp. Khalid teaches him the first step and the first monosyllable, receiving in return the first kiss which his infant lips could voice. With what joy Najib makes his first ten steps! With what zest would he practise on the soft sands, laughing as he falls, and rising to try again. And thus, does he quickly, wonderfully develop, unfolding in the little circle of his caressers—in his mother's lap, in Shakib's arms, on Khalid's back, on Mrs. Gotfry's knee—the irresistible charm of his precocious spirit.

In two months of desert life, Najib could run on the sands and sit down when tired to rest; in two months he could imitate in voice and gesture whatever he heard or saw: the donkey's bray, and with a tilt of the head like him; the cry of the cock; the shrill whistle of the train; and the howling of donkey boys. His keen sense of discrimination in sounds is incredible. And one day, seeing a Mohammedan spreading his rug to pray, he begins to kneel and kiss the ground in imitation of him. He even went into the tent and brought Khalid's jubbah to spread it on the sand likewise for that purpose. So sensitive to outside impressions is this child that he quickly responds to the least suggestion and with the least effort. Early in the morning, when the chill of night is still on the sands, he toddles into Khalid's tent cooing and warbling his joy. A walking jasmine flower, a singing ray of sunshine, Khalid calls him. And the mother, on seeing her child thus develop, begins to recuperate. In this little garden of happiness, her hope begins to blossom.

But Khalid would like to know why Najib, on coming into his tent in the morning and seeing him naked, always pointed with his little finger and with questioning smile, to what protruded under the navel. The like questions Khalid puts with the ease and freedom of a child. And writes full pages about them, too, in which he only succeeds in bamboozling himself and us. For how can we account for everything a child does? Even the psychologist with his reflex-action theory does not solve the whole problem. But Khalid would like to know—and perhaps not so innocently does he dwell upon this subject as upon others—he would like to know the significance of Najib's pointed finger and smile. It may be only an accident, Khalid. "But an accident," says he, "occurring again and again in the same manner under stated conditions ceases to be such." And might not the child, who is such an early and keen observer, have previously seen his mother in native buff, and was surprised to see that appendage in you, Khalid?

Even at Al-Hayat Najib is become popular. Khalid often comes here carrying him on his back. And how ready is the child to salaam everybody, and with both hands, as he stands on the veranda steps. "Surely," says Khalid, "there is a deeper understanding between man and child than between man and man. For who but a child dare act so freely among these polyglots of ceremony in this little world of frills and frocks and feathers? Who but a child dare approach without an introduction any one of these solemn-looking tourists? Here then is the divine source of the sweetest and purest joy. Here is that one touch of

Nature which makes the whole world kin. For the child, and though he be of the lowest desert tribe, standing on the veranda of a fashionable Hotel, can warm and sweeten with the divine flame that is in him, the hearts of these sour-seeming, stiff-looking tourists who are from all corners of the earth. Is not this a miracle? My professor of psychology will say, 'Nay.' But what makes the heart leap in that grave and portly gentleman, who might be from Finland or Iceland, for all I know, when Najib's hand is raised to him in salutation? What makes that stately and sombre-looking dame open her arms, when Najib plucks a flower and, after smelling it, presents it to her? What makes that reticent, meditative, hard-favoured ancient, who is I believe a psychologist, what makes him so interested in observing Najib when he stands near the piano pointing anxiously to the keyboard? For the child enjoys not every kind of music: play a march or a melody and he will keep time, listing joyously from side to side and waving his hand in an arch like a maestro; play something insipid or chaotic and he will stand there impassive as a statue."

And "the reticent hard-favoured ancient," who turns out to be an American professor of some ology, explains to Khalid why lively music moves children, while soft and subtle tones do not. But Khalid is not open to argument on the subject. He prefers to believe that children, especially when so keenly sensitive as his prodigy, understand as much, if not more, about music as the average operagoer of to-day. But that is not saying much. The professor furthermore, while admitting the extreme precocity of Najib's mind, tries to simplify by scientific analysis what to Khalid and other laymen seemed wonderful, almost miraculous. Here, too, Khalid botches the arguments of the learned gentleman in his effort to give us a summary of them, and tells us in the end that never after, so long as that professor was there, did he ever visit Al-Hayat.

He prefers to frolic and philosophise with his prodigy on the sands. He goes on all four around the tent, carrying Najib on his back; he digs a little ditch in the sand and teaches him how to lie therein. Following the precept of the Greek philosophers, he would show him even so early how to die. And Najib lies in the sand-grave, folds his hands on his breast and closes his eyes. Rising therefrom, Khalid would teach him how to dance like a dervish, and Najib whirls and whirls until he falls again in that grave.

When Mrs. Gotfry came that day, Khalid asked the child to show her how to dance and die, and Najib begins to whirl like a dervish until he falls in the grave; thereupon he folds his arms, closes his eyes, and smiles a pathetic smile. This by far is the masterpiece of all his feats. And one evening, when he was repeating this strange and weird antic, which in Khalid's strange mind might be made to symbolise something stranger than both, he saw, as he lay in the grave, a star in the sky. It was the first time he saw a star; and he jumped out of his sand-grave exulting in the discovery he had made. He runs to his mother and points the star to her....

And thus did Khalid spend his halcyon months in the desert. Here was an arcadia, perfect but brief. For his delight in infant worship, and in the new Love which was budding in beauty and profusion, and in tending his sick cousin who was recovering her health, and in the walks around the ruins in the desert with his dearest comrade and friend,—these, alas, were joys of too pure a nature to endure.

AL-KHATIMAH

"But I can not see all that you see."

"Then you do not love me."

"Back again to Swedenborg—I told you more than once that he is not my apostle."

"Nor is he mine. But he has expressed a great truth, Jamïlah. Now, can you love me in the light of that truth?"

"You are always asking me that same question, Khalid. You do not understand me. I do not believe in marriage. I tried it once; I will not try it again. I am married to Buhaism. And you Khalid—remember my words—you will yet be an apostle—the apostle—of Buhaism. And you will find me with you, whether you be in Arabia, in America, or in Egypt. I feel this—I know it—I am positive about it. Your star and mine are one. We are born under the same star. We are now in the same orbit, approaching the same nadir. We are ruled by our stars. I believe this, and you don't. At least, you say you don't. But you do. You don't know your own mind. The trend of the current of your life is beyond your grasp, beyond your comprehension. I know. And you must listen to me. You must follow my advice. If you can not come with me now to the States, you will await me here. I am called on a pressing business. And within three months, at the most, I shall return and find you waiting for me right here, in this desert."

"I can not understand you."

"You will yet."

"But why not try to understand me? Can you not find in my ideas the very essence of Buhaism? Can you not come up to my height and behold there the star that you have taken for your guide? My Truth, Jamïlah, can you not see that? Love and Faith, free from all sectarianism and all earthly authority,—what is Buhaism or Mohammedanism or Christianity beside them? Moreover, I have a mission. And to love me you must believe in *me*, not in the Buha. You laugh at my dream. But one day it will be realised. A great Arab Empire in the border-land of the Orient and Occident, in this very heart of the world, this Arabia, this Egypt, this Field of the Cloth of Gold, so to speak, where the Male and Female of the Spirit shall give birth to a unifying faith, a unifying art, a unifying truth—"

"Vagaries, chimeras," interrupted Mrs. Gotfry. "Buhaism is established, and it needs a great apostle. It needs you; it will have you. I will have you. Your destiny is interwoven with mine. You can not flee it, do what you may. We are ruled by our stars, Khalid. And if you do not realise this now, you will realise it to-morrow. Here, give me your hand."

"I can not."

"Very well, then. Good-bye—*au revoir*. In three months you will change your mind. In three months I will return to the East and find you waiting for me, even here in this desert. Think on it, and take care of yourself. *Au revoir*."

In this strange, mysterious manner, after pacing for hours on the sand in the sheen of the full moon, Mrs. Gotfry says farewell to Khalid.

He sits on a rock near his tent and ponders for hours. He seeks in the stars, as it were, a clue to the love of this woman, which he first thought to be unfathomable. There it is, the stars seem to say. And he looks into the sand-grave near him, where little Najib practises how to die. Yes; a fitting symbol of the life and love called modern, boasting of freedom. They dance their dervish dance, these people, even like Khalid's little Najib, and fall into their sand-graves, and fold their arms and smile: "We are in love—or we are out of it." Which is the same. No: he'll have none of this. A heart as simple as this desert sand, as deep in affection as this heaven, untainted by the uncertainties and doubts and caprices of modern life,—only in such a heart is the love that endures, the love divine and eternal.

He goes into Najma's tent. The mother and her child are sound asleep. He stands between the bed and the cot contemplating the simplicity and innocence and truth, which are more eloquent in Najib's brow than aught of human speech. His little hand raised above his head seems to point to a star which could be seen through an opening in the canvas. Was it his star—the star that he saw in the sand-grave— the star that is calling to him?—

But let us resume our narration.

227

A fortnight after Mrs. Gotfry's departure Shakib leaves the camp to live in Cairo. He is now become poet-laureate to one of the big pashas.

Khalid is left alone with Najma and Najib.

And one day, when they are playing a game of "donkey,"—Khalid carried Najib on his back, ran on all four around the tent, and Najma was the donkey-driver,—the child of a sudden utters a shriek and falls on the sand. He is in convulsions; and after the relaxation, lo, his right hand is palsied, his mouth awry, and his eyes a-squint. Khalid finds a young doctor at Al-Hayat, and his diagnosis of the case does not disturb the mind. It is infantile paralysis, a disease common with delicate children. And the doctor, who is of a kind and demonstrative humour, discourses at length on the disease, speaks of many worse cases of its kind he cured, and assures the mother that within a month the child will recover. For the present he can but prescribe a purgative and a massage of the arm and spine. On the third visit, he examines the child's fæces and is happy to have discovered the seat and cause of the affection. The liver is not performing its function; and given such weak nerves as the child's, a torpid liver in certain cases will produce paralysis.

But Khalid is not satisfied with this. He places the doctor's prescription in his pocket, and goes down to Cairo for a specialist. He comes, this one, to disturb their peace of mind with his indecision. It is not infantile paralysis, and he can not yet say what it is. Khalid meanwhile is poring over medical books on all the diseases that children are heir to.

On the fifth day the child falls again in convulsions, and the left arm, too, is paralysed. They take him down to Cairo; and Medicine, considering the disease of his mother, guesses a third time—tuberculosis of the spine, it says—and guesses wrong. Again, considering the strabismus, the obliquity of the mouth, the palsy in the arms, and the convulsions, we guess closely, but ominously. Nay, Medicine is positive this time; for a fifth and a sixth Guesser confirm the others. Here we have a case of cerebral meningitis. That is certain; that is fatal.

Najib is placed under treatment. They cut his hair, his beautiful flow of dark hair; rub his scalp with chloroform; keep the hot bottles around his feet, the ice bag on his head; and give him a spoon of physic every hour. "Make no noise around the room, and admit no light into it," further advises the doctor. Thus for two weeks the child languishes in his mother's arms; and resting from the convulsions and the coma, he would fix on Khalid the hollow, icy glance of death. No; the light and intelligence might never revisit those vacant eyes.

Now Shakib comes to suggest a consultation. The great English physician of Cairo, why not call *him*? It might not be meningitis, after all, and the child might be helped, might be cured.

The great guesswork Celebrity is called. He examines the patient and confirms the opinion of his cònfrères, rather his disciples.

"But the whole tissue," he continues with glib assurance, "is not affected. The area is local, and to the side of the ear that is sore. The strabismus being to the right, the affection must be to the left. And the pus accumulating behind the ear, under the bone, and pressing on the covering of the brain, produces the inflammation. Yes, pus is the cause of this." And he repeats the Arabic proverb in broken Arabic, "A drop of pus will disable a camel." Further, "Yes, the child's life can be saved by trepanning. It should have been done already, but the time's not passed. Let the surgeon come and make a little opening—no; a child can stand chloroform better than an adult. And when the pus is out he will be well."

In a private consultation the disciples beg to observe that there was no evidence of pus behind the ear. "It is beneath the skullbone," the Master asserts. And so we decide upon the operation. The Eye and Ear specialist is called, and after weighing the probabilities of the case and considering that the great Celebrity had said there was pus, although there be no evidence of it, he convinces Khalid that if the child is not benefited by the operation he cannot suffer from it more than he is suffering now.

The surgeon comes with his assistants. Little Najib is laid on the table; the chloroform towel is applied; the scalpels, the cotton, the basins of hot water, and other accessories, are handed over by one doctor to another. The Cutter begins. Shakib is there watching with the rest; Najma is in an adjacent room weeping; and Khalid is pacing up and down the hall, his brows moistened with the cold sweat of anguish and suspense.

No pus between the scalp and the bone: the little hammer and chisel are handed to the Cutter. One, two, three,—the child utters a faint cry; the chloroform towel is applied again;—four, five, six, and the seventh stroke of the little hammer opens the skull. The Cutter then penetrates with his catheter, searches thoroughly through the brain—here—there—above—below—and finally holds the instrument up to his assistants to show them that there is—no pus! "If there be any," says he, "it is beyond the reach of surgery." The wound, therefore, is quickly washed, sewn up, and dressed, while everybody is wondering how the great Celebrity can be wrong....

Little Najib remains under the influence of anæsthetics for two days—for two days he is in a trance. And on the third, the fever mounts to the danger line and descends again—only after he had stretched his little arm and breathed his last!

And Khalid and Najma and Shakib take him out to the desert and bury him in the sand, near the tent round which he used to play. There, where he stepped his first step, lisped his first syllable, smacked his first kiss, and saw for the first time a star in the heaven, he is laid; he is given to the Night, to the Eternity which Khalid does not fear. And yet, what tears, Shakib tells us, he shed over that little grave.

But about the time the second calamity approaches, when Najma begins to decline and waste away from grief, when the relapse sets in and carries her in a fortnight downward to the grave of her child, Khalid's eyes are as two pieces of flint stone on a sheet of glass. His tears flow inwardly, as it were, through his cracked heart....

Like the poet Saadi, Khalid once sought to fill his lap with celestial flowers for his friends and brothers; and he gathered some; but, alas, the fragrance of them so intoxicated him that the skirt dropt from his hand....

We are again at the Mena House, where we first met Shakib. And the reader will remember that the tears rushed to his eyes when we inquired of him about his Master and Friend. "He has disappeared some ten days ago," he then said, "and I know not whither." Therefore, ask us not, O gentle Reader, what became of him. How can *we* know? He might have entered a higher spiritual circle or a lower; of a truth, he is not now on the outskirts of the desert: deeper to this side or to that he must have passed. And passing he continues to dream of "appearance in the disappearance; of truth in the surrender; of sunrises in the sunset."

Now, fare *thee* well in either case, Reader. And whether well or ill spent the time we have journeyed together, let us not quarrel about it. For our part, we repeat the farewell words of Sheikh Taleb of Damascus: "Judge us not severely." And if we did not study to entertain thee as other Scribes do, it is because we consider thee, dear good Reader, above such entertainment as our poor resources can furnish, *Wassalmu aleik*!

IN . FREIKE . WHICH . IS . IN . MOUNT . LEBANON
SYRIA . ON . THE . TWELFTH . DAY . OF
JANUARY . 1910 . ANNO . CHRISTI . AND . THE
FIRST . DAY . OF . MUHARRAM . 1328 . HEGIRAH
THIS . BOOK . OF . KHALID . WAS . FINISHED

Also from Benediction Books ...
Wandering Between Two Worlds: Essays on Faith and Art
Anita Mathias
Benediction Books, 2007
152 pages
ISBN: 0955373700

Available from www.amazon.com, www.amazon.co.uk

In these wide-ranging lyrical essays, Anita Mathias writes, in lush, lovely prose, of her naughty Catholic childhood in Jamshedpur, India; her large, eccentric family in Mangalore, a sea-coast town converted by the Portuguese in the sixteenth century; her rebellion and atheism as a teenager in her Himalayan boarding school, run by German missionary nuns, St. Mary's Convent, Nainital; and her abrupt religious conversion after which she entered Mother Teresa's convent in Calcutta as a novice. Later rich, elegant essays explore the dualities of her life as a writer, mother, and Christian in the United States-- Domesticity and Art, Writing and Prayer, and the experience of being "an alien and stranger" as an immigrant in America, sensing the need for roots.

About the Author

Anita Mathias is the author of *Wandering Between Two Worlds: Essays on Faith and Art*. She has a B.A. and M.A. in English from Somerville College, Oxford University, and an M.A. in Creative Writing from the Ohio State University, USA. Anita won a National Endowment of the Arts fellowship in Creative Nonfiction in 1997. She lives in Oxford, England with her husband, Roy, and her daughters, Zoe and Irene.

Anita's website:
    http://www.anitamathias.com, and
Anita's blog Dreaming Beneath the Spires:
    http://dreamingbeneaththespires.blogspot.com

The Church That Had Too Much
Anita Mathias
Benediction Books, 2010
52 pages
ISBN: 9781849026567

Available from www.amazon.com, www.amazon.co.uk

The Church That Had Too Much was very well-intentioned. She
wanted to love God, she wanted to love people, but she was both ham-
pered by her muchness and the abundance of her possessions, and
beset by ambition, power struggles and snobbery. Read about the surprising way The Church That Had Too Much began to resolve her
problems in this deceptively simple and enchanting fable.

About the Author

Anita Mathias is the author of *Wandering Between Two Worlds: Essays on Faith and Art*. She has a B.A. and M.A. in English from
Somerville College, Oxford University, and an M.A. in Creative Writing from the Ohio State University, USA. Anita won a National
Endowment of the Arts fellowship in Creative Nonfiction in 1997.
She lives in Oxford, England with her husband, Roy, and her daughters, Zoe and Irene.

Anita's website:
    http://www.anitamathias.com, and
Anita's blog Dreaming Beneath the Spires:
    http://dreamingbeneaththespires.blogspot.com

Shadows of Ecstacy
Charles Williams
Benediction Classics, 2011
186 pages
ISBN: 978-1-84902-475-4

Available from www.amazon.com,
www.amazon.co.uk

Classic Charles Williams: A human-
istic adept has discovered that by
focusing his energies inward he can
extend his life almost indefinitely. He
undertakes an experiment, using Afri-

can lore, to die and resurrect his own body, thereby assuring his im-
mortality. His followers begin a revolutionary movement to destroy
European civilization.

"THE KINGDOM OF GOD IS WITHIN YOU"
CHRISTIANITY NOT AS A MYSTIC RELIGION BUT AS A
NEW THEORY OF LIFE
LEO TOLSTOY
Benediction Classics, 2011
298 pages
ISBN: 978-1-84902-474-7

Available from www.amazon.com,
www.amazon.co.uk

A new edition of Tolstoy's non-fiction mag-
num opus. Gandhi regarded this book,
banned in Tolstoy's native Russia, as one of the three greatest influ-
ences on him. The ideas Tolstoy that expounds so clearly were
revolutionary in his day and still are relevant and challenging today.

www.ingramcontent.com/pod-product-compliance
Lightning Source LLC
Chambersburg PA
CBHW022008170626
46808CB00001B/322